The White Venus

R.P.G. Colley

R.P.G. Colley

Fiction:

Love and War Series:
Song of Sorrow
The Lost Daughter
The Woman on the Train
The White Venus
The Black Maria
My Brother the Enemy
Anastasia

The Searight Saga:
This Time Tomorrow
The Unforgiving Sea
The Red Oak

Non-Fiction:

History In An Hour series

Other non-fiction:
The Savage Years: Tales From the 20th Century
The Hungarian Revolution, 1956
A History of the World Cup: An Introduction
The Battle of the Somme: World War One's Bloodiest Battle

The White Venus

Rupertcolley.com

Historical Note

On 10 May 1940, the armed forces of Nazi Germany invaded France, entering undefended Paris on 14 June. The Battle of France was effectively already won. Two days later, the 84-year-old Philippe Pétain was appointed prime minister. His first act was to seek an armistice with the Germans, which was duly signed on 22 June.

France was split into two; the north and west occupied by the Germans, while the south and east remained unoccupied. The unoccupied region was run by Pétain, now state president, who, together with his government, was based in the town of Vichy in central France. This situation lasted until 12 November 1942, when Hitler ordered the occupation of the whole country.

French people had to decide – whether to resist German occupation, collaborate, or in most cases, tolerate it and try to ignore it. Resistance included milder activities, such as pasting anti-German stickers on lampposts. The number of active resisters was minimal, although their numbers grew as the war progressed. Their work was co-ordinated, where possible, by General Charles de Gaulle, first from London, then from his base in Algiers.

On 6 June 1944, D-Day, Allied forces launched their invasion of Normandy and, from there, slowly pushed the Germans back. Paris was liberated on 25 August. By the end of September 1944, following four years under the yoke of Nazism, most of France was free.

The witch-hunt for those who had served the Vichy regime and their German masters began immediately.

Chapter 1

Xavier passed him the chicken. 'Go on then, you do it. Like you say, it can't be that difficult.'

Pierre gathered the hen in his arms and stroked its head, trying to keep it calm. Her sister hens and cousins ambled around the yard, pecking, their shadows long in the late afternoon sun, circling the various monuments dotted around – statues and memorials half completed. It was here, at the back of the house, that Pierre's father did his work.

'It's all right for you,' said Pierre, 'she's not part of your family.'

Xavier, sitting in an old rocking chair Pierre's mother no longer wanted in the house, guffawed. 'It's a chicken, Pierre, not your grandmother. Go on, two seconds and it'll be done with.'

'Yeah.' The chicken jerked its head. 'Right then, Madeleine.'

'Madeleine? You call it Madeleine?'

'Yeah. So what? All the chickens have names.'

'How quaint,' said Xavier, shielding his eyes from the sun. 'You give it a name, it's part of your family, as you say, like a family pet, then your dad tells you to kill it.'

'She's old. She's not laying any more. And Papa, well, he thinks I'm *of an age now*,' he said, adopting a pompous tone. 'That one's called Marion,' he said, pointing to another hen. 'And that one Marlene, Monique…'

'Wait, do they all start with M?'

'Mmm. Maman's idea.'

'Your parents are strange.'

'Papa wanted to name them each after top Nazis – Goebbels, Goring, Rosenberg, but Maman wouldn't let him. Said it'd be bad taste, especially if he was heard calling out the names.'

'She has a point. So, which one's Hitler?'

'He's the cock behind you – on the fence. But he's called Maurice.'

Xavier turned round to view the cockerel. 'So what would Madeleine have been?'

'I don't know. Perhaps Bormann.'

'Well, hurry up then, kill Martin Bormann, even though she's a girl. They could be here any minute.'

'And we can't be late for our special guests.'

'Exactly. The swine. They couldn't have chosen a hotter day for it. All this white stone – it hurts your eyes. How do you see to work?'

'Sunglasses, Xavier. Sunglasses. What d'you think?'

'What's this block of stone going to be?'

'It's sandstone. It's mine to practice on. Papa said I could have it.'

Xavier ran his hand down the stone. 'What's it going to be?'

'A chicken.'

Xavier laughed. 'Oh, really? A bloody chicken? A metre-high chicken? I'd like to see that when it's done.'

'Yeah, a chicken with a Hitler moustache pecking your eyes out.'

'Very funny. Well, look, your Madeleine's going to die of old age before you get to wring her neck.'

'OK. It can't be that difficult.' Pierre placed two fingers beneath the bird's head. Securing its body under his armpit and clamping it against his chest, he tightened his fingers. All he had to do was pull. Pull hard. He'd seen his father do it several times. It took but a second. One solid pull; that's all it took. The bird squawked. He had to do this. It was part of growing up. He had to have it done before his father came out. He regretted now having invited Xavier over to witness the occasion. He thought it would give him courage but instead it only made things worse. It was like inviting someone over to watch you lose your virginity. He felt self-conscious, pressurised by his friend's presence. Some things should be done in private. Bracing himself, he started to count down in his head. Five, four, three…

The door to the kitchen flung open. It was his father. Pierre's fingers slackened, his body slumped. 'They're here,' said Georges.

'What, already?'

'Come on, we ought to go.' Uncharacteristically, Pierre's father was wearing a collar and tie and his best beret, his shoes polished, his moustache waxed. 'Hello, Xavier. You can come with us if you like, or are you going with your parents?'

'I said I'd meet them there.'

'Let's go then. After all, we don't want to keep them

waiting.'

Pierre wondered what to do about the chicken. His father spotted his hesitation. 'What are you doing with Mirabelle?'

'Mirabelle?'

'I said wring Madeleine, not Mirabelle.'

Pierre dropped the chicken as if he'd burnt himself. The bird flapped its wings as it landed, causing billows of dust, and ran off, squawking.

His father sighed. 'Please don't tell me you were about to do away with one of our best layers?'

Xavier stepped forward. 'No, Pierre wanted to show me Mirabelle, that's all.'

'Thank the Lord for that.' He straightened his tie. 'Well, let's go. Let's see what the future of France looks like. You ready then, boys?'

*

It was like a macabre carnival. The whole population seemed to have converged on the town square. The clock on the town hall showed five. The sun beat down on the assembled crowd. Whole families had turned out together. Children ran around the square, their shadows chasing after them. The cafés, although still open for business, were empty; their staff in their black and white uniforms waiting outside, craning their necks like so many penguins. There was laughter but also a deep sense of apprehension. No one wanted to admit it but Pierre could feel it; could see it behind everyone's outward smiles. Ahead of them, in front of the town hall and the war memorial, they had erected a stage, a wooden platform, with large speakers to the side. Centre stage, a microphone in its stand. The war memorial, dating from the Franco-Prussian War of 1870-71, featured a bronze statue of a French soldier high on a plinth, one hand holding a rifle, the other shielding his eyes as he gazed into the distance. The locals affectionately called him 'Soldier Mike'. The French tricolour hung limp on its flagpole above the town hall; there was no wind to stir it.

People stood on the benches. Pierre's mother stood on tiptoe, the better to see. She too had dressed up for the occasion, wearing a bright blue dress that came with a belt and a simple straw hat. It was her 'going out' dress, her only one. She wore it rarely. A kingfisher brooch acted as a button. Pierre noticed her take her husband's hand. His father wouldn't like that. Sure enough, after a few seconds, he leant over to talk to his friend, thereby having the excuse of letting go. Kafka, his father's friend, chewed on his pipe, scowling as Georges whispered in his ear. Pierre heard Kafka utter the word 'bastards'. Georges rolled his eyes and nodded knowingly.

'Georges...' said Pierre's mother, remonstrating that her husband should allow his friend to swear in public.

Xavier nudged Pierre in the ribs. 'Well, this is better than murdering innocent chickens.'

'I wish they'd hurry up; it's getting hot.'

'Look who I see. Our lovely librarian.'

Pierre followed his friend's gaze. Involuntarily, he let slip the word 'shit'. His mother, thank God, didn't hear. Claire looked gorgeous. She was wearing a white blouse, its buttons like daisies, her breasts clearly defined, and a swirling yellow skirt. Her auburn hair, held with a band, reflected the sun. As if aware of Pierre looking at her, she turned and caught his eye. A flicker of a smile.

'Here he comes,' said Georges, breaking the moment. Pierre saw the mayor climbing the steps onto the platform. He looked back towards Claire, but she had gone.

The mayor, wearing his red robes, tapped the microphone. Clutching a sheet of paper, he waited as mothers called their children back. A wave of silence descended across the town square as the hum of conversation died away, broken only by the cawing of a pair of crows perched high on top of Soldier Mike.

'*Bonjour, messieurs, mesdames.*' The microphone squealed. The mayor stepped back, a clear look of annoyance on his face. Someone to the side of the platform offered advice. Adjusting his spectacles, the mayor, now standing a little further back, continued. 'My friends, citizens of this glorious town; we live in momentous times. France may have been defeated but she is still France and we are still her children. Yes, we have fallen at the feet of the enemy and yes, Marshal Pétain has asked the Germans for an armistice. The Battle of France is over. You may ask is it unpatriotic to accept so meekly the German in our midst, to bow down before him? I tell you instead to ask is it patriotic to want to throw thousands, hundreds of thousands, of young men to be slaughtered like lambs? Is it not patriotic to want to save our future generation from futile resistance? Most of us remember too well the horrors of the last war. A war we won, but at what price?' He shook his fist, causing his chin to wobble. 'So many men and boys killed; leaving behind a generation of young widows; children growing up without ever having known their fathers. Those of you who remember, look now at the children, the young men amongst us. Would you want them to suffer as we suffered twenty years ago in the name

6

of victory?' Pierre and Georges exchanged glances. His father, Pierre knew, had been in the war. His father had never mentioned it to him – not once. And Pierre had never, until this moment, thought to ask him. 'No,' continued the mayor, the sun reflecting off his glasses, 'this is no shameful defeat; this is peace. Compromised maybe, but better a compromised peace than a victory awash with so much blood.'

'Bollocks,' someone muttered. People nearest turned around. That someone, Pierre knew, was Kafka. Pierre's mother pursed her lips, tutted, noticeably affronted by Kafka's language. Georges grimaced, as if responsible for his friend's outburst.

'I, Claude Marchel, will remain your mayor. You elected me to serve four years. And four years I will serve. With your blessing, perhaps more. But now, as from today, I will have at my side, the *Ortskommandantur* at Saint-Romain. Together, Colonel Eisler and I will ensure the smooth running of this town and its surrounding area. We shall work together to maintain peace so that we, the good people of this proud town, can coexist in tranquillity with our guests.'

Pierre feared another outburst from Kafka. Thankfully, the man held his tongue. Pierre could see this Colonel Eisler hovering at the side of the stage, waiting for his cue.

'I have asked the colonel to deliver a few words.' Removing his spectacles, the mayor motioned the German to take his turn. Pierre noticed that the crows had gone but, with a start, he saw a line of German soldiers at the edges of the crowd. Left and right, they were there, stock still in their grey-green uniforms and steel helmets, their rifles at their sides. Georges had noticed too and visibly stiffened.

The mayor stepped back to allow the colonel centre stage. A tall man; in his fifties, thought Pierre, but still lean. Even from a distance, the man had a presence; his immaculate uniform a stark contrast to the mayor's ceremonial garb. 'Thank you, Monsieur le Maire.' Pierre had half expected a deep authoritative voice, and, although heavily accented, was surprised by its normality. 'This town and its surrounding area are now under the jurisdiction of the German High Command,' said the colonel without an introduction. He paused as if allowing his audience to absorb the import of what he had said. 'While we have nothing but scorn for your government and its feeble-minded politicians, we have nothing but respect for the French people.'

'So why in the hell did you invade us, then?' came a loud voice to the side. It was not Kafka, but the man was nodding his agreement. The colonel ignored the taunt and continued his speech, extolling the need for Franco-German cordiality. Pierre noticed the German soldiers nearest the dissenter shuffle forward, squeezing in the crowd. They had seen the man, Monsieur Touvier, the town's blacksmith, and they were watching him.

Pierre saw his mother take his father's hand again. 'All guns, in whatever form, are to be handed in to the town hall by noon tomorrow. There are to be no exceptions. Likewise, all radios are to be handed in by the same time. From today, we will be observing German time, so you will need to adjust your clocks and watches by one hour in advance.' Pierre felt rather than heard the collective groan. 'From today also, you will have to abide by a curfew. This curfew will change with the time of year but for now, with the days at their longest, it will be nine o'clock – German time. Anyone found outside their homes from nine to five the following morning will face consequences.' The colonel scanned the audience in front of him, looking at people, one to another, as if daring anyone else to make a comment. No one did. The soldiers nearby, Pierre noticed, were still watching the blacksmith.

'The day-to-day running of this town will remain with Monsieur le Maire. My staff and I will be based in Saint-Romain. Most of my men will be based there but a few will remain here. Some of those remaining will be billeted in your homes. It will not be for long – perhaps a month at the most. The noticeboard behind me has a list of residents who can expect a lodger. I expect those listed to make my men feel welcome; and I fully expect my men to treat you with the utmost courtesy. I bid you all good day. Heil Hitler.'

The rumble of voices began immediately, rising to a crescendo of speculation. The mayor returned to the microphone but his attempts to call for attention were ignored as his face reddened to the same colour as his robes.

'I hope we don't get someone staying with us,' said Pierre's mother.

'I'll bloody show him the door if we do,' said Georges, pulling on his moustache.

'Don't swear, Georges.'

'He's right, though,' said Kafka. 'Any German staying in my house will sleep in the outside toilet.'

'Kafka, you live alone – they won't send anyone to you.'

Pierre noticed two soldiers squeezing into the dissenter.

9

Holding his arms down, they took Monsieur Touvier to one side, trying their best not to cause a commotion.

'What are they going to do him?' asked Xavier.

'They're going to make him pluck chickens as a punishment.'

Pierre's mother called out to them. 'Boys, why don't you go check the noticeboard? Let us know the worst.'

*

Xavier had got there before Pierre, pushing his way through the throng of people crowding round the noticeboard. Pierre watched as people came away, either with a look of relief or dread emblazoned on their faces. Someone, he noticed, had wrapped a French flag round Soldier Mike's ankle. He caught sight of Claire again. He waved and although she was looking in his direction, did not see him, leaving him feeling rather foolish with his hand mid-air.

Xavier re-appeared from the scrum of people, looking slightly dishevelled but grinning.

'Well?'

'Don't worry, my parents are in the clear.'

'Well, that's nice. I'm so pleased for you. And, erm…'

'Oh, sorry, Pierre, I forgot to look for your name.'

'You're an idiot.'

His friend laughed. 'I'm only joking. I did look.'

'Oh, the suspense. Well, go on then, tell me.'

Xavier could not contain his glee as he imparted the news. 'Yep, my dear friend. You are to expect a Major something-or-other at some point in the next couple of days.'

'Oh great. Sod it. A major?'

'Yeah. What rank was your father?'

'No idea. So what's his name?'

'I've forgotten. Something beginning with an H.'

'Major H, welcome to our humble home. I'd better tell my parents.'

'Ah, don't worry. I'm sure he'll be a very nice Kraut, and I'm sure you'll all live happily ever after together.'

'Yeah, thanks, Xavier. You're still an idiot.'

*

Xavier had, at last, found his parents and disappeared with them into the throng of people now meandering back to their homes. Heading home down a side street, Pierre walked alongside his mother while his father walked behind, talking to Kafka. Pierre had told them the news – they were to expect a lodger. They took it rather well, he thought. 'What does it all mean, Maman?'

'The Germans? I don't know. Maybe the mayor was right; maybe it is for the best.'

'What? To have a bunch of Germans telling us what to do?' Further ahead, they saw two German soldiers peering through the baker's window.

'I remember the last war, Pierre,' said his mother quietly, as if the soldiers might hear her from twenty metres away. 'They were terrible, terrible years. The Marshal knows what he's doing; he'll find a way.'

'What, Pétain? That old goat?'

'Pierre, please. Keep your voice down. You don't know what you're saying. He'll keep us safe.' The soldiers, sharing a joke, were now heading towards them, ambling leisurely, looking around them as if sightseeing in the sunshine.

'But the lad is right,' bellowed Kafka from behind. 'Pétain *is* an old goat; he's sold us down the river.' The soldiers were getting closer but Pierre feared that Kafka was far from finished. 'In sucking up to the Krauts, he's signed a pact with the Devil.'

The soldiers had heard Kafka's shouting. They were watching him as they strolled past them in the lane. Pierre's mother turned to Kafka, 'Keep your voice down.'

'No, sorry, Lucienne; I cannot hold my tongue. Pétain has betrayed us and betrayed his country.' This time the Germans had clearly heard him. Pierre saw their faces harden. 'And so now we have to tolerate having these Krauts telling us what to do.'

'Hey, you; watch your tongue,' said one of the soldiers in German, a man with a boxer's nose, gripping his rifle in front of him.

'Sod off back to Germany.'

It took but a second – Kafka was on his knees on the tarmac, clutching his stomach. The soldier had hit him with his rifle butt. Lucienne screamed; Georges's face turned white; Pierre had taken his mother's hand. The soldier was leaning over Kafka, screaming at him: 'You filth! You talk like that again you're dead; you got it?' The second soldier kicked Kafka, catching him in the arm. People stopped, shocked, open-mouthed.

'Please don't say anything else,' Pierre whispered to himself.

The first soldier had his rifle poised, ready to butt Kafka a second time. Pierre held his breath, gripped his fingers over his mother's, but a voice rang out in German: 'Hey, stop right this instant.'

Kafka spat as a German officer ran onto the scene.

'Stop right now, Private. What's going on?'

The second private spoke. 'This piece of shit was insulting us, sir.'

'What was he saying?'

'I don't know, I don't know that much French.'

'He's got a bad attitude, sir,' said the other, lowering his rifle.

Kafka rose unsteadily to his feet, still holding his stomach.

'That's enough now,' said the major. Pierre released his mother's hand.

Georges helped his friend up. 'You're OK, Kafka?'

'I can manage,' he said, shrugging Georges off.

'Kafka? What sort of name is that? Are you a writer?' asked the major in perfect French. Turning to his soldiers, he said in German, 'OK, men, you can go now.' The two soldiers looked at each other. One shrugged and with a half-hearted Hitler salute headed off, the other following in his wake. 'I apologise for the men,' he said to Kafka. 'After a month of fighting, they're a little twitchy. Are you OK?'

Kafka puffed out his cheeks. 'A month of killing Frenchmen, eh? My heart bleeds for them.'

Pierre could see the major's goodwill rapidly draining away. 'What is your name?'

'Kafka; I told you.'

'Your real name?'

Kafka stretched, as if trying to rid his stomach of the pain.

'I asked you what is your name?'

'Foucault, Albert Foucault.'

'But they call you Kafka?'

'Looks like it. Can we go now?'

The major stared at him for a few moments. Then with a quick bow to Pierre's mother, turned to leave. They watched him head briskly back towards the town square.

'Oh, Kafka,' said Lucienne. 'When will you learn?'

'Thanks for all your help, Georges.'

'I – I wanted to but…'

'But what?'

Lucienne, still agitated, fanned herself with her hat. 'I think we should go now. Come, Pierre.'

But Kafka, rubbing his stomach, wasn't finished. 'Still a little smitten with the German race, eh, Georges? Still in awe of their biological superiority after all these years?'

Lucienne took Georges's hand. 'Let's get you home, dear,' she said, dragging him away, trying to save her husband from further embarrassment. 'And you, Kafka. Go home and have a bath, even in this heat. Hot water will do your stomach some good. Help ease the pain.'

Georges huffed. 'Take a few days off, Kafka. Go to your island on the lake, have a rest.'

'I might well do that. And thank you for your concern, Lucienne; I'll do exactly as you say, a hot bath, even in this weather.' He was smiling now, a smile without affection. 'I'll see you soon, Georges; and Pierre…'

'Yes?' said Pierre nervously.

'You know, you don't always have to grab your mother's hand at the first sign of trouble.'

Chapter 2

While Lucienne waited for the kettle to boil on their large, black stove, she washed her hands thoroughly, still determined, she'd said, to wash away the dirt of the previous day. Pierre was familiar with this habit of hers – this obsessive washing of hands whenever she felt under a strain. He remembered exactly when it had started…

Eventually, with the tea made, they sat and sipped in silence, Lucienne smelling of carbolic soap. His parents sat on the bench at the kitchen table, the table with its rose-patterned oilcloth, while Pierre sat back in the kitchen armchair. His eyelids felt heavy. His eyes scanned the familiar items on the chest – the crucifix at its top, the china cups hanging on hooks, the ones rarely used; the saucers on display with a picture of the Eiffel Tower on a white background, the Tower, adorned with a smiling face, leaning to one side as if exercising. There was one missing – Pierre had broken it years back; he must've been about eight or nine. It was the only time he ever recalled his mother spanking him. He cried, naturally, but not from the pain – there wasn't any, but from the fact he'd so upset his mother. On the wall opposite the chest, two framed photographs – one of a man on a tightrope and the other of a young boy aged about five wearing a flat cap too big for him and baggy trousers, the definition of a cheeky but sweet boy.

While his mother had made tea, he had sat there with his father. Neither spoke a word yet he'd wanted so much to ask. But his father seemed so diminished it didn't seem right to bring it out in the open. Kafka knew something that Georges would rather forget. Perhaps, at some point, thought Pierre, he would broach the subject with his mother. And then of course there was the little matter of his own abject humiliation. He tried to persuade himself that he had taken his mother's hand to protect her. But Kafka knew the truth. And so did he.

Finally, Pierre's mother broke the silence. 'What about your gun, Georges?'

'What about it?'

'You have to hand it in.'

'Why? Because they said so?' asked Georges, stirring his tea although he had almost finished it.

'Of course. We can't keep it, especially with a German staying in the house. If they find it…'

'There'd be serious consequences,' finished Pierre.

'Yes, thank you, Pierre,' said his father. 'For God's sake, it's only an old shotgun. I use it for the rabbits and crows. That's it.' Pierre didn't like to say that, despite numerous attempts, he'd never seen his father kill anything. 'And I've had it for years. It's virtually an antique.'

'Yes but they don't know that, Georges. You have to

hand it in. Think of us, all of us.'

Georges finished his tea. 'I'm not handing it in,' he said, placing his mug on the table.

Lucienne rose from her seat and went outside. 'She's gone to get it,' said Georges to Pierre. 'You wait.'

Sure enough, moments later, Lucienne returned carrying the shotgun at arm's length as if it was emitting a terrible smell. 'It is safe, isn't it, Georges? You haven't left it loaded or anything?'

'No, of course not. Bloody hell.'

She looked up worriedly at the crucifix. 'Please, Georges, don't use profanities.'

Gingerly, she placed the gun on the table. They looked at it. Pierre had never really considered it before. It was a fine piece of craftsmanship, he decided. Elegant, sleek yet solid. He knew nothing about guns but could see that this thing could cause some damage. He realised that his father knew he had to hand it in but couldn't face another indignity. 'I'll take it if you want.' The idea of walking through the town with this in his hand was thrilling.

His parents looked at each other and silently reached the same conclusion. 'Good idea,' said Lucienne. 'Yes, you take it. But do it now – in case this Major H turns up early.'

Pierre picked it up. He weighed it up and down. It was heavier than he expected. 'It's lovely.'

'Just take it, Pierre,' said Lucienne.

Pierre pointed to his father's wartime helmet that hung from the back of the kitchen door. It'd been there for as long as he could remember. 'Can I wear your helmet, Papa?'

'No, you cannot. Is there not a bag of some sort he

could put it in?' asked Georges.

But Pierre was already out of the door. As he closed it behind him he heard his father shout, 'Get a receipt for it.'

*

Pierre couldn't resist it. He called in on Xavier to show him the shotgun. His friend was suitably impressed. 'So what are you doing with it?'

'I'm off to shoot a few Germans. Do you want to come?'

'Right we are.'

'For every German we take out, there's one less to worry about.'

'Yep – simple. Let's go.'

It was strange walking down the street with a huge gun. People couldn't help but notice and many backed away. Monsieur Tautou, the carpenter, saw them. 'That's the spirit, boys.'

They took turns with the gun, carrying it as a soldier would on parade. The walk from Xavier's house to the town hall was but a few minutes but the boys took several detours so that soon hardly a street in the whole town had not been visited by the two boys and their heavy shotgun. 'Hey, Pierre, let's take it into the woods and see if we can kill something. Or we can sneak into the back of the mayor's house and kill his rabbits.'

'Xavier – it's not loaded.'

'Oh.'

'You think my dad would let me walk down the street with a loaded gun? Anyway, imagine firing this thing; it'd dislocate your shoulder.'

'Let's go to the library – go see the lovely Claire,' he

said in a sing-song voice. 'I'm sure she'd be impressed with something that size.'

'It's closed now.'

'Barriers, barriers. That's all you do; create barriers to everything I say.'

Pierre laughed. 'It's not my bloody fault that the gun's not loaded and the library is closed.'

Wrapped up in their banter, they hadn't noticed the pair of German soldiers approach them. 'What are you doing with that gun?' said one in German, his rifle trained on them.

The boys looked up. 'Oh, shit,' uttered Pierre, recognising the soldier with the flattened nose. 'What did he say?'

'I don't know.'

'Put that gun down,' said the first German.

'Don't you understand German?' shouted the second.

'I think he wants you to put the gun down, Xavier.'

'Yeah, you're probably right.' Carefully, he placed it on the road.

Pierre pointed in the direction of the town hall. 'We hand it in to the mayor.'

'What did he say?' asked the first German to his comrade.

'I think he says they're going to shoot the mayor.'

On hearing this, the first one leapt into action, lifting his rifle to eye-level and, advancing, aiming it straight at Pierre's head. 'Get down, you frog, on your knees now.'

'Whoa,' cried Pierre putting his hands up.

'Get down.'

The boys understood and went down on their knees, then, after furthering gesturing, lay on the road on their fronts.

'I think they're going to kill us,' said Pierre.

'But I haven't had my dinner yet.'

'You could ask him to come back later.'

'Stop talking,' yelled the first as the second German began frisking Xavier.

'We've got an audience,' whispered Pierre. Sure enough, a small gathering of people had emerged, forming a circle around the spectacle. Someone shouted, 'Leave them alone.' Someone else added, 'They're only kids.'

'No, we're not,' said Pierre.

The second soldier had begun frisking Pierre, kicking his legs apart, and running his hands down his trousers, into his pockets, and down his socks. Craning his neck, Pierre saw a light green skirt. Fantastic, he thought; Claire couldn't help but be impressed. Here he was, only two days in, and he was already a resistance fighter. If only she'd step a little closer with that swirling skirt.

'What are you doing?' she asked the soldiers in German.

'Are they friends of yours?'

'I know them.'

'We caught them on their way to kill your mayor. They confessed.'

'Really?' She laughed. 'Hello, Pierre, Xavier. So, you were off to assassinate the mayor, were you?'

'Erm, yes,' said Pierre.

'Don't listen to him,' said Xavier. 'Of course we weren't. Tell her, you idiot.'

Pierre told her the truth as the soldier frisked his shirt. People in the crowd sniggered as they turned to leave. Claire, in turn, told the soldiers.

'I'm not so sure,' said the first. 'They look suspicious to me.'

'Do you really think—'

'Nonetheless, we'd better escort them,' said the second. 'Just to make sure. Get up!' he yelled at the boys.

'What did he say?' asked Pierre.

'He said, "prepare to die, you filthy sons of dogs",' returned Xavier.

'He said all that in just two syllables?'

'Boys, you can get up now,' said Claire. 'These kind soldiers are going to escort you to the mayor's office.'

'What – Fritz One and Fritz Two? That's awfully decent of them,' said Xavier, brushing away fragments of tarmac.

'They don't have to,' said Pierre. 'We know the way.'

Claire shook her head and smiled.

*

Pierre felt rather excited, walking to the town hall with two German soldiers behind them, pointing their rifles. One carried his father's shotgun. He hoped everyone in the town would get to see them. Indeed, they received many admiring glances and shocked ones too. It was turning out not to be such a bad day after all. Outside the town hall, the Germans had already erected a notice: *Whoever commits acts of sabotage against members or property of the German armed forces, or found to be in possession of arms of any type, will be shot.* Xavier caught Pierre's eye, raising his eyebrows.

Inside the town hall, the reception area was brimming. With its high ceiling and marbled floor, voices echoed. Men in German uniforms marched in and out; well-dressed women carrying envelopes or pads of paper busied themselves; telephones rang; a deliveryman appeared pushing a large cardboard box on a trolley.

The two German soldiers deposited the boys at the main desk, handing the shotgun over to the receptionist. She took it, leaning it against the desk beside her as they briefed her. On the wall behind the desk, a large portrait of Marshal Pétain wearing his peaked hat decorated with gold braids, his grey moustache almost white, his eyes fixed resolutely on the viewer, his chin defiantly prominent. The boys looked at each other. Subtly, Pierre shook his head, warning Xavier not to say anything. As the soldiers left, the first one slapped Xavier on the back and said, 'There we are; wasn't too bad, after all.'

'What did he say?' asked Xavier.

'He said next time you're dead.'

'Severe.'

It took Pierre a whole five minutes to fill out the necessary paperwork and receive, in return, a receipt. As they turned to leave, his mother suddenly appeared, throwing open the double doors of the town hall and standing there, catching her breath while trying to find her son. 'Pierre, thank God,' she said upon seeing him. 'I heard you'd been arrested.' She threw her arms round him.

'Maman, please.'

'Were you arrested? I heard all sorts of tales of you being led away at gunpoint. What happened?'

As they left and Pierre began recounting the tale, Xavier told them to look behind. They stood and looked up at the flagpole above the town hall. The French flag that had been there as long as anyone could remember had gone. In its place, flapping gently in the breeze, was the swastika.

'It's no joke, is it?' said Xavier.

'No,' said Pierre.

*

Having said their goodbyes to Xavier, Pierre and his mother slowly walked the rest of the way home.

'Maman, what did Kafka mean by saying Papa was still in awe of the Germans?'

Lucienne stopped. She sighed. 'I don't know. Your father fought in the war. You know that, he's got the medals. And that helmet on the back of the door. They were in the same unit. But, like a lot of men, your father never talks about the war. I only met him in 1920. We married a year later, so I didn't know him as a soldier. But something happened; I don't know what but something between Kafka and your father. Whatever it was, your father has always seemed as if he is still in debt to Kafka. He says Kafka is his friend – but friends don't blackmail each other.'

'Blackmail?'

'I don't mean with money. Just – emotionally, somehow. I remember, about ten years ago, Kafka moved away for a while. I think he moved to the city to be with his father who was dying. He was gone for about six months. I'd never seen your father so happy. He was like a different man. Then, Kafka came back and it was as if a big shadow had fallen over him again. I tell Georges just ignore him but, of course, in a town of this size, it's almost impossible.'

They had come to the house now. They lived in a bricked bungalow painted green, with large windows and a wooden porch that had three steps leading up to the front

23

door. Either side, on each step, a blue enamel pot of flowers, which Lucienne watered every day. More pots hung from the porch. At this time of year, especially, their porch was ablaze with colour.

'Before we go in, let me say – don't mention any of this to your father. And be careful of Kafka. You know what he's like; we saw it yesterday. He's unpredictable. Stay away from him. For whatever reason, your father can't – but you, Pierre, you can.'

Chapter 3

The following morning, Georges was in the yard, working on another memorial engraving, while Lucienne had just returned from her daily visit to the churchyard and a shopping spree, complaining about prices already going up. Pierre was sitting on the bench at the kitchen table drawing – sketching out his ideas for a grand statue. He'd just had his daily dose of cod liver oil and the foul taste still lingered in his mouth. He decided then and there he would never take the stuff again. He was too old for it now. A tray with three Eiffel Tower china cups and saucers lay at the end of the table.

It was exactly ten o'clock when the knock on the door came. They had been expecting it but had not mentioned it. Lucienne, carrying a pallet of mushrooms, ran a hand through her hair. Quickly, she removed her apron, and smoothed out her blue dress. Pierre wondered why his mother had worn her best outfit again, right down to the kingfisher brooch. Again, she smelt strongly of carbolic soap. She opened the door. Immediately, Pierre recognized the German's voice speaking immaculate French.

'It's no inconvenience; do come in,' he heard his mother say. 'Mind your head.'

And then, there he was – this tall German officer standing in the middle of the kitchen, his big, shiny boots on the red tiled floor, his cap in hand, carrying a small suitcase. It was the major from the gathering; the one who had intervened in Kafka's argument.

'Such a lovely house... oh, hello there.' The man offered Pierre his hand. 'My name is Major Hurtzberger, Thomas.'

'Major H.'

'Yes; if you like. And your name is?'

'Pierre. I'll get my father.' He heard his mother offer the German a cup of coffee as Pierre stepped outside. It was another hot day. He found Georges with his goggles on, chisel and mallet in hand.

On seeing his son, Georges took off his goggles. 'He's here?'

Back inside, Pierre found the German looking at the ornaments and the pictures, paying particular attention to the photographs of the tightrope walker and the young boy in the flat cap. Sitting back at the table, Pierre watched as the three of them, his parents and the German, danced through a series of apologies and polite platitudes. 'It should only be for a month or so; I do apologize for the inconvenience.' He was over six foot, dark-haired, thin nose, pronounced cheekbones, and here he was, with his Nazi uniform with its German eagle, epaulettes, and medal ribbons, sitting at the kitchen table. The polite occupier; the enemy within their midst, being offered coffee.

Pierre twirled his pencil around his fingers. He noticed

that the German wore a gold signet ring on his left hand.

'What amusing cups,' said the major.

Lucienne laughed. 'Yes, it's the Eiffel Tower.'

'Yes, I can see.'

Georges shook his head.

Lucienne complimented the German on his French; mentioned that Pierre had done well in his English lessons at school.

'You speak English?' asked the German in English.

'No,' replied Pierre in French; annoyed to have been brought into the conversation.

'Don't be silly, Pierre. Go on, say something in English,' said his mother.

'Leave the boy alone,' said Georges.

'What is it you're drawing?' asked the major.

'Nothing really.' Subconsciously, he scribbled over his drawing, leaving an impression on the oilcloth beneath.

The kettle steamed on the stove while Lucienne prepared the coffee.

'Almost ready, Major.'

'Please, Madame Durand, you must call me Thomas.'

'No,' interrupted Georges. 'I think for the sake of propriety, we should stick to more formal use. I hope you understand, Major?'

'Y-yes. Yes, if you like.'

Changing the subject, Georges asked the German whether he had been to France before. He had once, as a child, with his parents, in about 1922, he said. Loire Valley – all those lovely chateaus. Had Georges been to Germany? 'No.' came the quick reply; too quick, causing a moment of awkwardness.

'You'll be pleased to know, you won't see too much of

me. I'll be working most of the day – every day.'

'No peace for the wicked?' asked Lucienne. She flushed red and subconsciously glanced up at the crucifix. Georges groaned.

'Well, yes. Erm. We're not all so wicked. And don't worry about food – I'll be eating all my meals at the canteen. I will endeavour to restrict my intrusion into your home to a minimum.'

'That's perfectly OK,' said Lucienne. 'You'll be sleeping in our third bedroom. You'll just have to ignore all the toys in there.'

'Toys? Oh, I'm sorry, I wouldn't want to take Pierre's room–'

'No, it's not Pierre's room. He's too old for toys now.' She poured him his coffee. 'Sugar, Major?'

'No, thank you.'

Oh, please, mother, don't say it. 'Sweet enough already, Major?' She'd said it.

He looked suitably embarrassed; as did she for saying it. Nerves. Pierre ground his pencil onto the oilcloth, breaking its nib. 'Are you all right, Pierre?' asked his mother.

'I need to go out. I said I'd go see Xavier.'

'Well…'

'You go, if you want,' said Georges.

'Yes, please, don't stay on my account,' said the major. 'You must all try to act as if I wasn't here.'

'Right,' said Pierre. A stern look from his mother stopped him from saying anything else.

*

'Well?' asked Xavier. 'Has he moved in?'

28

They were heading towards the town square. 'He's moved in all right. My mother couldn't be more creepy than if the Queen of Sheba had arrived. *It's no inconvenience, Major. Can I get you a coffee, Major? Sugar, Major? Sweet enough, Major? Can I stroke your hair, Major?* It's sickening.'

'You ought to send Kafka over. He'll sort it out. What about your dad?'

'He doesn't say much – as usual.'

'No guns today, boys?' asked a passer-by, Tautou, the carpenter.

'Why does everyone find this such a joke?' said Pierre. 'We're swamped by Krauts and we have to pretend nothing's changed.'

'What can we do?'

'You said it just now.'

'What?'

'Kafka. He'll know.'

'He's bad news, that man,' said Xavier. 'My father told me to stay away from him.'

'That's what my mother said. Everyone's frightened of him all of a sudden.'

'Good God, look at the cafés; we've been taken over.' They had reached the square and the cafés dotted round the perimeter were all doing a brisk business – but not a Frenchman amongst them; every outside seat seemed to be taken by Germans. The mood was jovial, much laughing as the soldiers relaxed, helmets on the back of their chairs, smoking and drinking their coffees in the sun. With a jolt, Pierre spotted Claire. She was outside Café Bleu standing next to a table full of Germans. She had their undivided attention. With a laugh and a wave, she bid them goodbye and made to cross the square, a smile on her lips, a bounce in her step.

She saw Pierre and his friend. 'Hello, boys.'

'Hello, Claire,' said Pierre. 'What are you doing?'

'Me? Nothing. Oh, that.'

'You were—'

'Keep your voice down. I'm going to the baker's. Come with me.'

The boys accompanied her to the baker's and accepted her offer of a macaroon each. They waited outside while Claire went in. A girl of about eleven passed on a red bicycle. 'I'm surprised the Germans haven't requisitioned that,' said Xavier.

'Ha; don't give them the idea.'

'Here we are,' said Claire, reappearing with a baguette and three macaroons.

'Are you buying our silence?' joked Pierre as they walked on.

Glancing up and down the street, Claire seemed to take the accusation seriously. Speaking quietly, she said, 'It's Kafka's idea. He told me to get friendly with the enemy. He'd said I'd be an asset with my German and… well, whatever. Better to know what they're up to, he said.'

'And what are they up to?' asked Xavier.

She waited for an old woman with a walking stick to pass by. 'That's not for me to indulge.'

'Are you working for Kafka now?'

'No, of course not, I still work at the library. I need to go. I have to open up. What's the time? My watch's wrong.'

Xavier shook his head. 'They've changed the time, haven't they? We're on German time now.'

'I forgot. Oh no, that means I'm an hour late.'

'Don't suppose anyone will notice.'

'Nonetheless, I have to go.'

The boys watched her go towards the library, her hair bouncing, her skirt flowing behind her.

'Wait here,' Pierre told Xavier. Running, he caught up with Claire.

'Did you not enjoy your macaroon?'

'Claire, can I work for Kafka?'

She stopped. She ran a finger softly down his cheek. Her touch, however soft, sent a little surge of electricity through Pierre. 'Don't,' was all she said before walking off again.

Pierre ran up beside her. 'I don't understand. Why on earth not?'

'You're too young, Pierre.'

'I'm almost seventeen.'

'Exactly. Anyway, think of your mother; what would she say?'

'She'd–'

'She'd be horrified.'

Pierre watched her leave, waving to a friend across the street. Claire was new to the village; she'd come from Paris, apparently wanting to escape the capital and its Germans. She'd merely swapped one set of Germans for another. Pierre wondered whether the Germans in Paris were any different to the ones in the town. More pertinently, he wondered how long she'd stay. A couple of soldiers passed by on bicycles, one of them wolf-whistling at her. Xavier appeared at his side. 'What was that about?' he asked. He had speckles of crumbs on his upper lip.

'She reckons I could work for Kafka,' he said.

'What do you mean *work for*?'

'You know.'

He wiped his mouth with the back of his hand. 'No.'

'No, nor do I. But I intend to find out.'

*

Producing a sculpture is, foremost, a matter of patience. Occasionally, the family of the deceased wanted something different from the stocks of memorials Georges had at the ready. They wanted a different kind of angel, or Virgin Mary, or Jesus. And they had the money to pay for it. This, then, meant you had to work to a deadline, for no family wanted their loved ones to be deprived of their headstone for too long. But even with a deadline, one had to have patience. Remember, this was a monument that would remain in place for evermore; long after they themselves were dead and forgotten. This was the message that Pierre's father had instilled in him. The sculptor's art was unique, he said frequently, in that it involved both hard, physical work, yet a finesse of touch. They were labourers and artists; lackeys and craftsmen. Theirs was a job that came with great responsibility. After all, they were putting the full stop at the very end of someone's life. They had been given a solemn obligation by the ones left behind; one that came with an expectation that, with their craft, they honour the memory of a life now gone with a memorial that would last for eternity; a testament to the worthy life once lived. In accepting the obligation, they, as sculptors, had formed a bond with the departed.

He hadn't heard the German open the back door but he knew from the chickens running away that he had company. 'So, is this how you spend the day?' asked the major, holding a cup of coffee.

'Yeah.' He kicked away the tarpaulin lying at his feet.

'It's a beautiful spot.' Shielding his eyes from the sun, the major scanned the view. Pierre noticed the signet ring on his left hand, holding the coffee cup. The design was of a horse with a wild mane. 'How big is that woodland?'

'Fairly big.'

'Hmm. You have two sheds?'

'Yes, that one over there with the bike against it is where we keep the stone, the marble and the granite and stuff. Papa calls it the warehouse.'

'Is that your bike?'

'Yes. And this shed is for tools and things.'

The major opened the door of the nearest shed. 'Oh yes, a workman's paradise in here. What a lot of tools, and so much paint.'

'Papa wants to paint both sheds.'

'What colour?'

'Red.'

'Certainly bright. Do you mind if I sit for a while?' asked the major taking a seat on the rocking chair. Pierre shrugged with what he hoped was marked indifference. He was aware of the major watching him at work, chiselling away at the stone. 'So, is this to be a memorial?' the German asked, removing his cap.

'Yes.'

Why, wondered Pierre, had he not told the German the truth? After all, it was not a big deal. He wasn't doing anything wrong. But the man was a German; he had no right to be in his house, his yard, let alone his country. There again, he was but a man, an annoyingly nice man who washed his cup after he'd finished with it; something neither his father nor he had ever done; a man who rose to

33

his feet whenever his mother walked in the room; why, he even put the toilet seat down and rinsed the sink after he'd had a shave. Pierre had been brought up believing the Germans to be a race of barbarians; brought up on stories of how they'd behaved during the last war; of atrocities committed; of nuns raped and children butchered. The image and reality differed in the extreme.

'It's not a memorial,' he said eventually. 'Papa reckons I'm not ready for a real memorial, although I have helped him lots. This is just for me.'

'Just for you and for your father – to show him you're perfectly capable.'

Pierre looked at the major – what right did he have to read his mind?

'And may I ask what's it going to be, this sculpture? Or is it an artistic secret?'

Indeed, Pierre had intended on keeping it a secret, but as neither his mother nor father had shown any interest it hardly warranted being classed as such. And the German had acknowledged that Pierre was embarking on a work of art.

'You don't have to tell me.'

'Venus.'

'Venus, indeed?'

Pierre got up, went to the tool shed and returned carrying a large book. Opening the pages at a bookmark, he passed it to the major.

'*The Birth of Venus* – Botticelli,' said the German. 'Sandro Botticelli. I have seen it.'

'You've seen it – in the flesh, the real thing?'

'Why yes. In Florence, the Uffizi. It's beautiful, of course. And so big. It's almost three metres long.'

'You've been to Italy?'

'Yes. In my early twenties. The Uffizi is the most wondrous place. One day you must go. It's perhaps even grander than your Louvre. Well, perhaps not so grand. You've been to the Louvre, yes?'

Pierre felt a prick of shame as he had to confess he had not; had not even been to Paris.

'Don't worry; you're still young. One day, when all this... this is over, you'll go – both the Louvre and the Uffizi, and you'll see Venus in the flesh, as you say, the real thing. Meanwhile, what you are doing is a grand endeavour; it's certainly ambitious. I'm impressed, Pierre.'

Pierre shuddered as a feeling of warmth cascaded through him, inducing such an unexpected wave of pleasure it left him momentarily disorientated. It was the way the major had said his name – not as a grown-up would but as an equal, a fellow lover of art.

'I have to go now; work to do.'

Pierre nodded; he wanted to say thank you but found it was simply too difficult.

The major stood and pulled the creases out of his tunic. 'I shall leave the artist to get on with his work.'

Pierre smiled.

Putting his cap back on, the major turned to leave. As he opened the kitchen door, he turned round. 'What do you plan on calling your sculpture?'

Pierre hadn't actually thought about a name. He stroked the dry sandstone and, on eyeing the thin layer of white dust on his palm, the name came to him in an instant. Grinning, he turned to the major and said, '*The White Venus.*'

Chapter 4

It was perhaps a week later. Already the family and their new guest had settled into a routine. True to his word, the major was out all day from eight, sometimes earlier, to about seven at night. He would return tired, having already eaten with his colleagues, sit quietly in the living room, reading a book, and retire early. On the fourth evening, much to everyone's delight, although Georges and Pierre tried not to show it, the major returned with a small joint of pork. The town, as a whole, was slowly becoming accustomed to the sight of the grey-green uniforms, the strangers within their midst. Sometimes people had to remind themselves that they were under occupation. The Germans went out of their way to be polite, speaking to the locals, accepting without complaint that shops charged them twice or thrice the going rate for every item on sale.

Meanwhile, while his father was out, Pierre worked on his sculpture, pulling off the tarpaulin each morning and chipping away at the stone, slowly bringing out a recognisable shape. It was still early days; it was going to be a long, rather daunting job.

One morning, Xavier burst in, barely able to contain himself. 'You have to hurry. They're coming through any minute. The whole town is gathering. Still working on your lump of stone, I see. Come on, hurry.'

Together with Lucienne, the boys joined the procession of people heading to the square. Again, thought Pierre, there was that same sense of carnival as the day the Germans had arrived. Was this the same feeling they had in medieval times when crowds gathered to watch an execution? Again, all the shops had closed down; the town had come to a standstill so they might witness the coming spectacle. It was well past one o'clock; Pierre was hungry. Strange, he thought, how quickly they had grown accustomed to the new time.

'Pierre, could you not have changed?' said Lucienne.

'I hardly think it matters, Maman.'

'Oh, but it does; impressions count on occasions like this – the whole town will be there, the mayor included.'

'And a lot of Germans,' added Xavier.

'Well, yes; best not to think of that.'

'Your Major H might be there.'

'I'm sure he wouldn't be involved in such things.'

Xavier pulled a face.

They joined the crowd of onlookers half way down Rue de Courcelles, one of the main arteries leading off the town square. Every few yards, standing guard, was a German soldier. Pierre recognised the soldier nearest to them, Fritz One. Xavier had seen him too. The man looked painfully hot in his tunic and buttoned shirt, standing to attention under the full glare of the sun. His colleagues opposite, at least, were in the shade.

Lucienne pushed through the crowds, suggesting they cross the road to the other side. The soldier put his hand up, preventing her from moving. The two of them, Lucienne and Fritz One, locked eyes for a moment. Pierre was impressed although he knew there could only be one outcome. Sure enough, she stepped back. Fritz One moved on a few yards. Muttering, Lucienne rummaged in her handbag and produced a fan. And there they stood; ten, fifteen minutes and more. Georges appeared, slipping through to join them. 'You look like you're going to the opera with that fan,' he remarked.

'Shush.'

It was only with his mother's shush, that Pierre realised the whole crowd was deathly silent. He heard the two o'clock chime from the town hall clock. Somewhere a dog barked.

And then they heard. A faint, faraway sound; the rumble of a motorbike and the shuffle of a thousand feet. Slowly, the sound became louder, the shuffle of feet nearer. Occasionally, a shout punctuated the air; occasionally a motorbike revved its engine. They were moving through the square; soon they'd be coming round the bend and down the street. Pierre's heartbeat quickened. But what was that noise; that new sound? With a jolt, he realised women were sobbing. And still the shouting; nasty, barked commands in German. People craned their necks as the first shadows appeared at the bend. A group of four German soldiers emerged, marching slowly, followed by the motorbike, mustard green in colour, with a machine gun mounted in its sidecar, its engine rumbling uncomfortably in first gear. And then came the mass, the pitiful mass of defeat. Lucienne held her hand over her mouth; Georges's eyes seemed to be on stalks; Xavier muttered a *merde*. There were so many of them, marching not as soldiers but as a shamble of ghosts, their khaki uniforms in tatters. Pierre watched, his stomach caving in with emptiness, as the parade of prisoners of war passed. And passed. The minutes ticked by yet still they came, hundreds and hundreds of men, Frenchmen; each and every one of these broken men had fought for France. The wailing of sobs spiralled like a funnel, gathering a momentum of its own. Pierre had never experienced such an outpouring of grief. He turned to see that his mother was openly crying. The Battle of France had waged a mere few weeks yet it had totally passed by their sleepy town. Although never too far off, it seemed to be happening somewhere faraway. Not any more, thought Pierre. He watched, uncomprehending, the dark, dirty faces, the haunted eyes. These men, united in defeat, were his countrymen, his brothers. Yet they did not seek the solace of the onlookers, the citizens. These men seemed unaware of their presence, unaware of anything. The crowd might as well not have been there. Marching alongside them, at regular intervals, were more Germans, their rifles drawn, bayonets glinting in the afternoon sun. But these weren't like the Germans in the town; their uniforms were black, altogether more sinister; somehow more serious. And still they came.

A woman standing next to Lucienne, Madame Philippe, the butcher's wife, slipped through the cordon of soldiers and placed a bucket of water at the side of the column. Her action was met by a murmur of approval. Lucienne fanned herself more vigorously. A PoW, his eyes wide as can be, scooped down with cupped hands. A soldier in a black uniform rushed up, shouting at him, and pushed him away. Despite this, another PoW tried also to snatch a few driblets of water. The German kicked the bucket over; it was too much for the prisoner who, exhausted, sank to his knees, causing the men behind him to crash into one another, to lose their rhythm. 'Get up, get up!' shouted the German. The Frenchman didn't get up. Lucienne took Pierre's hand. Xavier was crying. 'Get up, you bastard; get up.' Pierre knew he had to look away; knew he would forever regret it if he didn't. The German swung his rifle around and hit the prisoner with the butt, smashing it onto his back, followed by a vicious kick into the ribs. The Frenchmen fell onto his front and groaned. Pierre saw how hard the German's boots looked; steel toecaps capable of breaking bones.

The column moved on. No one stopped, sidestepping their fallen comrade. The German swung his rifle round again. A collective grasp echoed round as the German plunged his bayonet into the man's back. A splash of crimson but no sound. Using his foot against the Frenchman for leverage, he pulled the blade out; a streak of blood glistening on the steel. Women screamed. Many started crying. The German in his black uniform marched on, his rifle with its bloodied blade against his shoulder, the other arm swinging. Someone vomited. Men muttered words like animals, beasts, murderers. Madame Philippe tried to reach the stricken prisoner. She escaped the clutches of her husband, who implored her to get back, but failed to get past Fritz One, who pushed her back. 'For the love of Jesus, let me through,' she screamed. She tried again. This time Fritz One slapped her with the back of his hand. Madame Philippe fell, her hand against her cheek.

Lucienne put her arm around her. Madame Philippe's cheek was bleeding; a cut from a ring, thought Pierre. She glared angrily at her husband.

The hopeless column of men continued for another twenty minutes or more. No one took any notice of the dead man lying in a heap, the circle of blood on his back. Finally, the last men staggered by, followed by another motorbike and sidecar. The crowd watched quietly as they advanced down the street, round the bend and out of view. Everyone remained in place, too dazed to move, listening to the fading sounds of shuffling feet, boots and the motorbike. So many people, thought Pierre, but the air hung heavy with silence. The local Germans nodded at each other; their task for the afternoon done. Fritz One prodded Georges with his gun. 'Take him away,' he said in German, pointing to the body. Georges nodded. Monsieur Philippe, the butcher, offered to get an old door he had lying in his shed, pleased perhaps to appear to be doing something after his earlier humiliation. The door, he said, could be used as a stretcher. Georges thanked him; said he would wait. As the soldiers dispersed, Lucienne and Madame Philippe, and others, went to the body. Pierre watched them. They came away, shaking their heads, their eyes filled with tears. He was dead all right.

Kafka appeared and shook hands with Georges. 'Are you OK, boys?' Pierre and Xavier nodded. Turning to Georges, he said quietly, 'Was that convincing enough for you? We need to talk.'

'I need to remove our friend here first.'

'I'll help you.' While they waited, Kafka puffed on his pipe. He offered Pierre and Xavier a drag. They both declined.

Monsieur Philippe reappeared struggling with his door, its green paint peeling off. 'Can you manage?' he asked the men.

'We'll manage.'

'Good. Right oh. Er, I'll be off then.'

The stench filled the nostrils, a mixture of dirt and sweat. Xavier gagged as, taking a leg, he helped lift the body onto the door. 'God, it's heavy,' said Pierre, immediately regretting using the word 'it'. The trouser leg slipped away, leaving Pierre holding onto the man's leg. He recoiled at how dry it felt, how flaky the skin.

A small crowd of spectators had congregated, including Pierre's mother, clasping a handkerchief to her mouth, although he wasn't sure whether it was because of the smell or the emotion. 'Careful,' urged Kafka as they eased the body onto the wood. And there he lay; a nameless soldier heaped face down on an old green door. It didn't seem right.

'Take him to Monsieur Breton,' said Lucienne.

'No, take him straight to the church, hand him over to Father de Beaufort,' said another voice from the crowd.

'What do we do?' asked Kafka. 'The undertaker or the church?'

'Cut out the middleman, take him to the church.'

'The funeral parlour is there for a reason, Georges; to clean him up and all that.'

'The church is nearer.'

'Not sure we should use that as a criterion.'

'Perhaps we should have a vote on it.'

'But people are coming and going all the time.'

'Only men should vote.'

'And those over twenty-one.'

42

'Oh, for goodness sake,' said Lucienne. 'Georges, you were given the responsibility – you decide.'

Xavier whispered in Pierre's ear, 'Your mother should be the mayor.' Indeed, thought Pierre, feeling a rare surge of pride for his mother.

'The undertaker it is. Should we not turn him around?'

'You might be right,' said Kafka.

'More dignified.'

'OK, boys. We'll twist him clockwise.' The four of them tried to turn the body clockwise which meant Pierre and Xavier, at their end, going the opposite direction of the men. 'No,' said Kafka. 'What I meant...'

For the first time they saw the man's face; his dark but sallow skin, the hollow eyes, still open.

'He's from North Africa,' said Kafka. 'Algerian. Perhaps Moroccan.'

'He might have his papers in a pocket.'

'We'll leave that to Breton.'

'We need to close his eyes.'

But no one did. Instead, they stood and looked down at the man, the man from North Africa who had tried to keep France free. He had failed. They had all failed. Pierre thought of the German who had done this; how he so easily took another man's life; how he kicked away the water, denying the man everything. And then he had walked on; just walked away. Pierre couldn't understand; how could a man do that; how could life be so cheap? How did one become so hard? It was why France had lost. We're too soft. To win meant beating the Nazis at their own game; to toughen up. But how in the hell do you go about achieving that?

And so, it was to Monsieur Breton they went; one man

at each corner, the boys at the back with the feet, the lighter end. As they carried their heavy but precious cargo, people stopped. Men took their hats off; women crossed themselves and shielded the eyes of their children. Pierre felt as if the body, with his eyes still open, was staring at him. He tried not to look back. After five minutes, panting in the heat, they arrived at the funeral parlour but, like every business in the town, it was closed; the shutters pulled across the window. 'We'll have to wait,' said Kafka. And so they did; the body on its door, on the tarmac. Kafka re-lit his pipe. Pierre and Xavier pulled a face at each other; they were both thinking the same: it didn't need all four of them to wait for Monsieur Breton's return. But to say so seemed disrespectful. Neither could bring themselves to say it and so they remained. It was almost thirty minutes before Breton returned.

'My word, sorry to keep you waiting. What does it take to get a drink around here? Were you here long?'

'About–'

'Let's get him in, the poor chap, away from all these people. This way,' he said, unlocking the door. After the brightness of the day, it took a few seconds to adjust to the darkness inside. Monsieur Breton flung open the shutters, and blades of sunlight filled his reception area. 'Just bring him through to the back.'

Having laid out the body on Breton's marble slab, Georges took the door. The four men made to leave. 'Can I ask, gentlemen,' said Breton, 'to whom I should present my bill?'

'Your what?' snapped Kafka.

'I don't work for free, you know. Would you? Work for nothing?'

Kafka and Georges exchanged glances. 'He died for you,' bellowed Kafka, 'fighting for your country. Is that not enough?'

'No, frankly, it is not. I work in a relatively small town. Not enough people die; I barely scrape by. You may live off the fat of the land, Monsieur Kafka, but I have a family; I can not.'

'My heart bleeds, but may I suggest, Monsieur Breton, that for a man who fought for your freedom, you waive your fee in this instance?'

'Fought for my freedom? What sentimental nonsense. Did you see that rabble?' said Breton. 'What a sad sight. Made me ashamed to be a Frenchman. No wonder we lost.'

'I suggest you hold your tongue.'

'You suggest a lot, Kafka. But whatever you say, we lost and it's no wonder. Who knows, a bit of German discipline might do us some good. Our children could do with a dose of it. Help toughen up young lads like these two.' Pierre was surprised to find Breton feeling his upper arm. Was he meant to flex his bicep, he wondered?

It happened quickly. Kafka pushed Breton against the wall, grabbing the undertaker by his throat. 'That poor sod died fighting for the likes of you.'

'Fat lot of good it did us, eh, Monsieur Kafka?'

Kafka tightened his grip. Breton spluttered, his face reddening, sweat breaking out on his forehead.

'Papa, stop him,' urged Pierre in a whisper.

Georges grabbed Kafka's wrists and pulled them away. Kafka relented, let go, snorting. Breton coughed and eased the pain from his throat. 'You... you maniac,' he gasped. 'Get out!'

'We're leaving alright. You just make sure you prepare this body properly; no short cuts. Understand?'

Kafka stormed out. 'What fine company you keep, Georges Durand,' said Breton. 'What a fine example to these boys.' Pierre and Xavier glanced at each other.

'He's a patriot, Breton; something you don't appreciate. Come on, boys, let's go.'

Pierre opened the door as his father struggled out with the green door. As he was about to leave, Georges said, 'Monsieur Breton, if I can also suggest something, you could present your bill to the mayor.'

Kafka was waiting further up the road, his back to them, a haze of smoke circling above his head. 'Here, you boys take this,' said Georges leaning the door against a building.

'Where are you going, Papa?'

'Kafka and I have business to discuss.' Pierre watched his father walk up to Kafka. Together the two men headed off.

'Jesus,' said Xavier. 'What a day. Do you want a cigarette?'

'You smoke?'

'I do now. Nicked them from my dad. Here, I have two.'

With cupped hands, Xavier lit both cigarettes, passing one to Pierre. The smoke hit the back of Pierre's throat, taking him by surprise, making his eyes water. He swallowed down a cough. The whole sensation was rather unpleasant. His legs felt woolly; he felt the need to sit down. But no, he wasn't going to give in. It was time to be a man.

They'd almost finished their cigarettes when Xavier

said, 'Watch out, here comes your mother.'

'Shit. Where? Here, take this,' he said, hurriedly passing his cigarette to his friend.

'Pierre. Hello, Xavier, again. Here you are. Did you manage to take the…?'

'Yes.'

'I can't find your father anywhere and I would like to go home now. Would you escort me, please, Pierre?'

'The house is only over–'

'Pierre.'

'Yes, OK. OK.'

'Pierre, have you been smoking?' she asked, intensifying the use of her fan.

'No,' Pierre said, quickly.

'It's me, Madame Durand,' said Xavier stepping forward. 'I smoke.'

'You must be very addicted, Xavier, to have to smoke two cigarettes at a time.'

'Y-yes. Its… it's been a difficult day, Madame Durand.'

'Yes, it has. Come, Pierre, take me home now.'

'Yes, Maman,' he said, trying to suppress a sigh.

*

That evening, the atmosphere at home was equally subdued. They sat in the kitchen, Pierre and his father reading while Lucienne knitted, the click-clack of her knitting needles being the only sound. Georges lit a cigarette; Lucienne pushed an ashtray towards him, a gentle reminder not to drop his ash on the floor. Pierre was flicking through a book on French artists, skim-reading a passage on the life of Auguste Rodin. A shiny plate featuring Rodin's *The Kiss* took up a whole page.

Pierre studied it, turning the book this way and that, admiring such a piece of work that somehow combined the classical and the modern. He wondered what it must be like to kiss a girl. But the more he studied it, the less he saw and the greater the image of the bayonet, the crumpled figure on the road, the blazing sun, the German killer. Somewhere, faraway in Algeria, a woman, a mother, had no idea that today, in a small town in northern France, her son had been murdered. In cold blood.

They heard footsteps. Georges stubbed out his cigarette. A gentle knock on the door. 'Hello, only me.' The door opened. It was Major Hurtzberger. A round of 'good evenings' ensued, offers of something to eat, a cup of coffee perhaps. A coffee would be very nice, thank you. Do take a seat, Major. 'Pierre, get up, let the major have the armchair.'

'No, Pierre, it's fine, you sit. I'm alright at the table.'

But no, Pierre got up, insisted. He knew what was expected of him. The major sat, a buff-coloured folder on his lap, and let out a sigh of tiredness. He took his coffee. No one was quite sure what to say, so, for a while, they said nothing. Pierre's father picked up his book, and his mother resumed her knitting. The major leant back, cup in hand, his eyes closed.

Eventually, it was Pierre who spoke. 'A difficult day, today,' he said to no one in particular, repeating Xavier's phrase.

'Yes,' said the major. 'Quite a day. These things happen in war. I understand there was an incident. I hope you weren't witness to it.'

'Witness? It happened right there in front of us, Major,' said Georges. 'We had ringside seats.'

48

'Georges, don't trivialise it.'

'Oh dear,' said the major.

'Oh dear indeed.'

'I'm sorry you had to witness such a thing, Monsieur Durand. It was unfortunate. The men who were escorting the prisoners, the one who killed the man, they weren't Wehrmacht, like I am, like all the garrison here. They are SS.'

'They're still German. They're still one of you.'

'Yes but we have no jurisdiction over them. And they are, how shall I say, very committed to the cause…'

'Committed to the–'

The major put his hand up. 'Please, Monsieur Durand, I beg you to say no more.'

Georges look confused. 'Say no more? In my own home? I'll–'

'Georges, stop,' said Lucienne. 'I think what the major is saying is that however cordial we may act within these four walls, he is German, we are French, and it is best if we remember that.'

'Your wife, Monsieur Durand, is a wise and intelligent woman.'

'She is also,' said Lucienne, 'a very tired woman. I'm off to bed. Georges…'

'What?'

'You must be very tired too. And you, Pierre.'

'You're telling us when to go to bed now?'

'It might not be a bad idea, Papa.'

Chapter 5

The following morning, Georges left early to catch a bus to Saint-Romain and arrange a new delivery of marble; after all, he'd said, they'd have a new addition to the graveyard soon, once Monsieur Breton had done his work, and the poor blighter will need a headstone of his own. Pierre decided to make the most of his absence and work on his sculpture. The yard was mainly in shade. With a slight draft, he felt chilled enough to wear a smock. The chickens pecked around him – Mirabelle, Madeleine, Marion, and the rest. All the M's. He knew at some point he'd be joined by the major. Sure enough, after little more than ten minutes, the back door opened and the major appeared holding a steaming Eiffel Tower cup of coffee. The chickens flapped and fussed. 'Your mother makes a fine coffee,' he said. 'Good morning, Pierre. Should be another fine day. So how's it going with the White Venus? It's beginning to take shape, I see. You work fast.'

Yes, thought Pierre. It was a matter of confidence as his father always told him. The more you chipped away, the less there was of the stone left standing and the more important the work. This is the point where things could go wrong. But too much caution can be counter-productive; can act as a break on creativity. This is where you had to firm up your plan and have the conviction in achieving it. No holding back.

'Listen, Pierre, I was thinking. Once it's done, your work, would you like to see it displayed at the town hall?'

'The town hall?'

'I could have a word with the mayor. I'm sure he would be accommodating.'

'Well, yes, I suppose so. That'd be good.'

'Excellent! Consider it done.'

'But he might say no.'

'I'm sure he won't.'

Pierre might have imagined it but he thought he saw the major wink. He tried not to show it but Pierre was staggered by this. That it could be so simple. He knew full well that if he, or his father, approached the mayor with such a request, they'd be laughed at. But not the major. A click of the fingers and it's done. This, in a small way, was the meaning of power. He tried to resume his work but felt too conscious of the major's presence. At least it meant he didn't have to look at him, so he carried on, making inconsequential chips.

'Thank you,' he said – in a whisper.

'That's OK. I have a son like you, Pierre.' He took a large gulp of coffee and stared out over the fields towards the woods. 'He's quite a lot like you, really. Joachim. A bit older though. Just turned nineteen. In two years, for his twenty-first, I'm going to give him this.' He held up his hand, showing Pierre his signet ring.

'A horse?'

'Yes. Generations of my family were cavalrymen. It's a family tradition to be given the ring on one's twenty-first birthday. Well, the boys. Joachim's just joined the army. He had no choice really. Not now. He's already finished his training. When I joined up, we had months of training. Joachim had just a few weeks. Hardly ideal, in my opinion, but these are far from ideal times. The army needs men; the Führer needs men. And Joachim is a man now. He wanted to be a vet. I told him he'll have plenty of time to be a vet when it's all finished. When all this is finished. I'd have preferred it had he joined the Luftwaffe. Now there's a glamorous job. His mother would have preferred it too. But no, he's in the army, infantry, a foot soldier like me. Here, would you like to see a picture of him?'

Frankly Pierre did not but as the photograph was thrust at him, he had little choice but to 'oo and err', as his mother would say. The corner of the photograph was creased, otherwise it was intact. It wasn't just the boy but the whole family – the major and the boy standing behind his wife and a girl, seated. The girl must have been about ten, her hair in plaits, wearing a white, collared shirt with a cravat. For reasons he didn't understand, Pierre found the image revolting even though, as individuals, they each seemed pleasant enough. Father and son were in uniform, everywhere little swastikas, on all four of them – a badge, a brooch, a tie, an armband.

'It was taken about two years ago. Unfortunately, his mother and I are no longer together. Brigitte, my daughter, lives with her mother. Joachim was in the *Hitlerjugend*.'

'The what?'

'Hitler Youth. Brigitte is in the *Jungmädel*; that's for girls ten to fourteen. Or is it fifteen? I can't remember.'

'Yes, very nice.' The boy looked big, as tall as his father, broad in the shoulders, proud to be in his uniform. A fine Nazi family. He handed it back. The major looked at it, the familiar picture, smiled, and returned the photograph to his breast pocket.

'It's nice to carry a reminder.'

'Yes.'

'Yes, anyway, I ought to be going. Work to be done and all that. Do you ever use your bike?'

'Occasionally.'

He finished his coffee. 'Nice to talk to you again, Pierre. You're a fine lad. See you this evening.' He made to leave but then, at the kitchen door, stopped. 'I've been meaning to ask – who's that man on the tightrope in the photograph in your kitchen?'

'That was my Uncle Jacques. He was killed when I was small. Hit by a car.'

'Oh. And the photograph of the boy? The boy with the cap?'

A flash of memory shot through Pierre's mind – a teddy bear with a yellow waistcoat and green trousers. 'No one,' he said firmly.

'And those toys in my room?' he asked hesitantly. 'Do they belong…?'

'No one.'

The major considered his answer for a moment; nodded and left.

More images appeared unwanted – a haversack in the water, bubbles, a bucket of worms. He shook his head, trying to free his mind of the memory.

It was only after the major had left that the thought

occurred to Pierre that they had no need for any more marble. He checked the shed at the far end of the yard, the warehouse, as his father called it. He was right; there were several slabs of it, enough for many new headstones. So where exactly, he wondered, had his father gone?

*

Later, Pierre found the major talking to his parents. His father was still upset over the killing of the Algerian. 'There is such a thing as compassion, you know, Major Hurtzberger,' said Georges. 'Even in war.'

'Of course, I realise that.'

'My husband fought in the last war,' said Lucienne.

'I know – I can see the medals from here. And the helmet.'

Pierre was so used to his father's framed display of medals, he'd quite forgotten they were there.

'Yes, so don't tell me about the necessities of war, Major; I was there. I know what it's like to be expected to kill another man; I know what it's like to expect to be killed. I once tried to show compassion. Did your father fight? Was he there?'

'Yes.'

'Perhaps it was him then. Him or someone very much like him. After all, none of us are that different, are we? Whatever side we fight on; whatever cause. I tried to show a man, a German, compassion. I had a choice. That's what compassion is, isn't it? You have a choice and you make a decision. A moral choice for which you have a second to decide. I decided. I thought I'd done the right thing, taken the right path, as the church tells us. A moment of compassion, Major Hurtzberger. Unfortunately fate intervened...'

'Georges, come, dear, you're being too hard on yourself.'

'What appals me is that your man acted as if he had no choice. He had every choice. The prisoner was unarmed and harmless. A defeated man. Your SS man murdered him. That wasn't the act of a soldier; that was the work of a barbarian.'

'Monsieur Durand, I advise you to be careful. You put too much faith in me. I can appreciate your distaste–'

'Distaste?'

'Let me finish. We have reached an understanding, you and I, your family. I regret we've had to meet under such circumstances. But I will not tolerate such denigration of Germany's forces. I have my superiors to answer to. I'm sure, as a former soldier, you understand that.'

'Yes, I understand, Major Hurtzberger.'

With a bright smile, Lucienne asked, 'Another coffee, Major?'

He laughed. 'Most kind, Madame Durand, but no thank you.'

*

Pierre was queuing in the baker's. After twenty minutes, it was almost his turn. A number of people were behind him. Outside, several children played. Behind the glass-fronted counter were Madame Gide and her ten-year-old daughter, their hair bunched up in hairnets, their aprons dusted in flour, their fingers white with the stuff, looking increasingly flustered with the unending queue of demanding and complaining customers. Until just a few weeks ago, the glass cabinet boasted vast arrays of cakes and cream buns. Not any more. Now it was bread and nothing but bread. And not much of it. Everyone knew that it wasn't Madame Gide's fault but still they took the opportunity to chastise her, as if she, and not the Germans, was responsible. Pierre just hoped there'd be some left by the time he got to the front of the queue. They'd heard that the Germans would soon be issuing coupons so that everyone had a fair share. He just hoped they'd hurry up because Madame Claudel, the locksmith's wife, three in front of him, seemed to be buying up the whole shop. It was stiflingly hot inside, with so many people, and the sun streaming through the large window, exposing myriad streaks of grease on the glass. Behind him stood Madame Clément who kept tutting at the amount of time it was taking and complaining to Madame Picard behind her, while her child had a continual sniff which, after a while, Pierre found mildly irritating. If he'd had a handkerchief, he would have given it to her. Madame Picard pulled away her dog, a white terrier, from Madame Clément's child. But time, at least, now passed quickly as everyone discussed in hushed but animated tones what Monsieur Gide, the baker, had just heard on the BBC in London. While his wife and daughter continued serving their customers, he had been at the back clandestinely listening to the radio. He came out and told everyone, loudly, what he had just heard, and he was not happy about it. 'How dare he?' he said.

'Who?'

'I don't know; some general. Never heard of him. But he was on the radio – just now. Talking nonsense about carrying on the fight.'

'What did he say exactly?'

'I'll tell you, I wrote some of it down. Listen.'

The queue gathered together, becoming not so much a line but a circle of people, all eager to hear what Monsieur Gide had heard.

'Of course, I didn't get all of it but I got the gist.'

'Go on then.'

The baker adjusted his rimless spectacles and cleared his throat. He was enjoying this, thought Pierre; more concerned he should not lose his place in the queue. 'He said, "France is not alone". That with our empire and the British, we can defeat the Germans. He said, "Is defeat final? No." Then later, he said, "The flame of the French resistance must not be extinguished." Or something like that.'

'Was that it?'

'No, of course not, Madame Claudel, there was a lot more, but I'm not a secretary taking a dictation, you know. He spoke quickly.'

Madame Claudel huffed. 'So where he is, this general?'

'In London.'

'London?' came the chorus.

'Shush, keep your voice down.' Emerging from the sudden silence, Madame Clément's child continued sniffing. 'Pierre,' said Monsieur Gide, 'keep an eye out the door, make sure no Boches are passing.'

'What? Me? But I'll lose my—'

'Go on, boy,' said Monsieur Gide, waving his arm. 'If anyone comes, shout, *What, no more baguettes today?*'

'You want me to shout that?'

'Do as he says,' said Madame Bonnet, standing next to her husband, the chemist.

'Such insolence,' agreed Madame Clément.

'So what's he's doing in London, this man on the radio?' asked Monsieur Bonnet.

'Telling us to fight.'

'Oh, that's awfully decent of him. Easy for him to say that safely tucked away in England.'

Pierre stood at the door, keeping it ajar, trying to listen while glancing up and down the street. In the distance, he could see Xavier ambling with a hefty book under his arm.

'Gide, you must remember his name.'

'It sounded French.'

'No surprise there, Gide; we're all bloody French.'

'Monsieur Bonnet, please mind your language in front of my lady customers.'

'My apologies, ladies,' said Monsieur Bonnet, removing his beret in a sweeping movement.

'I think his name was Gaulle. Or *de* Gaulle. That was it – General de Gaulle.'

'I see what you mean, that *is* a French-sounding name. So this General de Gaulle in London says we're to rely on the British?' said Bonnet loudly.

'Keep your voice down, man. But yes, in essence.'

'The British?' shrieked Madame Picard. 'Well, we've seen what the British can do.'

'That's right,' said Bonnet. 'First bit of trouble and they're scrambling back home, sobbing all the way from Dunkirk. We lost the war because of them. Traitors.'

'They fought to the last drop of *French* blood before running away.'

'My husband says we lost the war because of the communists,' said Madame Claudel.

'How's that then?'

'And the Jews,' shouted Madame Picard. 'Despicable

lot.'

'Exactly. The Jews stole all the petrol.'

'The Bernheims are Jewish and they're quite nice,' said Madame Bonnet. 'Very nice, in fact.'

'Wolves in sheep's clothing,' muttered her husband behind his hand. 'Don't trust them, my dear.'

Pierre beckoned his friend over. 'Psst, Xavier, come here.'

'What are you doing?'

'Buying bread, you fool. What do you think I'm doing? Listen, I dare you to shout out, *What, no more baguettes today?*'

'Why would I want to do that?'

'Go on. Double dare.'

'What, no more baguettes today?' he said.

'No, that's no good; no one heard. Do it louder.'

Xavier shrugged his shoulders and repeated the phrase with volume.

Inside the shop, customers clashed into each other as a surge of panic took hold. 'Quick, they're coming.'

'Back in line,' urged Monsieur Gide. 'Back in line. Quick, quick.'

'I was before you,' Pierre heard Madame Clément say.

'No, you certainly were not.'

Another woman moaned, 'I wasn't this far back,' as she was pushed past Pierre and out into the street. 'This is outrageous.'

'Have you not bought enough already, Madame Claudel?' said a voice inside. 'There are other people, you know.'

'I have a big family.'

'And whose fault is that?'

'I beg your pardon?'

Still at the door, Pierre and Xavier started laughing. He heard Madame Picard's voice. 'Good God, your child has just wiped his nose on me.'

'It was an accident.'

'Disgusting child. Can't you wipe its nose?'

'But, Gide,' said Monsieur Bonnet, 'you still have loads of baguettes.'

'For goodness sake, did you not hear me say? That was my code for the boy Durand.'

'But he didn't say it, that other boy did.'

Suddenly aware of all the faces turning round, Pierre pulled on Xavier's sleeve. 'I think we should go,' he whispered. 'Quick, run.'

'Oi, you two, come back here, you scamps.'

A minute later, having escaped the bakery, they stopped running. Two German soldiers passed, walking slowly.

'Morning,' said Xavier between breaths.

No response. Pierre whispered, 'Tell them to check out the bakery.'

'You are a sod.' He waited until the soldiers were out of earshot, then asked, 'So, what was all that about?'

Pierre laughed. 'I'll tell you later. It's strange, though, everyone seems to have changed in the last few days.'

'The whole world's changing; hadn't you noticed? Soon there won't be a Europe; we'll just be one vast German Empire, the swine.'

'Yeah, you're right. So, what do we do about it?'

'Go to the library. My mum told me to hand this book back in.'

'It's big.'

'Marcel Proust.'

'That's big.'

'It's called *Remembrance of Things Past*. Looks dead boring to me.

'It's big.'

'Stop saying that. Anyway, why were you at the baker's?'

'Buying a skirt.'

'You are an idiot as well as a sod. Come on, you can come with me. You'll get to see Claire stamping books.'

'Do you think she'll say *shush* for me?'

'Tickle her feet, she might.'

The library stood alone – a small, solitary building beneath a looming oak tree at the end of a quiet street. It was known less for its books than for the surrounding garden that the previous librarian had tended with much care. The path leading up to the library entrance cut through an abundance of summer flowers, the names of which Pierre didn't know. But what made him stop in his tracks was the sight of his father walking briskly in front of him. He was about to call out but thought better of it.

'What's he doing here?' asked Xavier.

'No idea.'

'Maybe he fancies Claire.'

'Piss off; she's mine.'

'Yes, right.'

'She just doesn't know it yet.'

'Well, let's find out what your dad's doing there.'

*

After the heat of the morning, the library felt deliciously cool. Pierre and Xavier found Claire, wearing, thought Pierre, a fetching blue frock, behind the counter, running her finger down the spines of a pile of books. 'What brings you two here?' she asked. A skylight in the roof allowed in a slither of light, illuminating tangles of cobwebs; behind Claire's counter, mounted on the wall, another portrait of Marshal Pétain.

Xavier handed over the Proust while Pierre strolled round the library looking for his father. The shelves backed high against the wall, beneath the small square-shaped windows. A couple of stacks jutted out, books either side. It didn't take long to confirm that his father wasn't there.

'What are you doing?' he heard Xavier ask Claire.

'Rooting out banned books.'

'You're doing what?'

Pierre returned to the counter, now thoroughly puzzled. 'Pierre's Major H was here earlier,' she said.

'He's not my Major H.'

'He gave me this list,' she said, holding a piece of paper, 'and said if I had any of these books I had to remove them from the shelves.'

Xavier scanned his eyes down the pile of books. 'Shakespeare? Dumas? Are they banned?'

'They are now.'

'They should ban that Proust; it could be used as a weapon, it's so heavy.'

'Are you all right, Pierre?'

'Have you seen my father? We saw him come in here – just a minute before us.'

'Your father?' She shook her head. 'No, he's not been in.'

'But–'

'I said no.'

'And Victor Hugo?' said Xavier. 'Why would *Les Misérables* be banned?'

'Ask Pierre.'

'What?'

'Yeah, come on, Pierre,' said Xavier. 'Why's your major banned Hugo?'

'He's not my–'

'And why have you got him up there?' asked Xavier, pointing to the portrait of Pétain.

'Why do you think?'

'Pierre's major.'

'Exactly.'

'I will not rise to the bait.'

Claire patted his arm.

Pierre decided to try again. 'So, my father – he didn't–'

She lowered her eyes. 'No.'

'No.'

The door swung open, and there, wielding a baton, was the major. On seeing the assembled, he stopped in his tracks. The four of them looked at each other while an undercurrent of surprise, mild embarrassment and awkwardness skirted from one to another. 'Hello again, Pierre, Xavier. Well, this is quite a little gathering.' Turning to Claire, he clicked his heels. 'Mademoiselle, how have you got on with the list?'

'I didn't think you'd be back so soon, Major.'

'I couldn't resist your charms too long. Anyway, I was passing.'

Pierre noticed Claire's face redden; her finger twirling a coil of hair. 'I've made a start. We haven't got all these books.'

'I see. Some excellent titles here, Mademoiselle.'

'Yes,' said Pierre. 'Xavier here was just wondering—'

'No, I wasn't.'

Claire laughed.

The major leant against the counter. 'And do you have any of these books behind the scenes? A basement perhaps?'

'No, no, not at all,' replied Claire.

'I see.'

'Can I offer you a coffee, Major?'

'A library that serves coffee? That's progress.'

'No but… In my office, if you like.'

'We never get offered coffee,' said Xavier.

'Very kind of you, Mademoiselle. As much as I could linger within these walls of literary merit all day, I have things to see to. I bid you good day.' With another click of the heels, he saluted and left, tapping his baton against his leg.

'Did you see that?' said Xavier.

'He clicked his heels.'

'Twice,' said Pierre.

'*I have things to see to. I bid you good day, Mademoiselle.*'

'At least he didn't say Heil Hitler.'

'Shut up,' said Claire. 'Both of you.'

'I was sure you had a basement,' said Pierre.

'No.' Claire sniffed. 'Well, perhaps.'

*

They waited some distance away from the library on the other side of the road, behind a tree that stood alone on a square of grass. Lying on their fronts within the tree's shadow, they plucked at blades of grass. A few people passed but no one took any notice of a couple of teenagers lounging round on the green. Xavier lit a cigarette. Pierre took a few puffs and immediately began to feel sleepy. As he dozed off, he wondered what his father was doing in the library basement, especially as he was behind in his job of completing the headstone for the Algerian. Was that why he kept rushing off, pretending to be doing errands, when in fact he was meeting Kafka and the others?

But it was the way Claire and the major spoke to each other that really perturbed him. Perhaps Claire had been merely using her charms to distract the major from what was happening in the basement but Pierre feared it was more than that. They spoke as if they'd known each other for a while and Pierre didn't like it one little bit.

They'd been there for over half an hour when Xavier nudged Pierre hard in the ribs. 'That's Bouchette coming out,' he said. Monsieur Bouchette ran the local garage.

'We didn't see him go in,' said Pierre, rubbing his ribs.

'How do you know? You were asleep? A fine lookout you'd make. But you're right, we didn't. Look at him, looking left, right and everywhere. The idiot.'

'How not to draw attention to yourself.'

'He's got a book though. Let's hope it isn't *Les Miserables*. So where's your dad?'

'And who else is in there?'

Five minutes later, Monsieur Dubois emerged, wearing a blue beret, also carrying a book, heading in the direction of the town square.

'Bloody hell, he's carrying the Proust. He can hardly read a shopping list let alone something like that.'

'Wait, here's my father.'

They watched him hurry away from the library. The boys melted back behind the tree as Georges passed them, a book under his arm. 'He'd better be going home to work on the Algerian headstone; otherwise he'll have the mayor after him.'

'And look who it is…'

Standing at the library entrance, lighting his pipe, was Kafka. Throwing away the match, he looked up to the sun, smiled to himself, and walked off.

'The whole bloody town is up to something and we're not invited,' said Xavier.

'We'll just have to do our own thing then.'

'What – you and me? Our own two-man cell?'

'Exactly. I've got an idea. Meet me here at nine.'

'At nine? Kraut time? You've got to be joking. That's curfew.'

'All the better. Less people around.'

*

Sitting in the kitchen with his parents and the major, Pierre began regretting his haste. He pretended to read while wondering how he could extricate himself at this time of evening without arousing suspicion. His father and the major were talking music and books while his mother dried the plates. Despite saying otherwise, the major now seemed to be eating with the family most evenings. Not that they minded as he often returned from his work with something to eat – a cut of lamb, fresh vegetables, things that were harder to come by with each passing day. Pierre listened as his father extolled the delights of Beethoven and Brahms and German composers generally, while the major lauded Debussy and Ravel, and other great French composers. They seemed to be falling over each other in their praises. Lucienne, stacking the plates, winked at him.

'And you're reading Flaubert, I see, Monsieur Durand. You got that from the library?'

'Yes; this morning.'

'How strange. He was on my list.'

'List?'

'I'm going to bed,' said Pierre.

'Already?' said Lucienne. 'Are you feeling all right?'

'I've got a headache.'

'Well, wait there, I have some–'

'No, Maman, I'd rather just go to sleep. I'm tired anyway.'

'Tired?' said Georges. 'But you've not done anything today.'

'Nonetheless.'

'Pierre was also at the library this morning,' said the major. 'Weren't you, Pierre?'

'Were you?' said Georges.

'Not for long. Goodnight.'

Pierre took off his boots and placed them under his bed, putting on a pair of soft-soled running shoes. He sighed; this was a ludicrous idea. His door had no lock and he could hardly wedge it shut with the chair. He just hoped if his mother came in she would know enough not to say anything – at least not in front of the major. But he was committed now; he couldn't abandon his friend. He took some clothes out of his wardrobe, folded them over and put them on his bed, under the blanket. It was nowhere near enough. In the end, he had to use every item of clothing he had in order to create a human shape.

Earlier, Pierre had left a can of red paint together with a brush, a flat-headed screwdriver and a couple of pages from a newspaper behind the shed. Now, having put his tools of sabotage into his haversack, he slipped out of the yard and into the night. Still warm, the atmosphere outside was heavy with heat, and how silent the evening; not even the slightest wind to disturb the leaves. It was almost dark but, once his eyes had come accustomed, still plenty of light to see by. There were no street lamps – the Germans had seen to that. The people of the town certainly took the curfew seriously – not a soul in sight; all hidden away behind their shutters. The thought gave him courage – he and his friend were the only ones, out of all these people, prepared to make a stand against their occupiers. One day, maybe years ahead, he would be remembered and feted; for this, he decided, was but the start. They would tell no one for now and the whole town would wonder, as one, who was this hero in their midst; the mysterious fighter prepared to make a stand? Perhaps he would tell Claire. And she would fall in love with him. He visualised her yellow skirt, her soft legs. Calm down, Pierre, calm down, he told himself. He resisted the urge to run; after all, he was in no hurry. He heard the town hall clock chime nine o'clock. For a moment, he thought he saw movement up ahead. He stepped back into the shadows. Deciding it was nothing he moved cautiously on. He realised how much he was enjoying himself; every sense was on full alert, acutely aware of his surroundings, his heart pumping, and it felt great. He told himself he had to breathe deeply, to relax his muscles; he felt invincible yet, at the same time, knew he had to act with utmost trepidation.

He reached the tree where he had arranged to meet Xavier but there was no sign of him. A little bit of enthusiasm slipped away; he felt himself deflate. But it was only a couple minutes past nine. Xavier would show. He leant against the tree, facing away from the street, and waited. Nearby, an owl hooted. He counted the seconds in his head. Sixty seconds. Then another. The more he waited, the more he felt his courage draining away. He knew, if necessary, he could do this alone but he needed the reassurance of his friend's presence. On a more practical level, he needed a lookout. Bloody Xavier, where in the hell are you? He thought of home; thought of his bed, and wished now he was back there. What was he thinking of? Suddenly he saw his town, this place he'd known all his life, in a new light. It seemed bigger and in its utter silence a rather frightening place. A town of the dead, of the cowed. Sixty seconds more. He'd give him just one more minute while he tried to work out what to do. He would do it; damn him, he'd show him that he, Pierre Durand, had the bravery to act alone, a solitary act of defiance. It was better that way. He thought of Claire; he thought of his father, his mother. They'd be proud of him. The romantic within was coming back to the fore.

Leaving the safety of the tree, Pierre embarked on the walk up to the town square; his heart pumping furiously inside. Feeling a little sick, he tried to breathe away his nerves as each step took him closer to his fate. Constantly he looked round him, straining his eyes for even the smallest movement, checking for places he could hide in if need be. He was passing Monsieur Breton's, the undertaker's. The thought of the dead Algerian inside gave him renewed strength. If the Algerian could give his life for France, then the least Pierre could do was to make his small but symbolic stand for freedom.

The high-pitched noise made him jump. He squealed in fright as he fell back against the undertaker's wall, the can of paint clanking against the brickwork. He saw the glint of light in the eyes of the cat, a little black and white thing, before it scurried away. Pierre leant against the wall, catching his breath, and rolled his eyes heavenward.

He pushed himself on; his legs weakened by the fright. He was nearing the bend in the road now, buildings on either side and no doorways to hide in. Here he knew he would be vulnerable. He feared he heard voices – German voices. Peering round, the town square came into view – Soldier Mike, the town hall with its huge swastika banners hanging down, the square of grass, the decorative trees. And there crowded round a bench beneath one of the trees the silhouettes of about five German soldiers, talking, smoking, occasionally laughing. He stepped back. Doubt seeped through him again. What was he thinking; why was he doing this? What if they caught him; what would they do to him? He was only sixteen; they'd let him off, surely, with no more than a verbal clip round the ear. The voices – they'd stopped. Perhaps they were coming. He had to run back but instead he glanced round the corner. He saw them walking leisurely away in the opposite direction; their rifles against their shoulders. Oh, the relief. He had to act now – a moment's hesitation and he'd lose his nerve for good. He waited until the soldiers had moved out of view, then, holding his bag to his chest, sprinted across the cobble-stoned road and to the nearest tree. He'd made it this far. The bravado chased away the demons of doubt. The clock showed nine fifteen. Was that all, he thought; he felt as if he'd been out on his mission for hours. Checking to see the coast was clear, he dashed for the next tree. He plucked a leaf. From the tree, a quick run to the war memorial. It was only now that the thought occurred to him that the Germans might post a sentry at the doors of the town hall. But, as far as he could make out, they had not. He almost laughed. He'd got to the last tree, the last point of safety. The town hall door was just a few yards away, a little stretch of no man's land between him and it.

Checking again for movement, straining his ears, Pierre took a deep breath, thought of Claire's smiling face, and stepped out from behind the tree. Across the cobbled stones, he walked quickly, resisting the urge to run. Crouched down by the door, the entrance afforded him the comfort of darkness. Fumbling, he took out the can of paint and eased open the lid with the screwdriver. With paintbrush in hand, he suffered a moment of hesitation – the solid oak door seemed too good to deface. But seconds later he had painted an enormous red 'V'. He had done it. The rest came easily as he worked quickly. He thought of his mother; she'd be so proud, his dear maman. By the time he was painting the last 'e', he was giggling under his breath. Now he felt exultant; felt like screaming with joy. His work done, he wrapped the brush in newspaper and put everything back in his haversack, tying it shut, shaking with excitement.

Making sure again he was still alone, he stepped back and admired his handiwork. In glistening red paint, letters writ large, he had written *Vive La Framce*. He clenched his eyes shut as the realisation hit him. What a prized idiot; what a bloody fool. He thumped his thigh with frustration. He knew immediately how it had happened – it was the point he'd been thinking about his mother. The 'm' for *maman* had subconsciously gone where the 'n' should have been. Could he fix it? No, his nerves were frayed enough; he knew he'd used up his courage for the night, possibly a lifetime; he had to get home. His bed couldn't come soon enough.

He'd only made it as far as the second tree, the war memorial still ahead of him, Soldier Mike upon his plinth, when the stillness was shattered by the single shout: 'Halt!' Had he hesitated a single moment, he would have stopped. Instead, he ran. And ran. 'Halt!' came the voice again, this time even more urgent, more threatening. Gripping his bag to stop it clanking against him, he ran knowing his life depended on it, his vision blurred with tears. The sharp crack echoed through the air. He instinctively knew that it was a warning shot, fired high. The next one would be aimed at him. He sensed the German taking aim, closing an eye. Dead at sixteen; shot in the back. *Vive La Framce; Vive La fucking Framce.*

He felt himself trip; felt himself fall as if in slow motion, flying through the night air. He landed in a heap at the base of the tree – the very tree he had lain against with Xavier earlier in the day, so long ago; the tree where his friend was supposed to meet him. The side of his head had hit the trunk, the bark scrapping his ear, which now throbbed in pain. Panting heavily, lying on his front, he knew he was done for; finished. There were more panicked shouts in German – two or three of them, then several more, it seemed. He could hear the pounding of footsteps, boots on tarmac, a whole bloody battalion of them coming his way. In a rush of certainty, Pierre knew he had come to his last few moments. All he felt was a deep irritation that his final mark on the world should be a misspelt act of graffiti. Then came the unmistakeable rev of a German motorbike, more shouts, orders, rifles clicking, men ready for action. He almost laughed at the amount of effort they seemed to expending on his behalf. They came running – dozens of them. He closed his eyes, preparing for the bayonet in his back at any moment. But they were running past him; they'd missed him. Peering up from the grass, he felt as if they weren't making much effort to find him. He watched, bewildered, as they rushed by, making room for the motorbike and sidecar which roared through them and raced ahead. He lay on the grass, his ears pounding, and watched as perhaps a dozen soldiers disappeared into the distance, past the library and beyond, the sound of their boots fading away. His eyes remained rooted to the spot where they had disappeared from view. The burst of activity had left in its wake an eerie silence, an imagined echo of boots. Looking around he realised he was very much alone. Not a German in sight. Pierre's relief was tempered by a hint of anti-climax; a faint sense of disappointment that he hadn't been the focus of their attention. He told himself not to be so ridiculous. He wondered where they were going, what had seized them so utterly? There was nothing in that stretch of town apart from the railway line. Oh good God, he thought; someone was attacking the railway line. Someone had the gall to trump his graffiti. The swine.

The town hall clock struck half nine. It had been quite the longest half hour of his life. He rolled over and lay on his back, exhausted. But it wasn't over – a rustle of footsteps on grass had him scrambling to his feet, preparing for an attack.

'Pierre, Pierre,' came the familiar voice. 'It's me.'

Pierre breathed; realising he'd been holding his breath.

'Where the hell have you been?' he said, sitting back down.

'Keep your hair on,' said Xavier, crouching. 'I'm bang on time. Half past nine.'

'I said nine.'

His friend was wearing his father's beret. Far too small for him, the fool; it made his ears stick out. 'You said half nine.'

'No, I said nine.'

'This could go on for a while.'

'You idiot.'

'What happened to your ear?'

'It's a long story.'

'Anyway, we've been beaten to it,' said Xavier, looking round. 'Someone had the same idea and painted all over the town hall door. But you never guess what?' He laughed as he said it, 'The suckers have gone and misspelled France. Put an 'm' instead of an 'n'. I mean, how stupid can you get? What bloody idiots.'

'Yeah,' said Pierre, feeling his whole body sag. 'What bloody idiots.'

*

Someone had locked his bedroom window. As well as meaning he couldn't get back in, it meant someone, probably his mother, had been in his room. Anything beyond a cursory glance and they would have realised that it was a pile of clothes in his bed. He deposited his bag in the shed, closed the door and wondered how on earth he was going to get back inside. He heard the chickens cluck within their pen. Leaning against the wall, the Algerian's headstone. His father had done more than he thought, even as far as half the wording. He laughed at the thought of his father engraving 'France' with an 'm'.

If his parents knew he'd gone, they'd be waiting up for him, however long it took. Circling round the house, he tried the front door. Locked. Creeping past the major's bedroom, he knocked on his parents' window. No answer. He hadn't expected one. He had no choice; he would have to knock on the kitchen door and hope to God the major didn't answer. He swore in frustration.

He tapped gently on the kitchen door. Not even a mouse would have heard that, he thought. Stealing himself, he knocked a little louder, then louder still.

'Who is it?' It was his mother. How lovely to hear her voice.

'It's me,' he whispered back.

The door opened and Lucienne almost pulled him into the darkened house, into the kitchen, lighted by just a couple of candles. 'Where in the blazes have you been?' she shouted, taking Pierre by surprise.

'Maman, keep your voice down!'

'Oh, don't worry – no one's here. I mean *no one*. First your father went out, then the major, someone called for him, and then I discover you'd gone too.'

'What? Where did they go?'

'You think they told me? No. You all leave me and I'm left alone worried sick.'

'Don't worry, Maman, I'm sure the major will be back soon.'

'Don't try to be funny. So where were you?'

'What?'

'You heard me. Where were you?'

'I can't tell you. I'm sorry. Business.'

'Funny that; that's exactly what your father said. It's not a game all this, Pierre, it's… What's happened to your ear?'

'I fell over,' said Pierre, rubbing it.

'On your ear? And what's that blood on your fingers?' She took his hand and turned it over. 'It's paint. Why have you got… OK, you're right; I don't want to know.' With a heavy sigh, she went to the sink to wash her hands. 'Did you see your father?'

'No.' She looked at him accusingly over her shoulder. 'No, really; I promise.' After a while, he asked, 'Is there a power cut?'

'No.'

'So why the candles?'

'Your father told me. Wants the world to think we're in bed.'

'The world? It's empty out there; no one will notice.'

'I'm only obeying orders. Anyway, it's not empty – out there somewhere is your father and the major, and I don't imagine for one minute they are together.'

Chapter 6

Pierre laid on his bed, the curtains open, a hint of sun shining through, motes of dust dancing in the air. He fancied a cigarette. It was still only seven. In the distance, he could hear the rumble of several trucks – he'd learnt that the Germans always went out on exercise at this time, always at seven. He dreamt of Claire, as he often did first thing in the morning. He was kissing her, always kissing her, only the location changed with each day. Today, he was kissing her at her work, in the library; next to them the pile of banned books, his hand on her breast. It seemed sacrilege to be fondling the librarian's breast in front of such greats – Flaubert, Shakespeare, Proust. He really could do with a cigarette. The sound of his parents talking filtered into his consciousness. So at least his father had made it back. The tone of their voices sounded normal; they weren't arguing. His father had already been forgiven. Back to Claire. He groaned. He dreamt of her nibbling on his ear – no, that hurt too much. 'Kiss me,' she whispered while pushing away Proust. She had such lovely lips. Pierre realised he had an erection.

'Pierre – breakfast time.' Claire vanished in an instant. 'Oh, dear. I do apologise.' His mother backed away from the door. 'I should've knocked,' she said, now knocking. 'I'm so sorry.'

He grunted.

'I'm sorry?' she said, still hovering outside the door. 'I didn't quite catch that.'

'Nothing, Maman. Nothing.'

'Can I come in?'

If you must, he thought. 'Yes,' he said, readjusting his blanket. 'OK.'

She slipped into his bedroom and, glancing surreptitiously behind her, closed the door. She was wearing an apron – a rarity these days, since the major moved in. She opened her mouth to say something but stopped as she registered the state of his room – the poster of Rita Hayworth which she always regarded as provocative; his bureau scattered with books and papers; the overflowing bin full of pieces of rolled-up paper; his dusty mirror, partially obscured by a French flag; the chest of drawers covered with statuettes, a chisel, and model aeroplane and goodness-knows-what and, leaning against it, a guitar he no longer played. She didn't have to say it, he needed to have a tidy-up.

'Pierre,' she said, sitting down gingerly on the edge of the bed. As soon as she sat, she shot up again. 'Oh, sorry; do you mind if I sit?'

He shuffled up against the wall. 'Yes, what is it, Maman?'

She checked the door. 'Listen, Pierre, about last night. I haven't told your father you went out; he doesn't know.'

'And you think we shouldn't tell him?'

'Yes, I think it'd be for the best. At least for now, for a while.'

'Fine. Is the major in?'

'Yes, he's having breakfast.'

'Good. Can I get up now?'

'Oh yes,' she said, getting to her feet. 'Sorry, I didn't mean to disturb your... I mean, your... well,' she added, cheerfully, 'breakfast is ready.'

*

Pierre ate his boiled egg in silence next to his mother at the table while his father and the major, opposite, discussed violin concertos. No one mentioned the railway. Pierre could tell that the major's musical knowledge was far superior but he was going to great lengths to play it down, not wanting to embarrass his host. Why, the major said, he had seen the great Furtwangler conduct. Pierre had never heard of Furtwangler but the name sounded grand and his father was certainly impressed.

'Sleep well?' his father asked him, spreading jam on his toast.

'All right,' he replied, wondering why, of all days, he'd ask a question he'd never asked before.

'What happened to your ear?'

'I fell.'

'When? It was all right when you went to bed last night.'

'I just fell.'

'Leave him be,' said Lucienne, quietly. Georges shrugged and bit into his toast.

'I passed through the square late last night,' said the

major, a coffee mug in his hand. 'Someone had painted a slogan over the big doors of the town hall.'

'Delinquents,' said Georges.

'Petty vandalism; it was nothing.'

'What did it say?' asked Lucienne.

'It said *Vive La France* in big red letters.'

Georges laughed. Pierre concentrated on his egg and soldiers aware that his mother had shot him a look.

'Silly thing,' continued the major, 'is that somehow they misspelled France.'

'What?' exclaimed Georges. 'How do you misspell France? Ha, it must've been the work of a German. No true Frenchman would have misspelled the name of his own country, for goodness sake.'

'Well, I'm afraid it will be a Frenchman who will have to scrape it off.'

Pierre grimaced as he swallowed down his spoonful of cod liver oil.

'Are you all right, Pierre?' asked Georges.

*

After breakfast, Pierre went to the yard and, having gathered his tools from the shed and donned his goggles, began work. The yard was still bathed in shadow; it would be another hour or so before it caught the sun. His father had already been out and unlocked the chicken pen. He watched them pecking at their seed, uncomfortably aware that news of his graffiti would be spreading through the town by now. He took no pleasure that everyone would be wondering who had done the deed. No one could ever know – the shame would be too much. He wanted to go and see it, see his work in the daylight but decided to wait;

thinking it best not to rush out. Instead, he would spend a little time with his White Venus.

He'd been chiselling away for ten minutes or more when the major appeared, as he knew he would. 'It's progressing, I see,' said the German. 'She's beginning to take shape.'

'Hmm.'

'It's lovely to see; a work of art being created before our very eyes.' He sat down on the rocking chair but then promptly got up again, disturbing the chickens from their pecking. 'I admire your dedication. When Joachim was young he used to paint. He wasn't bad. He doesn't paint any more; doesn't have the time, poor boy. I received a letter from him yesterday. The army's keeping him busy. He tells me they'll be on the move soon. Of course, he can't tell me where. Could be Poland, North Africa, Holland. Perhaps even France. I would love that. I miss him, you know. His mother is very proud of him, I'm sure. I know you are French and he German but you would like him, my Joachim. You're very similar in many ways.'

Pierre watched him from the corner of his eye. The man seemed on edge, pacing up and down, hands behind back, kicking little stones with the toe of his shiny boots.

'It does seem very young to put a boy in uniform. He's nineteen, but nonetheless. You'd have thought we would have learnt from the last war, but no. I know he couldn't wait to play his part, to fight for the Führer. But it's a cause of constant anxiety. I'm sure you understand.' He looked up at the sky. 'It's another fine day. Not a cloud in the sky. A fine day for the beach. Do you ever go to the beach here? I suppose it's quite a distance. When I was a boy... Listen to me. I talk too much. I ought to go.' He paused, deep in thought. 'It's times like these,' he said, eventually, 'that you think back to your childhood and it all seems such a long time ago. My father had a little shed like this. He used to sit at the door after dinner and smoke his pipe, staring up to the sky, looking at the stars. My mother, bless her, wouldn't let him smoke indoors.' He laughed, peering inside the shed.

Pierre wished he would go. He had enough to think about without this foreigner unburdening himself.

'What a lot of paint in here.' Pierre tried to focus on the work in hand. 'Red paint too, I see.' The major readjusted his cap. 'Well, Pierre, time I was leaving. It's been lovely talking to you. Keep up the good work.'

'Yeah.'

Pierre watched him leave, watched him as the major paused at the kitchen door. Without turning, the German said, 'Be careful, Pierre. It's a dangerous place out there. Just... just be careful.'

And with that he was gone.

*

A while later, Pierre was joined in the yard by his father, wearing his overalls, a pencil behind his ear, a damp cigarette between his lips. Without acknowledging his son, he pulled out his little stool from the shed and sat down in front of the headstone. He looked at it for a few minutes, checked the wording written for him on a sheet of paper by the mayor, and set to work on the headstone, delicately engraving the letters.

The two men, each with a chisel and hammer, worked in silence. After a while, the temptation to go see his graffiti became too much. Laying down his tools, Pierre removed his goggles and wiped the dust from his trousers. He left without saying anything. His mother was doing the washing, having pulled out the mangle, despite the warmth of the day outside. The kitchen smelt of damp linen. He washed his hands batting off questions from his mother asking whether he was feeling OK. 'You're very quiet this morning, Pierre,' she said, holding one of Georges's shirts, her head tilted to one side as if to emphasise her concern.

'I'm fine, Maman,' he snapped.

*

A small crowd had gathered in front of the town hall, sniggering at the slogan on the doors, shaking their heads as if in disbelief. Standing back, too afraid to mingle among them for fear they would sense his guilt, Pierre couldn't help but agree – it looked ridiculous. Nearby, a couple of soldiers watched them, little smiles on their faces. Pierre recognised Fritzes One and Two.

Vive la Framce. The letters were not as big as he thought. 'What must the Germans think of us,' he heard someone say. 'It's embarrassing,' said another. Pierre recognized Madame Picard, a baguette poking out of her basket. 'If I find out my son did this, I'll put him over my knee.' 'But he's nineteen.' 'I don't care; this is a disgrace.' The town hall doors opened. People stepped back. It was the major accompanied by a policeman, a Frenchman, with, thought Pierre, unusually long sideburns, a folder under his arm.

Pierre felt ridiculously pleased to see his German, pleased for the distraction. 'Hello, Major,' he said, brightly.

Striding past, the major saw him, looked straight at him with cold eyes, but made no acknowledgement. Pierre watched the two men go. Maybe, he thought, he had had the sun in his eyes. The major shouted something at Fritz One who saluted in return. Fritz One approached the gathering and said something in German. He repeated it, this time more loudly. 'I think he wants us to move on,' said Madame Picard. 'Let's hope they catch the little bugger who did this,' said someone. Slowly the crowd dispersed. Pierre watched the major and the policeman enter Café Bleu on the far side of the square, taking a table outside. A new sign had appeared above its door – *We welcome our German guests.*

'Hey, you.' Pierre heard the soldier shouting in German. 'Oi, are you deaf?' said Fritz One, poking Pierre in the arm.

Pierre turned to see the German holding out something in his hand. 'What?' It was a strip of sandpaper. Motioning with his head towards the door, the penny dropped. 'You... you want me to...?'

'Take,' said Fritz One in French, thrusting it at Pierre. Pierre looked round, hoping somehow to be saved. 'Take.'

'What now? Me?' Reluctantly, he took the sandpaper. *'Merde.'*

Fritz One strolled back to his colleagues who had formed a small semi-circle, their arms folded, their helmets pushed back on their heads.

And so Pierre began work, starting not at the beginning but at the 'm', the letter that had so mocked him. The sun beat down on his back and he soon broke out in a sweat. His hand ached as he rubbed and rubbed at the paint which, predictably, proved mightily hard to remove. Every now and then, the door would swing open, causing each passer-by to stop and look disdainfully at what he was doing. No one spoke to him. The soldiers giggled. One of them shouted at him. He turned to find the German taking a photo. Finally, they tired of the attraction and melted away. Only Fritz One remained, to ensure Pierre didn't slack. After half an hour, drenched in sweat and thoroughly miserable, he asked for a break. '*Nein*,' said Fritz One, motioning for him to carry on. Pierre hoped to God the major couldn't see him from the other side of the square, basking in the sun with his coffee. Indeed, he hoped no one would see him at this, his greatest humiliation. But, of course, at some point every person he had ever known, or so it felt, passed by and asked him what he was doing. 'You can give me a hand, if you want,' he'd said to Xavier. But no, Xavier had things to do, slapped him on the back, wished him good luck and, mounting his pushbike, buggered off on his merry way. The worst, of course, was the appearance of Claire, looking gorgeous in a lime-coloured blouse, her brassiere clearly visible beneath the fabric, and a rose-patterned skirt, the picture of gaiety. 'Poor Pierre,' she said. 'They should find the idiot who did this and get him to do it. It's not fair you should have to. Must go. Bye bye!'

Half an hour on, and Pierre was only half done. He needed a drink and both his hands throbbed. Fritz One kept guard still, pacing up and down. Pierre looked across at the café. The policeman had gone but sitting in his place, laughing and talking with the major, was Claire. How comfortable they looked together. Pierre groaned. Could the day get any worse?

*

Some thirty minutes later, exhausted and thoroughly

dejected, Pierre had finished. He had managed to scrape the red lettering off but the words were still visible as he had also removed much of the blue paint beneath. The doors would need re-painting. He was thirsty and hungry. For now, Fritz One seemed prepared to let him go. He sat down on a bench near the war memorial. Realising he had a few centimes in his pocket, he decided to treat himself to a coffee at Café Bleu.

Claire and the major were long gone but most tables were full of German soldiers leaning back on their chairs, helmets to the side. Many were singing, clapping their knees in time. An elderly French couple occupied the table nearest the door, trying their best to ignore the boisterous Germans near them. Having been outside for too long, Pierre was relieved to experience the cool and darkened interior. It was the town's smartest café – a two-toned red-and-white linoleum floor, a bookshelf full of ornamental books, framed pictures of cockerels hanging from the walls above the dado rail, a standard lamp, and a glass case full of crockery. The place smelt pleasantly of real coffee and cigarette smoke. In an annex on one side, a couple of soldiers played table tennis, while others watched and cheered, their shirtsleeves rolled up. The only thing that spoilt it was a framed portrait of Hitler with his silly moustache and icy stare. He wondered whether its placing, next to the door of the gents' toilet, was accidental. He hoped not. He sat at a table for two beneath Hitler, decorated with a long glass vase and a single flower, and ordered a black coffee and a single cigarette. A waiter in black and white returned with his coffee, cigarette and a clean ashtray. 'What's that awful song they're singing?' he asked the waiter.

'Keep your voice down. That's their *Horst Wessel* song. They're always singing it.'

'Their what?'

'Named after some dead Nazi martyr.'

Pierre leant back and allowed the rush of nicotine to pulse through his veins. The coffee, syrupy and strong, helped revive him. Things, he concluded, were not going well. His first act of sabotage had backfired in ways he would never have imagined and he had been chastened in front of the whole town and particularly in the eyes of Claire. He would finish his coffee and then seek out Kafka and demand he be allowed to join whatever he had formed.

A laugh erupted from a table of soldiers nearby. Much back-slapping ensued. In a peculiar sort of way, Pierre realised he rather envied them. They were men, doing men's work, united by their uniforms. Pierre had nothing – no sense of belonging. Just a vague feeling that the honour of France had to be salvaged, but this gave him no satisfaction – it was too big a concept, too nebulous, to mean anything on a practical level. He needed direction, to belong, to have a leader. He needed Kafka.

He was suddenly aware of a soldier standing over him, barking at him in an unpleasant tone. 'Out,' said the soldier in German. 'Get out of this seat.'

'I'm sorry?' The man, all six foot of him, was a lieutenant.

'I need this seat. I need to work,' said the lieutenant in heavily accented French, waving a file at Pierre.

'Yes, you can sit here, if you want,' said Pierre, motioning to the chair on the other side of the table.

The German considered the offer. With a shrug of the

shoulders, he sat down.

Pierre finished his cigarette, trying to hide his discomfort at sharing a table with a Boche. The German ordered a hot chocolate in bad French, then, pushing his peaked hat further up his head, opened his file and started to read. Pierre considered the man while trying not to. He wished he had something to read. The German seemed incredibly young – not more than a few years older than himself, but his face looked hard, his skin tight. He thought of the major's son.

The German looked up and caught Pierre staring at him. 'What are you looking at, little froggy?' he said in German.

'I'm sorry?'

'You speak German? No? Good.'

Pierre smiled.

'So, what's it like to drink your coffee beneath a picture of the Führer, eh? That's how it should be,' he said, nodding.

Pierre nodded back. 'Yes.'

'You're a fawning little shit, aren't you?'

'Yes.'

The German laughed and Pierre found himself laughing too. 'Are you a little Frenchie froggy, yes?'

'Yes, yes.'

'Ha! That's my boy.' The German glanced up worriedly at Hitler's portrait. 'We should not speak like this in front of the Führer, you scum.' Abruptly, he stood up and, facing the painting, saluted his leader, his arm outstretched. 'I'm sorry, *mein Führer*, forgive me my language.'

It was time, thought Pierre, to make a hasty exit. Rising to his feet, he quickly realised, was a mistake – the German thought that he too wanted to pay his respects to Hitler.

'Salute the Führer.'

'Yes.'

'Go on then,' said the German, elbowing Pierre hard in the arm.

'Ow. What?'

The waiter appeared at his side, carrying a tray with a number of dirty cups and saucers. 'Lieutenant Neumann wants you to do the Hitler salute.'

'What? Me?'

The lieutenant barked, 'Show some respect, Frenchie boy,' his arm still outstretched.

'He doesn't look too happy,' said the waiter. 'I'd do as he says, if I was you.'

'I can't,' said Pierre, his stomach caving in. 'Not that.'

The German turned to him, his eyes ablaze with anger. 'You salute the Führer, you little French frog.'

'Just get it over and done with,' said the waiter. A German customer called him over. 'I won't say anything,' he said as he left, balancing his tray.

And so Pierre found himself in Café Bleu standing next to a rabid Nazi who resembled a fury on the verge of tears, in front of a painting doing a Hitler salute. It was the final humiliation; he just hoped to God no one had seen him.

*

Pierre worked furiously, hacking away at the stone, sweating beneath his goggles. He changed them for his sunglasses. The yard at this time of day offered not an inch of shade. The hens had taken to their pen. Only Maurice the cockerel remained outside. He wasn't going to let a bit of heat keep him from his duty. The incident with the Nazi had proved to Pierre that all Germans were bastards; that he'd been a fool to allow himself to be charmed by the major. He was a German, serving Hitler, and by default no better than the bastard lieutenant. He would no longer listen to the major's whinging and waxing lyrical about his precious son. He was a Nazi too; they were all bloody Nazis. They had no right to be in his country and he would do whatever it took to play his part in kicking them out. He was relieved his father wasn't around; he needed to be alone, to think. His father was always out now. He, at least, had found a purpose, a cause. His mother popped her head round the kitchen door, asked him if he was hungry. Hungry? He felt weak with hunger. Even his mother had a cause, albeit one she didn't relish, the cause of finding food on a daily basis. And it could only get much worse. At the moment, only luxury things like cakes, butter and real coffee, seemed to have disappeared, almost overnight. Now, only the cafés frequented by the Krauts, had them.

Back indoors, eating his bread and cheese and wishing it were so much more, Pierre's father returned, looking mildly perturbed. Although, mused Pierre, the emotional distance between perturbed and euphoric covered very little ground with his father. And he seemed continually entrenched in neutral, viewing a world that induced no feeling great or small, for the better or the worse. He remembered, before the war, his mother once returning with a brace of herring, a rarity, bought from a travelling fishmonger. She slapped the fish down on the kitchen table, remarking Georges was no longer the only cold fish residing in the house. A twitch of the moustache was probably the only response she got.

Georges sat down, stood up, paced up and down.

'Are you OK, Georges?' asked Lucienne.

'I'm fine, Lucienne.' He then did something that Pierre had never seen before – he reached out for his wife, took the bread knife she was holding and placed it on the table, then put his arms around his wife and hugged her. Why, wondered Pierre, did this unexpected and totally out of character show of affection worry him so?

*

Most of the population had never had a car. Georges once did, an old Daimler inherited from his brother, the tightrope walker, but even that had died a death a few years back. Now, all the family had was Pierre's bicycle. A few businesses owned a truck and that was about it. But they had mostly been requisitioned by the Germans – cars, lorries, motorbikes, the lot, together with the petrol. While the German staff drove round in their front-wheel drive Citroens, all that was left for the locals were the bikes. And whatever the farmers had – tractors mainly. The 'cemetery boys', as Pierre's father always called them, were allowed to keep their old wagon, and this battered four-stroke was now outside their bungalow, a small black monstrosity of a vehicle. The cemetery boys were, in fact, two bent old men, whose combined age, by Pierre's reckoning, must have been 160. Standing in the yard, hands on hips, soggy cigarettes on their lips, they admired Georges's handiwork, the Algerian headstone. Pierre made a half-hearted attempt at sweeping the yard, causing the hens to scatter in a cloud of dust and downy feathers. The two of them were mirror images of each other – both scrawny old men in dirty dungarees, skin as tough as leather, grey hair beneath their flat berets, thin moustaches, both smoking. 'Very nice,' said one, his voice gruff with age.

'It wasn't difficult,' said Georges.

'At least you spelt "France" proper.'

'And what have we got here, young Pierre?'

'It's my sculpture,' said Pierre, sweeping, wishing now he had left the tarpaulin over his work.

The man stroked his chin. 'Is it meant to be a woman?'

'Has she got any clothes on?' asked the other.

'It's classical.'

Both men laughed raucously. Even Georges guffawed while Pierre bristled.

'Classical, eh? Is that what you call it? And you feel qualified to carve the female form in all its glory, eh?'

Pierre blushed. 'I've – I've got a book on Renaissance art. It's Botticelli.'

'Botcha what?'

He was about to tell them its name but held back. He realised he hadn't even told his father its name, nor his mother. Only the major knew. He feared anyone else would only consider it pretentious, and mock him.

'Come on, boys,' said Georges. 'We need to press on.'

'In a hurry, are we, Georges?'

Georges didn't answer but it was enough to stir the men into action. They may have been ancient, mused Pierre, but they were strong. Between them, they hoisted up the headstone and, with Georges guiding them, urging them to be careful, carried it out through the yard door and round the front of the house, grunting, and onto the back of the truck. Pierre followed. The truck sagged with the weight of the headstone.

With the tailgate secured and with much wiping of hands, they were ready to leave. 'Where's your new family pet then, Georges?' asked the first chap, grinding his cigarette into the pavement with his boot.

'Our what?'

'I hear you've got your very own Kraut?'

'Oh, our family pet. Very funny. I don't know where he is. Have you seen him, Pierre?'

'Me? No. He's out.'

'Well, I worked that much out for myself.'

'So what's he like then?'

'I don't know; I have very little to do with him.'

Apart from long discussions about music, thought Pierre.

'You haven't poisoned his soup yet?'

'Leave him alone,' said the other as they climbed into their truck. 'They're not a bad lot, these Krauts. They'll sort out the commies for us, that's for sure. This country's gone soft. Not like your generation, eh, Georges?' He turned on the ignition and the old truck spluttered into life. 'Dig out your old bayonet, Georges; show them what we're made of.'

The truck bounced down the road, billows of black smoke in its wake. Emerging from the cloud of fumes, returning home with bulging shopping bags, was Pierre's mother.

'Do you still have your bayonet, Papa?'

'Don't be daft.'

'Hello, boys,' said Lucienne. 'Good news – plenty of marrows today.'

'Is that what you've got in those bags. Anything else?'

'No,' said Lucienne, lifting a bag as if in triumph. 'Just marrows. I've been to church as well.'

'Great. Well, I have to be off.'

'Where are you going?'

'Out.'

'Where?'

'To get my wages from the town hall – for the headstone.'

'Good, we could do with the money.' Lucienne went indoors, huffing. That, thought Pierre, was a hint that he should have carried her bags. Instead, he ran after his father, quickly catching him up. 'Papa, can I come with you?'

His father looked straight ahead. 'To the town hall?'

'No, I mean... I want to help.'

'With what?'

'With... whatever it is you do.'

His father laughed – heartily, a laugh that pierced Pierre.

'Go home, boy. Help your mother stuff a marrow. Have you slaughtered Madeleine yet?'

Pierre stopped and watched his father saunter down the lane, shaking his head. As he returned home, the White Venus beckoning, he remembered his father and Kafka remonstrating with Monsieur Breton, the undertaker, for wanting to claim payment for his work on the Algerian.

He passed through the kitchen where he found his mother stroking a marrow as if it were a cat. 'Are you OK, Pierre?' she asked.

'The world is full of hypocrisy, isn't it, Maman?'

'Yes, Pierre, I suppose it is.'

*

An hour later, Pierre was on his way to the library. His father's dismissive laugh was bothering him still, disrupting his concentration. Georges still hadn't come back and the longer he took the more agitated Pierre felt. Giving up on the White Venus, he covered it with the tarpaulin and decided to head for the library – to see if he could find his father there, plus, of course, the library always had the additional bonus of Claire's presence.

He slipped out of the house before his mother had chance to allot him an errand. He knew the library would probably be closed – it was often closed. No one in this town ever read. They'd probably read even less now, now that the major had stripped the shelves of all the interesting books. He thought of calling on Xavier but decided against it. He wondered whether fifty, sixty years hence, he and Xavier would resemble the cemetery boys. What a thought and not altogether an unpleasant one. Assuming of course they weren't all German citizens by then. He passed the baker's – the queue seemed to be longer with each passing day. He noticed Xavier's pushbike leant up against the wall. So his mother also got him to do the bread run. He resisted hiding his friend's bike, just to see the expression on his face.

He could see from a distance that the library doors were closed. He thought, nonetheless, he'd go investigate. Madame Picard was walking her dog, the little white terrier, on the grass, a small yappy little thing with a short tail. He saw it do a shit right near the tree he and Xavier had sat against.

Sure enough the library doors were locked. Yet one of the windows above him was slightly open. Disappointed, he walked round the building treading delicately on the gravel path but to what purpose he wasn't sure. He arrived back at the point he started from. He'd not seen or heard anything. He noticed a brick had fallen out from the sidewall. Without a second thought, Pierre had wedged his boot in the hole and clambered up the wall, grabbing the windowsill. It wasn't easy; he could feel his foot slipping. With some effort, he managed to lever himself up and was able to peer through the window. Inside it was dark but there at the counter he saw a figure, perhaps two. His foot slipped and he fell. He looked about. Madame Picard had gone; no one else was around. Someone was inside the library; he had to see who it was. He climbed up to the window a second time, pushing his boot into the hole as far as it could go. Holding onto the windowsill, he pressed the side of his face against the glass. He gasped. Something like a sledgehammer hit him on the chest. His legs turned to jelly. Unable to prevent himself, he fell, landing in a heap on the gravel path. His eyes blurred over. A pain gripped his heart.

'Are you all right there?' It was Madame Picard who had reappeared out of nowhere. Her dog sniffed at him. He scrambled to his feet, fighting back the urge to scream, fighting the urge to kick the sodding dog, the ugly mongrel. 'Are you... are you crying?' said Madame Picard, relishing the moment.

She stepped back on seeing the look of rage on his face.

He walked quickly, muttering the word 'bitch' over and over again, his fingers digging into his scalp. He could feel the bile at the back of his throat. He shook his head, as if trying to free his mind of the image. But it remained, imprinted, refusing to fade away. The image was of Claire – on the counter, her eyes closed, running her fingers through his hair; her skirt ruffled up, her legs around him as he fucked her, his trousers down at his knees. The bitch. They'd kill her if they knew; they'd kill her for that; they'd bloody string her up for fucking a German, a fucking German, the fucking major.

Chapter 7

Pierre stared at his sculpture, wondering whether to carry on with his work. What held him back was the fear that the major would make his usual morning appearance before he went off to work, or to fuck Claire. Pierre couldn't bear the thought of seeing him. He'd spent the previous evening shut in his room, reading and sketching. He could hear his father and the major talking about art. He pricked up his ears whenever he heard his name mentioned – usually in the form of compliments from the major, about his artistic eye, his feel for sculpture. He waited for his father to say something of his own accord. But no. Nothing. Today for the first time in weeks, there was no sun. Overcast but still warm. His mother had been urging him to go to the town hall and ask if they had any jobs. So far, he'd resisted. His father's work, although well paid, was sporadic. It was, after all, a strange way of making a living – to wait for someone to die. Fortunately for Georges, his catchment area included the nearby town of Saint-Romain, five kilometres away. It was where the

Germans had set up their headquarters; they'd requisitioned a large office block next, apparently, to the dentist's. But she was right; he needed his own job.

The kitchen door opened. Pierre made to leave. He saw the major. 'No work today?' he asked.

'No,' said Pierre, barging passed.

'Pierre,' called his mother. 'If you're passing the baker's…'

And so he found himself, again, queuing up at the baker's. Outside, on the door window, the Germans had put up a notice announcing a blanket ban on anyone attending the funeral of the Algerian, due the following day. *Any citizen attempting to attend the funeral will face harsh consequences*, it read in bold red letters.

Inside the bakery, Pierre saw Xavier a few places ahead of him. They saluted each other. Monsieur Gide, the baker, was reading aloud from his newspaper. Marshal Pétain, apparently, had now been confirmed as president. 'He's too old,' said Madame Picard. 'He doesn't know what day of the week it is.' 'You don't know what you're talking about,' came a reply from further up. 'He's the right man for the job. At least he's here, unlike that de Gaulle man, spouting nonsense from his cosy London home.' 'You know, Pétain's found him guilty.' 'Who? De Gaulle? How can he? He's not even here.' 'You can try someone *in absentia*, it's called. And they've found him guilty of treason and he's to be shot.' 'In London? Will the English do that?' 'No, not the English. If he steps foot in France again he'll be arrested and then shot.' 'Shush, here come the Germans.' 'They've got Touvier.'

Pierre recognised the young lieutenant from Café Bleu, Lieutenant Neumann, walking ahead of two privates, his rifle over his shoulder, his belt buckle glinting in the sun. The soldiers were leading a dishevelled Monsieur Touvier, the blacksmith. Pierre slunk back behind Madame Picard; he didn't want the lieutenant to see him. Touvier, his overalls streaked with the dirt of his trade, was clasping his beret, his eyes looked wide with fright. But as they passed the bakery, Touvier shook himself free of his minders, and shouted at the queue. 'You have to resist, all of you; before it's too late, you have to–'

The lieutenant punched him hard in the stomach, bringing Touvier to his knees. He groaned, clutching his stomach while the queue gasped as one. One of the privates kicked him in the ribs. Touvier fell but was immediately scooped up by the other.

'Leave him alone,' shouted Monsieur Bouchette, stepping out of the baker's. Taking his revolver from its holster, the lieutenant strode up to the Frenchman who stood transfixed while those inside melted back. Without a word, the lieutenant pointed his revolver, pressing it against Bouchette's forehead. The two men glared at each other. Bouchette's courage took Pierre's breath away. The thought of that cold barrel against bare skin made him shiver. Slowly, Bouchette put his hands up. With quick movements, the lieutenant returned the gun to its holster and clicked shut the button, all the time keeping his eyes fixed on Bouchette.

He motioned at the privates to follow him. Now gripping the spluttering Touvier more firmly by his arms, they dragged the unfortunate blacksmith away.

The queue breathed a sigh of relief as Bouchette returned indoors. 'Are you OK, Monsieur Bouchette?' 'You're so brave.'

Pierre and Xavier acknowledged each other with raised eyebrows.

'Monsieur Touvier is right,' said Bouchette. 'We can't just let the Boches ride roughshod over us.'

'What did they want with Monsieur Touvier?'

'Perhaps it was to do with the other night. You know, on the railway.'

For his bravery, Monsieur Bouchette was allowed to jump the queue to be served ahead of everyone else. He left, with two baguettes under his arm, to a round of applause.

*

Xavier and Pierre walked home together, Xavier pushing his bike, a baguette each. 'You should do that,' said Xavier.

'What?'

'Stand up to the Boches like that.'

'What and get my head almost blown off?'

'Yeah, but just think how impressed Claire would be. Girls love that sort of thing.'

Pierre's stomach ached at the thought of Claire. 'So, you're an expert on girls now?'

'It's obvious, isn't it? What's the matter? You all right?'

'Yeah.'

'We could go out later, maybe—'

'No. Can't today.'

*

On returning home Pierre told his mother about the blacksmith. She called Georges in from the yard and made Pierre repeat the tale.

His father blanched. 'Shit. When did this happen?'

'About half an hour ago. Maybe more.'

'And you've only just come back?' He sprang over to the front door, turning the key and bolting it locked.

'I didn't want to lose my place in the queue.'

'You didn't want to… Oh Lord.' He began pacing up and down the kitchen. 'Someone's talked.'

'Georges, what's the matter? What are you talking about?'

He looked at his wife and Pierre, glancing from one to the other. 'Look, that night up at the railway.'

'Oh no, please, Georges, don't tell me you were involved.'

He nodded. He seemed to take no pleasure from confessing his involvement because, Pierre knew, Lucienne would be furious. He waited for the barrage of anger but instead his mother collapsed in tears. 'Georges, no, I begged you.'

'I had to. I've waited twenty-two years for this; I couldn't turn away – not now.'

'I don't understand – twenty-two years for what?'

'I can't explain; they could be here at any moment.' He started pacing again, running his fingers through his hair.

'Who? The Germans?'

'They've arrested Touvier. That means I'll be next. Maybe the others.'

'What others?' asked Lucienne, biting her nails.

'Don't ask. The less you know the better.' He stopped, as if an idea had just hit him. 'Listen, I need to go and lie low for a while.'

'Where would you go?'

'I don't know,' he screamed. 'That's the problem; I don't bloody know.'

'Why don't you stay at Monsieur Touvier's?' suggested Pierre. 'He lives alone, and they're hardly likely to return there, not now that they've taken him.'

'My word; that's not a bad idea. Lucienne, go pack me some clothes. Not too many. Thank you, son.' Georges briefly hugged him. He felt awkward but Pierre experienced a tremor of pleasure.

'It's OK, Papa. It's OK.'

'You're a good lad.'

Lucienne called through from the bedroom, 'Georges, will you want…'

The urgent rap on the door stopped her short. The three of them stood stock still as if frozen.

'Open up,' came the accented voice from outside, pushing at the door.

Georges's eyes darted left and right. 'I'll make a run for it.'

'Darling, no; they might shoot you.'

His body sagged. 'You're right. Pierre, let them in.'

It was strange, thought Pierre, how heavy his arm felt as he lifted his hand to turn the key in the door and undo the bolt.

The Germans barged past, pushing Pierre to one side, as a flurry of grey-green uniforms flooded into the living room. 'Georges Durand?' shouted the lieutenant, his revolver drawn. The two privates seized Georges's arms, twisting them behind his back. He made no resistance. 'You come with us.'

Lucienne screamed, her hands at her face, her wide eyes full of incomprehension. The soldiers pushed Georges towards the door.

'Where are you taking him?' screeched Lucienne.

'He come with us,' said the lieutenant, brandishing his revolver at Lucienne.

She stepped back, her eyes full of tears.

Georges managed to stop at the door, next to Pierre. 'Don't fight back, son, it's not…'

With a yank of his arm, the privates pushed him outside. The lieutenant pointed his gun at Pierre and, at that point, recognised him from the café. 'Heil Hitler,' shouted the lieutenant, his arm stretched out, before following his men out, laughing to himself.

Pierre caught his father's eye a second before the door slammed shut. He seemed calm, thought Pierre; resigned almost.

The sudden silence weighed heavily. Lucienne stood, her arm extended, as if seeking her husband's hand, her features drawn. She seemed to stagger through to the kitchen and plonked down on the armchair. Pierre knew he had to say something, to try and reassure his mother with empty words. Placing an awkward hand on her shoulder, he said, 'It'll turn out all right, Maman. Just wait and see.'

'Yes, Pierre; you're right. I know you are.'

*

Many hours later, near bedtime, Major Hurtzberger returned to the house. It had been an awful afternoon. Lucienne was beside herself with worry, frequently breaking down in tears, frequently washing her hands. The claustrophobia of her grief was too much for Pierre, who felt totally ill-equipped to handle the situation. He knew circumstances dictated he should hug his mother but having grown up in a less-than-tactile family, it was beyond him. Instead, he found himself agreeing with everything his mother said, even though she said the same things again and again, and making her so many cups of coffee, she complained of a headache. By early evening he was hungry. But how could he mention dinner on a day like this? Fortunately, around seven, his mother went for a lie down to help ease her head and Pierre attempted something he had never tried before – to cook. But the scrambled egg he cooked himself was burnt, littered with fragments of shell, and quite revolting. At least with his father gone, he was able to help himself to a larger portion of baguette than normally allowed. The pan proved almost impossible to clean but it provided a distraction. His mother had made him promise that he wouldn't go out. It was approaching curfew now, anyway.

He wondered where his father was at that moment. What would they do to him? Would they hurt him, torture him? He had heard such dreadful rumours. How long would they keep him? And what did he mean when he had said he'd waited twenty-two years? Waited for what? Twenty-two years – that made it 1918. The war.

An hour later, Lucienne re-emerged, her hair, usually so neat and carefully brushed, out of place; her eyes red. 'There is nothing to do except wait until the major returns,' she said, sitting at the kitchen table. And so they waited, in silence, for an age. When he went to put the light on, his mother asked him not to, she couldn't face the brightness of artificial light. So denied even the chance to read, Pierre sat in the armchair and, along with his mother, waited for the major's return. He still hadn't really spoken to their house guest since he saw him with Claire. He realised that his anger with Claire, the all-encompassing hurt he had felt, had rapidly faded. Jealously had evaporated, leaving, in its place, a deep sense of disappointment and revulsion – disappointment with the major and revulsion at having caught him in the act. However much he tried, Pierre couldn't rid the revolting image from his brain. And the more he tried to purge his memory, the more ingrained the image implanted itself. The major had said he and his wife were separated, not divorced, thus he was still a married man. He would have thought that the major, so much older and so cultured, would have been above such baseness.

With the kitchen in total darkness, Pierre began to resent his mother for forcing him to endure this ridiculous situation. Had it not occurred to her that he might not want to sit in the dark for hours on end? When, at some point, he said he wanted to go to bed, Lucienne asked him not to; asked him to wait with her, her voice coming through the dark.

Sitting in the armchair, Pierre had drifted off into a light sleep when his mother said, 'He's here.' Sure enough, he could hear the major's now distinctive footsteps on the gravel outside, then on the wooden steps. Lucienne buttonholed the major the moment he stepped through the door, bombarding him with questions about her husband. 'Is there a power cut?' He flicked the switch. Pierre blinked as his eyes adjusted to the sudden light. 'Why were you sitting here in the dark?'

'Major, I asked you about my husband. Your colleagues… comrades, whatever you call them, came and took Georges away.'

'Oh dear, oh dear.'

'Oh dear? Is that all you have to say? They came in

here, just barged in, and pushed him out of the door and took him away. Did you know about it, Major; did you know he was about to be arrested?'

The major sat down at the table. 'Not really. I'm sorry to hear this.'

'Not really? Is that a yes or a no? Did you know, Major?'

He took off his hat. 'OK, I admit, I knew it was imminent.'

'Imminent? Did you order his arrest?'

'No, the order came through from Colonel Eisler.'

'The officer based in Saint-Romain?'

'Yes, the *Ortskommandantur*. Lucienne, you must understand – Georges, the blacksmith and a couple of others, tried to damage the railway line. They did not succeed but that doesn't diminish the gravity of what they did. We, as the German authorities, take this sort of thing very seriously. Georges knows that. Everyone does. Why, they even had a third party paint the door of the town hall as a sort of diversion. This third party was spotted – a young man but, lucky for him, he evaded capture.' The major glanced at Pierre. 'They were prepared to sacrifice a younger member of their community to obtain their objectives.'

'I heard about the paint. It caused some amusement.'

'Yes. Probably not the intended reaction.'

'This is beside the point, isn't it?' barked Pierre.

'I couldn't ask for a cup of your fine tea, could I, Lucienne?' Why did his mother's name always sound so odd when the major used it? He felt pleased that his mother was still calling him by his title.

'Major, I don't think you understand how worried I am,

and Pierre, both of us. What can I do?' The major remained silent. 'Apart from make you your blessed tea?'

'That would be nice.'

'Where are they keeping him?'

'Headquarters, Saint-Romain. It's where they take anyone wanted for questioning.' Pierre hoped it was just questioning.

Lucienne got up to make his tea when the major said, 'Lucienne, listen, I have a suggestion for you.'

Immediately, she sat down again. 'Yes? Yes, what is it?'

'It probably won't work but no one's tried it before, at least not to my knowledge. Colonel Eisler is a hard man; he has to be, it comes with the job. But he's not an unreasonable man.' Pierre could sense his mother's spirits lifting. 'Go and see him. Don't phone up first; you'll only be told no. So just go to Saint-Romain, both of you, and demand to see the colonel. Be prepared to wait; all day if need be. Be prepared to return the following day, the day after that. Eventually, Colonel Eisler will grant you an audience.'

'An audience? Is he the pope?'

'Tell him Georges is a soldier. Once a soldier, always a soldier. We all have respect for a man in uniform, even the enemy. Tell him you're all supporters of Pétain. Buy one of those postcards of him and have it in your purse and make sure the colonel sees it. Tell him Georges was led astray, that he hadn't been aware of what he was being told to do. Make him sound a little simple even. Simple but honest and honourable. It might help if you could borrow a small child; Pierre is too old. It probably won't make any difference but who knows? Colonel Eisler, I know, is a family man.'

108

'Thank you, Major. Should I take a present?'

'No, no. He will listen to a reasoned argument but a present could be misconstrued. The colonel is beyond bribery. Pierre, you'll go with your mother, yes?'

'Of course he will,' said Lucienne. 'We'll go tomorrow, straight after the funeral.'

'Funeral? The Algerian's? You know there are notices prohibiting attendance?'

'Major, I am prepared to listen to all your rules but not when they contradict the rules of God. That poor man is to be buried far from his home without his family present. It is our spiritual duty to pay our respects.'

'To a Muslim?'

'To a child of God, whoever that God may be.'

'Amen,' said Pierre. His mother and major looked at him. They'd quite forgotten he was there. Pierre had always found his mother's 'God first' approach to life suffocating and often tedious but right now, for the first time, he saw how profound her faith was.

'One more thing,' said the major.

'Yes?'

'I did not say a word of this. You understand? Not a word.'

'Yes, we understand. Thank you, Major. I'll make that tea now.'

Chapter 8

The Germans, as the major had pointed out, had banned the citizens of the town from attending the Algerian's funeral yet the ubiquitous notices only helped to spread the word. One person after another said they were planning on being there. If his mother was going then of course, thought Pierre, he had to go too. He had a neat shirt and a pair of dark trousers but had to borrow one of his father's jackets. It looked absurd – far too big. But there was nothing for it, he could not, insisted his mother, attend a funeral without a jacket. She too wore her only black outfit. She even had a hat with a black feather in it. 'You never know when a funeral hat will come in useful,' she said.

It felt as if the whole town was there, squeezed into the graveyard. Everyone he had ever recognized seemed to be here. He had noticed this, since the start of the occupation, a greater sense of community. Yes, people still argued over whether Pétain was a saviour or a traitor, but people talked as never before. He saw Claire. He wanted to look upon her and hate her. But in her black blouse with a pretty bow, and her knee-length skirt, and her hair tied back, she looked beautiful. He was too young for her; he knew that. If only he'd been a couple years older. If only he was a man; a part of the action, not, as he so often was, a spectator. But then, if he had been a couple years older, he'd probably be in a prisoner of war camp by now, somewhere deep in Germany. Either that or dead.

And for once, the Germans had been rendered impotent by this show of community togetherness. Not even they had the gall to break up such a large gathering under the eyes of God. Yet, still, they were making their presence felt. Dozens of them watched from the perimeter, making sure the mourners acted accordingly.

They were on the north side of the church. He felt at ease here. It was the southern side that he wanted to avoid. The little cross lost among all the other gravestones. Once a year, his mother dragged him and his father there where they would stand for ages, silently gazing down at the grave that took up so little space, and contemplate.

Father de Beaufort had insisted that the service within the church be limited to invitees only, in other words, the dignitaries of the town. Now, outside, under the intense early afternoon sun, he had to raise his voice in order to be heard.

'It is a sad gathering I see before me today...' Father de Beaufort liked to claim he was descended from Pierre Roger de Beaufort who, as Gregory XI, was France's last pope, back in the fourteenth century. No one ever contradicted the claim.

'We all know why we find ourselves in this situation; why we have been defeated. It is, without a shadow of

111

doubt, a punishment inflicted on us from God Himself. We, as a nation, have become lazy, swayed by temptation. Too many are content to wallow in sin, materialism and pleasure-seeking. They have turned their backs on God. Liberation will only come when we heed this lesson, when we return to God and beg His forgiveness and seek His protection. Until then, we are not worthy of Him, and we deserve this penance of occupation.'

Many in the congregation shook their heads, disagreeing with the priest's version of events. If Father de Beaufort noticed their disagreement, he paid no heed. 'Now, dearest brothers and sisters, let us pray for our beloved brother, Mohammed El Harrachi, from faraway Algeria…' Pierre wondered what, at this precise moment, Georges would be doing. Pierre had never really thought of his father as an individual, a person with a history. He realized that Georges, while not a bad father, had never been a particularly good one either. He'd been brought up almost by a stranger, a man about whom he knew nothing – not where he was born, what his parents were like, where he had lived as a child. All he knew was that still, after all these years, he felt as if he belonged to an incomplete family; as if there was forever a place at the table, waiting for someone who would never return. And what would Georges be like when they let him out? Would he come home a different man? Perhaps, thought Pierre, he might see his life in a new light; come to treasure what he had around him; come to appreciate that he had a son, a son who loved his father very much.

'…whom the Lord has called forth from this world and whose body has been given to us this day for burial.' His mother sniffed next to him, clasping her rosary beads, twisting them around her fingers. He could recall no shows of affection from his father, or a raising of his voice. Perhaps if he had it would have been proof of a man who cared. Instead, he was man who drifted through life, happy to be on the sidelines, content to be left alone. He had no need for anything or anyone, the town, his associates, the church, his only son. So why had he been dragged into Kafka's net? What hold did Kafka have over him?

'May the Lord receive him into His peace, and, when the Day of Judgment comes…' He would go with his mother to see this Colonel Eisler; he would walk into the lion's den, and demand his father's release. Well, maybe not demand. Pierre knew well enough already that you could never demand anything of the Nazis. Was the major a Nazi? Was he a believer, like that brutish lieutenant, like Fritz One? Or was he just a man doing his job?

'… To raise our brother up to be gathered among the elect and numbered with all the saints at God's right hand. Amen.'

Father de Beaufort sprinkled a handful of soil on the coffin. 'We commit this body to the earth…'

Pierre wondered what Mohammed El Harrachi's parents were like. Was he their only son; did they shower him with affection; would they grieve for him for the rest of their lives? The word was that they would have been informed by now. That the town hall would have got his details from Paris; that they had written to them. It didn't seem right, somehow, that they were all attending the poor man's funeral while his mother and father, back in Algeria, had no idea that today, this day, their son was being buried in a Catholic churchyard, attended to by a Catholic priest.

113

Perhaps, thought Pierre, one day, when all this was over, they might travel across the sea from North Africa and across the length of France to this forgotten spot and kneel down here, in this graveyard and pray for their Muslim son. He hoped, one day, they might.

Chapter 9

Lucienne would have gone to Saint-Romain to see Colonel Eisler straightaway but the funeral meant they had missed the second and last bus for the day. The following day was a Sunday – and there were no buses on a Sunday. They knew no one who had a car, except the cemetery boys and their truck, and Sunday was their one day off. Pierre did wonder how a job in a graveyard could take up six days a week and guessed that, as very old men, they probably worked slowly and drank large quantities of tea throughout the day. Thus two days had passed. It was Monday. Lucienne, just back from church, was anxious, watering the garden, washing her hands frequently. Having worn her black dress for the funeral, she'd worn it each day since. 'I will wear black everyday now until they release your father,' she'd declared. 'Today we must go see this Colonel Eisler. Each day we leave it is another day Georges has to spend in that place.'

And so, it was at eleven o'clock that Lucienne and Pierre caught the bus the five kilometres to Saint-Romain, his mother carrying a parcel containing a clean shirt. Inside the breast pocket, on a slip of paper, she'd written Georges a note. What it said, she didn't say but Pierre could guess.

The bus was packed, stuffy and quiet, except for the noise of the engine and, strangely, the sound of turkeys. Every seat was taken, people standing, holding onto the bars, as the bus lurched from one stop to another. A young man with a walking stick offered Lucienne his seat. Politely, she declined. His need was greater than hers, her expression said. Pierre stood. Beneath him, on her mother's lap, sat a girl of about four sucking on her hair. Her mother, a well-to-do woman, using Lucienne's phrase, slapped her hand away. Next to them, was an old woman in black, at her feet three wicker baskets. Inside each was a turkey, making a dreadful din, their heads peering out. The smell wasn't pleasant either. The mother of the girl was clearly agitated by this. At each stop, more people got on but no one alighted. Those standing shuffled closer together. Considering the short distance, the journey was taking an age. Pierre had become separated from his mother, whom he could see, in black, fanning herself with her operatic fan. He heard the mother of the small girl ask the old woman, 'Can't you stop those birds from making that dreadful noise?' 'And how do you propose I do that?' snapped back the old woman. The girl began sucking her hair again.

Finally, the bus rolled into Saint-Romain, made its way to the centre and stopped. With a collective sigh of relief, everyone disembarked. Lucienne and Pierre and others were held up behind the old woman, also in black, as she struggled with her baskets and their heavy cargo. Lucienne nudged Pierre in the ribs, telling him to help her.

'Can I…?'

'I can manage. I've got muscles, you know.'

Lucienne shook her head as they got off the bus. 'Well, that is not something I would want to do everyday,' she said. 'Right, let's find the dentist's. The major said the office was next to it.'

'How are you feeling?'

'Oh, Pierre, I'm terrified. I'm trembling all over. Does it show?'

'No.'

'That's good then.'

Saint-Romain was so much larger and busier than their sleepy little town, thought Pierre, with its grander buildings, its shops and stores, the trams, advertising hoardings, ornate lampposts adorned with hanging baskets of flowers. Lucienne entered a tobacconist and bought a postcard of Marshal Pétain. She knew the way and soon they found themselves in a maze of narrower streets, with high buildings either side; balconies, many draped with laundry; little cafés, their outdoor tables brimming with smiling Germans; people on bicycles; a hotel with a swastika hanging above its front door.

'Do you know what you're going to say, Maman?'

'Yes. No. Whenever I try to rehearse it, I become too nervous and I can't think.'

'Do you want me to do the talking?'

'No, Pierre, you're just a boy.'

'Yeah. Thanks, Maman, just a boy.'

'Oh dear. Pierre, don't be so sensitive; I didn't mean… But this is serious.' She stopped. 'Oh my, here we are.'

They looked at the swastika-adorned building on the corner across the street. Lucienne clutched her handbag to her chest. It was an imposing work of neo-classicism: grey-bricked, three stories high, with a balcony at the top and adorned with large, elaborately decorated windows. A gravelled path surrounded it. A Nazi kept guard at the double doors at the top of a few steps, beside which hung another flag. On either side of the doors was a large pot of rhododendrons – a dash of colour, thought Pierre, in the drab grey.

'Oh, Pierre,' said Lucienne, her voice breathless. 'I don't think I can do this. It could make things worse. Those rhododendrons could do with a watering.'

'But it's what the major told us to do. We have to do it; we don't have a choice.'

She nodded, her jaw tightening. 'Come, let's go.'

The soldier at the door watched them as they crossed the road. As they approached, he slipped his rifle off his shoulder.

'Hello,' said Lucienne. 'We'd like to see Colonel Eisler please.'

'The *Ortskommandantur*? Do you have an appointment?'

'No.'

'But we're prepared to wait,' added Pierre.

'Why do you need to see him?'

'I – I can't tell you; it's very important I see the colonel. Most important.'

The soldier considered them for a moment. 'Wait here,' he said.

Pierre watched the cars pass on the street, pedestrians going about their business. He saw the woman from the bus, pulling her daughter by the hand, urging her to hurry up. The girl was sniffling, wiping her eyes.

The soldier returned. 'Your bag, please.' He rooted

inside Lucienne's handbag. 'Arms up.' He ran his hands up and down both of them, quickly but expertly. 'Follow me.'

Pierre held the door open for his mother and followed her in, wondering what on earth they were stepping into. The atmosphere inside was not dissimilar to the town hall back at home, thought Pierre – people in uniforms running round, carrying papers, folders, the click-clack of typewriters, muffled conversations, the echo of shoes on marbled floors, pillars painted white, a huge portrait of Hitler. Everything but the floor was white and polished, the floor consisting of black and green squares. A receptionist with pink nail varnish and startlingly bright red lipstick, introduced herself as Mademoiselle Dauphin and took their details. The soldier showed Lucienne and Pierre into a waiting area behind a glass screen, white-walled and high-ceilinged, and told them to wait. Sitting on the wooden bench were three elderly Frenchwomen, each wearing a headscarf. Lucienne asked them if she could take a seat. Reluctantly and wordlessly, they shuffled up and allowed Lucienne to perch on the end. Pierre leant against a pillar. He wished he could smoke. He wondered whether they were all here for the same reason, to plead on behalf of their husbands or sons. Another German kept watch over them. He could have been no older than nineteen, thought Pierre; the same age as the major's son. An hour passed before Mademoiselle Dauphin appeared to call the first woman through. No one said a word. Lucienne rested her handbag on her lap, playing with its catch. The German guard was relieved by another. Pierre would have sat down, but another woman came in, a dishevelled younger woman, and sat down on the bench. 'How long have you been here?' she asked the woman next to her.

'Hours,' came the quick reply. 'Oh.' She looked like a woman who wanted to talk but, sensing the atmosphere, held her tongue.

Finally, after over two hours, Mademoiselle Dauphin returned. 'Madame Durand?'

Lucienne and Pierre followed the woman across the hallway, up two flights of red-carpeted stairs and down a long corridor. She stopped to talk to a soldier standing guard outside a door, a strange looking man but for reasons Pierre couldn't work out. The man was, Pierre realised with a shudder, SS, wearing a black uniform with a swastika armband. The SS man knocked and they waited. A voice came from within. 'Wait,' the receptionist said to them, before entering, leaving the door ajar. 'Madame and Monsieur Durand, sir,' Pierre heard her say.

'Show them in.'

'You can go in,' said Mademoiselle Dauphin to Lucienne. Pierre nodded at the soldier who stepped in with them and closed the door. It was only then that he realised what was odd about him – his eyes were of different colour.

Pierre and his mother were greeted by the colonel, also wearing the uniform of the SS, sitting behind an expansive mahogany desk, his glasses perched on his head, his grey hair thin but neatly combed. His peaked hat sat on his desk, alongside a telephone, an ashtray, an empty vase, a bottle of water and a couple of glasses, piles of folders and a brass desk lamp with a hexagon-shaped shade. Behind him an opened window that reached the floor, its turquoise-coloured net curtain fluttering in the draft. The noise of traffic sounded in the distance. Next to the window, another portrait of Hitler. How often he had found pictures of Hitler ridiculous, with his stupid moustache. But here, in this office, behind the colonel, Pierre could feel the man's power, the intensity of his eyes, the aura of invincibility. He suddenly felt rather small.

'Take a seat,' said the colonel.

Lucienne thanked him nervously. There being only the one chair, Pierre stood behind his mother. He wished he could sit down; he was tired of being so long on his feet.

'Your name is Madame Durand, and you are Pierre Durand. Is that right? How old are you, boy?'

'Sixteen,' he croaked.

'What?'

'Sixteen, sir.' He found the unmoving eyes of the Führer staring down at him unnerving.

'And you've come presumably on account of your husband.' He checked the name against his paper. 'Georges Durand. Is that correct?'

'Yes, sir,' said Lucienne. 'You see, Colonel, Georges, my husband, is a good man.' She spoke quickly. 'He fought in the last war. I know that was against you but he fought honourably, like a proper soldier. He wore his uniform with pride, like all good soldiers, whether they are French or German. He was led astray. He is a good husband, a good father, and–'

She stopped midsentence; the colonel had raised his hand.

'This is all very well, Madame, but it is not his conduct in the last war that concerns me but his conduct now, during *this* war. Destruction of German property is a grave offence and an affront that I take very seriously. Now, do you really think that by simply telling me that your husband is a good man, as you call him, that I shall just click my fingers and say, "OK, I'll have him released"? What sort of people do you take us for? I advise you not to answer that.'

'Colonel, we are great supporters of the marshal. I never go anywhere without a picture of him in my handbag.' She fished out the postcard and held it up for the colonel to see.

'What can I say?' he asked with a hint of an exasperated smile.

'Colonel, would I be allowed to give my husband a clean shirt? I've heard you permit such things.'

'Yes, that's perfectly acceptable. We may be severe sometimes but we're not savages. A man needs a clean shirt every now and then. If you want to pass it to me.'

Lucienne passed him her carefully wrapped parcel. The colonel undid the packaging and held the shirt aloft, inspecting it. He found Lucienne's message straightaway. Lucienne flushed red. He cast his eyes over the note, screwed it up and threw it in a bin at his feet.

'I'll make sure he gets it,' he said, handing it to the guard. 'You can put your postcard away, Madame Durand. Now, I shall tell you what happens next. We are investigating the attempted derailment of our train, and those found guilty will be retained here as punishment for up to six months. On release, they will be monitored. Any further transgressions would likely result in more severe punishment. I hope I've made myself clear?'

'Yes, thank you, Colonel.'

'You may, on occasion, like today, bring in provisions, small food parcels and such like. Do not ever attempt to smuggle in messages again otherwise your husband's stay here will automatically be extended.' Pierre made a conscious effort not to look at his mother. 'Now, if you don't mind, I have a lot of other business to see to.'

'Yes, of course.' Lucienne rose to her feet, her face flushed. 'Pierre...?'

'Before you go, however, I'd like a word with your son. In private.'

'Oh.' Lucienne looked at Pierre. 'In private?'

'Please.'

Lucienne looked flustered as she gathered her things. Pierre stood still, trying to maintain a look of impassivity, while wondering what on earth the colonel wanted.

The guard held the door open for Lucienne, who retreated with a final, worried look at her son.

'Right then,' said the colonel. 'Take a seat. Cigarette?' He pushed forward a pack towards Pierre.

Pierre looked at it. He was tempted but his mother would smell it on him. 'No, thanks.' The colonel took one and, finding a box of matches, lit it.

'So, when are you seventeen?' he asked, blowing out of column of smoke.

'Four months.'

'Old enough. Good.' He sat back in his chair and considered the young man opposite him.

Pierre felt as if he was being assessed and tried to hold the German's gaze. Failing, he glanced up at Hitler. A little jolt of apprehension ran down his back.

'What I am about to say is between you and me,' said the colonel. 'Is that understood? Not a word.' Pierre nodded. 'I wasn't being entirely honest with your mother. The fact is your father has been identified as being one of the ringleaders of this puerile attempt at sabotage. Now, if we show leniency, it would merely encourage others. This cannot be. Your father is due to be executed.'

'Shit, no.' The word tumbled out. His hand went to his mouth. Pierre looked aghast at the colonel, not totally sure he'd heard correctly.

'Tomorrow morning. Five o'clock.'

'No. Please. It wasn't that serious, no one–'

'It's not for you, young man, to tell us what we deem to be serious.' The colonel blew out another puff of smoke. Pierre felt a wave of nausea cloud his thoughts. 'But you can save him.'

'I'm sorry?'

'You heard me correctly. I said you can save your father from the firing squad tomorrow morning.'

'What can I do?' He tried to think but it was as if a thousand contradictory thoughts were rushing through his mind.

'Your father, I believe, was acting under orders. Someone else was the brains behind this little operation and I want to know who before he tries something else, something more adventurous, let's say.'

Immediately, Pierre thought of Kafka.

'Would you know who this man might be?'

Pierre tried to think of what his father would want him to say. 'No, I'm sorry.'

'Pity. We asked your father but he refused to name any names. I admire his stubbornness.'

'Did you–'

'We asked him. Let's leave at that, shall we?'

'Can I have some water?'

The colonel reached over and poured Pierre a glass. Sliding it over the table, he continued. 'I could ask you just to go home, find out the name and bring it to me. But that'd be too simple. I want more.'

Pierre gulped his water down. 'More?' He placed the glass on the desk and realised his hand was shaking.

'Yes, more. I want you to go to this man and offer yourself as your father's replacement. Become one of them, this merry band of resisters. Find out what they're doing; become party to their plans. Then report back to Major Hurtzberger.'

'The major?'

'Yes, he has been briefed. He'll be expecting good things from you. If you agree, I will guarantee no one save myself and the major will know, and I will order a stay of execution.'

'But I can't. I'm only sixteen; they won't let me in.'

'Who's they?'

'I don't know. Whoever they are.'

'Come, come, you're almost seventeen. You told me. Need I remind you what's at stake? By just having this conversation, you've kept your father alive for a further five days.'

'Five days?'

The colonel looked at his watch. 'Five days. That's how long you have to inform the major that you have infiltrated the group. Now, I've kept you long enough. You'd better not keep your mother waiting any longer. Off you go.'

The guard appeared at Pierre's side, casting a sinister shadow over him. 'Can I see my father?'

'No.'

'How do I go about–'

'That's for you to work out.'

The two of them locked eyes. Pierre felt the man's power invade his being.

'Five days, don't forget,' said the colonel.

'Can… can I take a cigarette for later?'

The colonel smiled an icy smile. 'Here, take the pack.' He threw it over.

As the guard escorted Pierre to the door, the colonel spoke. 'Remember, young man – not a word to anyone, including your mother. Especially your mother.'

*

With the colonel's cigarettes in his back pocket, Pierre descended the stairs, the guard behind him. He found his mother in the waiting room, now empty except for Lucienne and another guard.

'Pierre. Is everything OK?'

'Yes. Let's go home,' he said.

Outside, under the beating sun, they headed back towards the bus station, their shadows behind them. Everywhere were Germans, laughing, taking photos of each other, shopping for jewellery and souvenirs.

'Idiots,' growled Pierre under his breath.

Lucienne glanced behind her. Satisfied they were out of earshot, she asked Pierre why the colonel had wanted to see him.

'I can't say.' He hoped his voice was firm enough to dissuade her from pressing him.

She stopped suddenly. She reached out for his hand. He refused to give it. With her hand resting on his sleeve, she spoke quietly. 'Pierre, please, what did he want? You were in there for such a long time; I'm worried for you.'

'I'm not allowed to say and, anyway, you don't want to know.'

'He's asked you to do something. For the love of God, you're sixteen; you're a boy.' Her eyes narrowed, her shoulders flexed. 'How dare he.' She turned abruptly, and made to walk back.

'What are you doing?'

'If you're not going to tell me, the colonel can.'

He reached out for her. 'No, you can't do that.'

'We'll see about that.'

He had to jog to keep pace with her. 'What are you doing?' he repeated. He ran in front of her, then stopped her as she tried to sidestep past him. 'Maman, this is not one of my old teachers you're dealing with, it's a...' He stopped himself before saying something unflattering about the Germans.

'Tell me then.'

'Look at me. Yes, I am young, but I am no longer a boy. This war has made men of us all. You just have to trust me.'

She seemed to diminish in front of him, her verve draining away. 'They took my husband and now, somehow, they have you. Promise me, Pierre, whatever it is, you'll be careful.'

He tried to smile a reassuring smile. 'Yes, OK, I promise I'll be careful.'

Chapter 10

Pierre could only stare at his work. Chisel in hand, he had neither the strength nor the will to apply it. It was early; the yard was still mostly in shade. The hens pecked at the grain he had just scattered while Maurice, the cock, strutted around. The sculpture had broadly taken on the height and shape that he had been aiming for. One could see that it was a woman. But now came the part where more detail was needed – to separate her arms from her body, to slim down her neck, her ankles. Having come this far, he felt a strange responsibility for her. He had to give her characteristics, features. Had to give her life. She provided him the means to escape but he realised now, that she was as dependent on him as he was on her. He stroked her shoulder. 'Give me time,' he whispered. 'I'll get you out of there.' They had questioned him, the colonel had said; they had tortured him. 'Give me time.'

'And now you talk to her.'

Pierre screwed his eyes shut. He wanted to be left alone. He no longer enjoyed this routine – the major's daily intrusion into his thoughts. Pierre turned. The major stood there, in his uniform, his cap, coffee mug in hand. It annoyed him that his mother would have made him that coffee. Coffee was a fast disappearing product yet here they were – offering it to the sodding Germans. A wolf in sheep's clothing. The major's expression was not one of conviviality. His features had hardened, his eyes cold. Pierre knew their relationship had changed. He was one of them now. The major knew. They both knew. He had four and a half days. He remembered the colonel's icy smile, his aura of power. He saw it too now in the man who stood before him. He hated him. He hated him for being in his home, for being there when his father was not; for coming between him and his White Venus. He hated him for having sex with Claire, for sullying his romantic boyish dreams.

The major sipped his drink, his eyes still fixed on Pierre. Pierre's fingers gripped the handle of the chisel. How easy it would be, he thought. And think of the satisfaction. The chest; he would aim for the chest. He felt every muscle tense, felt himself rocking on his feet, ready to pounce.

The major spun on his heels and left. Pierre stared at the kitchen door as it swung shut. The chisel slipped out of his hand.

*

Standing outside, Pierre realised he had never been to Kafka's house before. He lived in a small grey-stoned bungalow on the outskirts of the town. Behind it, a vast expanse of woodland. The windows and shutters were open; everything quiet. To the side of the house, was a garage, its doors open. From the house to the garage, scattered everywhere, were bits of rusting machinery – old car engines, tyres big and small, a bashed-up car door propped up against the house, discarded boots, garden tools, an empty birdcage, a wooden chair without its seat. Gently, Pierre knocked on the door. Kafka's face appeared at a small window, pushing aside the net curtain. 'For Pete's sake.' A moment later, he was at the door. 'Jesus, you gave me a fright. What brings you here? You'd better come in.'

He found himself in the living room – an upright piano with brown keys, an Eiffel Tower on the dresser, a large stove, a collection of pipes in a rack.

'I heard about your father. Hard luck, that was. I sort of guessed I'd be next. Guess your father is tougher than I thought. Anyway, what brings you here?'

'I want to take my father's place.'

Kafka seemed taken aback by the boy's impertinence. 'You want to take your father's place,' he said slowly. 'In what exactly?'

'In your group.'

'In my...?' With two quick steps, he was on Pierre, clasping his shirt, pushing him back against the wall. 'What do you think you're saying? What group?'

Fighting for breath, Pierre gasped, 'I thought...'

Kafka released him. 'You thought wrong. You stupid little fool. Get the hell out of here before I put you over my knee.'

Pierre felt the surge of humiliation but with it, came the anger, an outpouring of indignation. 'I am a patriot,' he said, his eyes prickling with tears. 'I watched them take my father away. I can't stand by and do nothing. I have to do something, anything. If you won't take me, then I'll find someone who will.'

'Oh, mighty words from one so young; so fine and dandy. And how do you propose this, eh? Go up to any bugger on the street and say, "I want to be in your gang"?'

'If need be.'

'Right. Easy as that. Go ahead and try it. Everyone is scared to death; no one will act. The Krauts have beaten them into submission. Collaborators – each and everyone of them. Active, tacit or horizontal – collaborators. So, you go and politely ask them. You'll be sharing a cell with your old man before you can say jackboot. Get out of here. Come back when you've become a man.'

Pierre tried to find a retort, his mind struggling with half-hearted insults. By the time he finally said, 'I'll show you, you stinking swine,' he was back at home.

*

Xavier knocked on the front door. 'Fancy coming out?' he asked.

'No, I bloody don't,' said Pierre.

He seemed taken aback by Pierre's abruptness.

Afterwards, as Pierre paced round the house, flitting from one room to another, he realised he'd been unfairly rude to his friend. His mother was out – where, he didn't know. He went into his parents' bedroom, rooting through their belongings. He had no idea what he was looking for, and he knew he was clutching at straws. The colonel's five days were already ticking by. His only idea had come to nothing. He didn't have a second option, no back-up plan. He hoped his father's belongings would provide some form of inspiration. There was nothing. A few letters, a couple of books, and that was it.

He tried to think of everyone he knew. Would Monsieur Bonnet be a secret resister? Hardly likely. And what about Clément? Perhaps. Who knows? Kafka was right – how does one go about asking the question?

He sat at the kitchen table, then stood up again. Finding a pack of playing cards, he sat back down again. Shuffling the cards, he tried to think. He kept glancing up at the clock. He laid out a card. The ten of spades. Spades. Without thinking, unconscious of where his feet were taking him, he went outside into the yard and to the shed. Yes, there were a couple of spades, a pick, an axe, a brush, the cans of paint, gardening gloves, secateurs, a jam jar full of screws, another of nails. He heard the front door. His mother was back. He found her in the kitchen, still wearing her headscarf despite the heat of the day. She had bought a few potatoes and a cabbage. 'Oh, Pierre. There you are. The major said he might be able to procure half a chicken for us tonight, save us having to kill one of ours, so I thought I'd get some veg. We might be eating like kings tonight.'

'Good.'

'But, my, it's so expensive. Prices are shooting up. I don't know how we'll manage. You must get yourself a job. You're the man of the family now, Pierre.'

'Funny that. I thought that was Major H.'

'We rely on his generosity. We have to be thankful for that.'

'Great. They take everything away; and give us back a little. And for that we have to thank them.'

Lucienne sat down with a heavy sigh, removing her headscarf. 'I hadn't thought of it in those terms. How quickly you're growing up.'

'Yeah, well, like you say, I'm the man of the family now.'

'Oh, and more coffee. The major said he could get more coffee. He likes his coffee in the morning, does the major. Poor Georges. I wonder how he is.'

'Nails.' Pierre slapped his forehead.

'I'm sorry?'

'That's it, the nails.'

*

The major did indeed bring back half a chicken. The smell of it cooking in the oven was both tortuous and wonderful. Lucienne ensured they had only small portions – enough for cold chicken tomorrow, she'd said. They ate in silence. Gone was the former joviality. OK, it may have been forced but at least it had been there. But since Georges's arrest, smiles had given way to fixed expressions, conversations on music to brief exchanges on the weather, the pretence of host and guest all but gone.

Afterwards, having eaten well, they sat in the living room and read. The major flipped through his papers, scanning each in turn before filing them neatly in his folder. Pierre picked up his book on renaissance art and scanned the pages for the umpteenth time. But, meanwhile, his mind tried to work out his plan of action. He had to be patient, had to hold his nerve.

'Are you tired, Pierre?' His mother's voice brought him back to the present.

'What? No.'

133

'It's just that you keep looking at the clock.'

'Am I? Oh. Sorry.'

'You don't have to apologise.'

'No.'

They all went to bed early. Night had still not fully fallen. Pierre lay, fully dressed, on his bed, the jar of nails in his haversack behind the door. It seemed weeks, months, since the night of the graffiti. But that was child's play compared to what lay at stake now. In some ways the task that lay ahead of him was easier. But it was more important. His mind raced through numerous scenarios and slowly he dozed off.

*

He awoke with a start. Finding the torch that he put beneath his pillow, he shone it on his alarm clock. Two o'clock. Quietly, he opened his bedroom door. He could hear the major snoring. Good. His mother, a heavy sleeper, would also be out for the count. The time was perfect. Outside, the night had retained the heat of the day. He slipped out of the yard, rounded the house and onto the street. He'd stuffed the jam jar full of socks and underpants to stifle the rattling of the nails. He looked left, right and around. Everything was inky black, no hint of a moon to illuminate the way. All the better for not being seen. Slowly, wearing his soft-soled shoes, he crept up the street, heading towards the town centre, his eyes adjusting to the blackness. The deep silence felt oppressive. There wasn't even the rustle of leaves. There was nothing. If only he could slow down the pounding in his chest. He wished he'd recruited Xavier but then, perhaps not. He had to do this alone. It wasn't difficult, he told himself repeatedly. It wasn't difficult.

Soon, he was on the bend of Rue de Courcelles, the road leading to the town hall, the road the prisoners of war had come down. This is where he wanted to be. He peered round the corner. Nothing; the road was clear. Ahead loomed the town square with Soldier Mike silhouetted in the foreground. He had to work quickly. Undoing the lid, he stuffed his underwear back into his bag. Gently, he poured out a handful of nails. Too worried to throw them, he almost placed them across the road, one handful at a time. His father wouldn't thank him for this – nails, like everything else, were now hard to come by, stupidly expensive for what they were. But, dear father, it's for a good cause. Within a couple of minutes, he had scattered the entire jar of nails on the tarmac, covering a good expanse of road. Satisfied, he returned the jar to his bag and crept quickly away.

Less than ten minutes later, he was back in his bed. Mission accomplished. He lay there, staring into the dark, his heart refusing to slow down. It was two twenty. The whole thing had taken only twenty minutes. The major was still snoring. He felt euphoric. In the grand scheme of things, this was a minor act of sabotage, but that didn't matter.

What mattered was the intent.

Chapter 11

Pierre woke early – soon after six. It was cloudy. This, Pierre concluded, was a good thing – less chance of the Germans seeing the nails glinting in the sun. Not so good was seeing the major, also up early, half dressed, lighting the gas flame on the cooker to heat up his precious coffee.

'You're up early,' said Pierre.

'Yes, early meeting.'

Pierre's chest tightened. The major's route took him up Rue de Courcelles. He would see the nails. The morning convoy of German trucks, taking the men out on their morning exercise, or manoeuvres, whatever they called it, always passed by at seven. Shit, he had to detain the major for almost an hour.

'What time is your meeting?'

'Seven.'

'Is it important?'

'What? The meeting? What an odd question to ask. Of course, it's important. Everything the German command does in the name of your country is important. Now, if you'll excuse me, I need to get dressed and shaved. Keep an eye on the coffee, would you?'

As soon as the major closed his bedroom door, Pierre turned off the gas, then switched the knob on again but without the flame. Taking the kitchen clock off the wall, he opened the glass and pushed the minute hand back ten minutes. He returned to his bedroom. Sitting on his bed, he tried to think. Nothing he said or did would keep the major from his meeting. Such a simple plan, puncturing a few German tyres, interrupting their routine, however briefly, seemed perfect for a solitary show of defiance. He hadn't counted on the major, of all people, upsetting his scheme. Minutes later, he heard the major come back to the kitchen and curse in German. The major called out his name.

'Pierre, what happened to the flame?'

'Why? Has it gone out? Oh, must have been a draft.'

The German looked round the room, as if seeking out a draft. He glanced up at the kitchen clock, then checked his wristwatch. 'Strange, your clock must have stopped – just in the last few minutes.' He re-lit the gas flame. 'Still time for a coffee, I think.'

At quarter to seven, the major pulled on his boots, put his cap on, checked his reflection and made to leave.

'Have you heard from your son?' asked Pierre.

'Yes, he's fine. Sorry, Pierre, I have to go.'

'I'll come with you.'

'What?'

'I feel like a walk.'

'Hurry up, then.'

They walked in silence. Pierre struggled to keep pace with the German. He could think of nothing to say and felt annoyed that his plan was about to go awry. As they turned onto the road, a hint of sun appeared behind the clouds. 'Could be a nice day again,' said Pierre.

The major ignored him. As they approached the bend, Pierre thought he heard the rumble of engines. He strained his ears – yes, the convoy was on the move, he could hear the trucks revving up in the distance, shouted orders. Yet, he and the major had almost come to the spot. He had to stop the German. He could only think of one thing. He screeched and started hopping.

'You all right?' asked the major.

'Ow, no. I think I've twisted my ankle.'

'How did you manage that?'

Pierre leant against the wall banking the road, holding up his left leg. 'It hurts.'

'Here, let me have a look.'

Pierre rolled up his trouser leg. The convoy was coming, the big German trucks rolling down the road, one by one. The major clasped his hands round Pierre's ankle. 'I can't feel anything,' he said.

The first truck was now at the bend. This was it. The noise was surprisingly loud – a screech of brakes, a skid, men yelling from within.

'What was that?' said the major. They looked up to see the first truck with a swastika painted on its side coming to a juddering halt as its tyres burst. A second truck crashed into it, forcing the first one off the road, tumbling down the ditch. The sound of many men shouting and swearing filled the air. Together, Pierre and the major ran up the road, Pierre forgetting his pretence of pain. 'It's an ambush,' shouted the major, drawing his revolver from its holster. 'Pierre, get back.' The scene was chaotic. Three trucks skewered across the road, their tyres rapidly deflating with a loud hiss; dozens of German soldiers pouring from the vehicles onto the road, their rifles at the ready, their eyes wide with fright and determination. They fell to their knees, the weapons trained on the surrounding area. The truck in the ditch had come to a halt, smashed up against a hefty tree trunk, a suspended wheel still spinning as men piled out. Then, everything stood still – dozens of Germans waiting for a burst of machine gun fire. Major Hurtzberger circled round, his every sense on full alert. Pierre, his back pressed against the wall, had to concede it was an impressive display. Satisfied that they hadn't been ambushed, the major asked the sergeant if everyone was all right.

'Look at all these nails,' said the sergeant.

'Swine,' said a corporal.

'We need to clear this up,' said the major. 'Rally up some locals. Where's Pierre?'

Pierre's heart sunk – not again. Instead, the major told him to go home. As he turned to leave, a number of villagers had already appeared, keen to know what had happened. Xavier slapped him on the back. 'Oh dear,' he said. 'What a mess, eh?'

'I wouldn't hang around, if I was you.'

'Fair point. Come round to mine, if you want.'

*

An hour later, having shared a measly boiled egg breakfast, Pierre and Xavier decided to venture back out. The sun had appeared, the day was already stiflingly hot. As they walked up Rue de Courcelles, they could hear a distant sound of crying.

'What's going on?' asked Pierre.

'I don't know but it doesn't sound good.'

Exchanging worried glances, they picked up speed, climbing up the hill. What they saw as they approached the bend made them both stop in their tracks. Lined up, either side of the road, were a number of German soldiers, rifles at the ready, screaming orders. Between them, on their hands and knees, were about a dozen villagers. They were being forced to pick up the nails, every last one of them. Some of the women were crying, snivelling.

'Have you noticed something?' whispered Xavier.

'They're all old.'

The Germans had selected the elderly and the fragile to do their work. Their trousers or skirts had shredded at the knees; many were bleeding.

'Faster, faster,' yelled a German.

Monsieur Roché was among them, his knees red with blood, his face covered in sweat. He made the mistake of protesting. 'We didn't do this. Why pick on us?' A German soldier swung his rifle round and with its butt hit him on the side of the head. Pierre grimaced at the sickening sound as the butt impacted the skull. People screamed as Monsieur Roché collapsed. 'Any more comments?' asked the German, his eyes gleaming with bloodlust.

'What do we do?' asked Xavier.

'We have to help.'

'How?'

'No idea.'

Together they strode up the hill. Pierre hoped to see the major – surely when he told them to round up some locals he hadn't meant this. It was barbaric. The villagers were at least eighty, thought Pierre, all of them. One of the old women looked up at him, her face soaked in sweat and tears.

He recognised the fanatical lieutenant leaning against one of the trucks, smoking. Three of its tyres had been replaced and a couple of soldiers were about to embark on the fourth. The other trucks, including the one in the ditch, had already gone. Monsieur Roché, Pierre noticed, hadn't moved, the side of his skull bleeding profusely.

'Hello. We want to help,' said Xavier, his voice cracking.

'*Was ist das?*' said the lieutenant.

Xavier pointed at Pierre and himself and at the old folk grappling for nails under the hot sun.

The German barked at a private, who came running towards the boys. 'What do you want?' he shouted in French.

'We want to help,' said Pierre, stepping back.

The private translated his request. The lieutenant laughed and responded in a quick, shrill voice.

The private snarled as he translated back. 'If you wimps aren't out of here in five seconds, you'll be spending the next six months with the Gestapo. Now sod off.'

The boys scampered back down the hill, the moans and groans of the villagers and the abusive shouts in German ringing in their ears.

'Bastards,' said Pierre, once they were out of earshot.

'Whoever pulled that trick needs his head examined.'

'What an idiot.'

*

Later on, once Xavier had returned home, Pierre was relating the sorry saga to his mother, who listened with her hand over her mouth. 'Poor Monsieur Roché; he must be eighty-five if he's a day. Is he all right?'

'I don't know. He needed a doctor but the Krauts weren't about to call one.'

'What's happening to our world?'

A knock on the door interrupted his tale. It was Kafka, his pipe dangling from the corner of his mouth. 'You and I need words,' he said, on seeing Pierre.

'My mother's here.'

'Let's go for a little walk then, shall we?'

They traipsed in silence through the field behind the house, lifting their knees to navigate the long grass, and headed for the woods. Pierre wondered what Kafka had in store. Kafka glanced behind as they left the field. Sheltered from the blazing sun by the trees, they stopped to catch their breaths, leaning on a prostrate tree trunk. Pierre was pleased not to have to look at the man. Instead, he concentrated on the dappled spots of sunlight decorating the forest floor. Above them, sparrows and finches sang.

Kafka lit his pipe. 'Old Roché is dead,' he said, discarding the spent match.

Pierre screwed his eyes shut. 'Shit,' he muttered. 'The sods.' He thumped his thigh in frustration.

'Who do you blame, eh? The Krauts or the person who laid the nails?'

'The Germans, of course. They killed him, not... whoever it was.'

'Still, I wonder who *that* person was.'

'I don't know.'

'But you blame the Germans?'

'Of course,' he said, stroking the bark.

'Well, you would say that.'

Pierre held his tongue. This is what he wanted, after all, but he wasn't sure how to proceed. What if he'd read the signals wrong? He wouldn't put it past Kafka to lure him into a trap.

Kafka stood up. Facing Pierre he leant towards him. Pierre recoiled from the stench of his tobacco breath. 'Whoever did this did so with the best intentions. Anything we do, however small, that shows the Germans that we don't accept their presence here is a step in the right direction. OK, Roché's death was unfortunate and unforeseen, but what's done is done. Now listen, take a book, any book, and meet me at the library at six this evening. The Krauts will be enjoying their dinner, scoffing our food and wine. Not a word to anyone. OK?'

Pierre nodded.

'I'm off. Wait here. Five minutes.' And with that, he was gone. Pierre watched as he strolled away, zigzagging through the trees, plucking at leaves as he went. The image of Roché lying on the asphalt, the side of his head congealed with blood, flooded his mind. 'What's done is done,' he said aloud. After all, he'd got what he wanted. He was a step closer to saving his father.

Surely, he thought, nothing else mattered.

*

Pierre's feet felt heavy as he made his way to the library. Under his arm, his father's copy of Voltaire's *Candide*. He had not been back to the library since he had spied the major and Claire having sex on the counter. The thought of it still made him feel sick. It was like an unmovable stain on his memory. Indeed, he still had not spoken to or even seen Claire since. But, unsurprisingly, it was Claire he saw first on entering the dark interior of the library, behind the counter, serving an elderly woman. His heart lurched on seeing her, pierced by a stab of anger mixed with jealousy. She looked gorgeous in a thin red cotton blouse, her hair tied back with a yellow bow. He could hear them, Claire and the old woman, discussing the wicked killing of Monsieur Roché and the pointless vandalism that led to it. His romantic imaginings were interrupted by the image of Monsieur Roché, his skull smashed in. If it hadn't been for him and his nails, Roché would be still alive.

Pierre flushed with shame. He browsed idly through the books, eying the counter, thinking of Claire's bare arse sitting on it. One day, he thought, when he was older, he would make Claire his. He would woo her, gradually breaking down her defences and winning her heart. He, Pierre, was far too good a man to simply seize her and rape her as the major had done.

With the old lady gone, he approached Claire. 'Follow me,' she said, darting out from behind her counter, her hair bouncing with her steps. She seemed to be expecting him. She led him across the library to a door at the far end, and, holding it open, pointed up the stairs. 'Second door on the left. Knock four times.'

'Not the basement this time?'

'No.' She left him to it, allowing the door to close on him. Pierre grimaced, annoyed that she hadn't said a pleasant word to him, not even an acknowledgement. He climbed the few steps slowly, wondering what on earth he was letting himself in for. He thought of his father, hoping the image of him would give him strength. It did no such thing. It'd been four days since they took him; and yes, he wouldn't want him to come to any harm, but, with aching guilt, he noticed how he was getting on with life without him.

He stopped outside the second door on the left – peeling green paint, a round, wooden door knob, a brass sign with the word 'Private'. Wouldn't this, he wondered, have been a better place to have sex? But then, with the library doors locked, one wouldn't anticipate anyone climbing up the outside wall to peer in.

He knocked. Four times. The door opened with a flourish and Pierre was surprised to see Monsieur Dubois with his blue beret and blue corduroy jacket glaring at him from behind his spectacles. A quizzical look passed between them until Kafka's voice came from behind. 'Let the boy in.'

Three men sat round an oval-shaped table in a dingy room, a small window high up let in minimal light, the brown painted walls were bare except for a large portrait of Marshal Pétain at the far end. The air hung heavy with cigarette smoke. 'Sit down, boy,' said Kafka.

'*Merde*, when you said you had a new young recruit, I didn't think he'd be still in his diapers.' This was Bouchette, whom Pierre recognised from his stand against the lieutenant at the baker's, thin-lipped, dressed in dungarees, twirling a penknife round his fingers.

'Leave him be; this is Georges Durand's boy.'

'That makes it OK, then, does it?'

'Is Durand still locked up?' This was Monsieur Dubois.

Bouchette began cleaning his fingernails with his penknife. 'We need men, more men, Kafka, not children,' he said.

'How old are you, son?' asked Dubois, drumming his fingers rhythmically on the table top.

'He's seventeen. Almost.'

'Well, Louis was only eighteen,' said Monsieur Bouchette. 'You knew Louis, didn't you, Pierre?'

Pierre nodded. Louis Bouchette, an obnoxious know-it-all, once pushed Pierre off his bicycle for no apparent reason except to get a laugh from his equally-obnoxious friends. But he'd been killed just a few weeks ago, caught up in the Nazi advance, and for that Pierre chastised himself for thinking ill of the dead, a hero of the Battle of France. Madame Bouchette, rumour had it, hadn't stop crying since.

Kafka held up his hand. 'OK, look; I know he's young but I reckon he's got fire in his belly. Think back to when you were seventeen, gentlemen. What if the previous generation of Krauts had taken your father? Isn't that motivation enough?'

Bouchette, still cleaning his fingernails, asked, 'And what exactly are your skills, boy? Any particular talents?'

'He's young. That in itself is good. He'll be able to get around easier than us lot. I can't step out of the front door without some sodding Boche asking me for my papers.'

'Yeah, but that's because you swear at them.'

'Not so much now. I keep my head down.'

'We can't talk while he's here,' said Bouchette, pursing his thin lips. 'We don't know whether we can trust him yet. Listen, son,' he said, turning to Pierre, 'one word to anyone that you've been here and...' He made an exaggerated throat-slitting gesture with his penknife.

'No need for that, Bouchette. Anyway, I have a job for him. A little mission with Claire. Nice and simple.'

'The leaflets?' asked Dubois.

'Exactly.'

'That's good.'

'Pierre, Claire knows what to do. Go speak to her.'
Pierre nodded. 'Off you go, then, boy.'

Conscious of being watched, Pierre made his exit. It was only after he closed the door and was half way down the stairs that he realised he hadn't said a word.

Back in the library, Pierre saw that Claire had customers – two German privates leaning on the counter, their helmets pushed up their heads, grinning. The three of them spoke animatedly in German. Pierre headed straight out, still carrying his book.

*

Later that afternoon, Claire appeared at Pierre's house. Lucienne had been outside, watering the plants and flowers in front of the house, and showed Claire in.

'Claire,' she said, bringing her into the kitchen, 'what a lovely surprise. Can I get you a glass of water? It's so hot, don't you think? Is it Pierre you've come to see?'

'Yes. And thank you, a glass of water would be lovely.'

Lucienne grinned at Pierre, making no attempt to disguise her delight that her son had attracted such a pretty girl into the house. Pierre and Claire exchanged embarrassed glances, both aware that Lucienne had misread the reason for Claire's appearance.

'It is very hot still, isn't it?' said Pierre, feebly.

'Mm. What's the helmet?'

'Oh that. It's my father's. From the war. Well, the last one, that is.'

'I see.'

'Here's your water, Claire. That's a pretty outfit.'

Pierre groaned – his mother was trying too hard.

147

'Oh, yes. Thank you.'

'The red suits you. And that hat…'

'Maman, didn't you say…'

'I'm sorry? Oh, yes; you're quite right. If you'd excuse me, Claire, I have to pop out.'

'That's fine. Thank you for the water.'

Lucienne picked up her handbag and hovered at the door. 'How long should I pop out for?'

'Half an hour,' said Pierre.

'Five minutes,' said Claire at the same moment.

Lucienne raised her eyebrows. 'I'll be back in fifteen minutes then.' She gave Claire a self-conscious little wave. 'Yes. Well. Have fun,' she said, closing the door behind her.

Claire sipped her water, peering at Pierre over the rim.

Pierre shrugged his shoulders. 'Sorry about that.'

'Don't worry. Mothers are all alike.'

'Yes. Mine has been on edge since… you know.'

'Understandable.' She looked round the room, taking in her surroundings. 'How did your meeting go?'

'The meeting, yes. It went well, I think. I, er, made my case – you know, why they should trust me. I think they were impressed.'

'Really? Strange, it's usually impossible to know what Kafka's thinking.'

'No, no, he said I'd made a useful contribution.'

'To what?'

'I… I don't know. Anyway, he said I was to speak to you.' He tried desperately not to think of the major fucking Claire on the library counter. He tried to make the image disappear, shaking his head.

'You all right?"

'Yes. What? No, I'm fine.'

She looked at him as one might look at something peculiar. She placed her glass on the table. 'He's set us an assignment. We're to have a day out together.'

'Great!' Immediately, Pierre slunk back from his overenthusiasm.

She rolled her eyes. 'Yes,' she sighed. 'Together. As a couple. Even though I'm almost four years older than you.'

'That's not such–'

'Pierre, please. I think…'

Pierre felt himself sag. 'Go on.'

'Listen, you're a nice boy, but I'm twenty years old, and I have a….'

'What?' A boyfriend?'

She removed her hat, placing it on the kitchen table. 'Yes, if you like, a boyfriend.'

'What's he–'

'Pierre, we're got a job to do. It's important, and we have to do it properly.'

The image returned – the major's trousers down at his ankles. Pierre clenched his eyes shut, despite knowing he looked ridiculous.

'Please, don't get upset.'

'No, it's not that. What… what is it we have to do?'

'A day out – you and me, to the seaside. You have your papers, yes?' He nodded. 'All we have to do is take a single sheet of paper with us.'

'And it takes two of us to do that?'

'Normally, no. But Kafka's sees it as training. I'm there to watch you. Make sure you cope with it.'

'Doesn't sound that difficult. Have you got this piece of paper?'

'Not yet, no.'

'When do we go?'

'Tomorrow. Ten o'clock from Saint-Romain. So we need to catch the nine twenty bus. Is that OK with you?

'Yeah. Can't wait.'

'Good' She stood up. 'Bring some money – not much. And perhaps get your mother to do a sandwich or something. I'll see you tomorrow at the bus. Don't be late.'

Claire was at the door, adjusting her hat, when it opened. She gave out a little shriek, stepping backwards. It hadn't been fifteen minutes yet, thought Pierre. But it wasn't his mother returning – it was Major Hurtzberger.

The major stood at the door looking like a person who had walked into the wrong house. No one spoke. The three of them hovered awkwardly, unsure what to say. Eventually, it was the German who broke the silence, 'Am I interrupting something?'

'No,' said Claire breathlessly. 'I'd just popped by. I was worried about Monsieur Durand. Georges.'

Pierre watched them intently, determined to spot any tell-tale signs of affection in their body language.

The major looked slightly flustered, thought Pierre with a degree of satisfaction. 'Ah yes, poor Monsieur Durand. Well, don't go on my account,' he said. 'I've just returned for something I'd forgotten.'

'I was leaving anyway. Goodbye, Pierre. Send my regards to your father – if you should see him.'

The major clicked his heels as Claire squeezed passed him. '*Au revoir, Mademoiselle.*' He watched the door closing. Turning to Pierre, he said with a wink, 'Pretty girl.'

'She's only nineteen,' said Pierre, reducing her age to make his point.

'Ah. Nineteen? Bit old for you, then.'

Yes, and a bit young for you – how he wished he had the nerve to say it. The major disappeared into his room and returned, seconds later, with his buff-coloured folder.

'So, as we seem to be alone perhaps we should have a chat.'

'About girls?'

The major laughed. 'I'm flattered you should think of me as a man who can advise you on such things, but sadly, no.' In a flash, his face hardened. 'I think you know what I mean. I had a meeting with Colonel Eisler, and he informed me that you may have something to report to me.'

Pierre's insides tensed up. He swallowed, hoping his mother would choose this very moment to return. This was the conversation he had been dreading. He thought of his father, the reason why he was doing this. 'No,' he said, as firmly as he could muster. 'I have nothing to report.' He resisted the temptation of addressing the German as 'sir'.

The major looked at his wristwatch. 'The colonel mentioned five days. I think we've had some forty-eight hours already. Still – plenty of time. But, listen,' he added, lowering his voice, 'don't try to cross the colonel. He's not the sort of man you can play games with. He's a seasoned soldier who knows how to get what he wants. And he's ruthless. I won't ask what Claire was doing here, apart from enquiring about Georges, of course, but please, I beg you, be careful. You're a good boy and I like you, I think you know that, and I wouldn't want to see you – or your father – come to any harm. Anyway,' he said, returning to his normal tone, waving his folder, 'I must go.'

*

Pierre stepped out into the yard. The White Venus looked pitifully incomplete. He sunk in the rocking chair and rubbed his eyes. *I have a boyfriend.* Her words rang through his head. Yes, you have a boyfriend. He so wanted to hate the major, felt that it was his duty to do so – he was a bloody Kraut and he was having sex with the girl he loved, even if the girl had made her feelings perfectly clear. But what he really hated was the fact that he liked the man, despite everything, he admired him. There was something about him. He was authoritative, strong, at times intimidating but… but he was also kind. He thought of Joachim, somewhere faraway, proud to be his father's son, proud to be wearing his new uniform. He realised how envious he felt – how he would love to don a uniform, to play a proper part in defending his homeland, instead of embarking on trips to the seaside with a girl he loved but who viewed him below contempt. But, more than this, he envied Joachim having a father like the major. He looked skywards and watched a cloud the shape of Corsica drift by, briefing obscuring the sun. He gazed at the white stone, and her clumpy features – her bendy figure, ill-defined and rather awkward, unsure of her place in the world, dependent on others.

His mother had returned – he could hear her pottering round in the kitchen. He decided to ignore her. The Corsican cloud had passed; the sun returned. Lucienne came out to find him. 'Ah, there you are. How did it go with Claire?'

'Fine.'

'What was it she wanted?' she asked, shielding her eyes from the sun.

'Nothing really.'

'No? She's never called on you before. Are you OK? She's a lovely girl is Claire, so pretty, but... oh dear, how do I say this? Pierre, don't you think that perhaps she's a little old for you? After all, she is twenty-two, I believe, and you're only–'

'For the love of God, why does everyone talk about her age?'

'Pierre,' said Lucienne, straightening her back. 'Please don't use the Lord's name so–'

'It doesn't matter how old she is – she's not my girlfriend.'

'Oh.' Lucienne huffed, annoyed to have misread the situation.

'Maman, do you miss father?'

'What sort of question is that?' She began fanning herself with her hand. 'Of course–' A loud knock on the yard door interrupted her. 'Who could–'

'*Bonjour*? Madame Durand?' came a voice from the other side. Pierre recognised the voice – it was one of the cemetery boys.

Lucienne opened the door. 'Oh, hello. My, what–'

'It's heavy, Madame Durand, let us through.' Lucienne stood aside as the two old chaps carried in a rectangular slab of marble.

Pierre got to his feet. 'Is this for me?' he asked.

'Sure is, sunshine,' said the first. They placed the stone down on its edge leaning against the yard wall and straightened their backs. The first one removed his beret and wiped the perspiration from his brow. 'Good day, Madame Durand,' he said with a small bow.

'Good afternoon, gentlemen.'

'It's getting hotter every day, don't you think?' said the first.

'Must be German weather,' said the second.

'Is this for Monsieur Roché?' asked Pierre.

'Yes, indeed, God rest his soul.' Both men crossed themselves in unison.

'Poor man,' said Lucienne.

'Have you got the paper, Albert?'

'No, Hector, I gave it you to, remember?'

'Did you, my God?' Both men searched their pockets but found nothing. 'Wait, I may have left it in the truck. Excuse me.'

Lucienne, Pierre and Albert stood in the yard, Albert rocking on his feet. An embarrassed smile passed his lips. He eyed Pierre's sculpture. 'So, how's it going with your Botcha-whatsit?'

'Botticelli.'

'Do you approve, Madame Durand?'

'Of what, Albert?'

'Your son depicting the female nude.'

'He's learning his art, aren't you, Pierre?' she said. 'One day, he'll be a famous sculptor.'

Thankfully, Hector returned, waving the piece of paper. 'It's your instructions,' he said, passing it to Pierre. 'Monsieur Roché was a widower and had no next of kin, so the instructions and the text have been written up by the mayor.'

Pierre scanned his eye over the sheet of paper. 'He's kept it simple for you, lad,' added Albert. 'What with your father not...' He glanced worriedly at Lucienne, unable to finish the sentence.

'You'll be paid the full rate,' said Hector, 'so no worries on that score.'

'That's very good of the mayor,' said Lucienne.

'We'll tell him.'

'When's the funeral?' asked Pierre.

'Three days' time but don't worry, lad, it doesn't have to be done by then. Anytime, really. Right, we'll leave you to it.'

Lucienne thanked them and closed the yard gate behind them. 'Well, that's good, isn't it? We could do with a little money.'

'Yeah, great.' I caused his death, he thought, and now I get to earn some money from it. He folded the paper and slipped it into his back pocket.

'Is everything OK, Pierre?'

'Yeah, great,' he said again. 'I'll make a start on it later today.'

Chapter 12

Pierre and Claire waited in line, trying to board the front of the train at Saint-Romain. The time was a few minutes to ten. There were, it seemed, hundreds of Germans milling about, most of them very young, perhaps just a year or two older than Pierre. The train was huge – an old steam locomotive brought back into service, its pistons spitting hot water and steam, its funnels churning out dense clouds of smoke which swathed the platform. Most of the carriages were reserved for the Germans, large signs announcing *Für die Wehrmacht*, allowing only the first two for the locals. Pierre and Claire managed to squeeze on and found a pair of seats together in a compartment. Both had haversacks containing their homemade lunches, a flask, a book and a magazine each given to Claire by Kafka. Claire's magazine was called *Carrefour*, and Pierre's *Signal*. Both were pro-German, pro-Pétain and his collaborationist government. Folded into Pierre's book, alongside the mayor's instructions for Monsieur Roché's headstone, was the piece of paper. Monsieur Bouchette, arriving on his bicycle, had slipped it to him at the bus stop in the town. No words were exchanged. Pierre didn't dare look at it, thus he still had no clue what was written on it and why it was so important. Part of him fancied it wasn't important at all, and it was all part of his initiation test. What exactly he was to do with this piece of paper, he had no idea. But Claire did. She knew precisely.

The train compartment was stuffily full: Pierre, Claire and four others. Opposite Pierre sat a large, middle-aged couple with an Alsatian dog. 'Toby, sit,' roared the man, wearing an old jacket with elbow patches.

'Speak to him nicely, Claude,' said the woman.

Unseen to his wife, Claude dealt Toby a swift kick.

The woman asked Pierre to open the window. He was glad to oblige.

On the other side of Claire sat an older gentleman, dressed in a suit and tie, a newspaper on his lap, his frail-looking wife opposite him, her hair in a hairnet.

Pierre gazed outside and watched the comings and goings of more passengers, of soldiers, of the train guard in his black uniform and green flag, the grey smoke hovering under the rafters of the station roof. The time was now ten – time for departure. They had a ninety-minute journey ahead of them. They heard Germans shouting at one another, and the sound of train doors slamming shut. The guard, waving his flag, blew his whistle. Slowly, with more puffs of smoke, the train crept forward and edged out of the station into the morning light.

As soon as the train was out in the open country, picking up speed, the woman opposite brought out two hard-boiled eggs from her bag, passing one to her husband. They sat, peeling their eggs, with a sheet of greaseproof paper on her lap on which the woman had sprinkled salt. Pierre had his own hard-boiled egg in his bag but he hadn't thought of asking his mother for salt. He tried not to watch them as they dipped their eggs. Toby lay on the floor, licking his chops constantly.

Pierre had hoped to talk to Claire, to get to know her a little better, but he felt too self-conscious to strike up a conversation now. Anyhow, Claire, sitting next to him, was engrossed in her book, fanning herself. He wondered whether the fan was to keep herself cool or to flap away the stench of egg that, despite the open window, was now permeating the compartment.

Pierre noticed the man, Claude, wipe away his fragments of eggshell, half of which landed on the dog. He needed a shave, thought Pierre, specks of grey clearly visible in his stubble.

Pierre wanted to read but the heat of the compartment and the early start had made him feel drowsy.

He was woken up by the opening of the compartment door. A French ticket inspector leant in. 'The Boche are acting odd this morning,' he said quickly. 'They're searching everyone's bags, and being very thorough about it.' Pierre's heart punched him from within. The dog, Toby, growled. Then, looking down the corridor to make sure he wasn't overheard, the inspector added, 'Just as well they don't check the toilets. And mind that dog.' Then, just as quickly, he was gone, sliding open the door to the next compartment.

Claire looked at Pierre, her eyebrows knotted. But it was Claude, opposite, who spoke. 'I think I need the toilet,' he said.

Claire nodded. 'Yes,' said Pierre. 'So do I.'

'Let's go, then,' said Claude, picking up his haversack.

Together, with their bags, they headed to the toilet at the front of the train. Fortunately, no one had beaten them to it but there was only the one. 'After you,' said Claude.

Claude locked the door behind them. With the smell of the filthy toilet pan overwhelming them, they squeezed in together. 'Christ, open the window.' Pierre tried but it was stuck. 'What's your name?'

'Pierre.'

Claude offered his hand. As rough as sandpaper, thought Pierre. 'Claude. Nice to meet you.' His breath reeked of egg.

'And you.'

'Question is, should we trust the inspector. This might be a trap, you know.'

Pierre hadn't thought of this. His heartbeat quickened. Pulling on his bag strap, he asked, 'What should we do?'

They heard raised German voices at the far end of the corridor, doors opening. 'Too late now,' whispered Claude. 'We'll just have to sit it out.'

They waited, pressed into each other, Claude considerably taller, Pierre's eyes level with the man's mouth; the stench of stale smoke, drains and egg filling their nostrils. The floor was stained brown with years of piss, the tiny sink with its rusty tap marked with dark stains. Pierre could feel the sweat running down his back, like a thousand tiny insects creeping down his skin. The Germans were getting closer, more doors opening, barked orders, French protestations, doors sliding shut – all in quick succession. He wished he'd stayed now; the searches were quick. Claude jumped at the sound of his dog barking. He mouthed the word shit. More feet, more voices. How many of them were there? There seemed to be dozens. The dog didn't bark again.

Claude delved into his haversack, and pulled out a notebook. He began ripping out the pages from the binding, trying not to rip the paper in half. 'Let's hope the flush works,' he whispered.

Pierre found his single sheet of paper. Yes, there was writing on it, words leapt out – "We will not be defeated / Pétain has sold you out / Drive the Hun invader off our soil." He wondered whether it should say "*from* our soil". The footsteps were closer. Pierre realised what was happening – there were several parties of Germans, overlapping each other. Perhaps, after all, it was better to be here in this stifling toilet with eggy Claude. The man had his papers held above the toilet pan, ready to drop them in. It was too small a toilet, thought Pierre. Even if the flush did work, it would never get rid of all that paper in one go. With a sudden heaviness in his stomach, he knew they would never explain why the two of them were here together, in the toilet.

The door handle rattled. Sweat poured down his brow. A shrill, German voice. Claude's pupils dilated with fear, his mouth open, his dirty tongue lolling from his lips. Outside, the ticket inspector's voice – 'It's out of order.'

A pause. Silence except for the rumble of the train. Footsteps moving away. Claude's shoulders fell. More footsteps but no more rattling of the door handle. Claude let his head fall back, exhaling a deep breath. Pierre clutched his heart, felt his sodden shirt.

'Oh, mother of God,' muttered Claude. 'Come on, let's get out of here before we suffocate.'

Back in the compartment, Pierre almost fell into his seat. He sat there, breathing hard, unable to talk, Claude opposite, a mirror image of relief. Claude's wife had her hand clasped over Toby's mouth. The dog, though muffled, was still trying to growl.

Claire placed her hand on Pierre's thigh. 'Well done,' she said quietly. Pierre looked round at everyone. The elderly couple were smiling. The man winked at him. Claude's wife stroked her dog. Claude let out a little laugh. Everyone laughed quietly with him.

'Good work, young man,' he said to Pierre. Pierre beamed.

Claude's wife leant over, grinning. One of her front teeth was missing. 'Would you like an egg?'

'No. No, thank you. I'm fine. Just fine.'

*

Claire knew where to go. They headed towards the main street of the harbour town. Squinting his eyes against the sun, Pierre could see the sea in the distance. Seagulls flew above. Everywhere, the road signs were written in Gothic script. The street, fully in the shade, was lined with cafés, mostly full of Germans sitting outside under the parasols, enjoying rounds of coffee and cigarettes while playing cards. A couple of cafés had signs saying *Germans only*. Pierre shook his head. At one, he noticed a table full of German officers drinking champagne, the bottles resting in ice buckets. The atmosphere, as at home, was holiday-like with much laughing and soldiers taking photos of each other. Turning off the main street, Pierre followed as Claire wound down a couple of side streets full of boarded-up shops before coming to a stop outside a front door with a lion head brass knocker. Above it, a balcony with curved railings. 'This is it,' she said, pulling on the knocker. 'Don't say a word until I say.'

A man in a vest appeared on the balcony momentarily before disappearing again. Pierre could hear footsteps on the stairs and seconds later the same man was at the door.

'Sorry to bother you,' said Claire, 'but we're lost. We're looking for the Church of Our Saviour.'

'Where?' He wore shorts, was bronzed, solid muscles in his arms.

'Oh.' Claire stepped back. 'I think… it doesn't matter.'

'Hang on a minute.' He returned inside, shouting. 'Victor, there's a woman at the door, something about a church.'

A distant voice responded, 'Keep your voice down, you fool.' More quick footsteps on the stairs and another man appeared, older, taller, round glasses, and blond eyebrows despite his dark brown hair, wearing baggy trousers and a buttoned shirt with a frilly collar.

'Excuse my friend here.' The man eyed both of them but he had, thought Pierre, a kind expression. 'What were you saying, Mademoiselle?'

Claire repeated herself, word for word.

'Ah yes, as beautiful as anything you'll find in Florence. Come in.'

The man stepped aside to allow them through. 'This way; follow me.' The house seemed bigger inside – with a marbled floor, and an arched doorway to the side. He took them upstairs, a spiral staircase with an ornate iron bannister. Pierre noticed his well-polished shoes. 'Welcome, my name is Victor. That was Alain you saw just now.' Pierre turned round but Alain had gone. He realised the exchange about the church and Florence had been a pre-arranged code.

Victor led them into a room on the first floor, a large room with an array of settees and armchairs, a big fireplace, its bricks burnt black, a stone floor with a deep red rug. 'Take a seat. Can I get you both a coffee?'

Victor shouted for Alain, telling him to make a round of coffees. 'No sugar, I'm afraid. And the coffee is of inferior quality. But you know how it is,' he said with an exaggerated shrug of his shoulders. He asked them about their journey, about life in the town and what their Germans were like. Pierre told him about the major in his house, glancing at Claire who sat impassively.

'He doesn't sound too bad then. There's a big difference between your ordinary German and his Nazi colleague. You're lucky, but still – be careful. When push comes to shove, he's still a German. We're having an easy time of it here – relatively. I think they've all got heatstroke; they all seem rather lethargic, poor dears. I doubt it'll last long. So, while the lion sleeps, the deer will play.'

'Is that a saying?' asked Pierre.

Victor laughed. 'No, I've just made it up but I give you permission to use it as often as you wish and pass it off as your own. Well, thank you for coming to see us. I have to say I didn't expect two of you but still, it's lovely to see you both. So, are you two...'

'No,' snapped Claire.

'No. Right. OK.'

'So, erm,' Pierre tried to think of something to change the subject. 'Why are half the shops boarded up?'

'Lack of customers. We don't have any money to buy

anything any more. Only the shops that appeal to the Boche survive.'

'Souvenir shops.'

'Yes, that sort of thing.'

The door creaked open, and in came Alain carrying a tray bearing three steaming cups. 'Ah, here he is; that's what we like to see.'

'Messieurs, Mademoiselle, your coffee,' said Alain.

'If you can call it that. Thank you, Alain.' The two men exchanged furtive smiles. Victor watched as Alain exited, as if admiring him, thought Pierre.

'Cigarette? No?'

The coffee was fine, thought Pierre; he had become used to this ersatz stuff.

Victor screwed a cigarette into a holder and lit it with a large, silver lighter. 'So, what have you brought me?'

'We have the text for the flyer,' said Claire. 'Pierre, have you got it?'

Pierre fished out the piece of paper from his book and handed it over to Victor.

Adjusting his glasses, Victor unfolded the paper. 'Bernard Roché, fourth June 1861 to... I don't understand.'

'Sorry, that's the wrong paper.'

'Thank God for that.' He drew on his cigarette, producing a cloud of purple smoke. 'For a horrible moment I thought you wanted me to print a death notice. Oh, he died yesterday.'

'This is the text.'

Claire cleared her throat. 'Kafka, my boss, of sorts, said you could print a thousand of them.'

They waited while the man read. 'Yep,' he said, pushing

his glasses back up. 'Shouldn't be a problem. It reads well. Perhaps a couple small grammatical errors but I can fix that. You can reassure your boss that I've got the transport heading your way at the end of the week. You'll have five boxes – two hundred in each.'

'Thank you.'

'Now, a bit early perhaps, but how about a spot of lunch?'

*

An hour later, Claire and Pierre sat on the sea wall, watching the sea lapping on the beach, the sun beating down on their backs. Not too far away, a group of Germans were drying themselves off after a dip in the sea. 'They really think they're on holiday, don't they?' said Claire, watching the men with, thought Pierre, a little too much interest. 'Drinking our best coffee, shopping, sunbathing. It's sickening.'

'At least we're doing something about it now.'

'Yes, it all helps.'

'Excuse me.' A German-accented voice made them jump. They turned to see another fresh-faced German struggling with a town plan. 'Sorry to be startling you.' He spoke slowly, each word separated by a space. 'Do you know the way to *Le Café de la Mer*?'

'Yes,' said Claire. Pointing the way, she gave him a complicated set of instructions.

The young soldier bowed and thanked her.

'I didn't know you knew this place so well,' said Pierre.

'I don't. I just made it up.'

'Oh.'

'Did you see those café signs earlier – Germans only?

Well, I'm damned if I'm going to tell him where a café is that I'm not even allowed to go into.'

'It shouldn't be that difficult – with all those Gothic signs everywhere. Poor chap; he'll still be walking round in circles for hours to come.'

Claire winked at him.

'The men in the house – they were nice, weren't they? Especially Victor.'

'I thought he was a bit creepy. Nice lunch though.'

'Yeah, saved me from having to eat my mother's hardboiled egg.'

Claire laughed. 'I think we've had enough stinky eggs for one day.'

'You should have been in the toilet with him. No escape.'

'I can imagine.'

'So, did they search you?' he asked.

'They searched my bags. Took everything out and went through it. Even my lunch. So I was happy not to have eat my sandwiches that had been manhandled by a German with dirty fingernails. In fact...' She retrieved the sandwich, unwrapped it from its greaseproof paper, and left it on the sea wall a few feet away. Sure enough, within seconds a seagull swooped down and snatched it. They watched it as it flew round before disappearing, other seagulls in its wake. 'That poor woman had to restrain the dog, Toby. I thought for a moment they might shoot it.'

The Germans had dressed and strolled by in their bare feet, trouser legs rolled up, squinting in the sun. Each one stole a look at Claire. A young mother passed them, holding a toddler by his hand, a bucket and spade in her other hand. The boy, with his pudgy knees, wore a wide-

166

brimmed straw hat. 'Look at all the birdies, Patrick. Look, there's one over there with a sandwich. Can you see? Oh, it's gone.'

This, thought Pierre, would be a good time to broach the subject of the major but however he tried to start the conversation, he couldn't think of the words.

'Come,' she said, after a few minutes of awkward silence, 'let's have a paddle.'

'What?'

'In the sea.'

'I… I'd rather not.'

'Why on earth not? Come, I'll beat you, last one in is a rotten egg.' Hurriedly, removing her shoes, she raced towards the water, giggling.

Pierre followed, slowly; his shoes scrunching on the sand and pebbles. He watched as Claire hiked up her skirt and waded through the gentle waves. 'It's cold,' she screeched, holding out her hand.

Pierre shuddered. All that water. Yes, it looked inviting in its calmness yet it still repulsed him.

'Ow, the stones are sharp. Come on, what's the matter for goodness sake?'

'I don't like water,' he said, knowing how feeble it sounded.

'There's nothing to be scared of,' she said, splashing

Reluctantly, he took off his shoes and socks and gingerly stepped forward, allowing the water to reach his ankles. Yes, it was cold, but it wasn't that that made him shiver. The teddy bear with its yellow waistcoat and green trousers flashed through his mind again.

'I can't,' he said, spinning round. 'I just can't.'

*

167

Ten minutes later, they were back on the sea wall, Claire with her bare legs stretched out, allowing her feet to dry off in the sun.

'So, what was that about, then?' she asked.

The mother and toddler sat nearby, building a sandcastle, the little boy slapping the sand with joy. Claire smiled, pushing tendrils of wet hair from her face, while Pierre tried to distract himself from her sodden blouse.

'I have a thing about water.'

'Why, you can't drown if you only go up to your legs.'

'I know.'

'Can't you swim?'

'No,' he said quietly.

'But it's more than that, isn't it?'

Almost imperceptibly, he nodded.

'Well? You can tell me, if you like.'

He shook his head, ashamed that, after all this time, water still had the same effect on him. 'I can't tell you. I'm sorry.'

*

They caught the train home, again sharing a compartment with others. This time they were left undisturbed. Much to Pierre's delight, back home, Claire accepted his offer to walk her back.

'Well,' said Claire, 'that was a really entertaining day; I enjoyed your company. Thank you, Pierre.'

'Pleasure. We must do it again one day. Soon.'

'We'll have to see what else Kafka has in store for us.'

They'd reached her bungalow, an old white-stoned house with small windows, a weather vane in the shape of a cockerel on its chimney, a gravelled front garden with a set of iron table and chairs. 'Here we are,' she declared. 'I'd invite you in but I'm exhausted. All that sea air. And my feet are killing me.'

'It's fine. I'm tired too.'

She hesitated, as if changing her mind. 'Another time then.'

'Yes, another time.'

Chapter 13

'The thing is people are getting soft.' Pierre had been instructed to have a walk with Kafka. They walked briskly through the woods, Kafka in front, a large bag round his shoulder, following a narrow path. The sun slanted through the branches, and the ground, after weeks without rain, was hard. The birds were in full song. 'People seem to have accepted this invasion as if it was a good thing.'

'People say the Germans will deal with the communists. And the Jews.' Pierre regretted his afterthought.

'We can deal with them ourselves. We don't need foreigners coming in sorting out our affairs. People see the Germans as a sort of deliverance; they forget they invaded our country and for what? On the whim of a madman. Take your house guest, for example. The villagers like him; he's a cultured man, he holds the door open for the ladies. Your mother seems to have grown used to his presence. I know all this; I keep my eyes and ears open. They forget, he's not here as our friend; he's here as an invader, a bloody invader.' They jumped over a stream. 'It's up to people like you and me to keep the flame of resistance alive. How will history remember us? You have to ask yourself that. In years to come will your children thank you for having been a collaborator?'

They walked in silence for a while. Pierre picked up a stick and beat at the long grass bordering the path.

'Keep up,' said Kafka over his shoulder. 'So, your trip went well?'

'Yes.'

'Yeah, Claire told me all about it. You did well. Victor prints newspapers. The Krauts have got him printing their rubbish but by night he supplies the whole region with flyers and "subversive literature", as our German friends call it. He's rich; he can afford to do it for free. He's got quite a network already.'

They'd been walking for over half an hour when Kafka declared, 'Here we are.'

At first, Pierre couldn't see what Kafka was referring to – but there, under the shade of a large cedar tree, was a small wooden hut. Its walls were made up of huge logs, it had a window covered in tarpaulin. Kafka undid the padlock and beckoned Pierre in. Inside, daylight permeated the gaps between the logs and through the roof. There was a bed covered in a brown blanket, a table and chair, a shelf half full of food tins, and, on the wall, a large framed portrait of Marshal Pétain peppered with holes. 'Welcome to my second home,' said Kafka. Reaching into his bag, he placed more tins on the shelf. 'Emergency supplies.'

Pierre watched, wide-eyed, as Kafka produced a rifle from under his bed. 'Yeah, I know, I didn't hand it in. I'd be shot for having this around. It's an old M16 carbine. Old but still effective. I stole it from the army in eighteen.

I used to be a sniper, you know. In my day, I could hit a centime from seventy metres. My eyesight's not what it used to be, but, though I say so myself, I've still got an eye for a target. This,' he said, lifting the rifle as if testing its weight, 'is the only rifle we have but one day we'll have more. I'm working on it. So, as you're now officially one of us, I thought you need to be prepared.'

'You want me to fire it?'

'Not the rifle, no, but this... another souvenir from the army.' From his pocket, he produced a revolver. 'That's why I've brought you out here. I wasn't taking you on a walk for the good of your health.'

Pierre watched as Kafka took a tobacco tin also from under his bed and fished out a handful of bullets. 'Let's go outside. Take the photo with you,' he said motioning at Pétain.

Pierre followed Kafka out, the picture under his arm. 'Right, there's a hook on that tree there. See it? Hang the photo up on it.' Pierre did as told, then re-joined Kafka, standing behind him.

Kafka loaded the revolver, took aim at the portrait and fired. The shot cracked through the trees, causing a cacophony of noise as thousands of birds, or so it seemed, took flight, squawking and flapping. 'Did you see that? Right in the old git's forehead. Dead. If only it was that easy. Right, your turn. Take the gun.' He passed Pierre the revolver. 'Always keep it pointing downwards until you're ready.' Pierre did as told. 'It holds five rounds. I can only spare a few, so listen. Hold it solidly, keep your arms straight. The recoil on these things isn't too bad.' Pierre concentrated as Kafka went through his instructions. Finally, Kafka declared that Pierre was ready to have a shot. 'Aim above your target and slowly lower it, then, just at the right moment, pull the trigger.'

Pierre held his breath and did as instructed. But he was unable to fire. Sighing, he tried again.

'Steady now,' said Kafka just behind him.

This time, Pierre pulled the trigger. The revolver jumped back in his hand, despite Kafka's reassurance. What he hit, if anything, he had no idea.

'Not bad. Try again,' said Kafka.

The second attempt hit the tree above the portrait with a satisfying dull thud. 'Hey, you're a natural,' exclaimed Kafka. 'We'll make a sniper out of you yet.'

Pierre grinned, felt his chest expand.

'Come on, let's head back and I'll tell you what's next.'

They returned to the hut. Pierre waited outside while Kafka went in, re-emerging a few seconds later, padlocking the door. 'Even if the Krauts managed to discover this place and ransacked it, they'd never know who it belonged to.'

'They're not likely to come out this far on foot.'

'No, exactly.'

Pierre followed Kafka back, back over the stream and down the zigzag path; this time trying to familiarise himself with the landscape, in case he ever needed to return alone. He noted a tree engraved with the initials 'RJ', and another fallen, its trunk blocking the pathway. With the town in view, nestled in the valley, they trudged back across the fields. As they drew closer, Kafka said, 'If anyone asks, we'll say we just went for a walk for a man-to-man talk. I'm looking after you now, we'll say; now that your father's gone.'

'I miss him.'

'I dare say. But they won't keep him long. I've heard they've got limited room, and they can't shoot all of them. Well, they could, I suppose, but I doubt it.' He stopped, gazing at the houses nearby. 'We'll go our own ways here. Listen, you've passed your first test but there'll be much harder, sterner ones to come. You still in?'

'Yes,' replied Pierre, despite wanting to scream no.

'Good man. Come to the library tomorrow morning at eleven. Make sure you're carrying a book – just in case, you know.'

Pierre nodded.

'See you tomorrow. *Au revoir.*'

*

Returning home, Pierre decided to make a start on Monsieur Roché's headstone. He slipped out the instructions from his pocket and re-read them. He did think the wording was rather brief – just the basics. And no hint about how Roché had met his end – clubbed to death like a baby seal by a German. It contained just the text – no clue as to what sort of lettering, whether it was to be big or small, straight or sloping. He realised he felt daunted by the task. It wasn't difficult but it was a responsibility and he had to get it right. It was the least he could do for Monsieur Roché. He wished his father was here to advise him. He fed the chickens some corn and watched as they fell onto their food. He poured fresh water into their trough, swept the yard, tidied the tools in the shed. Anything to delay actually starting his work. It was always the most daunting part – just starting; making that first engraving onto the pure, virgin surface of the marble. Taking his tape measure, he measured out the width of the stone, and how much space he needed for the first line, then the second, and so on. He wrote out the words lightly in crayon. Dissatisfied with the spacing, he rubbed out the crayon with a rag dabbed in white spirit, and tried again. This time, he decided, he had it right.

Poised with his chisel and hammer, he heard the front door open and clattering in the kitchen. It had to be his mother. Seconds later, she emerged at the kitchen door, her headscarf still on. 'Oh, Pierre, there you are. Where have you been?'

'Oh, nowhere really. I needed a walk to think about how to do this stone.'

'That's OK then. I do worry when I don't know where you are. You are being careful, aren't you, Pierre?'

'Yes, Maman.'

'I can see you're busy, so I'll let you get on. I'm going to Saint-Romain later today to take your father some fresh clothes and a bit of food.'

'Don't put a message in anywhere.'

'Of course not,' she huffed.

'I'll walk you to the bus stop.'

'No need but if you want to, that'd be nice.' She paused. 'Your father – he'd be very proud to see you doing this work.'

'I know.'

She smiled a maternal smile, and returned indoors.

'Right then,' said Pierre to himself. '"In Loving Memory of..."'

*

An hour later, and Pierre had finished. His mother, ready to go to Saint-Romain, joined him outside.

'So, how's it going?' she asked.

'All done, I think.'

Together, they admired his handiwork. 'You've done an excellent job. Simple but dignified. And there's not much of that around any more – dignity.'

Pierre tried not to think of Roché's undignified end. 'Yeah, I'm pleased. Poor old Monsieur Roché. I'll take you to your bus now, if you're ready.'

It was early afternoon. The streets were deserted, the shops closed; not a French person in sight. 'It's like a ghost town,' remarked Pierre.

'Things have changed so quickly. Only the cafés and restaurants seem to thrive nowadays. They're busier now than they ever have been.'

They passed through the town centre and, sure enough, the cafés were open for business and, as usual, doing a roaring trade with their German customers.

'Oh, isn't that our major?' said Lucienne, pointing ahead.

'*Our* major?'

'With that pretty girl. Claire.'

'Oh. Yes. So it is.'

'Pierre, I know what you're thinking but she is a little old for you. Can't you find someone your own age?'

'Where, Maman? They all left, didn't they, during the fighting.'

'They'll be back one day.'

Now, they passed through the square and onto the road on the other side that led to the bus stop.

'I don't think Claire should be cavorting quite so openly with the Germans,' said Lucienne. 'Especially our major.'

'Maman, stop calling him "our" major. He may be nice and all that, but he's still a German.' Pierre remembered Kafka's words. 'He may be cultured and hold doors open for you but don't forget, he's still part of the people who invaded us on the whim of a madman.'

'Invaded. You make him sound like a barbarian, like a Viking, raping and pillaging.'

'But that's exactly what he is.'

'What? Has the major raped someone? I should hope not. And I would have noticed if he had stolen anything from our pantry. There's little enough as it is.'

'No, I don't mean... It doesn't matter. Look, here's your bus. You don't want to miss it.'

'No. Thank you, Pierre. I'll be back in time to do some dinner. Major Hurtzberger brought us some sausages today. That'll make a nice change, won't it?'

*

'Claire told me more Germans are coming in to borrow books, at least the ones who can read French.' Kafka was at the head of the table, addressing the meeting which, this time, numbered six of them.

'I'm surprised they can read at all – French or German,' said Bouchette, idly playing with his penknife.

'She reckons they're bored.'

'Oh dear. Maybe we should lay on some entertainment for them.'

'Right. Yes. What did you have in mind? No, don't answer that. I'm worried in case you take me seriously and we start doing Punch and Judy shows for them.'

A polite tittle of laughter circled round the room.

'Anyway,' said Kafka, 'my point is that I reckon it's too dangerous to meet here any more. Pétain's portrait up there is a good cover but it's not enough. We need somewhere else. Any suggestions?'

Pierre put his hand up. 'What about—'

'Shut up, Pierre.'

'Sorry,' he muttered. Obviously, Kafka didn't want anyone knowing about his hut.

'What about the crypt?' said Dubois, wiping his spectacles.

'Yes, not bad.'

'The Germans are so atheist they never go in the church. We can go in, one-by-one, and sit at the front to say our prayers—'

'Or pretend to.'

'Or pretend to, and once we feel it's safe, we can pop down. Lots of exits too. Not out of the crypt but out of the church. And I'm sure Father de Beaufort won't mind.'

'Good idea. That's what we'll do. Can you speak to Father de Beaufort, Dubois? He's more likely to listen to you.'

Dubois nodded.

'Right, to the main business. No doubt you'll have noticed all the trains passing through at night from Nantes on their way to the Reich, filled to the brim with French goods. We need to do something about it, to hold them up for a few days.'

'Not again?' said Bouchette. 'Look what happened last time. Pierre's father was arrested.'

'And Touvier,' added Dubois.

'So what? They're stealing from us, stealing the fruits of French labour.'

'He's quite right,' said a man nicknamed Lincoln, a gaunt man with long, black sideburns who, people felt, resembled the American president. No one seemed to remember his real name. 'As patriots, we have a duty.'

'But the whole line is guarded, especially round here, after our last attempt,' said Dubois.

'Yeah, but only by collaborators, bloody traitors.'

'Have you a plan, Kafka?' asked Lincoln.

'What do you think? Of course I bloody have. It doesn't involve all seven of us–'

'There's only six,' said the other new man, Gide, the baker.

'Plus we can always call on Claire.'

'A girl?'

'She's keen, and that's what counts.'

'For God's sake, man, what have we come to?' said Bouchette, stabbing his penknife into the table top. 'Children and girls. Next, Kafka, you'll be recruiting from the nunnery.'

'If I thought it would make a difference, I would.'

'And what if one of the nuns turned traitor?' asked Gide.

'I would deal with her. No hesitation. A traitor is a traitor. I'd shoot my own mother if I thought she was sleeping with a Kraut.'

'Isn't she dead?'

'That's not the point.'

'We don't have a nunnery,' said Dubois.

Kafka shook his head. 'Jesus, it's like a chimp's tea party.'

Bouchette whispered to Dubois, who laughed.

'Right,' said Kafka, 'here's the plan. We go tomorrow night, two hours after curfew. Memorise all of this, if you're capable of that. Don't write a single word of this down.'

*

The sausages, Pierre had to concede, were delicious. With a large helping of potatoes and French beans, the three of them retired to their armchairs, relaxed and opened their books or knitting. An hour before, the major had returned from his work with a framed watercolour – an Alpine scene portraying long-horned cattle on rolling lush grass with snow-peaked mountains behind. He said he'd bought it in Saint-Romain and was giving it to Lucienne as a present for all her hospitality. Lucienne oozed gratitude; said she loved it.

'I'll hang it up for you,' said the major. 'Perhaps after dinner.'

'Well, that would be lovely. Thank you.'

Now, after dinner, Pierre found himself alone with the major, or Thomas, as he seemed to have become. Pierre dreaded what he knew was coming next. It didn't take long.

'So,' said the major, quietly, drawing out the word. 'The colonel is expecting a response tomorrow, Pierre.' He didn't look up, keeping his eyes fixed on his book.

Pierre tried to picture his father, tried to remember why he was doing this. He had plenty to tell; enough to save his father and secure his release.

'I don't know anything.'

'And you think the colonel will accept this? I don't.'

'But I do know someone who is working against you – nothing big or dangerous, just leaflets, that sort of thing.'

'Oh?'

This was difficult, thought Pierre but, after all, he had to save his father. It didn't make it any easier.

'Pierre – you have to tell me. Remember what's at stake.'

'I know. It's… I met a couple of men – in a town on the coast.'

'Go on.'

Bracing himself, Pierre told the major about Victor and Alain and their printing press. The major, having placed his book on the floor, listened intently, nodding his head.

'Leaflets, you say?'

'Yes.' Pierre felt himself go red.

'And where are these leaflets? I haven't seen any?'

'They haven't arrived yet.'

'When are they due?'

'I don't know. I think within the next few days.'

He paced up and down. 'This is good.'

'What will happen to them?'

'Don't worry about that.' He slunk back into his armchair and reached down for his book. Reclining, he rested it on his lap, and closed his eyes.

Pierre sighed. He seemed strangely aware of his own naivety, aware of how ill-equipped he was in dealing with this. He felt as if he'd walked into a minefield and had no idea how to extricate himself.

Chapter 14

'It's Monsieur Roché's funeral today, isn't it, Pierre?'

'Yes.' Pierre was eating scrambled egg on toast for his breakfast – he was beginning to hate eggs. He had no appetite, too worried for Victor and his friend and what might happen to them. His mother hovered over him; the major was at the mirror, adjusting his tie.

'Thomas, are you about to go to work?'

'Soon.'

'Would you have time to put that lovely picture up?'

He glanced at his watch. 'Yes, of course. Shouldn't take long.'

'Pierre, you've got nails in the shed, haven't you?'

'Yes – in a jam jar.'

It was only when the major went out into the yard that Pierre remembered.

Within a minute or two, the major had returned, holding the jam jar in his hand. 'It's empty.'

'Oh yes, I forgot, I lent them all to Xavier.'

'You *lent* them?'

'Gave.'

'All of them?' asked his mother.

'Yes, his father needed them for... for something.'

'But it was full before,' said the major holding up the jar, peering into it as if he might have missed one. 'There must've been a hundred nails in here.'

'It was a big job.'

'Let me have a look in the shed,' said Lucienne. 'There must be one lying around. It does seem strange though, Pierre. All those nails.'

The major waited for her to leave. Turning to Pierre, he said, 'It was you.'

'What?'

'Don't play games with me.'

'I... I had to do something – to get into the resistance.'

'An old man died as a result.'

'That wasn't my fault.'

'Wasn't it?' he snapped. 'Every action has a consequence. You're old enough to realise that.'

'I didn't want that to happen.'

'But it did. As a direct result of what you did. I should tell Colonel Eisler.'

Pierre's heart caved in at the sound of the name.

Lucienne returned. 'Couldn't find any. I don't understand, Pierre – why did you have to give them all to Xavier's father?'

'Well,' said the major, re-adjusting his tie, 'if Pierre could ask Xavier's father if he could give us one back, I'll put the picture up tonight.' He put on his cap. 'I'd better go.'

*

It was the afternoon of Monsieur Roché's funeral. Pierre and Xavier were slowly making their way to the church, surprised at how empty the streets were. Lucienne had left earlier. Xavier had elected to wear his father's tight beret.

'Why do you wear that thing? It makes your ears stick out.'

'Your ears stick out by themselves.'

'No they bloody don't.'

'Anyway, you're telling me that you want one nail. Just. One. Nail. Don't you have any left? None at all?'

'No.'

'One nail?'

'Yes.'

'OK. I'll bring round one, solitary nail a bit later. So, why you're so keen on going to this funeral?' he asked.

'I told you. It's because I'm doing his headstone, so I feel I should attend and pay my respects.' He could never admit the real reason, the sense of responsibility that hung so heavily on his conscience.

'Should we be wearing black?'

'Yes. No. I don't know. We hardly knew him.'

'I didn't know him at all. I'm only going to keep you company – remember?'

'Let's go and see. We can always rush back.'

They heard the church clock chime two. As they approached, they could see a strong German presence and, in front of them, remonstrating, a few villagers. 'This doesn't look good,' said Xavier, slowing down.

'The church doors are open.'

'There's the coffin.'

Pierre narrowed his eyes. The coffin, on a trolley, was just inside the church doors. Draped over it was a French flag. The next moment, a German soldier passed by, whipping off the flag. 'Arse.'

'Look out, here comes your mother.'

'Pierre.' Lucienne emerged from the throng. 'They won't let us through.'

'Why not?'

'Hello, Xavier. I don't know. They say only family can attend the funeral.'

'But he doesn't, I mean, didn't have any family,' said Xavier.

Pierre could see the German lieutenant leaning against a jeep to one side while his men stood in front of the church gate, their rifles held across their chests.

Bouchette and Dubois were among the villagers. 'This is outrageous,' shouted Dubois, dressed in a black suit, approaching Lucienne. 'They're saying we can't even pay our respects now?'

'They don't want a repeat of the Algerian funeral,' said Pierre.

'Buggers. Oh, sorry, Madame Durand.'

The villagers began dispersing, intimidated by the German presence. 'Let me try. I'm doing the headstone; they'll let me through.' said Pierre. He approached the soldiers at the gate as everyone else left, Bouchette and Dubois among them. Beyond the gate, Pierre could see Father de Beaufort arguing with a German soldier who was smoking, sitting on the grass next to the gravelled path, with his back propped up against a headstone. The soldier threw away his cigarette and rose, slovenly, to his feet.

'Hello,' said Pierre to two German privates, adapting a deep tone. 'I am preparing the headstone for the deceased.

I'm supposed to be here. Can I come through, please?'

The soldiers stared blankly beyond him, resolutely gripping their guns. Behind them, Father de Beaufort had stubbed out the fizzing cigarette end with his shoe, and was walking back into the church, his robes flapping behind him.

In his side vision, Pierre saw the lieutenant spit. 'It's you again, Frenchie,' he said in German.

'I want to go to the funeral.'

The lieutenant idly produced his revolver, clicked the hammer back and, without warning, fired at Pierre's feet, hitting the gravel path with a sharp ping. A cloud of dust exploded around his shoes as Pierre jumped back. 'OK, OK,' shouted Pierre, scurrying back to join Xavier and Lucienne.

He found his friend almost doubled-up in laughter.

'Are you all right, Pierre?' said his mother, reaching out for him.

'I'm fine, thanks,' he said, jutting out his jaw.

'Well, they sure listened to you,' said Xavier, guffawing.

'Yeah, very funny.'

Lucienne shook her head. 'Come on, I think we should go home.'

*

The night was eerily still, broken only by the distant hoot of an owl. Pierre looked up as the slither of moon disappeared behind a cloud. Kafka had told him to meet up at eleven in the ditch beneath a small junction box on the railway line. He was told to keep an eye out for the French guards the Germans had posted as patrols along the track. The railway was a good couple of kilometres' walk away. He glanced at his watch. It was quarter to. He walked slowly, continually checking behind him, pausing at corners, conscious of the sound of his footsteps on the road. He knew that if caught out this long after curfew, he would never be able to explain it. He'd reached the point where he had to leave the road and follow a path with a field on one side and the woods on the other. Here, at least, he felt more secure – the trees providing him ample cover. He realised how heavily he was breathing – not from the excursion but from the tension. Glancing behind, beyond the field with its corn swaying gently in the breeze, he could make out the outline of the town, the church spire looming in the dark sky. How peaceful the world seemed. A bat flew by. Pierre wanted to smile, wanted to console himself with the thought that nature had no truck with the misdeeds of man. But the thought provided no consolation. He pressed on, his feet as heavy as clay.

Beneath the trees he could no longer make out the time on his watch. He could see the junction box ahead of him, up on the embankment. No sign of a patrol. The last stretch, from the edge of the woods to the line, was across an expanse of barren grass. He ran across, stooping, half expecting to hear a shot ring through the air. As he approached, he saw the figures of others crouching against the bank. They weren't Germans – that was all he needed to know for now.

'Good boy.' It was Kafka. Someone shook his shoulder in a paternal sort of way – it was Monsieur Dubois, wearing his blue corduroy jacket with a wide leather collar. Next to him, Monsieur Gide. Pierre felt relieved to see them all. Safety in numbers, he thought. But no Lincoln or Claire. Pity, he thought, she'd be missing out. Behind

Dubois, crouching, was Monsieur Bouchette. The man gave Pierre a wave. They were lying in a ditch at the bottom of the bank – above them, the junction box.

'Right,' said Kafka. 'Everyone ready?' He spoke in a whisper yet it still sounded too loud. 'Good. Let's go.'

As previously instructed, Pierre and Dubois edged about fifty metres to the right, while Bouchette and Gide covered a similar distance to the left – leaving only Kafka, with his explosives, in the middle. Dubois led the way. A thin veil of rain began to fall. Continually crouching, Pierre's back began to ache. After a while, Dubois told Pierre to stay put while he went further along. Kafka had devised this system of lookouts – an outer one and an inner one, each armed with a white handkerchief and, if that failed, a whistle. The whistles, Kafka had told them, had been provided by a sympathetic school teacher in Saint-Romain, while the explosives had been commandeered from a quarry left to waste since the Germans' arrival. Dubois and Bouchette, as the further lookouts were each armed with a cosh. Kafka held onto the only firearm they possessed – his wartime revolver.

Pierre watched as Dubois made his way along the ditch. With a start, he realised someone was on the track; two men heading their way. Dubois, too far down, hadn't seen them. The men, strolling along, had rifles slung behind their backs, their silhouettes made hazy by the rain. Pierre had his handkerchief at the ready but he couldn't use it – Dubois had his back to him and it would only attract the patrol. The whistle was just as useless. He looked back, hoping to see Kafka but the man was out of view. His mouth felt dry. Creeping forward on the damp grass, he kept the two men in sight. They had stopped. Holding his breath, Pierre stopped also. Dubois, at last, had seen them too. He also halted, waiting, Pierre guessed, for him to catch up. One of the men was patting his pockets, as if looking for something. Pierre crawled forward on his knees, using his hand on the grass to help him keep balance. The patrolmen were lighting cigarettes, talking quietly but loud enough for Pierre to hear what they were saying. They were talking about the war memorial, Soldier Mike. The Germans had ordered its destruction. Why, wondered Pierre, would they want to do that?

With a wave of the hand, Dubois urged Pierre forward but he felt unable to move any further. The two patrolmen moved slowly on – they were now half way between Pierre and Dubois, Dubois behind them, making hand signals which Pierre tried to decipher while not wanting to take his eyes off the men on the line. Dubois was creeping up the embankment. Pierre felt at a disadvantage – the men were in front of him; if he moved now, they would see him. Dubois had reached the train track. One of the men turned. Dubois screamed as he sprinted with, thought Pierre, surprising speed for a man in his forties. Both men reached for their rifles. Pierre tried to climb the bank but his legs, shaking uncontrollably, gave way beneath him and he slipped down the wet grass. 'Shit,' he muttered, trying to maintain his balance. With frightening clarity, he suddenly realised he would rather be shot than be found simpering at the bottom of a ditch. With renewed determination, he ran up the bank, knowing that any moment could be his last. Clambering to the top, his mouth gaped open at what he saw. The three men were sharing a cigarette.

'Pierre,' whispered Dubois, beckoning him over. 'Come

here. Come meet my brother-in-law.'

His knees gave way as the relief flooded through him. With a stab of shame, he realised he had tears in his eyes. Surreptitiously wiping them away, he hoped Dubois and the patrolmen wouldn't notice in the dark and the rain.

'Don't worry,' said Dubois. 'We're safe here.'

But, thought Pierre, are we not exposed up here on the track?

'Hello,' said the two patrolmen, shaking Pierre's wet hand.

'You gave us a fright there,' said Dubois's brother-in-law.

'Likewise,' said Dubois.

Pierre couldn't see their faces. He hoped they couldn't see him. 'I don't understand.'

'Gustave and François are, how shall we say it, unwilling collaborators.'

Gustave sniffed. 'I'd rather we didn't use that word, unwilling or not.'

'We didn't ask to do this,' said François.

'Don't worry about Pierre,' said Dubois, wiping the rain off his spectacles. 'He's just a kid.'

Just a kid? thought Pierre. I'm out here, aren't I?

Footfalls on the track made them step back. 'It's only Kafka,' said Dubois.

'What's going on?' asked Kafka, his revolver at the ready.

'Put that away, you fool. We're among friends here.'

'No man doing Germans' work is a friend of mine.'

Dubois flung his cigarette away. 'Oh, do shut up.'

Bouchette and Gide had joined them. The seven of them climbed back down the bank.

'Have you chaps heard?' said Gustave on reaching the bottom. 'The Germans are planning to pull down Soldier Mike.'

'What on earth for?' screeched Bouchette.

'I don't know.'

'It's obvious, isn't it?' said François. 'It's a memorial to the 1870 war – against them.'

'Yeah, but they beat us that time.'

'And that will be the only time,' said Kafka.

'You're going to have to hit us, you know,' said François.

'My sister won't thank me for it,' said Dubois.

'Oh, I don't know.'

'Why do we have to hit them?' asked Pierre.

'Come on, boy, think about it. So they can say to the Krauts that we overpowered them.'

Kafka put his revolver back into his jacket pocket. 'I'll happily oblige. I'll take you,' he said, pointing at François. 'Pierre, you can hit the other one.'

'Me?' The idea of hitting someone without the benefit of a fight seemed preposterous.

'It'll be good for you. So, how shall we do this?' he said, stepping up to François.

'I don't know but…' The man fell back as Kafka's fist caught him on the jaw. He remained on his feet until a second punch floored him. He landed on the grass. After a while, he sat up, puffing his cheeks, and holding the side of his face. 'Whoa. Hopefully that'll do it.'

'Your turn, Pierre.'

Pierre considered Gustave. The man raised an eyebrow. 'Get it over and done with,' he said.

Clenching his fist, clenching his jaw, Pierre stared at

him, trying to summon a feeling of hatred. But it wasn't working; he felt himself go slack. 'I can't do it.'

'You have to,' said Dubois.

'You'll be doing me a favour,' added Gustave softly. 'Believe me, I'd rather be hit by you than a Nazi.'

Not wanting to give himself time to think about it, Pierre swung his fist. It caught the man on the side of the nose. He shook his knuckles, surprised at how much it hurt. Gustave, meanwhile, did not move. With a groan, Pierre realised that his punch had barely registered.

'Come on, boy; you can do it,' said Kafka behind him. 'Imagine he's a Kraut, imagine he's just raped your mother; no, not your mother. Claire. Yes, Claire. This bastard in his Nazi uniform who has no right to be in our country has just forced himself onto Claire. Poor Claire; defiled by a...'

Gustave staggered back. Having hit him, Pierre held his fist under his armpit. Gustave laughed. 'That's better,' he said, dabbing his lip.

Kafka stepped up to him just as he was recovering his balance and struck him again. 'Just for good measure,' he said.

Gustave flew back, landing heavily. This time he didn't move. Dubois went to him, bending over his stricken friend. 'Jesus, Kafka; you've knocked him out cold.'

Kafka winked at Pierre. 'You'll learn,' he said. 'Right, back to work. Our little homemade device is in place. Now, just a gentle little explosion. Oh...' He took the patrolmen's rifles, handing one each to Dubois and Bouchette. 'We'll take these, thank you very much.'

Chapter 15

Pierre lay in bed, watching the second hand of his bedroom clock go round. It was almost eight. He knew he had to get up; he had work to do – now that Monsieur Roché's headstone was finished, he wanted to get on with his Venus. He replayed the events of the previous evening through his mind. They'd left François dozing in the rain next to his unconscious friend. The story for their German employers was that both had been taken by surprise and knocked out. By the time they came to, it was almost morning; too late to check the rail track. Kafka had cursed the lack of rope to tie them up with. The first German train, which would have left Saint-Romain at six, should have been derailed. Pierre hoped their battered faces looked convincing enough.

*

Hair is a difficult thing to fashion on stone. Success is in the detail. But not too much. Too much and it detracts from the rest of the work; too little and it begins to resemble so much rope. Consulting his book containing Botticelli's masterpiece, Pierre saw the amount of work that lay ahead of him. The hair of Venus ran down her back, round to her front, finishing at her pubic mound. It amounted to hundreds, no, thousands, of strands. It was easy for Botticelli, he concluded – he had only to work on the front. For him, Pierre, it was far more daunting a task, because it had to look right front and back. The more he pondered, the greater his sense of unease. Best, he thought, to make a start, to allow the chisel to do its work, and to see where it took him. He'd propped Monsieur Roché's headstone up against the yard wall. His mother said she would call on the cemetery boys to ask them to come pick it up. Then, he could make his way to the town hall and pick up his wages. The thought pleased him no end – a man's wage for man's work. His father would be proud.

It had been over a week now since Georges's arrest. It disturbed Pierre how quickly he had become accustomed to his absence. He reasoned that it was not necessarily due to a lack of concern. It was just that he could not imagine what ordeals he would have had to endure; what indignities may have been heaped on him. And he, Pierre, had been given to the chance to save him and he knew, following the railway sabotage, that he was already failing him. He only hoped his information on Victor and his friend made a difference.

The kitchen door burst open. It was the major, already returning from work, and Pierre knew straightaway that he wasn't pleased.

'Did you know about last night?' snapped the major.

'Last night?'

The major considered him for a few moments, as if trying to see whether a lie hid behind his idle tone.

'I've just found out. I came back because I thought you might, perhaps, know something.'

'No.'

'I believe you do. The railway line has been sabotaged. Two guards beaten up.'

'I didn't know.'

The major's eyes scanned the yard as if looking for evidence. He stiffened, his eyes momentarily narrowing. 'OK; you can lie to me if you want to but I warn you, you cannot lie to the colonel. And it is to the colonel you have to report.'

The major was right – it was easy lying to him, but he baulked at the thought of being confronted by Colonel Eisler. 'I have to go see him?' he asked, aware of the quiver in his voice.

The major heard it too. His eyes beamed, pleased to have caught Pierre out so easily. 'He wants a word with you right away.' He looked at his watch. 'You'd better go now. Take your bike.'

Pierre gazed at Venus. Her hair would have to wait a little longer. He wondered whether he ought to change, to dress up for the occasion. No, he decided, it wouldn't make any difference. 'I'd rather take the bus.'

'You'll have to wait too long. No, cycle. It'll be quicker.'

Well, it wasn't far, he thought, and the ride might help calm his nerves. He ought to tell his mother. He made for the kitchen.

The major called out to him.

'Yes?'

'Don't even attempt to conceal the truth; don't play games with him. His eyes will see into you.'

*

Colonel Eisler eyed Pierre menacingly from across the mahogany desk, his fingers twiddling a fountain pen. On the desk stood a vase of flowers; many of its petals had fallen, forming a circle of colour round its base. The brass desk lamp with its hexagon-shaped shade was lit despite the light pouring through the huge French windows. 'I think you know why you're here,' said the colonel in a gentle tone.

'I didn't know anything about it,' said Pierre, trying to maintain the colonel's gaze.

The colonel raised an eyebrow. 'You didn't know anything about it,' he repeated slowly. 'Not good enough. You had your instructions and you have failed me.'

Pierre had to stop himself from shrugging his shoulders.

The colonel continued. 'As it is, the saboteurs caused minimal damage. We are dealing with amateurs here. The railway line will be fixed in no time but my point is your failure to keep the major and me informed. I thought you knew what was expected of you. Well? What have you got to say for yourself?'

'I'm sorry.'

'You're sorry. Is that it?'

'I tried but I can't find out who is part of this group.'

He slammed the table with his palm causing Pierre to jump. 'You have to try harder. What you do think this is? A friendly chat with your headmaster? First we have the incident with the nails and now this. Major Hurtzberger

196

told me about the printing press and the flyers. You'll be pleased to know that their little operation has been broken up, and both men are now in the custody of my seaside colleagues. So, that was good; enough to save your father from the firing squad for a while longer but it's not enough. It didn't tell me anything I didn't already know. Have you forgotten we have your father within these walls? I have come to admire him; he is a stubborn man. Foolish but stubborn. He is our hostage but he is only useful to us if, in return, we have a grasp of what's going on in your town. If not, as I told you before, he will be executed. We, the might of Germany, have conquered huge swathes of Europe. Do you think I will allow this little community of ne'er-do-wells to derail my work here?'

'No.'

'What?'

'No, sir.'

The telephone on his desk rang. He looked at his watch, snapped it up, grunted something in German, and slammed it down again.

'Right,' he said, returning his attention to Pierre, 'it's time.' He rose from his chair and squared his cap. He clicked his fingers. 'Follow me.'

Pierre felt a wave of fear; he hadn't expected this. A soldier, standing guard outside the colonel's office, closed the door behind them, then followed the colonel and Pierre down the corridor. Together, they descended one flight of stairs in silence, and along another corridor where they came to a halt next to a window half way along. The soldier opened the window, pushing up the top half, then stepped back. Peering out over the balcony, Pierre saw beneath him the courtyard, the floor made up of red bricks, the occasional potted plant dotted round, along one side a laurel hedge, at the far end a stone wall partially covered by creeping stands of ivy. In itself, it was a pleasing view yet for reasons he couldn't fathom, Pierre's blood ran cold. Something, he knew, was wrong.

They waited but for what, Pierre had no idea. The colonel stood, his arms behind his back, watching him, his face stern. Pierre felt himself wilt. The whole building seemed to hum but despite so many people within its walls there were no voices to be heard. A flock of swallows flew by overhead; somewhere, on the street, a lorry sounded its horn. The soldier behind him cleared his throat. And still the colonel remained motionless. Then came the noise from beneath him, of a bolt being pulled back, of a heavy door being pushed open. Craning his neck over the balcony, Pierre saw a number of German soldiers appear, one after the other, their rifles against their shoulders. Six, seven, eight of them. They drew up in one line, facing the ivy wall, a few feet away. Then, more slowly, a man accompanied by a priest, his hands behind his back, followed by an officer and two more soldiers. It took a few seconds for it to register. 'No,' Pierre yelped as his knees buckled. The colonel stepped forward to hike him back up. Pierre reached for the windowsill to steady himself. The man was his father and he was being led to his execution. The priest, a Frenchman, walked alongside him in his black robes, his bible open, reading quietly in a soothing voice. Whether Georges was listening, whether he found it any comfort, Pierre could not tell.

'Do not to say a word,' said the colonel. The soldier was directly behind him. Pierre felt a nudge in his back, a revolver.

He tried to control his breathing; clutching at his heart. Feeling lightheaded, he feared he was about to fall.

His father was placed against the wall. His hands had been tied behind his back. Pierre's mouth gaped open at his appearance – his father looked ten years older, his skin taut and grey, heavy bags beneath his eyes. His clothes, streaked with dirt, hung off him. He hadn't said a word; not a flicker of emotion had crossed his face. He seemed almost not to care. 'Look at me,' thought Pierre. 'Look up, look up at me.'

The officer stepped forward and, from a sheet of paper, read a few words aloud at Georges. The firing squad took their positions, rifles drawn, at the ready.

'I'm sorry,' muttered Pierre, aware he was crying. He spun away, unable to look. The guard jerked his revolver up, aiming at Pierre's forehead. 'Turn around,' ordered the colonel.

'No, please, no.'

The guard clicked off the safety catch.

Feeling unable to stand, Pierre turned back to see the priest cross Georges. He placed his hand on Georges's head, muttered a final few words, then stepped back.

The officer's voice echoed across the courtyard as he ordered his men to take aim. Pierre swayed on his feet. He heard the round of rifle fire just as he blanked out.

*

Pierre opened his eyes and realised he'd fallen against the colonel who now had his arms round him, propping him up. The sound of gunshot still reverberated through his head. His limbs felt heavy, his heart more so.

He felt the colonel's hand resting on his head. 'It's OK

now, Pierre. There is but a hyphen that separates life and death. Look outside.'

Pierre wanted to pull himself away but found he had not the strength.

'Go on; look outside,' repeated Colonel Eisler. 'Tell me what you see.' The German helped Pierre find his feet and most gently pushed him back towards the open window.

Pierre wanted to protest but couldn't find his voice. He felt nothing; his mind devoid of thought, his heart laden with so much weight. Even the smallest movement felt as if he was struggling through the heaviness of nothingness. It took him a few seconds to register as he tried to focus his eyes. Yet, there, standing in the courtyard, as if nothing had happened, was his father. He still wore the same dulled expression as if he was unaware of his surroundings; of what was happening around him. But yes, he was standing, he was breathing. He was alive.

Behind him, with head bowed, stood the priest, his bible, held in both hands, closed. Pierre noticed the officer glance up at the balcony and from the corner of his eye, Pierre saw Colonel Eisler nod. A soldier prodded Georges from behind with his rifle and slowly he stepped forward. Pierre watched, numb, unable to understand, as his father was led back the way he came. A few seconds later, he heard the door close, the bolt pushed back into place. The courtyard was empty. Yet Pierre continued to stare, unsure now whether the drama had been a figment of his imagination. One of the potted plants had been kicked over.

*

Pierre sat in the colonel's office, unaware of having been

led back. Colonel Eisler sat opposite him, staring, his head cocked to one side, a look of concern in his face, his hands on the armrests of his chair. The French windows had been opened, the heavy turquoise-coloured curtains swaying slightly in the wind. The desk lamp had been switched off. Sunk in the chair, Pierre felt tired, exhausted even. He concentrated his gaze on the vase of flowers, on the petals around it. The vase, also turquoise, was embedded with the shape of a woman with a long flowing dress that disappeared into the glass. Pierre studied her hair, following its contours as it circled round the vase.

'Pierre.' He looked up. The colonel had removed his cap. He looked younger for it; less severe. 'You've had a shock, I understand. Forgive me but it was necessary.' He paused perhaps waiting for Pierre to respond. 'You were not taking me seriously. I believe you saw it as a game of some sort. I had to make you realise that war is not a game and that I am serious. Go home now. Find out who is in this town gang of yours and report back to me via Major Hurtzberger before they manage to do some real damage.'

Pierre tried to speak but could only manage a nod of the head.

'Next time, your father's execution will be for real.'

*

Riding home on his bike was an effort; he could hardly concentrate. He had stumbled out of the building and had to return to sign out with the receptionist with pink nail varnish. Wherever he could, he freewheeled, zigzagging down the streets of Saint-Romain, passing a parked convoy of German trucks, and out into the countryside. The clouds hung low but it was still warm. He wondered whether his father was aware that the execution would be fake. Somehow he thought not. His father had stood up to them; and even at the supposed moment of death, he refused to break. His courage was admirable. Should he tell his mother? Tell her what a brave husband she had? No, he couldn't. Not yet. So why did Kafka mock his father so? He'd like to see Kafka withstand a week in Nazi custody with such dignity.

Some three kilometres from home he faced a steep incline. Any other day, he knew he'd be able to cycle up without too much effort but this was far from any other day. Half way up, short of breath, he dismounted. In his trouser pocket was the packet of cigarettes the colonel had given him on the first visit. Dropping his bike on the grass verge, he sat down and leant against a tree. He lit a cigarette and closed his eyes. The thought of his father remaining in that place, at the mercy of the colonel, was too much to bear. The colonel had made his point – he would, from now on, do whatever he could to save his father. Sod France, sod patriotism; his father was his father, his flesh and blood. Nothing else mattered any more.

Having smoked his cigarette and cleared his mind, Pierre re-mounted his bike and cycled up the rest of the hill. Having reached the top, a nice downhill road led to home. He paused and looked upon his town in the valley with the church tower at its centre. From here, from this vantage point, it seemed as if God had casually dropped the whole place from on high. He never felt so pleased to see it. He raced down, pedalling hard, joyous with the wind blowing through his hair. He felt like screaming but couldn't find it within himself to let go of his emotions to such an extent. Having reached the bottom of the hill, the road flattened out as it snaked into the town itself. This was the road the PoWs came through, he remembered. Would he ever forget? He slowed down as the road plateaued. Then, from seemingly nowhere, he felt a terrific smash against his right side. He screeched as he fell and landed heavily on his left arm, his bicycle skidding on its side away from him. A man in a cap appeared from behind him, running. Pierre sprung to his feet, the pain in his arm vanishing in an instant. 'What are you doing?' he shouted as the man grabbed his bike. The thief tried to make off but, losing his balance, had to try again. Pierre was on him, barging into him, pushing the man off. He pulled the bike from him, its pedals hitting the man in the shins. Now, he feared the man would turn on him.

Instead, he remained on the ground, his cap lying next to him. 'I'm sorry,' he said. Slowly, he got to his feet. He was tall with black hair, shaved at the back but long at the front, his fringe covering one eye. He tossed his hair back to reveal strange eyes. His black trousers were covered in dust, a jacket pocket torn. 'I'm sorry,' he repeated. 'I shouldn't have done that.' He offered his hand.

Pierre, sensing a trick, ignored it. He didn't recognise the man's accent – he wasn't a local. 'Where are you going to?'

The man eyed him, perhaps, thought Pierre, wondering whether to trust him. He didn't look much older than himself – perhaps eighteen or nineteen. Eventually, he answered. 'I need to get to the Free Zone,' he said, looking round as if they might be overheard. But there was no one around – just large expanses of fields flushed with corn, grass verges adorned with wild flowers, the sound of bees.

'The Free Zone? That's miles away.'

He shrugged. 'That's why I need a bike.'

'Well… I suppose you could take mine.'

The man smiled. 'That's awfully generous of you but I feel bad enough as it is; I couldn't now. Are you hurt?'

'No.' Pierre looked down at his left arm. His sleeve was ripped, the skin beneath grazed. 'Who are you?' he asked.

'I can't tell you that.'

'You're not French.'

'No. Belgian. Listen…' The man ran his fingers through his hair. 'I need… I need your help. They're looking for me. You could turn me in; you'd probably get a decent bounty.'

'I wouldn't do that.'

'No, I guessed that. You offered me your bike after I tried to steal it from you.'

Pierre thought of Kafka. How much he would relish this. 'I know a man who could help.'

'You do?'

'The town wouldn't be safe now. If you stay here, I'll come and fetch you about six o'clock. That's the time the Krauts eat their dinner. It's the best time. Do you have a watch?'

The man nodded. 'I'll find somewhere to hide in those woods.' He scooped down to retrieve his cap. 'I couldn't ask you to bring me some food, could I? I've a bottle of water but that's it. And this man of yours… I don't have any money on me.'

'It'll be fine.'

The Belgian smiled. 'I'm lucky to have found you.'

'If you can't tell me your name, I'll call you Tintin – he's Belgian, isn't he?'

'Tintin's a great name. You're a good man. So, what's your name?'

'I can't tell you that.'

*

Pierre cycled straight to Kafka's and found him wearing overalls, painting his porch. The old car door propped up against the house was still there, along with the empty birdcage and discarded boots.

'Ah, young Durand. What brings you here? You can give me a hand if you want.'

'I found a Belgian,' said Pierre, propping his bike against a tree.

'A Belgian bun?'

'No, a…' He hated it when Kafka mocked him. 'A Belgian on the run.'

'Ha, it rhymes. Have you indeed? Good for you.' Kafka stepped back to admire his work.

'He needs our help.'

'Does he? In what way?'

Pierre stood next to him. The new green paint reflected the sun. 'He's on the run from the Germans. He's trying to cross the demarcation line.'

'He's got a long way to go.'

'That's what I said. He needs somewhere to stay until things quieten down.'

Kafka placed his paintbrush on the upturned paint tin lid. 'OK, tell me everything.'

The two men sat on the porch as Pierre related his tale, of how the Belgian, Tintin, had tried to steal his bike, of how he said he would return at six. Kafka picked up a bamboo stick and jabbed at the ground, making little holes in the dry soil. Pierre could tell Kafka was excited by the prospect of doing something.

'And how do you know he's trustworthy?'

'I don't; not really. Although when I knocked him off my bike he could have fought back – he's bigger than me. And desperate.'

'True. I'm impressed; you've done well.'

Pierre smiled.

'I'll speak to Bouchette and Dubois. You can leave it to me now.'

'But you'll need my help. He might not trust you if you all turn up looking for him.'

'Hmm. All right. Meet us at a half past five at Bouchette's garage. We'll be within striking distance of him from there.' He threw away the bamboo stick. 'Meanwhile, I'll work out what to do with this Belgian.'

*

Pierre returned home, waving to Xavier as he passed.

'Pierre, where have you been?' Lucienne was outside the house watering the flowers as Pierre jumped off his bicycle.

'Nowhere. Just things to do.'

'Your sleeve – it's ripped. What happened?'

'I fell off.'

'Is that all? Does it hurt? You're up to something. Tell me, what is it?'

'Nothing, Maman. I need to get on.'

Having escaped his mother, Pierre paced up and down the yard disturbing the chickens. Already, the certainty he felt cycling home had drained out of him. This was the sort of thing he should report to the major but he'd taken an immediate liking to the Belgian with his strange eyes. How could he deliver him into the hands of the Nazis? God knows what they would do with him. He remembered enough from Sunday school to know that he'd been assigned, albeit unwittingly, the role of the Good Samaritan.

*

'We have to be careful. After the railway attack, the Boche are more nervy.' Kafka, Bouchette, Dubois, Claire and Pierre had gathered in Bouchette's kitchen. Monsieur Gide, apparently, had declined to have anything else to do with Kafka's group, finding the derailment episode too traumatic. On the kitchen table, a fishing rod and a small bucket of maggots. It was half five.

'How's the coffee?' asked Bouchette. His wife had made them each a cup. Every time one of them took a sip they couldn't help but grimace.

'Disgusting,' said Dubois.

'It's made of beetroot and chicory.'

'What happened to all your wine? Did the Germans take it?'

'Ha, no! The idiots. I buried it in the garden.'

'All of it?'

'Every last bottle.'

'What do you think of the coffee, Pierre?' asked Claire.

'It's… it's fine.'

'Not like the coffee your friendly Hun supplies, eh?'

'Leave him alone,' said Kafka. 'The boy's done good work today.' Pierre noticed Kafka's fingers were stained with green paint. How did Claire know the major gave his mother coffee? The answer, he guessed, was obvious.

207

'So how do we know if he's genuine, this Belgian?' asked Claire.

'We'll interrogate him tonight.'

'And if he's not?'

'Then we'll deal with it,' said Kafka, patting the revolver in his jacket pocket. Dubois and Bouchette exchanged glances, raising their eyebrows.

'Do you always carry that thing with you?' asked Dubois.

'Only on special occasions.'

The Bouchettes' Alsatian dog wandered in. It made for Pierre's bag and sniffed it, pushing his nose against it. 'Oi, Daisy, leave it alone,' said Bouchette. 'What have you got in there?'

'Two chicken legs. For the Belgian.' He placed the bag out of reach on the kitchen table.

'I'd like to see you explain away chicken legs if the Germans stop and search you.'

'So, what's the plan, boys?' asked Dubois.

'Hide him in the crypt,' said Claire. 'Father de Beaufort wouldn't mind.'

'Are you mad?' exclaimed Kafka. 'That means bringing him into town. Too dangerous. No, what we'll do is take him to Lincoln's farm. I've already spoken to him. He said we could hide him in his barn. It has a loft.'

'Perfect,' said Dubois. 'Then what?'

'We need to find someone in Sainte-Hélène to take him.'

Bouchette slapped his dog. 'That will take him four kilometres closer to the demarcation line.'

'It all helps,' said Kafka. 'Right, we'd better go. Pierre and I'll pick him up now, take him to Lincoln's. Claire, you can come with us. A woman's presence might help calm him down. We'll all meet here tomorrow at ten.'

Dubois and Bouchette nodded.

'Not at the crypt, then?' asked Pierre.

'No, we got short shrift from the father,' said Dubois. 'He went all strange when I mentioned Kafka's name.'

'Idiot,' said Kafka.

Madame Bouchette reappeared, a rotund woman wearing a bulging floral dress. 'Any more coffee, gentlemen?'

'No, no, no.'

*

Bouchette's garage lay on the outskirts of the town on the road to Saint-Romain. There was always a chance of a German convoy returning but Pierre knew they'd be able to hear that in advance. The chances of a German patrol, this far out, was, he hoped, slim, and, as he'd said to Tintin, they'd be having their dinner now. The three of them walked quickly, keeping to the side of the road. Kafka carried the fishing rod, Pierre the bucket of maggots. This was to be their alibi if stopped. Less than a kilometre on, they'd come to the place where Pierre had had his encounter with the Belgian.

'Let's hope he appears soon,' said Kafka.

'I told him six. Five minutes.'

'I know.'

Sitting on the verge, they waited, their shadows on the road in front of them. Ahead of them, a field of corn, bordered on the far side by the woods. Pierre stared into the bucket and watched the constant movement of the maggots, with their slimy yellow and green bodies.

'Revolting things,' said Claire. 'Any news on your father?'

'No.'

The church bells rang six o'clock. They waited, the silence broken only by the sound of bees and the squawk of a blackbird. Two white butterflies danced before them.

'Good God, is that him?'

Pierre looked up – coming towards them, across the field, was the Belgian, his cap pushed down over his eyes. 'Yes, that's him.'

The three of them stood up. Pierre waved. The Belgian waved back.

'He doesn't look like a man in a hurry,' said Kafka.

'Hello,' said the Belgian, his hand outstretched. Shaking hands, Pierre introduced Tintin to 'his friends who can help'.

'Nice to make your acquaintance,' Tintin said to Claire, removing his cap. He offered his hand to Kafka but Kafka, like Pierre earlier in the day, refused to take it.

'So who are you?' asked Kafka.

'My name, as christened by your young friend here, is Tintin. I was fighting with the 35th Infantry Regiment.'

'What happened?'

'We were totally overrun.' He shook his head at the memory. 'We suffered badly. Many killed. It was horrible. Truly horrible. I was lucky; I was taken prisoner. Then I escaped.'

'How?'

'On a march. A week ago. We were being transported. I don't know where. Three of us made a dash for it. The others were gunned down, shot in the back, but, as you can see, I got away. I've been on the run ever since, stealing food, sleeping in forests. I stole these clothes. From a washing line.'

'A good fit.'

'I was lucky.'

'I'm told you're a Belgian.'

'Yes but I've lived in France since I was ten. Look, I know it must be difficult for you, but can you help me? I thought of getting to the Free Zone.'

'And then what?'

'To get to Spain eventually, then perhaps from there, to England. I'm a captain; I have a lot of experience. I want to offer my services to the English army. Anything to fight these pigs.'

Kafka eyed the man, looking at him up and down, considering what to do. 'OK, this is the plan. We'll take you to a farm a couple of kilometres from here, belonging to a friend of ours. You can sleep in his barn for a night or two while I arrange transportation to the next town.'

'Thank you; that'd be...' Unable to finish his sentence, Tintin bowed.

'Come on,' said Kafka. 'We ought to get going. We'll need to go back through the field. It's on the other side of the woods, nice and isolated. If we should get stopped, we've been out fishing. You lead the way,' he said to Pierre.

Claire walked alongside him. 'Is it just me, or does this feel wrong somehow?' she whispered.

'He seems genuine to me.'

'I suppose. Ignore me, I'm being paranoid.' After a pause, she added, 'He's got very clean fingernails.'

*

Ninety minutes later, Pierre was back at home. They'd taken Tintin to Lincoln's farm. It was obvious that Kafka had browbeaten Lincoln into taking the Belgian. Reluctantly, Lincoln had led them to the barn. Inside was a loft, reachable by ladder. Having settled Tintin there, and left him with Pierre's chicken legs and half a bottle of red wine and a hunk of cheese, courtesy of Monsieur Lincoln, they descended back down the ladder and removed it. Kafka told them all to meet again at Bouchette's garage the following morning at ten. It had all gone well. Almost too well.

Pierre lay on his bed and tried to read his biography of Botticelli but something was troubling him. His mother came in, asking whether he'd taken the chicken legs she'd been saving. Pierre confessed and apologised. He heard the major return, heard him and his mother talking. He knew he had the power now to save his father; he merely had to tell Major Hurtzberger that they were hiding a fugitive in Lincoln's barn. But he knew he wouldn't.

That night, Pierre slept fitfully. When, finally, he managed to doze off, he dreamt vivid dreams that involved maggots and bicycles and eyes and dogs. The maggots, millions of them, were everywhere, climbing up his legs, wriggling on his stomach, crawling across his neck. He sat up, his hands frantically flapping them away, his body quivering with revulsion. Realising he'd been dreaming, he breathed a sigh of relief. He felt thirsty. Turning on his bedside lamp, he swivelled his legs out of bed, nodded at his Rita Hayworth poster and made for the kitchen. He waited for the tap water to run cold as he took a glass from the draining board. He drank the water down, relieved to feel the cold water cascading through him. Returning to bed more relaxed, he fluffed up his pillow and lay back, switching off the light. He lay there with his hands behind his back, hoping sleep would soon return. As, slowly, he drifted off, the Belgian's strange eyes came into view. One was blue, the other green. He saw them, appearing in the dark, peering intently at him from beneath the Belgian's cap. They seemed to be mocking him. The cap transformed into a helmet – a German helmet. Two different-coloured eyes beneath a German helmet.

The realisation hit him with the force of a hammer. He screeched, sitting up in bed. He had seen the Belgian before – in an SS uniform.

Chapter 16

Pierre woke up with a start but it took him a few seconds to work out why. The memory came flooding back. He remembered all too well – the guard with his different-coloured eyes beneath his helmet opening the door to Colonel Eisler's office; his mother and he entering. He jumped out of bed and swiftly pulled on his clothes. He had to warn Kafka and the others. They were to meet at ten but were due to arrive in ten-minute intervals. Too many men arriving at the same time could raise suspicions. It was Kafka's new idea. Pierre had been instructed to arrive last at ten thirty. He realised as he was getting dressed that mixed in with the dread was a sense of excitement. The gang would be pleased with him, pleased that Pierre, through his sharp observation, had spotted a trap.

He managed to escape the house without his mother noticing. The major had left earlier. A steady drizzle fell. The meeting in Bouchette's kitchen was already well under way when Pierre arrived a few minutes before ten thirty.

Kafka was, as usual, holding forth. 'We'll have to search him, of course.' He looked up as Madame Bouchette showed Pierre in. 'You're wet. Were you seen?' he asked.

In his haste to get there, Pierre hadn't thought to check. 'No,' he said firmly, as he took his place opposite Claire. She winked at him.

'What were you saying?' said Kafka to Bouchette.

'What? Ah yes.' Bouchette twiddled his penknife between his fingers. 'I have a mate in Sainte-Hélène. Owns a garage like me. And like me he has bugger all to do nowadays. Bloody Germans, how they expect us to survive when they close down our businesses, I don't know. I'll go over and see him today; see if he can help us move our Belgian friend.'

'Good; that'll get him off our hands,' said Dubois.

'He'll still have a long way to go,' said Claire.

'We can only help so far,' said Kafka.

Madame Bouchette appeared carrying a tray laden with steaming coffees. 'Here were are, gents; I know how much you enjoyed it last night.'

A round of muttered thanks circled the table.

Pierre cleared his throat. 'Ahem, erm, the Belgian; he's not who he says he is.'

'What?' screamed Kafka. Claire choked on her coffee.

'He's German.'

'Good God.'

'Are you mad?' said Dubois, his face red. 'How do you know?'

'You said he was a Belgian,' said Bouchette.

Pierre hadn't seen Kafka come over to him until he felt himself being hoisted out of his chair by his lapels. 'You assured us; how do you know he's German?'

Claire rose from her chair. 'Kafka, leave him be, let him speak.'

Kafka thrust Pierre back down.

'I'm sorry, I didn't realise. It was only last night when I was asleep. I woke up and I remembered I'd seen him in…' He stopped. He couldn't tell them where he'd seen the Belgian.

'In what?' asked Dubois, his face redder still.

'In a German uniform, SS. It's his eyes.'

'SS?' shrieked Bouchette. 'Oh shit.'

'Yes,' said Claire. 'His eyes are odd.'

'Couldn't you have remembered this earlier, you idiot?' Pierre slunk down, fearful that Kafka was about to strike him.

'There, there,' said Bouchette. 'Let's not get upset. It's not Pierre's fault he didn't recognise him at once. Indeed, we should be grateful he remembered at all.'

'Exactly,' echoed Claire.

'But are you sure, Pierre?' asked Dubois. 'It's important you get this right.'

'I've never seen eyes like his. One of them is green and the other is blue.'

'It would also explain why he was so clean-shaven,' said Claire.

'Yes, you're right,' said Kafka. 'He's got thick black hair; and he said he'd been on the run for a week. He'd have a full-blown beard by now. That man has had a shave within the last day or two.'

'And it would explain how he miraculously managed to find perfectly-fitting clothes to change into, and why, for a man living off the land, his fingernails were so clean.'

'Yes, good girl, Claire; you'd make a great detective.'

The five drank their coffee in silence. Daisy, Bouchette's dog, entered, pushing open the kitchen door. Claire stroked it. 'She's got very thick fur for this weather.'

It was Dubois who broached the subject that was on all their minds. 'So, what do we do with him? We can hardly return him to the Germans.'

Kafka took another sip of his coffee. 'There's only one thing we can do.'

'Exactly,' said Bouchette. 'So I suggest we get it over and done with as quickly as possible.'

'Claire and Pierre should go home,' said Dubois. 'This is no job for women or boys.'

'No,' said Claire. 'I want to be there. I'm part of this group; I need to be there.'

Kafka nodded. 'She's right. And Pierre, you're almost a man now.'

Pierre nodded, unable to speak.

*

Again, Pierre was obliged to arrive last at Lincoln's farm. He waited in Bouchette's kitchen while, one by one, starting with Kafka and Claire, the others went ahead. Politely, he turned down Madame Bouchette's offer of more ersatz coffee.

She sat down with a sigh in a squashy armchair in the corner of the kitchen. Balancing two dirty cups on her hefty bosom, she said, 'I was sorry to hear 'bout your father.' It sounded as if he'd died. 'It's a nasty business all this, mark my words. I don't like it one bit. Do you mind if I smoke? Don't tell my old man, though. He'd have my guts for garters.' She lit a handmade cigarette and blew a billow of smoke through her nostrils.

'Won't he smell it?'

'He won't be back in here until he wants his lunch. Anyhow, the windows are open. You won't tell, will you?'

'No.'

'Our secret.' Daisy wandered in and nuzzled her mistress. Placing the cups on the floor, she beckoned the dog onto her lap. Pierre couldn't help but think she looked ridiculous sitting in an armchair with a huge Alsatian dog on her. She shook her head. 'First they take your father, God rest his soul–'

'Madame Bouchette, he's not–'

'Then that poor Monsieur Touvier.' She tapped her ash directly on the dog where it rested on its fur. 'It's probably best we don't have no horses left for there'd be no one to mend their shoes. And they killed my Louis. I hate them.'

Pierre nodded sympathetically. 'Madame Bouchette, I have to go now.'

'Yes, yes, you go. Don't let me hold you up.'

She ruffled Daisy's ears.

*

Pierre made his way to Lincoln's farm. The drizzle of earlier had turned into steady rain. The clouds moved quickly across the sky. The road was empty, the rain keeping everyone inside.

Leaving the road, he followed the path alongside the cornfield to the farm, relieved to reach the shelter of the trees. Lincoln's farm lay in a little dip and walking down the path towards it, the sight of it, cloaked in mist, depressed him.

He skirted past the farmhouse, across the yard, watched by a black and white goat, and made straight for the barn.

The barn had two double doors, both painted black, one big, one small. The drain, he noticed, was blocked; rainwater was pooling beneath the drainpipe. It was only now that the thought occurred to him that he might be walking into a trap. Trying not to make too much noise, he eased open the smaller door and peered in. Inside, he saw the ladder lying on the floor, undisturbed since the previous evening. He crept in. Shafts of light broke through the doors. Bales of straw were stacked high to the far end. Nearer by was an assortment of crates, boxes and bins. A cat slept in a wheelbarrow; various tools were propped up against the barn wall – a couple of brooms, a hoe and an axe. A coat hung on a hook. The cat lifted its head as Pierre crept by but wasn't perturbed enough to give up its place of comfort. The door behind him opened. Quickly, he looked round for somewhere to hide. But then he saw Claire's silhouette. He breathed a sigh of relief. Lincoln, Dubois, Bouchette and lastly Kafka followed her in.

'Is he still up there?' asked Dubois, wiping the rain off his spectacles.

'I don't know,' said Pierre. 'I've only just arrived. Where were you?'

'In the kitchen.'

Tintin's head appeared at the square gap above them. 'Good morning, friends,' he called down.

'Keep your voice down,' said Lincoln, who was wearing a long raincoat that reached his ankles. 'Here, boy, help me with the ladder.' Together, Pierre and Lincoln hoisted the ladder up to the loft. Tintin skated down, jumping off the last few rungs.

'Here,' said Lincoln, 'breakfast.'

'Lovely. Thank you. Wine?'

'No coffee. Sorry.'

'That's fine.' He bit into the baguette. 'Mm, bread and wine. Anyone would think it was my last supper. Most welcome.'

Pierre and Claire exchanged glances. Pierre noticed that Tintin's stubble had noticeably grown overnight. Kafka was right – if it could grow this fast, how come he'd been so clean-shaven the day before?

'Nice wine. And this sandwich – delicious. Listen,' he said, his mouth full of bread, 'I was thinking – perhaps you chaps could do with some help. Rather than going south or to England, I'd happily stay here and volunteer my services.'

Kafka cleared his throat. 'That's good of you. We'll certainly consider it. Look, we'll need to search you,' he said.

'What?' His hand, gripping the baguette, stopped half way to his mouth.

'I'm sure you understand.'

'I assure you I'm who I say I am.'

'You haven't told us your name,' said Bouchette.

'I just thought the less we know of each other the better. I told you, I'm a captain in the 35th Infantry Regiment, I fought–'

'You're very young to be a captain,' said Dubois.

'I'm twenty-three.'

'Come on,' said Kafka. 'Arms up.'

The Belgian glanced at each of them. Placing his wine on the ground and passing his baguette to Claire, he stretched out his arms. Bouchette and Dubois stood with their arms folded while Lincoln hung back near the barn door. Kafka delved his hands into the Belgian's jacket pockets. He pulled out a penknife, a box of matches and, from the inside pocket, a photograph. 'My mother,' said the Belgian.

'Pull out your trouser pockets.'

'Is this really nec—'

'Do as I say.'

The Belgian pulled his trouser pockets inside out — empty but for a trail of dust and crumbs.

Reaching behind him, Kafka checked his back pockets. 'What's this then?' he said, retrieving a folded piece of card.

Kafka was standing too close to the Belgian to notice the fist. He doubled up as the punch caught him in the stomach.

'Stop him,' yelled Bouchette.

Dubois fell as he tried to seize the man. Pushing Claire aside, the Belgian reached for the axe leaning against the barn wall. The cat leapt from its wheelbarrow.

'Hey, steady with that,' said Lincoln.

The Belgian swung the axe in front of him. 'OK, let me go, and no one will get hurt.'

'No,' said Kafka, his revolver trained on the Belgian. 'Put that down or I'll shoot you.' He clicked off the safety catch.

The Belgian seemed to consider his options for a moment before dropping his axe.

Pierre tiptoed across and retrieved it.

Without taking his eyes off the Belgian, Kafka passed the card to Claire. 'Here, read this.'

Claire's eyes widened as she scanned the writing. 'It's an SS identification card.'

'Is it indeed?' said Kafka, a note of triumph in his voice.

'Oskar Spitzweg, born ninth November 1920. It's got a Nazi stamp on it.'

'You rat,' said Lincoln, spitting. 'To think I gave shelter to a sodding Nazi. SS at that.'

'You're only nineteen, not twenty-three,' said Claire.

'So what do we do with him now?' asked Dubois.

'We let him go,' said Bouchette. 'So that he can report us to his superiors who'll come and arrest us and then execute the lot of us.'

'Exactly,' said Kafka. 'That's what will happen if we let him go.'

Dubois ran his fingers through his hair. 'That means only one thing…'

'You don't have to,' said Tintin, stepping forward. Kafka lifted his revolver. The SS man paused and lifted his arms higher. 'Look, I won't say a word. Please, you have to trust me.'

'Huh,' snorted Bouchette. 'Trust a German?'

'Not just a German,' said Lincoln. 'SS. Remember? Let's see that card.' He scanned it, shaking his head. 'Just looking at it gives me the willies. You look like one evil sod.'

'But I'm not. Not really.' He was sweating now, his face red. 'You saw the picture of my mother.'

The men laughed. 'I imagine even Hitler loved his mum,' said Claire.

'Please, you can't kill me like this – in cold blood.'

'Oh the irony,' said Dubois.

'Here, Pierre, take this,' said Kafka, handing his revolver over. 'If he should so much as blink – shoot him.

Got it?'

Pierre nodded and tried to control his trembling hand.

The four men moved to the centre of the barn where they fell into a heated discussion. Pierre gripped the gun, feeling vulnerable. Claire stood next to him; their eyes fixed on the German. His eyes looked left and right. 'So I know your name now as you know mine. Tell me, Pierre, what would you do if I made a run for it?'

'He'd shoot you dead,' said Claire.

'I doubt it. Ever handled a gun before, Pierre? I thought not. It's not as easy as it looks, is it?' He took a step forward.

'Get back. Get back, I say.'

'What, and wait for those fools to kill me? They wouldn't have the balls.'

'Those fools fought in the last war,' said Claire. In the corner of his eye Pierre swore he spotted them playing rock, paper, scissors.

A sudden flurry of movement to his side took Pierre's attention. The cat. A mouse. The German sprang, leaping through the air. Pierre fell back, the German fell over him. The gun fired. Claire screamed. The men came running, shouting. Pierre still had the gun. The German tried to release his grip, slamming Pierre's hand against the barn floor, before slumping on top of him. Pushing him off, Pierre staggered to his feet. The German stirred, rubbing the back of his head. 'Good work, Claire,' said Dubois. Claire stood, panting, grinning, the spade in her hand. Behind her the cat dragged its victim away, its tail twitching.

Bouchette patted her shoulder. 'That was one hell of a swipe, girl.'

'Get up,' ordered Kafka. The German straightened his back. 'Are you listening?' The German nodded. 'We may be enemies but we are not monsters. However, we have decided we have no option but to execute you. Monsieur Lincoln owns a rifle and has volunteered to carry out this unpleasant duty.'

Lincoln had gone; presumably, thought Pierre, to fetch his gun.

The German stood hunched. The man was crying. 'I had so many plans,' he said. 'After the war, I was planning to resume my studies in Bremen. Architecture. I never wanted to be a soldier. I had dreams of designing lovely buildings, meeting a pretty girl and settling down. Nice house, children, you know.' His eyes widened as Lincoln returned, carrying his rifle. His legs buckled. Kafka helped him stay on his feet. 'I am as helpless in the face of death as that mouse was with the cat.'

'It's a bit old,' said Lincoln apologetically as he approached them. 'It's a Berthier from the war. My brother gave it to me.'

'Oh God,' said the Belgian. He began muttering in German, crossing himself.

'I think it'd be best if you stand next to the wall,' said Kafka to the German. 'Come on.'

'Yes, thank you. Thank you.'

Pierre tried to swallow. He couldn't believe he was about to witness a man being killed. It seemed unreal. Lincoln looked as if he might be sick. He too was muttering, talking about his brother. No one was listening. Bouchette and Dubois had stepped back. Dubois was shaking, Bouchette covered his mouth with his hand.

Claire wiped her eyes. 'We should have a priest,' she

said. 'Look at him; he needs a priest.'

'I know but what can we do?' said Kafka. 'I'm sorry,' he said to the German, who, gulping, tried to speak. 'Lincoln, you ready?'

'Here, hold this a minute, boy,' said Lincoln to Pierre, handing him the rifle. Lincoln approached the German, now standing with his back against the wooden slats of the barn wall. He offered the German his hand. 'I'm sorry I have to do this.'

'You have no choice,' said Oskar. 'I see that now.'

After a moment's hesitation, the two men embraced. The German sobbed into Lincoln's shoulder as the Frenchman patted his back, repeating, 'Forgive me, forgive me...'

'Please, do it now. Get it over and done with.'

Pierre handed Lincoln back his rifle. The German hung his head, reciting a prayer in German. Lincoln lifted the gun, took aim. Everyone took a further step back. Lincoln, Pierre noticed, was shaking terribly. 'Go on, do it,' whispered Claire.

The crack of the rifle shot sounded. Oskar screamed. He fell to his knees, clutching his shoulder and grunting. Blood seeped through his fingers. Lincoln spun away; his eyes clenched shut.

Claire patted her pockets and found a handkerchief. 'Here, let me,' she said to Oskar. The man fell on his back. Claire scooped up his head and rested it on her lap. He removed his hand and allowed Claire to press the handkerchief against his wound trying to stem the flow of blood.

Lincoln let the rifle fall to the ground where it landed blowing up a cloud of straw dust. 'I can't do it again.'

Oskar screwed up his face. 'Please, Mademoiselle, post the handkerchief to my mother.' Claire glanced at the others. Kafka was removing his revolver from his inside jacket pocket. 'I want her to have this handkerchief with my blood on it. The street is Winter Strausse in Bremen, number fourteen. It hurts. Will you remember that?'

'Yes, yes, I'll remember.'

Quietly, Kafka walked up to Oskar.

'Tell her I died for Germany; tell her I died with her name on my lips.' He looked up at her. He had no idea Kafka was next to him, slightly behind.

Kafka lifted his arm.

'I'll tell her; I'll write to her. I promise.'

'Thank you, Mademoiselle.'

Pierre closed his eyes. The shot rang out. Claire screamed. Somewhere birds squawked. Pierre forced himself to look. Claire, her jaw quivering, her hands against the sides of her head, was sprayed with the German's blood, her coat splattered with fragments of brain and tissue. Frantically, she tried to wipe it off.

Kafka strode back to his friends. Pierre was sure he was grinning. The nausea rose in his throat. They each patted him on the back; Lincoln, with great solemnity, shook his hand.

Pierre turned round and vomited.

*

Kafka allowed Pierre and Claire to return to the town immediately. He, and the others, would stay behind and bury Oskar Spitzweg in the grounds of Lincoln's farm. 'Should we not get Father de Beaufort?' asked Bouchette.

'No,' said Dubois. 'It could complicate matters.'

'Perhaps after the war?' suggested Claire.

Pierre pushed the small barn door open. He saw Lincoln's wife at a distance throwing grain for the chickens while stroking the head of the goat. 'She must have heard,' said Pierre.

'Yes, but it's easier to pretend it's not happening.'

The rain had stopped, the dark clouds dispersing revealing islands of blue sky. Pierre walked with his head down, his hands in his pockets; Claire alongside him, her coat filthy with blood.

'I hope never to have to come back here,' said Pierre. 'That was horrible.'

'But necessary.'

'Do you think so?'

'Of course. It would have been us at the end of the rifle barrel had we let him go.'

They walked in silence until they were back on the road leading down to the town. The day didn't feel real somehow, as if time had suspended itself. Outside, everything looked normal, the sky, the fields, the woods, the town ahead. Yet the world looked uglier; it felt different, and Pierre felt older, his feet heavier.

Claire muttered something to herself.

'What did you say?'

'I was just repeating the address. Number forty, Winter Strausse in Bremen.'

'Number fourteen not forty.'

'Is it? Are you sure?'

'I couldn't forget it if I tried. One day, after the war, in years to come, I might go visit it.'

'And what would you say?'

'I don't know. Perhaps I won't even knock. I'd just

stand outside and watch.'

'You're being sentimental. The man would have had us shot in a blink of an eye.'

'Different-coloured eyes.'

'That's what made you remember, wasn't it?'

'Yes.'

'You know the Germans are pulling down the war memorial the day after tomorrow. It's been announced. The barbarians.'

'It won't look the same without Soldier Mike.'

'Listen.'

'What?'

'I can hear boots.' It sounded like a group of German soldiers running, just round the bend in the road, their heavy boots slamming against the tarmac.

'They might ask for our papers,' said Pierre. 'They might ask where we've been.'

'They'll see the mess on my coat.'

'Get rid of it.'

'Too late. Quick, kiss me.'

'What?' Before he had time to prepare himself, Pierre felt Claire's arms around him, her lips on his. He closed his eyes. He felt quite lightheaded with the mixture of emotions – the tension of German soldiers about to pass them, the execution and the unexpected delight of kissing Claire. He felt her hand on the nape of his neck. His back muscles relaxed at her touch while the sound of the thumping boots became louder, pounding in his brain. Opening his eyes a fraction, he saw them pass, about eight of them, exercising in full uniform, with heavy packs on their backs. They waved and cheered as they ran by. One of them whistled, another put his thumbs up. Pierre waved back but made sure to keep his lips to Claire's. The sound of their boots receded but he held Claire tightly, not wanting the moment to end. But it did. Claire pulled back. 'That did the trick,' she said.

'Perhaps we should carry on in case they come back.'

'Come on, this is no time to be flippant. Oh, you've got blood on your coat as well now.'

'It's stopped raining so we can take them off.'

He walked with a lighter step, wanting to take her hand, holding his coat over his shoulder. He knew the kiss had been meaningless but still, he felt marvellous.

He hadn't realised that Claire had stopped. He turned. She had her hand on her forehead. 'You OK?' he asked.

'Those soldiers – they may talk. They might tell their comrades.'

'About what?'

'About you and me just now. *Merde.*'

'I don't understand. What would it matter?'

But of course he understood only too well.

*

Having said goodbye to Claire outside her house, Pierre ambled home, in no hurry to return. He wondered about her life in Paris, how different it must have been from her life here. He wondered whether she wanted to return there; whether, indeed, she might take him one day.

Taking a detour via the library green, he leant against the tree he and Xavier often used to sit under. The grass was wet. He hadn't seen his friend for a while. He rather missed him, yet when he thought of the games and antics they used to get up to, he realised none of it appealed any more.

A truck full of soldiers rumbled past behind him. So Tintin the Belgian had been Oskar Spitzweg the German SS. And now he was dead. It must have all been planned. Yes, of course it was – he remembered the major insisting on him cycling to the colonel's office. So, Spitzweg, on duty there, would have known he would be cycling by on that road around that particular time, tipped off by Major Hurtzberger, and had enough time to set up his little ambush. After Pierre had been pushed off his bike, he was too stunned to react that quickly, and his left arm throbbed in pain. The man had plenty of time to make his getaway on the bike, but no, he purposely got the pedals stuck, allowing Pierre time to get up and seize him. But why? The man had offered his services to them. Perhaps that was it – simply to infiltrate and report back to the colonel.

Bremen. He wondered what sort of town it was, whether it was big, a city, or small like Saint-Romain. Did he drink coffee in its cafés, did it have a cinema, did he have lots of friends there? A girlfriend? One day, soon, Oskar Spitzweg's mother would receive a letter from northern France enclosed with a handkerchief stained with her son's blood. How does one cope with that? Did he have brothers in uniform? Sisters? What would Claire say in her letter? Would she say he'd been captured and executed with tears in his eyes, regretting the life that had eluded him, his plans to study, to become an architect? Would she say he was buried in unconsecrated ground on a bleak farm without the attendance of a priest? Nineteen years old, almost twenty, born after the last war, born in a time of peace. What an age to die.

He flung himself down on the armchair in the living room. The major had put up the painting of the Alpine

230

scene. Pierre wasn't sure that he liked it. He saw, hung up on the coat rack, the major's cap. Normally, at this time, he would be still at work in the town hall. Something felt strange, an odd atmosphere in the house. As soon as he stepped through to the kitchen, Pierre knew something was wrong. He found his mother and the major in an embrace. Involuntarily, he let out a sound of surprise. He stepped back, hoping to escape back out but his mother heard him.

'Pierre, come in,' she said quietly, disentangling herself from the German. There was nothing unusual in her expression, no sign of shame. Pierre realised their embrace was not improper. Something was wrong. 'Thomas has had a letter.'

The major's eyes were red. He looked older, his face drained, his hair dishevelled.

Pierre sat down at the kitchen table. The major withdrew and disappeared into his bedroom, gently closing the door behind him.

'What's... what's happened?'

Lucienne sat on the bench next to him. 'It's the major's son, Joachim. He's been killed.'

'Oh.'

'Yes.'

*

Pierre spent the rest of the morning working on his sculpture, trying not to think about the major's son or the executed SS man. He found comfort from the familiar presence of the chickens near him. Madeline, Marlene, Monique... The work was going well, he chiselled away feverishly, keen to distance himself from the real world.

231

He remembered that the major had promised to have the finished sculpture displayed at the town hall. He hadn't mentioned it since. Perhaps, when the opportunity presented itself, he would remind him. He imagined the sign next to it – 'The White Venus by Pierre Durand, 1940.' His father would burst with pride. His mother would tell everyone in the town. If only things were so easy.

Concentrating as he was, Pierre hadn't realised the major had come out into the yard and was standing behind him.

'You made me jump.'

'My apologies.' He lit a cigarette, closing his eyes as the smoke filled his lungs. 'It's coming along nicely, I see,' he said nodding at the sculpture.

'Yes. I'm doing the hair. It'll take a while.' Pierre wondered if he should mention his son; he had no idea what the etiquette was concerning a bereavement.

'Yes. It looks like a lot of work. I admire your patience.'

'Thank you.'

'My son, Joachim, he had too little patience. Always in a hurry, wanting to do whatever came next in life.'

'Yes.'

'Always in such a damned hurry. Too keen to do the Führer's dirty work. Your mother told you?'

'Yes. I'm sorry.'

'Hmm.' He sat down in the rocking chair. 'North Africa. Killed in action. "I regret to inform you…" Fighting for the Führer. At least that's what the telegram said. It makes it sound as if it was a worthy death. Nineteen years old. No death is worthy at that age. Goodness knows how his mother is coping. I ought to…

Never mind.' He stood up again, struggling to extricate himself from the rocking chair. 'I need to go back to work. It's just another day; a day like any other.' He threw away his cigarette, half smoked. The hens jumped and squawked. 'Pierre, I have… There's something else.'

'Yes?'

'I've been told… I mean, they, my superiors, have told me…' He looked to one side. 'I'm being transferred. They'll give me a few days leave, but when I return to France, I'll be heading for another garrison, one in Paris, I think.'

'Oh.' A heavy silence settled on Pierre's heart; a form of guilt that he should be pleased, pleased to ridding his home of this invader, but, instead, a blanket of sadness wrapped over him. He stared at the sculpture, his hand, holding the chisel, poised; his mouth hung open. 'Oh,' he said again. The news, so sudden, had taken him unawares; he'd never considered the possibility. Of course, it was obvious but still… 'I…' Summoning the courage, he turned to face the major. 'I'd be sad to see you go.'

The major smiled a smile filled with painful regret. His eyes turned heavenward, running his fingers through his hair, clenching at strands so tightly to have hurt. He shook his head and was gone.

Pierre leant over and scooped up the major's half smoked cigarette.

Chapter 17

Kafka slammed the table. 'What idiots we were; we should have kept him alive.'

'No – the only good German is a dead German,' said Bouchette, his hand beneath the kitchen table, stroking Daisy.

'Don't you see, you fool; if we'd kept him alive, we would have had a bargaining tool. One German SS for our boys holed up in Saint-Romain.'

'No, you're the fool here. If you can think you can outfox the Germans at games like that, you're mad. Can you imagine the swap? Off you go then, Oskar, go join your mates over there while our lads come back to us. Can you imagine? They'd slaughter us; they'd shoot us down in an instant.'

'He's right,' said Dubois. 'If there's one thing their madman of a leader has taught them, it's that you don't win wars by gentlemanly agreements.'

'That's your problem, Kafka,' barked Bouchette. 'You think only of the here and now; no thought to the repercussions.'

Kafka sprung out of his chair. 'And your problem is that you're cowards.' With his knuckles on the table, he spoke quickly. 'All we've done so far is down to me. The railway sabotage, the capture and killing of that Kraut.'

'Right, yes, the railway sabotage that they fixed within a couple of hours, and the killing of one solitary boss-eyed Kraut hardly dismantles a regime, does it?'

'He wasn't boss-eyed,' said Pierre. 'It was just that his–'

'Yes, whatever, it doesn't make much difference,' said Bouchette.

Claire winked at Pierre.

'And now, Lincoln's bowed out.'

'Another coward,' said Kafka.

'We need more men,' said Dubois.

'And we will have more men,' said Kafka, sitting down. 'I've been sounding people out; we have a lot of support.'

'Is that so?' shouted Bouchette. 'So where are they, these mythical men?'

'They'll be ready when I tell them, don't you worry.'

'Oh but I am; I'm very worried.'

'Let's be honest,' said Dubois, 'we're out of our depth. The Krauts think we're simple hillbillies and frankly I reckon they've got a point.'

'Speak for yourself,' said Claire.

'Yes, sorry, Mademoiselle.'

'Any coffee, gentlemen?' asked Madame Bouchette, popping into the kitchen.

'No.'

Daisy barked. 'Shush, girl,' said Bouchette, slapping the dog.

'Hey, what's happened to those leaflets?' asked Dubois.

'Claire said we'd have them by now.'

Kafka shrugged. 'That's a point. Do you know, Claire?'

She shook her head. 'They must've got held up.'

'Not good.'

Pierre tried to hide his grimace as he thought of Victor and Alain hauled away by the Gestapo on his say so.

'So, what's next?' asked Dubois.

Kafka grinned. 'Our next hit.'

Bouchette threw his hands up in the air. 'I'm not risking my neck for another pointless—'

'No, this will be big,' said Kafka sharply. 'This will show we mean business.'

'Oh, so that's all right, then,' said Dubois. 'And what did you have in mind?'

'A bomb. Right at the heart of their operations.'

'What?' screeched Bouchette. 'That's preposterous.'

'Hear me out. We quietly leave a bomb in a briefcase at the town hall reception. You know I used to work in the quarries. The Krauts may have closed it down but they didn't empty it. Never even bothered to look. I know for fact there's still a mass of explosives down there. You know how busy it gets in the town hall and tomorrow they're tearing down Soldier Mike so no one will notice. But, just in case, we'll create a diversion or two.'

'Tomorrow? You're mad,' said Dubois. 'Quite mad. Have you thought of the consequences? For every Kraut we kill; they'll kill ten of us – at random. I've heard it done, not far from here—'

'This is war, for pity's sake. Yes, there'll be casualties but we can't lie back and let the bastards trample over us. This is just a small outpost for them. By our actions they'll think it's not worth the candle and move on. Christ,

Bouchette, they killed your son. We have to fight back.'

'If you want to go down in history as a martyr, Kafka, that's your lookout.' Bouchette's face had turned quite red. 'Shed your own blood, not the blood of innocents.' He looked round the table, seeking support. 'I can't be party to this; I'm going home.'

'This is your home, you idiot,' said Dubois.

'Yes, yes, I know that; I meant hypothetically.'

'What about you two? Claire? Pierre?'

'There is a risk, yes,' said Claire. 'But it's war. I'm prepared to help. As a woman, they'd suspect me less.'

'Good girl. Pierre?'

He would have said no, but following Claire's show of hand, he felt he had no choice. 'I'm prepared to help in any way,' he said quietly.

'Ha! So you see, Bouchette, even the kid and the girl you've so dismissed in the past are prepared to play their part.'

Bouchette slapped his dog in frustration. 'OK, OK, tell me the plan – in detail; then I'll decide.'

*

Pierre felt sick. He accompanied Claire in silence to the library. Despite hints of sunshine coming through the high windows, the place still felt dank and dark. A thin layer of dust had settled on the books. 'Yes, I know,' said Claire. 'The place needs a thorough clean.'

'Do many people come inside?'

'Not often. The odd German. People are too busy trying to survive to worry about reading. Especially now that your major forced me to remove all the good books.'

Once, recently, Pierre would have resented Major

Hurtzberger being referred to as *his* major; now, the thought struck him, he felt rather pleased with the association.

'I have a few minutes before I need to unlock the front door. I'm going to write that letter today – to Bremen.' She jumped up onto the counter and crossed her legs. Pierre tried not to look at those legs. If only he had the excuse to kiss her again. 'So, Pierre, what do you think of Kafka's grand plan?'

'Bouchette is right – it's a mad idea. The notion of walking into the town hall, nonchalantly leaving a bomb and making our escape seems absurd.' Would it cow the Germans, he wondered? No, of course not. Since their arrival, the Germans and the French had settled into a state of acceptance. They weren't the barbarians people feared they would be; they had, in fact, gone out of their way to be polite and accommodating. Life was harder, that couldn't be denied; the lack of petrol, radios and the rising prices, the introduction of coupons to purchase items, these things ground people down. Yes, one knew who had the power and that the Germans, at any time, could turn nasty but for those who chose to accept their presence or simply ignore them, and that counted almost everyone, then life was bearable.

'Kafka seems more unhinged with each passing day,' she said, filing her nails. 'He has to be stopped. How many innocent people, French people, would be caught by the blast?'

'So why did you agree to it?'

'I could ask the same. I wanted to hear his plan.'

'Me too.'

'We have to stop him; you need to tell your major.'

Now, Pierre had the perfect reason for approaching the major; something that, hopefully, would secure the release of his father. This time, he knew he wouldn't hesitate.

'Well, time to open the doors. Brace yourself for the rush…'

*

Back at home, Pierre found his mother at the kitchen table, her head in her hands, a glass of water next to her. More worryingly, on the table, in front of her, were his father's war medals, unclipped from their frame.

'Mama, what's the matter?'

'Oh, Pierre. I'm sorry, I didn't want you to see me like this.'

'It's fine.'

'It's just got on top of me today. Your father. I need him back.' Pierre had to fight the temptation of telling her that it would soon be over, that Georges would soon be home, that he had the means to make it happen, but he knew he couldn't say it. 'I think it's seeing the major in his sadness; it brought it all home for me. Do you think your father's OK in there? You hear of such dreadful things.'

'I'm sure they'll let him go soon.'

'Oh, I so hope you're right. And the major, Thomas, why do I feel for him so? He's lost his son, a German soldier, one of them. Yet I see only a father grieving. A friend. It feels terrible saying that.'

'I know; I feel the same.'

'He's our enemy, isn't he? Goodness knows how many Frenchmen he's killed.'

'Perhaps none.'

'We don't know, though, do we?' She took a sip of

water. 'Well, this is no good. They may have taken my husband but I still have to prepare something to eat. I'd better put these medals away. Your father never looks at them. He would have thrown them away by now if I hadn't stopped him.'

While his mother clattered around in the kitchen, tidying things that didn't need tidying, sweeping the spotless floor tiles, Pierre stepped outside into the yard and turned his attention to his sculpture, trying to blank everything from his mind. It would be a few hours yet before the major returned. In some ways, he was pleased to have seen his mother in such a state. Without realising it, it had bothered him how calm she'd seemed; as if her husband's arrest had not affected her. What he took as indifference was, in fact, strength. But now, at least, he knew she cared.

That evening, Pierre and his mother sat in the living room, not the kitchen; Lucienne with her knitting and Pierre reading. A standard lamp standing on the fireplace hearth shone despite the day still being light; above the fireplace was a framed print of a Renoir painting – *Young Girls at the Piano*. A large bookshelf contained only a map of the area and a few books, a few French classics that no one read but Lucienne insisted on keeping, if only for appearance's sake – Guy de Maupassant, Jules Verne, Flaubert and others Pierre knew nothing about. A pair of binoculars hung from the back of the door.

The major returned, unfastened his belt buckle, removed his cap and plonked himself in an armchair with a heavy sigh. 'I'm sorry I'm late. I hope dinner's not ruined. I do apologise, Lucienne. A lot of work on at the moment. I'm expected back in two hours as well. More manoeuvres.'

'I do understand, Thomas.'

'It's a good thing, really. It acts as a distraction from… you know.'

'Yes, of course. Wait there, I'll get your dinner. Nothing's ruined.'

'Thank you, Lucienne. I'll go have a wash.' He turned to Pierre, removing his boots. 'And how are you, Pierre?'

'Fine. I guess.'

'I shall miss this place, this house. After a day's work, it's like coming home.' He smiled. 'I shall miss you all.'

'Major, I need to speak to you.'

Lucienne, wearing her apron, appeared at the doorway. 'Would you like to eat here or in the kitchen, Thomas?'

'I think perhaps in here for a change.'

The major went to have his wash and returned as Lucienne came into the living room with his dinner and a small glass of red wine on a tray. 'There you are,' she said, 'chicken stew.'

'The chicken I brought yesterday?'

'We wouldn't eat nearly as well if it wasn't for you. What shall we do after you've gone, Thomas? Anyway, I'll leave you two to it.'

'Give me a minute, Pierre,' said the major as he tucked into his dinner. 'Delicious.' After a few minutes, he asked Pierre what he wanted to speak about.

'Well… you know Colonel Eisler said I had to speak to you if I heard anything. I've heard something.'

'This sounds serious.'

'Yes, there're some men who plan to bomb the town hall.'

'Good God.' He gulped down his wine. 'Are you sure?

How do you know this?'

'I was... I was approached.'

The major placed his glass carefully on the table. 'To do what exactly?'

Pierre glanced at the Renoir painting. He had never liked it. It reminded him of his own failure to learn the piano. Eventually, his parents, disillusioned with their son's lack of musical aptitude, had sold it, replacing it, instead, with something easier – a guitar. That hadn't worked either. They just had to accept their son had no musical ability whatsoever. The little girls in this picture looked too pleased with themselves, irritatingly self-assured with their pretty dresses and their concentrated expressions.

'Pierre – I asked a question. To do what exactly?'

'To work with Claire to create a diversion.'

'Claire? How did she get involved?' He played with the stem of his glass. 'When? What time?'

'Tomorrow. Eleven o'clock.'

'You've done right in telling me. And who are these men?'

'Do I have to tell you everything?'

'You either tell me everything or you tell it to the colonel.'

'Will it...'

'Yes?'

'Will it be enough to get my father released?'

'I can't promise, but I'll speak to the colonel. He usually listens to me. And after all, you've done as he asked. Now...' He took another mouthful of wine. 'You'd better tell me everything.'

Chapter 18

Kafka was right. The town square was packed with soldiers and civilians. Even the mayor was present, standing outside the town hall wearing his robes, a tricolour sash across his chest, his face as red as the colour in his sash. The mayor had made his protestations, he had tried, at least everyone believed so, but he had failed. To remove the statue would be sacrilege, a violation to those who had fought in the war seventy years ago. There were still village elders who were alive and could remember, as children, the calamitous events of 1870 and 1871. Word went round that the official response from Colonel Eisler was that the steel within the statue would be better used as German bullets.

Two German soldiers stood guard at the town hall doors, searching a woman's handbag. Kafka had planned two diversions; the first, involving himself and Bouchette, aimed to divert these guards. The sun, although shining, was cool. A pleasant wind filtered through the square. Pierre, who had joined the crowd of spectators, watching with Xavier, felt the tension in his head and his shoulders. The town hall clock showed ten to eleven, German time. Ten minutes. With plenty of shouting and bellowed instructions, the Germans had thrown ropes round the statue's neck, torso, knees and ankles. 'Shame on you,' came a shout from the crowd of French onlookers. 'Leave him alone.' 'Monsieur le Maire,' came another voice, 'can't you do anything? Can't you stop them?'

'My dear people, don't you think I've tried?'

A few Germans approached the crowd, their hands on their rifles, and eyed them while, behind them, their colleagues were busy securing the ropes to a truck. Murmurs of discontent circled the crowd, a constant hum of disgruntled voices.

'Can you imagine what the square will look without our statue?' said Xavier quietly. 'I never really appreciated him before.'

'I know; he was just – there.'

'Exactly. I shall miss him. So, how have you been? Haven't seen you for ages.'

'Oh, you know. Busy.'

'Have you heard – some of the Krauts are being transferred to Paris. What about your major? Is he one of them?'

'I don't know. Maybe. He's not my major.'

'Whatever, it will mean fewer for us to contend with. Oh shit, look, they're bringing out the blowtorches.'

A fresh chorus of complaint rose from the villagers. But it wasn't the Fritzes lighting up their blowtorches that caught Pierre's eye but the sight of Dubois appearing in the square, carrying a small, brown-coloured briefcase, his glasses perched at the end of his nose. Kafka had decided to entrust the placing of the bomb to Dubois, not Claire as originally decided. Claire reckoned Kafka didn't trust her sufficiently enough to carry out such a task. 'After all,' she'd said, 'I'm only a woman.' He watched as Dubois mingled with the crowd, bumping into someone he knew, shaking hands and shaking his head. That means, thought Pierre, that Kafka wouldn't be far away. He craned his neck, trying to find him. A different truck, one with a broken windscreen passed by, a swastika painted on its side, full of soldiers going somewhere, its exhaust clattering loudly, leaving a dense cloud of fumes in its wake.

'Hello, boys.' Claire had appeared, squeezing in between them. 'Not a day we'll want to remember, is it?' She looked lovely, thought Pierre, very Parisian, wearing a polka dot skirt with a frilly white blouse, her hair tied back with a blue bow, carrying a petite red handbag with a shiny, silver clasp.

'We'll hardly forget it, though,' said Xavier. 'Not with the base left behind as a constant reminder.'

'Plinth,' said Pierre. 'Not base.'

'Ah, thank you. I stand corrected.'

Two of the Germans, wearing goggles beneath their helmets, were now working at the statue's ankles, weakening them with their blowtorches. The crowd edged forward. The Germans guarding them pushed people back, making sure they were aware of their rifles. 'Heathens,' shouted someone from the back. 'Barbarians,' came another.

The mayor, still within the sanctuary of the town hall, had been joined by Father de Beaufort. The priest, in full regalia, shouted over, 'Citizens, citizens, these men are under orders. Don't persist in abusing them. No good will come of it.'

Claire nudged Pierre and motioned with her head that it was time to go. The clock read three minutes to eleven. His heartbeat quickened. 'OK,' he mouthed.

He slapped Xavier on the shoulder. 'We have to go. We'll be back later.'

'Eh? Where you going?'

'We've just got to see the town hall reception about something.'

'Don't you want to see them pull the statue down?'

'We won't be long.'

'Well, all right. Mind how you go.'

'Yeah. Thanks.'

'Cheer up, my friend, it can't be that bad.'

'No.'

The ankles of the statue had taken on an orange glow as the flame did its work. 'You OK?' whispered Claire.

'No.'

'No, nor am I.'

His mouth felt dry; he felt the need to be sick. There were so many people around. Kafka thought this would be a good thing; lots of activity. But Pierre knew that among all the Germans many would be waiting for them, ready to pounce. Somewhere, among all these uniforms, was the major. He wished he could see him; wished he had the reassurance of his presence. He knew he had done the right thing but the thought that Kafka and the others would be captured, perhaps killed, weighed heavily, a weight on his back, his crooked back.

A soldier, sitting in the truck, was revving the engine while his colleagues, with much yelling, checked the tension and positioning of the ropes. The crowd hissed as one, a sinister sound that soon gathered momentum and volume. As Pierre and Claire approached the town hall, circling round the hissing protestors and the animated German soldiers, they caught sight of Bouchette wearing, despite the sun, a heavy overcoat, torn on one pocket. Not far from him, wearing expressions of weary resignation, were the priest and mayor, church and state unified in their disgust of the symbolic rape of their town which they had been powerless to prevent. Pierre and Claire had been told by Kafka not to turn round, not to appear as if they were looking for someone. But Pierre did turn round. Not far behind him, he saw Dubois with his briefcase taking an interest in the proceedings as the German driver slowly eased his truck forward, picking up the slack on the ropes. 'Go on, forward,' shouted a German. 'Put your foot down, slowly. Slowly, mind,' yelled another above the continuous hiss.

Claire took Pierre's hand. This meant Kafka had appeared. Yes, there he was – approaching Bouchette, hands in pockets, hoping not to be noticed. Kafka would strike up a conversation with Bouchette, which would soon descend into an argument and a fight. Claire and Pierre headed for the town hall entrance. They were to keep the receptionist busy while Dubois slipped in with the briefcase containing the bomb.

Pierre and Claire sidled up the town hall steps, avoiding the mayor and the priest who, watching the truck straining with the ropes, were in deep discussion, and up to the large open doors. Both doors still bore the scar of Pierre's graffiti, *Vive La Framce*. How long ago that seemed now. 'Halt,' said the first guard, a plump man, his eyes obscured by his helmet. 'Your business?'

'Hello,' purred Claire. 'I need to apply for my clothing coupons. I was told I could do it here.' In the corner of his eye, Pierre could see Kafka and Bouchette talking.

'And you?' said the guard to Pierre in a thick German accent.

'I'm her boyfriend.' Even in his state of nervousness, it felt great saying that. Claire suppressed a grin.

'Your handbag.' Pierre could sense Claire wince as the German delved his fat fingers in. The conversation between Kafka and Bouchette had increased in volume, catching the attention of Father de Beaufort. A burst of laughter erupted behind Pierre. One of the ropes had snapped. The soldier statue, although at an angle, wasn't prepared to be pulled down quite yet. The mayor clapped then, abruptly, stopped.

'OK, you can go in,' said the guard stepping aside. Pierre followed but the man held up his hand. 'Not you.'

'Can't I–'

'No. You wait here.'

Claire, the other side of the guards, looked back at him. With a shrug of the shoulders, she disappeared into the darkness of the town hall.

Pierre trudged back down to the bottom step.

Kafka and Bouchette were now pushing each other. 'You're a son of a bitch,' yelled Bouchette.

'And you expect her to stick by a useless old git like you?'

The truck engine revved again.

Bouchette pushed Kafka back into the road. Regaining his balance, Kafka leapt forward and struck Bouchette. Bouchette staggered back, his hand on his lip.

The guards, thought Pierre. The guards should have reacted by now, allowing Dubois the chance to slip into the building. Instead, a number of soldiers stepped away from their colleagues and ran towards the quarrelling Frenchmen, rifles at the ready. Kafka had seen them too. He drew his revolver from his jacket pocket. A shot rang out through the square. People screamed and ducked. A soldier fell, clutching his stomach. Others drew their rifles, ready to fire. The German truck with the broken windscreen, now empty of soldiers, chose that moment to make its return journey. It passed between the Germans and Kafka and Bouchette. The two men ran down the side of the town hall. The Germans screamed at the driver who, on misunderstanding them, stopped. The soldiers had to run round the truck, losing valuable seconds. Pierre heard a scuffle to his left. Three soldiers had bundled Dubois to the ground. Dubois bawled as one of them put him in an arm lock. Another hit him in the stomach. His shrieking stopped. The third took the briefcase. The crowd gasped. The soldiers chasing Kafka and Bouchette fired round after round, then resumed running. A couple of others ran to their stricken colleague. The mayor and the priest had backed against the wall. The priest crossed himself.

Two soldiers emerged from the town hall, between them, with her hands held above her head, was Claire.

Pierre jumped as he felt a hand slap against his shoulder. Fritz One, the German with boxer's nose, was arresting him.

The tremendous sound of metal on gravel made everyone stop. A cloud of exhaust fumes floated up. The Germans cheered; the crowd booed, the mayor and the priest shook their heads. Soldier Mike had fallen.

*

The room was small. Pierre sat at a table. Opposite him sat a German major – not *his* major but an SS major wearing a black uniform, who introduced himself as Hauff. The table was bare except for a table lamp, a dirty glass ashtray and the major's papers. Above them a bare light bulb emitted a feeble glow. There were no windows. On a long table adjacent to the wall were various jars and trays containing instruments that made Pierre shudder – knives, pincers, hammers. Had his father sat in this very chair? Had those instruments been used against him? In the corner, a broom and a mop and bucket. Major Hauff puffed on a pipe, producing a sickly sweet smell. Next to the door, stood a private, his hands behind his back.

'So, let's go through this again.' The man had a gaunt face, heavily lined. A pair of metal-rimmed spectacles merely added to his gauntness. 'You say after Colonel Eisler made his offer, you tried to enlist in this group run by Albert Foucault, who goes by the name of Kafka. Why does he call himself that? Does he have literary pretensions?'

'I don't know.' Pierre pulled at his collar. The room, airless and claustrophobic, was hot.

'Speak up.'

Pierre cleared his throat. 'I said I don't know.'

His lips, Pierre noticed, were chapped, while his nose had a pronounced bump half way down. 'You say after his refusal, this Kafka, you tried to prove yourself by sabotaging a convoy of German vehicles with a jarful of nails.'

250

'Yes.'

'Hmm.' He scribbled something on his paper. 'Most enterprising. It was lucky for you that no one was hurt.' Pierre thought of Monsieur Roché, beaten to death, but thought it best not to say anything. 'Very lucky.' Carefully, the major placed his pen on the table and straightened his back.

'So, where is this Kafka?'

Pierre glanced at the private in the corner. 'I don't know.'

'Do you want to know about your friends? Albert Bouchette is dead. He was shot as he tried to make his escape.' Pierre caught his breath. Poor old Madame Bouchette, her son killed and now her husband. Major Hauff continued, 'And Albert Dubois – perhaps your Kafka would have accepted you sooner had you changed your name to Albert.' He guffawed at his own joke. 'Where was I? Yes, Albert Dubois is in custody. He's been most helpful – to a point. He told us Foucault has a little hideaway in the wood outside your little town. He's escorting Major Hurtzberger and a couple of privates to this hut. Let's hope they leave a trail of breadcrumbs, eh? Major Hurtzberger, I believe, is billeted in your home? And then we have your girlfriend, Claire Bouchez—'

'She's not my girlfriend.'

'No? She should be. She speaks very fondly of you. Mademoiselle Bouchez told us much the same as Dubois. You'll be pleased to know we have released her. Dubois, however, will be executed.'

'Oh.' The image of his father's mock execution haunted his subconscious, the courtyard, the priest, all those guns. 'Even if he helps you find Kafka?'

'Yes, I'm afraid so. What did you expect? If it wasn't for you, he would've blown the town hall to smithereens. Well, maybe not smithereens; it was quite a small bomb; the damage would have been minimal. The work of an amateur. But that, and I'm sure you'll agree, is not the point.' He tapped his pipe against the ashtray. 'I will say, Colonel Eisler is most grateful for your co-operation. Indeed, we all are.'

Pierre would have said thank you but the words caught in his throat. Instead, he mumbled, 'Can I have some water?'

'No.' The major ran his fingers over his chapped lips and grimaced. 'Now, let me ask you again, and think carefully – where is Albert Foucault?'

Pierre shook his head. 'I promise you I have no idea. I would have said his hut in the woods but...'

'Yes, exactly. And there's nowhere else he might have escaped to?'

He thought of Lincoln's barn. 'No,' he said firmly.

'If anything comes to mind, you'll let us know.' The major re-read his notes. 'On a separate note, did your little gang, this gang of Alberts, run across a comrade of ours, a lieutenant by the name of Spitzweg, Oskar Spitzweg?'

'No.'

'Pity. A good fellow, young. Good-looking chap. Odd eyes though. He was sent on a mission to follow you. Yes, you, Durand. He went out and we haven't seen him since. So your paths didn't cross?'

'No, sir.'

'Interesting.' Pierre saw the major write a large 'X' on his paper. 'Right, the colonel has instructed me to inform you that your father will be released today.'

252

Pierre sat up in his chair. 'Really?'

'He is a man of his word, is our colonel.'

'Can I see him?'

'You want to thank the colonel?'

'No, I meant my father.'

'Your father? No. But you'll see him later today no doubt. Now...' He scanned his paper, adjusting his glasses. 'I think that is all. You may go, Monsieur Durand. Private Dassler here will see you out.' The private stepped forward.

'I can go? You mean... just like that?'

'Unless you want to stay?'

'No, no.'

The major picked up his pipe. 'No, I thought not.'

*

'He's here! Pierre, he's here; your father's back!' Lucienne, still wearing black, her hands clasped as if in prayer, welcomed Pierre back. 'Isn't it marvellous?'

Pierre stepped into the living room, his heart beating wildly. The curtains were drawn, the lampshade, with its weak light, on. 'Papa?'

Georges was standing next to the fireplace, circling his cap in his hands, a slight smile on his lips. 'Hello, Pierre.'

'Papa.' How small his father seemed, so diminished, his hair greyer, his eyes dulled. He'd lost so much weight, his clothes, like rags, hung off him. His skin, it seemed so thin, so fragile, as if it might tear. There were no obvious signs he'd been tortured but he tried not to look too hard. It was the smell that hit him, a stench of dirt and sweat. But Pierre cared not a hoot. It was his father; he had returned from the dead, from the hands of the Gestapo; his brave

253

father, this man he had never really thought about, had never appreciated, the man who had fought against the Germans as a young man, who had, no doubt, seen horrors that Pierre couldn't begin to imagine, and, in the process, had his faith in God destroyed; and who now, in his middle age, was still fighting them. The Germans had bowed him, had killed a part of him, this much was already obvious, but they hadn't finished him. For he was back, at home, where he belonged, with his wife, his son, and even the son he had lost. He was back in his home with its years of memories, of routine, of comfort, with his little knick-knacks, his mementoes of times past, his books, his photographs, even his armchair. 'Papa.' He felt himself move as in slow motion, a step towards his father, Georges's arms outstretched, ready to embrace his older son, tears smearing the dirt on his haggard face, tears of joy, yes, and tears of relief. They fell into each other, Georges's hand against the back of Pierre's head, his whole body now convulsed in sobs, great, giant sobs. His father's grip weakened. Quietly, he slipped away from his son and, with awkward steps, manoeuvred himself to his armchair and fell upon it, exhausted, faint. He put his head into a hand and with his eyes clenched shut, continued sobbing, his delicate frame shaking.

Pierre felt his mother's hand in his. 'Come,' she whispered. 'Let's leave him be for a while.'

Pierre nodded and, following his mother, retired to the kitchen.

*

Georges was having a bath, a very long bath. He'd eaten a whole baguette with ham and cucumber, and had been sick soon afterwards. 'It's to be expected,' he'd said. 'Even ham and bread is too rich after the water soup they give you in that place.' Pierre had fallen asleep on the sofa while his mother fussed about in the kitchen, humming to herself. She'd changed out of her black dress and was now wearing a light green outfit. She'd applied lipstick and painted her nails. 'I want to look nice for my husband,' she'd explained to Pierre. 'Isn't it just so wonderful to have him back?'

'Oh, that's better.' Pierre opened his eyes and smiled. His father had re-emerged from the bathroom in a fresh set of clothes that Lucienne had laid out for him, his hair was washed, his skin free of the prison grime. 'I feel half human again.'

'Sit down, Papa.' The clothes that once appeared a little tight now dwarfed him.

'I don't mind if I do. What's that hideous painting?'

'What? Oh that. It's, erm… a present from the major.'

Georges considered it for a while. 'Is it, indeed? Oh well. Something smells good.'

Lucienne appeared from the kitchen. 'Oh, Georges, you look so much better.'

He laughed. 'I feel it.'

'I've got my old husband back.' She sat on the armrest and pecked him on the cheek. 'Welcome home, my love.'

He patted her hand. 'It's good to be back.'

'Now, dinner won't be long. Mutton chops, mashed potatoes and runner beans. Oh dear, it won't be too rich for you?'

'I should be OK. I'll just have a small bit.'

'It's thanks to Thomas we've got the chops.'

'Thomas? Oh yes, the major. Food, paintings, whatever next? Still here, is he then?'

'Yes, I'm afraid so. But tonight's dinner, as so often, is courtesy of our Major Thomas. He should be home by now.'

'Home?'

'Well, his... home from home. He said he'd bring back a nice bottle of red; said we should have a little celebration for you, Georges.'

'I don't want a fuss.'

'Perhaps but we have much to thank him for – your release was entirely down to him. Isn't that what you said, Pierre? That Thomas had a word with that colonel and secured father's release?'

'Yes, Maman.' One day, he thought, one day, when he was much, much older, he may tell her the full story.

But not yet.

They waited a while for the major until Georges, understandably famished, could bear it no more. And so they ate dinner, their mutton chops, mashed potatoes and runner beans, without the major and without his wine. Georges did indeed have a small portion, and felt quite emotional, only to be followed by another small portion and a third. At ten o'clock, tired after an exacting day, they retired to bed. Pierre felt more content than he had in a long time. His brush with the Gestapo was over; he had no need to worry about Kafka again; and he had survived. It was only now, now that it was all over, that he realised quite how frightened he had been of Kafka. His was not a fight for France against the invaders; it was a personal crusade, a vendetta carried from the previous war against all things German; and in his desire for vengeance, he had no qualms about using others. Bouchette, Lincoln, Dubois, Claire and he, Pierre, had been all sucked in. They had been expendable to Kafka's wishes. Bouchette and Dubois had been unlucky. But it was over now. Kafka was in the past and his father was home. For the first time in ages, Pierre could go to sleep and not worry, and dream of pleasant things.

The only concern, the only slight niggle in his thoughts, was why had the major not returned home.

Chapter 19

Pierre woke up thinking of Monsieur Dubois. He wondered whether he'd been executed yet. Poor old Dubois; a decent man, trying to do his best but led down the wrong path by Kafka.

After breakfast, he went out into the yard and started work. His father had gone to report himself at the town hall. He was obliged to do so every morning, he'd said. A while later, he returned and stepped outside to see Pierre.

He circled round the sculpture, his shadow long in the morning sun, but much to Pierre's disappointment, said not one word about it. Instead, he enquired about the blessed chickens. 'You're feeding them?' he asked. 'Their water looks a little dirty.'

'I changed it yesterday.' In fact, it'd been three days.

'Your mother told me the major's son's been killed.'

'Yes, out in Africa somewhere.'

'Hmm. I wonder where the major is. Thomas, as your mother calls him.'

'I don't know. Did you sleep well then?'

Georges's shoulders dropped. 'Did I sleep well? Ah, I slept like a king; it was heaven. A proper bed. Although I still feel tired. And a proper breakfast. I feel human again. The food at Hotel du Gestapo leaves a lot to be desired. I dread to think what Monsieur Michelin would make of it.' He sniggered to himself as he stepped inside one of the sheds.

Pierre changed the chickens' water, slightly irked that his father had found him out.

The knock on the front door was alarmingly loud. 'Blimey, someone's in a hurry,' said Georges, popping his head out of the shed.

'Perhaps it's the major,' said Pierre, surprised by how much he hoped it was.

Pierre followed his father back into the house. The living room felt crowded as Georges and Pierre were confronted by three Germans. Their presence seemed to take all the space. Lucienne, wearing her headscarf and outdoor jacket, ready to go out, had already let the visitors in. Pierre recognised the officer, Lieutenant Neumann. Lucienne, fidgeting with her ring, said, 'These gentleman want a word with you, Pierre.'

'Where is he then?' barked the lieutenant. 'Has he been back?'

Pierre found himself stepping back. 'Who? The major? No.'

'Have a look round,' said the lieutenant to the two privates. While they searched the house, the lieutenant eyed Pierre with narrowing eyes. 'My French – it's good now, no?'

'Very good.'

'We were expecting the major back last night for

dinner,' said Lucienne. 'Weren't we, Georges?'

'Where is your friend, Foucault?'

'Kafka?' said Georges. 'I haven't seen him for weeks.'

'And you?' he said to Pierre.

'Nor me, not since the…'

'Shoot-out?'

'Yes.'

The two privates returned to the living room, shaking their heads.

'If you hear anything, you tell us straightaway. You understand, yes?'

'Yes, of course, Lieutenant,' said Lucienne. 'Straightaway.'

The lieutenant nodded and left; the two privates following in his wake.

Pierre and his parents watched them leave, then turned to each other. 'Oh dear,' said Lucienne. 'This sounds serious. Where could they be?'

'I don't know,' said Georges, 'but something tells me they're together somewhere.'

'You mean Kafka has kidnapped Thomas?'

'Seems mad, I know, but then Kafka *is* mad. Always has been. You can never know what idiotic scheme he'll come up with next. Doing nothing has never been his way; he'd rather do anything, however stupid, than do nothing.'

'I don't like this one bit,' said Lucienne. 'Oh well. I was about to go the bakery and a few other chores. You two need anything? No?' She kissed both her men. 'I'll be back soon.'

*

His father went off to have another bath, 'purely for the indulgence,' he'd said. Taking his bicycle, Pierre decided to

260

visit Claire. After all, they were accomplices now. He found her coming out of the chemist. 'Look,' she said. 'Shampoo. Quite a rarity these days. Come, let's talk.'

They walked towards her home, Pierre pushing his bicycle. 'So, how are you, Pierre? How did you get on with the Gestapo?'

He shrugged his shoulders. 'They were fine. Just asked me a few questions.'

'Me too. We must be the only people in France who have walked straight out of a Gestapo interview intact. They asked me where Kafka's disappeared to. And your major. They actually believed me when I said I didn't know.'

'The same.'

'Do you think it's a coincidence – both of them disappearing at the same time?'

'I don't know. Probably.'

Madame Clément passed by, her shopping bag full of vegetables. They waved at each other. 'The Germans knew about the bomb,' said Claire. 'Someone told them.'

'Yes, someone must've talked.'

She smiled. 'Well, it couldn't have been Bouchette or Dubois, and it certainly wasn't Kafka, and it wasn't me. So…,' she said, drawing out the word. 'That only leaves you, Pierre.'

'Does it?'

'Come on; don't play games with me.' She stopped and placed her hand on his sleeve. 'I approve, you know, you did the right thing.'

He leant his bike beside the wall of a house that backed onto the street. 'Monsieur Bouchette was killed. I didn't want that to happen, and now they're going to execute

261

Dubois.'

'It was their choice, Pierre. Remember what we said in Bouchette's kitchen? "Shed your own blood, not the blood of innocents." Those were Bouchette's very words. No one but me realises it, but think of the people you saved, the innocents.'

'Apparently the bomb was small and would have done minimal damage.'

'Yes, but think of the reprisals.'

'I suppose.'

'You suppose nothing. Come here, you... you brave man.' She pulled him in by the lapels of his jacket and gently, very gently, kissed him on the lips. Pierre felt a warmth cascade through him. His fingertips tingled, his heart burned with a feeling he'd forgotten – the feeling of joy. She wrapped her arms round him. Emboldened, he followed suit. Her kiss became more urgent. This, he realised, was the real thing, the real Claire, so unlike the kiss on the roadside leading into the town. She pulled away and lowered her eyes, momentarily abashed.

He tried to suppress a grin. 'I thought I was too young for you.'

'Not any more, you're not,' she said quietly, looking up at him through her fringe.

*

Back at home, Pierre found his father sitting in his armchair, deep in thought. 'Oh, Pierre, I was miles away. You OK? Good. Listen, Pierre... Sit down. I need to tell you something.' Pierre took a chair opposite him. 'I never thought I'd tell anyone this tale; I'd promised myself never to mention it, but I think you need to know what sort of man Kafka really is.'

'Are you sure?'

'I've never told your mother this.' He paused, his eyes drifting away. 'It was night time, the first of January 1918. New Year's Day. Kafka and I had been in a patrol with some boys from our battalion. Kafka's main job was to be a sniper. I have to give it to him, I've never met a man who can fire a rifle as accurately as that man. Something to behold. Well, on the way back from this patrol, we became the subject of a German attack. Shells, machine guns, the lot. We fought back. A few of ours were killed. Kafka had seen his mate have his head blown clean off. It upset him terribly; made him determined to fight back in any way he could. His mother had recently died, and he was close to her. So he was already churned up. Then the bombardment stopped as suddenly as it had started. When the smoke cleared, Kafka and I found ourselves alone. The others, if they hadn't been killed, had gone on without us. We didn't know where we were. The attack had disorientated us. We didn't know which way was forward, which way was back. It was pitch black, and bucketing down. We were utterly lost and, I don't mind admitting it, Pierre, we were scared…'

'What happened?'

'We tried to find our way back, naturally. We must've gone the wrong direction because we found ourselves in an area that had seen a lot of shelling. German dead lay everywhere and bits of German, an arm here, a leg there. We'd already been fighting for a year or more so we took it in our stride. But when I think about it, as I do everyday, it was enough to turn your stomach. At the time, though, I was just impressed that our artillery had done such an effective job. Kafka and I knew we had to turn tail and make our escape before we were seen. And that's when we came across him – this German boy, lying wounded in a ditch. His hand hung off by the tendons; he was barely conscious and had lost a lot of blood. He could have been no more than nineteen, maybe twenty. Not much older then you, Pierre. Fair hair, clean-shaven, bright blue eyes. He had a ring on the hand hanging off. His other hand clutched a crucifix. I read his name on his dog tag – Otto Zeiss, a corporal. He didn't have long but at the time, I thought we could save him. I wanted us to carry him back to our lines. I thought our medic boys would simply amputate the hand, cart him off as a prisoner and he'd be fine. I was already thinking, you see, of the future. I wanted to be able to live with my conscience after the war, and to be able to say "yes, I saved a man, the enemy; my place in heaven is assured". Kafka was having none of it. He wanted to kill him off there and then. He could only think of the here and now; angry that his friend had met such a horrible end at the hands of the Hun. We argued; we pushed each other. I said, you cannot kill him in cold blood. He said the man had killed his friend and many others besides; he deserved to die like a dog, without mercy. I knew then that the boy was as good as dead because there was no way I could carry him by myself. So I begged Kafka to make it quick; to allow him, at least, a merciful death. He called me a German-lover, a secret enthusiast of all things German, and said, "He'll have the death he deserves". Oh, Pierre, I'll never forget it. I was powerless to stop him. He stuffed a handkerchief or a rag in the boy's mouth and then went at him with his bayonet – in the legs, his knees, the testicles. I tried to stop him, to

264

pull him off. The tortures that poor boy endured. Only when he had lost consciousness, did Kafka administer the fatal blow. He pocketed the boy's ring and that crucifix, and ripped off his dog tag, and threw it into the darkness. It was the final humiliation – his parents would never know; only that he was missing, and would have to endure the agony of waiting and not knowing.'

Georges fell silent, his head in his hands. Fishing a handkerchief from his inside pocket, he blew his nose.

'The war unhinged Kafka. It was me who gave him that name by the way. He was reading *Metamorphosis* when I first met him. He must have read it a dozen times during the time I was with him in the trenches. I hadn't known him beforehand. He lived a few towns away. But getting to know him in the army during the autumn of sixteen, he was your usual happy-go-lucky chap.'

'I… I don't understand. Did he want to torture him?'

'Just killing him wasn't enough. He'd wanted to hurt this German boy; he wanted to take revenge for all the misfortunes that had fallen on him. I remember, a few months before, we were behind the lines, enjoying a few days off. We were exercising in some woods. Kafka caught a rabbit. Rather than kill it, he stunned the creature and took it back to our lodgings where he put it in a crate or a cage the farmers use for their dogs. Then, he took a serrated knife to it and hacked off one of its feet. The poor thing screeched to heaven come. I remember him saying, "A rabbit's foot is meant to be lucky, isn't it?" Then, the next day, he hacked off another foot. By the following day, someone had killed the poor creature out of mercy. Kafka was livid; someone had spoilt his fun.'

'Do you think he's kidnapped the major?'

Georges rose to his feet. 'Either that or perhaps the major's captured Kafka a long way from home and is on his way back through the woods.'

'Perhaps one of them is wounded.'

'I don't know, but I intend to find out.'

'What? How?'

'I know his hideaways. Come help me get some food from the kitchen.'

They'd moved into the kitchen. Pierre watched as his father filled a small haversack with a baguette and a sausage. 'But why, Papa? Why do you need to get involved?'

Georges stopped. 'You're right – I don't have to. But I need to. I could have saved that German. I could have informed his parents. What I did that night, Pierre, was cowardly and I've never been able to forgive myself. Not a day has passed when, at some point, I haven't thought of Otto Zeiss. Every night now, for twenty-two years, I've gone to bed with his face in my mind, the memory of that horrible day. I should've saved him from that monster who lives in our midst. I cannot let him do the same to the man who saved my skin from the Gestapo. I know this sounds dramatic, but it's time to atone for my sins.'

'It wasn't…'

'Yes?'

'No, nothing.' It wasn't just the major who saved you, father; it was me, forced to turn on my countrymen, forced to work for the enemy; it was me who saved you. But he couldn't say it.

Georges sighed. 'Your mother, she thinks I'm a godless person. She has no idea. I have great faith; I just never show it. I don't allow myself. I believe God looks over us,

266

takes note of our actions and our… inactions. It's just that I am still, even now, too ashamed to step into His house; too ashamed to let Him into my heart. He knows. He knows I could have stopped Kafka from killing that man.'

'But, Papa, it was war–'

'Murder is murder, Pierre. The circumstances excuse nothing. Kafka is a murderer and I, by my complicity, am no better.'

'No, Papa, you can't say that, you can't mean that.' He remembered the expression on Kafka's face after he'd shot Tintin, a look of diabolical pleasure.

'Oh but, my son, my dear son, you have suffered too. What sort of father have I been to you? What sort of example have I set you over the years? I've ignored you, haven't I? I've been no father to you, just a presence. I didn't want children; I admit that. I didn't want to pass on my genes. But of course your mother… She wanted children, lots of children. Of course, we had the two.' He found a bottle from under the sink and filled it with water. 'He'll be waiting for me; I know that. He'll see it as a game. And if I don't get there in time, he'll cut his fingers off one by one.' He bounced his haversack by its strap. 'That's everything, I think.'

'Can I come with you?'

'No.'

'But what if you don't come back?'

'Pierre…' he placed his hand on his son's shoulder. 'If I don't come back it's because the fates have decreed it. It'll be my own fault.'

'What do I tell mama?'

'Tell her… tell her the truth, that I've gone to look for Major Thomas. Tell her I've gone to look for Corporal

Zeiss.'

With that, he was gone.

*

Pierre spent the next few hours trying to kill time. He was tempted to go see Claire again but, somehow, after their kiss, he feared he wouldn't know what to say to her any more. Instead, he visited Xavier and together they went for a cycle ride round the outskirts of the town. They lay in a field, leaning against an elm tree and idled away the time. Pierre found he had little in common with his old friend now. 'I'll give you a race,' said Xavier.

'What?'

'To that rock over there. And back.'

'Don't be so childish.'

He returned home in the late afternoon. His mother had been back and gone out again. A pan of chicken stew simmered on the stove. Taking a wooden spoon, he helped himself to a sip, burning his lips in the process. Rather watery, he thought. He went out into the yard and sat in the rocking chair and considered his sculpture. He wasn't sure he even liked it any more. Her arms seemed too big, her legs too bulky. It lacked finesse. His amateurism stared back at him. Why did adults, proper adults, always say what they thought he wanted to hear? Why did they always hide behind deceit dressed up as kindness? Who did it benefit? Picking up a stick, he jabbed at the ground. Otto Zeiss. He would probably have been the same age as his father. He would have had a family by now, living a comfortable life somewhere in Germany. Perhaps in Bremen. It had already been several hours since his father left. With each passing hour, his unease intensified. And now, hearing the front open, he would have to tell his mother.

'Pierre, Pierre,' she rushed into the yard, untying her headscarf. 'Where's your father?'

'He… he went out. Earlier.'

'Where on earth to?'

'I don't know.' He ran his finger along the tip of the stick.

'Pierre, you do know. I can tell. Where is he?'

'He's gone to find the major.'

Her hand went to her mouth. 'Oh no. No, no, no.' Rubbing her eyes, she asked. 'How long will he be?'

'Well, I wouldn't know, would I?'

'Oh dear, oh dear. Why does my heart feel so heavy? If the Germans can't find him, then what makes your father think he can?'

'He does know the area better than any German.'

'Pierre, if that's meant to reassure me, I'm afraid it doesn't.'

*

Georges still hadn't returned by bedtime. Lucienne had been unable to keep still all evening. 'This is so hard to bear.' She pulled back the curtain, looking up and down the street. 'It's long past curfew. I had my husband back with me for one night and now he's gone again. It seems so unfair. If anything, this is worse. At least, before, I knew where he was. It's the not knowing that is so trying.'

'I know.'

'Could you not have stopped him?'

'How? I didn't know he'd be gone for so long.'

She sat down on the sofa and immediately sprung up

269

again. 'No, I suppose not. I wished I smoked, or drank. Anything. You go to bed if you want.'

'What about you?'

'I'll wait up a while longer. He must be back soon.'

'It is strange. First Kafka, then the major and now–'

'Yes, thank you, Pierre.' She re-arranged the vase within the living room niche. 'I don't care about Kafka; I don't care so much now about the major. I just want your father home.'

Chapter 20

Pierre ate his boiled egg breakfast in silence. His mother, wearing black again, maintained a silence borne out of worry. She busied herself in the kitchen, continually washing her hands. When, earlier, Pierre had tried to suggest Georges would surely be back today, she snapped back at him. How on earth could he know? Deciding that saying nothing was the best option he concentrated on his egg. Once this war was over, he thought, once everything was back to normal, he would never eat another egg in his lifetime. Nor the cod liver oil.

He decided he would venture out to Kafka's hut as soon as he was done with breakfast. Best not tell his mother. If they weren't there, he thought, surely it would provide a clue as to where they were. Problem was finding it. If only he'd paid more attention that time.

Lucienne snatched away his plate and eggcup before he had chance to finish. He thought it best not to complain and, instead, gulped down his cod liver oil.

An urgent knock on the door stopped them in their tracks.

'Oh dear,' said Lucienne. 'Not again.'

'I'll get it,' said Pierre. Taking a deep breath, he opened the door. He barely had time to register, when the lieutenant barged into the living room. This time, at least, he was alone. 'Where's your father?' he snapped.

'I – I don't k-know.'

Lucienne came in from the kitchen, gripping a tea towel. 'We – we both don't know.'

The lieutenant eyed them both, his eyes narrowing. With quick strides, he marched into the kitchen, the bedrooms, the yard. Moments later, he was back. 'Where is your father?' he repeated, screaming.

'We really don't know, Lieutenant,' said Lucienne, her nervousness dripping from her voice.

'He's not reported in. He has kidnapped Major Hurtzberger. We will find him. He will be shot for this.'

'He hasn't kidnapped the major,' said Pierre quickly. 'He wouldn't–'

The slap took Pierre by surprise. Lucienne screamed. Falling back, he was more shocked than hurt.

'We will find him, we will hurt him, then we will shoot him dead. *Sie verstehen?* You understand?'

Both of them nodded, too fearful to say anything more. The lieutenant clicked his heels and left as abruptly as he'd appeared.

'Pierre, are you OK, my love? Does it hurt?'

Yes, he thought, it bloody did hurt. 'No, not at all. I'm fine, Maman.'

They sat in the living room, neither able to talk. Every now and then Lucienne would mutter an 'oh dear, oh dear.' He had to find his father before the Germans did, thought Pierre; that much was obvious. But where? Where could he have gone?

A distant voice seized their attention. Both of them cocked their heads.

'What is that?' whispered Lucienne.

'I don't know. Wait…' He went to the living room window pushing aside the net curtain. The sun shone weakly, failing to melt away the clouds drifting across the sky. Straining his neck, he saw, coming slowly up the road, a German motorbike and sidecar mounted with a machine gun. The driver looked slightly ridiculous – wearing goggles despite driving at walking pace. His companion, in the sidecar, was standing up, shouting through a loudhailer. People passing in the street had stopped to listen. Lucienne joined Pierre at the window.

'What's he saying?'

'…At twelve o'clock. Attention, attention! By orders of the Ortskommandantur, all citizens without exception are ordered to congregate in the town square at twelve o'clock. Twelve o'clock. Any citizen not accounted for will face harsh penalties. Attention, attention! By orders of the Ortskommandantur, all citizens…'

'Oh dear,' said Lucienne. 'I don't like the sound of this.'

'It must be something about the disappearance of the major.'

'And your father.'

'Maybe about Kafka too.'

Lucienne sat at the kitchen table, pulling at a thread in her tea towel. 'Oh dear, oh dear; I don't like this one bit.'

It was nine o'clock. Pierre wondered whether he had time to hunt out Kafka's hut and make it back in time. No, he decided; it'd be too risky; he could easily get lost. He would simply have to postpone it until the afternoon.

*

273

At five minutes to twelve, Xavier appeared. 'Hello Madame Durand. Hi Pierre. Do you mind if I join you?'

'Don't you want to go with your parents, Xavier?' asked Lucienne.

'They've gone ahead. They wanted a seat at the front.'

'That's brave of them,' said Pierre.

'Are they providing seats?' asked Lucienne.

'Huh, that's what I said.'

'We'd better go,' said Pierre. 'See what they've got cooking now.'

They joined a procession of villagers making their way to the town square. People raised eyebrows at each other in the form of acknowledgement but no one spoke. Everyone could sense the anxiety in the air. Shops were closed for the hour. As they turned the corner coming into the square, Xavier nudged Pierre in the arm. 'Look,' he said, pointing. There, on a tree, were two posters. Both posters bore the word, printed large, "Missing". The top one had two pictures – of the SS man, Oskar Spitzweg, and Major Hurtzberger; the second had the names of Pierre's father and Kafka – Albert Foucault. Beneath the names, also in large writing, was an offer of an unspecified reward. Peering closer, both posters warned of severe penalties to anyone withholding information or harbouring the four men. Every tree, Pierre noticed, every shop front, every lamp post, had these posters.

People had already gathered, milling round the square but no one pushed. Mothers held onto the hands of their children. A few chairs were provided for the elderly, including Albert and Hector, the cemetery boys. German soldiers lined the perimeter. At the front, Pierre spotted the mayor and the staff from the town hall. This time there was no stage, no decking, no microphone. He spotted Claire, looking gorgeous in her polka dot red dress, speaking to a couple of friends. The town hall clock chimed twelve. As the last peal faded away, Colonel Eisler, flanked by two privates, appeared from the town hall. A hush descended on the crowd. The colonel scanned the audience, his expression hard and resolute, emotionless. Lucienne reached for Pierre's hand. As subtly as he could, Pierre ignored it.

One of the privates handed the colonel a loudhailer. 'Monsieurs, mesdames.' He held in his other hand a sheet of paper. Behind him, standing to attention, were another group of soldiers, their steely expressions fixed on the villagers in front of them. 'I do not intend to keep you long. You will have seen the posters concerning the sudden disappearance of two of our men and two of yours. I am deeply concerned for the welfare of my men. I believe their vanishing is no coincidence. I also have reason to believe that these bandits, Foucault and Durand, are responsible for the disappearance of Major Hurtzberger and Lieutenant Spitzweg.' Pierre winced at hearing his father being described as a bandit. 'If my men are indeed being kept against their will, the consequences for their captors, and for you, will be severe. I will not tolerate such actions. If you have any information or suspicions, you must inform the town hall staff straightaway. Your information will be treated with the utmost confidentiality. If the provided information bears fruit in any way, you will be heartily compensated. You have until midday tomorrow. If our men are not located by this time tomorrow, there will be consequences.' He paused. Not a sound. 'I would like to call on the following citizens to step forward.' Putting on his glasses, he unfolded his sheet of paper. He read out the names of six villagers, three men, including Monsieurs Picard and Gide, and three women. The last name was that of Claire. What was this, thought Pierre? Why Claire; what did they want with her? The six of them shuffled forward and made their way to the front, Claire glanced behind, anxiety etched all over her face. On making themselves known, two German privates herded them together, pushing Monsieur Gide, the baker, roughly in the back. Gide put his hands up.

The colonel removed his glasses. 'Unless we can account for all these missing men within the next twenty-four hours, these six citizens will be shot.'

A shocked gasp passed through the crowd. Madame Picard screamed her husband's name. Another fainted and had to be caught. Someone behind Pierre muttered, beasts. Resting the loudhailer against his side, the colonel turned to the hostages. 'You,' he said, pointing at Claire. 'Come here.' His voice was still audible.

Pierre held his breath. Cautiously, Claire approached the colonel, her eyes downcast. Even from here, thought Pierre, one could she was trembling.

'I need a seventh person. Choose someone.'

She looked up at him, her mouth open, shocked. Slowly, as if death had already half claimed her, she turned and gazed at the crowd. Instinctively, it drew back, frightened of her. Colonel Eisler had transformed her into the Grim Reaper. She had come amongst them to dispense death. So many people, but not a single sound save for the gentle mewling of a baby in its mother's arms. Many were shaking their heads, beseeching Claire not to choose them. And Pierre was one of them. If you choose me, he thought, we're as good as dead; I'm the only one capable of finding them. Claire stepped into the crowd splitting it into two as people backed away, like Moses and the waves. She cast her eyes left and right; her skin ghostly white, as if she was looking for someone specifically. His stomach caved in as the realisation hit in – she was looking for him. If he begged her she would only see it as cowardice and he would be damned in her memory for eternity – she wouldn't realise. He had to remain free to save her, to save them all. Xavier glimpsed at him, his eyes filled with terror; a look reflected everywhere. And still she came, closer and closer. People were crying while shuffling away. Mothers hid their children; some of the men stepped in front of their wives, while most did not. Monsieur Bonnet, Pierre noticed, furtively stepped behind his wife. Claire ignored them all, looking for Pierre. And she found him.

'No, not Pierre,' said Lucienne, pressing herself into him, trying to ward death off.

She stood so close to him, he could smell her breath. Her eyes were dry, it was almost as if her brain had stopped functioning, as if her soul had already departed her physical presence. 'Help me,' she whispered. 'Tell me… Tell me what to do.'

Aware of every pair of eyes fixed on him, he whispered back, trying not to move his lips, 'I don't know but I can save you. Give me time, I'll save you.'

It registered. Her eyes widened a fraction. She stepped away. Pierre felt his knees give way. Three paces on, she lifted her hand and pointed a finger.

'Nooo,' screamed Monsieur Clément, shattering the unearthly silence. 'No, I don't deserve to die.'

'I'm sorry,' said Claire quietly.

'You chose him,' shouted Madame Clément, pointing at Pierre. He felt the eyes of everyone bore into him. They knew she was right; he felt their raw hatred. Lucienne took his hand. He gripped it. 'You chose him. I saw him – he asked you not to.' She began crying while her husband, next to her, started shaking. 'You – you can't do that,' she spluttered between sobs.

Two German privates approached, their boots resounding on the stones.

'No, please, I beg you,' said Clément, his knees buckling beneath him. 'I beg you, Claire. There must be someone else. Please, I thought we got on.' Claire took a step back, her work done. Clément knew it. 'You bitch, you fucking bitch.'

'You can't take him,' yelled Madame Clément at the soldiers as they almost picked her husband up by the elbows. 'This is not fair; it's not fair.' She began thumping the back of one of the soldiers as they dragged her husband, still cursing Claire, through the crowd. 'It should be him, that boy,' cried Madame Clément. 'That boy. Please.'

The soldier spun round and, without warning, punched her. Her body jerked back as if the life had snapped out of her. 'Chrissy,' yelled her husband. 'Chrissy…' His voice deteriorated into sobs. He tried to wrestle his arms free but stood no chance against the bulky Germans. Madame Clément lay in a heap on the ground, not moving. Those nearest to her seemed too frightened to help her, as if she was the carrier of a disease.

The soldiers deposited Monsieur Clément at Colonel Eisler's side, where he fell, and took their places a few yards behind. Without being told to, Claire obediently followed them, her head bowed, and took up her place beside her fellow hostages. The crowd re-converged, a mixture of terror and relief sweeping through it.

'Get up,' shouted the colonel. If Clément heard through his sobs, fear had stripped him of the ability to move. The colonel unclipped his holster. 'Get up,' he repeated, brandishing his Luger in his right hand.

This time, Monsieur Clément heard. Looking up, he saw the revolver pointing down at him. With great effort, he clambered onto his knees and up.

The colonel clicked his fingers. A soldier passed him back the loudhailer. Holding it in his left hand, he switched it on. 'I need these missing men here at precisely twelve o'clock tomorrow in this very place, otherwise these six men and women will be shot.' Monsieur Clément's weeping had been amplified by his close proximity to the loudhailer, sniffling in the background as the colonel spoke. 'All citizens will be required to attend the executions.'

Why had he said six? thought Pierre. There were seven hostages now.

'Be warned,' said the colonel. 'We are not playing games here.' Then, sweeping his right arm straight, he fired his Luger. The sound of the shot rebounded throughout the square. People screamed. Like a collapsing puppet, Monsieur Clément fell at the colonel's feet, dead, a crimson hole in his forehead.

Colonel Eisler cast his eyes over his audience. 'I hope I have made myself understood.' And with that, he handed the loudhailer back to his attendant, and returned to the town hall, the mayor in his wake. Monsieur Clément lay on the ground, his dead eyes open, a pool of blood forming beneath his head.

'Claire… Claire,' muttered Pierre. He watched, open-mouthed, as, together with the others, she was led away, German soldiers surrounding them.

He wanted to rush over, to save her now. He felt Xavier's hand on his shoulder but there was nothing he could say.

Nearby, Monsieur Gide's wife began crying. 'This is not fair,' she screamed. Her companions tried to calm her. 'Bertrand! Why pick on my Bertrand?'

'This is too awful,' said Lucienne, her face etched with anxiety. 'What can we do?'

'Hope something happens,' said Xavier. 'Something will turn up,' he said to Pierre.

'You think so?'

'Well…'

Someone pushed towards them – Madame Picard. 'Did you see that?' she shouted at Lucienne, her hand pointing at the Germans behind her. 'They took my Gerard. This is your husband's fault, isn't it?'

'No.'

Her son, a man in his late twenties, as wide as he was tall, tried to pull her back. 'Where is he?' hissed Madame Picard. 'Where is he, you bitch? Him and that stupid friend of his.'

Pierre could tell his mother was on the verge of tears. 'Madame Picard,' he said, stepping forward. 'This won't help–'

'Proud of your father, are you? Well, let me tell you,' she said, turning to Lucienne, 'if they murder my Gerard, I won't rest until I find your husband and rip him to pieces.' She spat at Lucienne, catching her fully on the cheek.

Taking her brusquely by her arm, Madame Picard's son yanked her away. Delivering her into the arms of another, he turned back. Squaring up to Pierre, he growled, 'She's right. Your father's as good as dead.' Pierre watched as he disappeared, with his mother, into the crowd. He realised he was shaking.

Lucienne, also trembling, searched her pockets for a handkerchief. Xavier offered her his. She took it without thanks. 'Pierre, take me home please.'

Chapter 21

Back at home Lucienne took to her bed. She had a headache, she'd said. Pierre, on the other hand, knew he had to find his father. The Germans were assuming Georges was in cahoots with Kafka; that, between them, they had somehow kidnapped the major and Lieutenant Spitzweg. It was vital he found Kafka's woodland hut as soon as possible. He decided against leaving his mother a note. Taking his bicycle, he'd cycled through the town, past the shops and through the town square. The crowds had melted away, gone home, like his mother, to lie down, to hope, to pray. Soldier Mike's plinth remained in place, fragments of bronze scattered around its base. The cafés had reopened. There were no locals, only Germans, filling every outdoor table, playing cards or dominoes, laughing. It was as if nothing had changed.

He visualised Claire's face as she was led away, her eyes wide with fright. The thought made him speed up. It was down to him, and him only. To save them all. He had to find that hut. But why? They wouldn't be there. He remembered Major Hauff, at the Gestapo headquarters in

Saint-Romain, saying that Monsieur Dubois was leading the major and a couple of privates to Kafka's hideout. Dubois would be dead by now, that was for sure, executed by a German firing squad. He thought of his father's mock execution. He tried to remember everything his father had said about Kafka: *The monster who lives in our midst. Kafka is a murderer and I, by my complicity, am no better.* He thought about Kafka and the rabbit, hacking off one foot at a time. Was it possible that Kafka had taken Major Hurtzberger as a hostage? But why would he do that? To what end? Did he really think he could outwit the might and ruthlessness of the Germans? *The war unhinged him,* his father had said. So much to remember. Yet, he pressed on, pedalling hard, knowing that he had to do something; that doing nothing would be unbearable.

He'd come out of the town now, and had begun cycling up the hill, on the other side of which was where Oskar Spitzweg had knocked him off his bike. *I know his hideaways.* He braked abruptly to a halt, almost falling off. Letting out a cry, he could hear his father saying it: *I know his hideaways.* He'd said hideaways in the plural; that must mean he had more than one.

His breath came in short bursts, but whether from cycling hard or the realisation, he didn't know. *Hideaways.* The lake. He'd heard it some point, a lake hideaway. Yes, it was that first day, when the whole town, like today, had gathered to 'welcome' their invaders. Kafka had been hit to the ground by Fritz One when the major had stepped in. Afterwards, as they wound their way home, his father had mentioned it – *Take a few days off, Kafka. Go to your island on the lake, have a rest.* An island on the lake. Good God, yes; that was it. But no, he couldn't go there; he couldn't face seeing the lake. He'd never been back; not since that day, had sworn he would never go back. He didn't even know where it was; he'd blanked it out. He knew that it was kilometres away, a good ten, twelve kilometres. He could hardly breathe. The thought of it was too much to bear. All that water; that deep, dark water. Yet, he knew he had no choice; he had to face it; he had to go. There was a map back at home, on the bookshelf in the living room.

*

He laid the map out on the kitchen table. His mother was still in bed, fast asleep. Yes, there it was – the lake. Too small to have a name but still, large enough to be quite clear on the map. There was no sign of Kafka's island but, thought Pierre, it was probably too tiny to show. Taking a piece of string he found in a table drawer, he measured the distance as the crow flies – six kilometres. Half on the road, half through the woods. With all the bends and curves in the road and through the forest, it was likely to be twice that distance. It'd take, what, two hours?

He never thought he would have to return to the lake. Not wanting to, he cast his mind back six years, entering a dark place he'd spent his whole youth trying to blot out. He realised he could remember every last detail of it. He walked over to the photograph of the young boy in the flat cap. Taking it off the wall, he sat back down. Rubbing the dust off with his sleeve, he ran his finger across the glass. He'd never done this before, had never wanted to look at him. The boy was smiling, acting up for the camera. He looked so happy, so full of cheekiness, yet Pierre saw his vulnerability. 'I'm sorry, Michel. I'm sorry.'

* * *

I remember every last moment of that day. I wish I could forget the details, but no, they are part of me, ingrained. I tell myself we had a nice day that day. But we hadn't. Not from the moment Papa called us over from the house and asked whether we wanted to go fishing with him. He often went out fishing but always on his own. He'd never asked us before, so I suppose we felt it was a special treat.

The day started off well. I remember. Like I said, I remember every last moment. Michel and I are playing in the field behind the house. On the other side of the field, the edge of the woods, a dark, forbidden place Michel is frightened of. He is only six, after all. I'm not afraid – but then, I am ten. Double figures. It's about nine on a chilly February morning. The grass is wet; the whole world smells damp. The clouds move quickly in the wind. I have an idea. I fetch a kite from the house, a kite as purple as the foxgloves that grow in the hedgerows nearby. Michel is desperate to have a go by himself, but, I tell him, it's easier when there are two of you. Papa says it's a good kite-flying day – a 'medium wind', he calls it, enough of a wind but not too much. Michel, in his funny shorts that fall below the knees and the clunky shoes he always insists on wearing, whatever the weather, runs around in circles, his arms outstretched, pretending to be an aeroplane. He's skinny, my brother, dark hair, almost black, like mine, but a little longer, curls at the front. Maman says it's a cowlick which always makes him laugh. *Aeroplanes don't sound like that*, I tell him.

How do you know?

Come on, do you want to hold the kite?

He leaps over, his cardigan flapping. *Here*, I say to him, *hold the kite while I unroll the string.*

With my back to the wind, I tell him to walk with the kite. After about twenty metres I shout stop.

Right, throw the kite.

Now?

Yes, now, go on.

He throws it up. Quickly, I pull on the string, hoping the tension will help it launch. It doesn't. It falls.

Michel stamps his feet. *That's rubbish*, he shouts.

We'll try again.

After twenty minutes or more, Michel and I have had little joy with the kite. Once, we managed to get it air bound. Michel leapt with excitement, clapped his hands. The next moment it plummeted faster than a stick thrown from a bridge. It is a relief when we spy Papa at the yard gate, waving at us. We run over. Michel, with his heavy shoes, falls over in the long grass. He doesn't hurt himself. Pity.

You boys want to come fishing with me today?

Oo, yes please, we both reply.

If only we had said no.

*

Papa takes us in the car. We have everything we need – the rods, a tin with an extra line and hooks, the bobbers and sinkers, a horrible box of worms, our coats, boots, gloves and rain hats, and, most importantly, a packed lunch each. Maman had packed it all, a haversack for Papa and a smaller satchel each

286

for Michel and me. But I was cross. I had wanted to sit in the front and, as I'm the oldest, felt it was only right. Michel put on his trembling lip act and Papa fell for it, as always, and allowed him to sit in the front, while I sat crossly in the back, arms folded. We hardly ever get to go in the car. Maman doesn't drive because ladies don't, and Papa only uses it for work and things. But he loves his car, as we all do – it's a 1928 Daimler, C class, he says. He inherited it from my Uncle Jacques, the tightrope walker, who was killed by a car. I don't remember him.

It's a fair walk, though, boys.

But we're driving there, says Michel.

Papa laughs. *No, I mean from where I park the car.*

It's not through the woods, is it?

Yes but don't worry, my little cabbage. I'll look after you. Papa slaps Michel's knee.

Oo, I say from the back. *Think of those dark woods, Michel, anything could be–*

Stop it, Pierre. Leave your brother be.

After a few minutes, Papa takes a turning off the main road, and down a smaller one and finally comes to a stop. *Here we are,* he says, rubbing his hands excitedly. *Let the day begin.*

Papa, it's raining.

Come now, Michel, you're not going to allow a little rain get between us and our lovely fish.

And it's cold.

Leaning forward from the back, I make a suggestion. *We could wait in the car until it stops.*

Not you as well. Nope, come on, the rain's good for you, and you'll soon warm up.

287

And so, reluctantly, we leave the warmth of the car, both my brother and I regretting our earlier show of enthusiasm.

We follow my father through the woods. Michel is trying not to show that he's frightened. At first, I laugh at him, jeering him. But now I feel sorry for him. *You can take my hand if you want,* I say, offering it to him.

Thank you, he says in a little, quiet voice. He takes my gloved hand.

Papa races ahead. *Papa, wait for us; we can't keep up.*

He stops, waits for us. *Come on, boys,* he says. *By the time we get there, the fish will have gone to bed.*

Do fish have beds? asks Michel.

Of course.

How much further, Papa?

Oh, not so far now.

I can tell he is lying. We carry on. I can also tell Papa is regretting bringing us.

Who's got the worms? asks Michel.

Papa.

Good.

Do you want me to take your bag?

Yes, please.

We walk in silence for a while getting further and further behind again. Eventually, Papa stops and waits for us. *For goodness sake, Michel, pick up your feet. You can walk faster than this; a girl could walk faster than this.* He stomps ahead.

You OK, Mickey?

He looks up at me and smiles. He likes it when I call him Mickey, like Mickey Mouse. It cheers him up for a few moments.

Papa, I shout. *Are we lost?*

No, I've done this hundreds of times. We're almost there now.

Almost there, I repeat for Michel's sake.

I want to go home.

I know. So do I.

* * *

Pierre placed his elbows on the table and rubbed his eyes. For so long now, he'd managed to file away the memory in a locked compartment in his brain labelled 'Do not open'. But now, like Pandora's Box, the lid had opened and it all came flooding back in all its dreadful, sickening detail. But he had to close it again, had to think of the present, of how to save his father – from Kafka, from the Germans. He remembered more of his father's words: *I believe God looks over us, takes note of our actions and our inactions.* Yes, thought Pierre, God will look over me; He'll look after me.

*

This time, Pierre decided to take some provisions – the map, a bottle of water, a hunk of cheese and an apple. And this time, he did leave a note for his mother: *Just popping out. Back soon.* He heard her stir; she was waking up. Quickly, he slipped out of the house, quietly closing the front door behind him. He didn't want to see her.

Ten minutes later, cycling hard, he'd reached the top of the hill, outside the town. He stopped and looked back on it. How peaceful it looked from up here, just a normal, rather quaint French town with its comings and goings. People lived here all their lives. He hoped he wouldn't be one of them; there had to be more to life. For them, a trip to Saint-Romain constituted the height of cosmopolitanism. He'd heard someone say that, now, without cars, the kilometre had returned to what it had been in the nineteenth century – a fair distance. How lovely it would be, he thought, to escape this place, to stroll through the streets of Paris, hand in hand with Claire; to sunbathe together on the beaches in the south. He had to tear himself away from his daydreams. A part of him felt as if he was saying goodbye to his town, goodbye to his life as he had known it; something told him he would return a changed person.

Remounting, he pushed on. It was two o'clock. Twenty-two hours left. A while later, he took a left fork, onto a smaller road, no more, really, than a dirt track, uneven and potholed. The sun was strong now, his shadow on the track in front of him. On the bend, up ahead, he spied a vehicle. He slowed down. It was parked up on the verge. Approaching it, he realised he recognised it – it was the truck used by the cemetery boys. He peered inside – nothing untoward, nothing to give an indication why it was here, seemingly abandoned. He tried the door handle. Unlocked. The keys had gone. The glove compartment contained various bits of paper and rubbish. Had the cemetery boys given the major a lift to this point? But then, why hadn't they taken it back to town? Why leave it here, abandoned? He'd seen them, two hours earlier, in the town square. Its presence here meant something. The back of the truck was empty save for a tarpaulin, a couple of spades and a plank of wood. He took a sip of water. It was time to move on.

* * *

And here we are! bellows Papa from far ahead. *We've made it; plant the flag.*

Why do we have to plant a flag? Michel asks me.

It's just Papa being funny.

Oh.

Yes, we've come to a lake. I thought we were getting close, by the way the trees were thinning out. We catch Papa up standing on a stretch of sand, gazing across the water. Now, out from the trees, the rain comes down harder.

It's lovely, don't you think?

No, says Michel.

What's the matter with you two? I always used to go out fishing with my old man. Loved it.

Is this a beach? I ask.

Looks like it, doesn't it? We could come back with your mother during summer and sunbathe. She'd like that. Come on, we can't fish from here. We need to get to a bank just over there, he says, pointing vaguely to his left.

Not more walking, says Michel.

It's not far. Just a bit further.

That's what he said last time, I say quietly to Michel.

And the time before that.

I heard that, says Papa.

We seem to go be going back into the woods. But now, we re-emerge next to the lake a bit further on. There's a wall, like a harbour wall. Grey stones. It's not long, perhaps twenty metres or so, and wide.

This is it, boys! says Papa, swinging off his haversack.

I peer over the edge. There are bunches of reeds. The water comes up high. It looks deep and dark. I don't like it. Michel joins me. *Get back, Mickey, it's dangerous.* He does as he's told.

Right, let's get started, says Papa.

Can't we have lunch first? asks Michel.

Papa spins around in a way that makes us step back. *Look, you little nincompoops, stop complaining. I've had enough, got it? One more moan and I'll throw you in the lake.*

He is angry now. He unties the top of his haversack and throws out everything from inside, muttering things Michel and I can't hear but don't like. Michel's chin disappears into his collar.

Papa calms down a bit and gets everything ready – the rods and lines and the rest of it. We empty our satchels too and put our lunchboxes to one side.

You've brought Munchie?

Hmm.

Munchie is Michel's old teddy. He wears a yellow waistcoat and green trousers. Michel likes to take it on expeditions. *Why did you do that? He's all scrunched up now.*

He shrugs his shoulders. *I don't know.*

Let's put him back in your bag. He'll keep dry there.

It's strange, I think; most of the time Michel gets on my nerves and I get annoyed that I have to play with him so much. It's not playing; it's looking after. But out here, with this horrible lake, and the dark skies and the rain, and that scary wood, he looks so small. I feel sorry for him.

*

We sit with Papa for ages, our feet dangling over the wall, the wind blowing round our heads, the rain in a steady drizzle. Papa casts the line and lets us have go at holding the rod. He tries explaining things to us, like how much worm we should use, how to attach the sinkers and things, but it's too complicated for Michel and I am too cold to concentrate. We've had our lunches; ham sandwiches and cheese, so we don't even have that to look forward to any more.

We've been here, sitting on this wall, for a while now, and my bottom is starting to get cold. I'm too frightened to ask if we could get up and move around. I hope Michel will ask – being younger he'll be more likely to get away with it.

Michel sits there stirring the worms round with a stick. Papa won't like that, I think, but Papa hasn't noticed it yet.

Oh, I think we've got something.

We sit up, peering across the lake, trying to find where the line meets the water. I can't see it.

Papa, Papa, squeaks Michel. *Can I hold the line; can I hold it? Please.*

Papa hesitates. I know what he's thinking – he wants to encourage him but knows if he does, we will certainly lose the fish, I mean, the catch. *We'll hold it together. There, put your hands over mine. That's it. Now, all we have to do is... Wait a minute. Oh, no, I don't believe it. Shit. We've lost it.*

Papa.

Yes, Michel? he snaps.

You said...

Yes, I'm sorry. I shouldn't use words like that.

Thank you, Michel. Look, why don't you two go and have a wander. See if you can find any wolves.

Wolves? cries Michel.

He's joking, I say.

Are there wolves in the woods?

I'm on my feet. What a relief. *No, there are no wolves around here. It's too cold for them.* Actually, I have no idea if that's true. Maybe they like cold weather but it sounds good and Michel believes me.

I don't want to go into the woods without Papa.

Don't be silly. Come on, we might find a unicorn, and unicorns are nice. I head the opposite way from the one we came.

Unicorns don't exist, silly.

Go on, Michel, says Papa. *Follow Pierre. He'll look after you and by the time you get back, I'll have caught a fish so big it could be a whale.*

He's joking again, isn't he?

Yes, Papa's always joking.

Don't go too far, boys.

Come on then, Mickey Mouse; let's find ourselves a unicorn.

He could give us a ride.

Good idea. Where would you like to go?

He thinks about this for a while. *The moon,* he says.

Yeah, the moon. That's a good idea.

* * *

The road petered out and soon came to an end at a hedge and a gate. Beyond it, the woods lay ahead. Pierre dismounted and left the bike against the hedge. How daunting the woods looked, the hider of so many secrets.

He followed a path, either side of which lay a carpet of bright purple woodland flowers. He followed the path into the forest where, to begin with, the trees were few and far between. A couple of dragonflies whizzed by. The woods soon became denser, more foreboding. But at least it was cooler.

He followed the path until it split into two. Consulting the map, he decided to take the right fork, heading due north. It was only now, now that he began to feel confident that he would find the lake, that he realised he had no idea what to expect and no idea what to do once he got there. Surely, with Claire and the others due to be shot, Kafka would listen to reason. But part of him knew that Kafka was probably beyond reason.

After a further twenty minutes of walking, Pierre came across another fork in the path. This one, however, he recognised – the tree with the engraved initials, 'RJ', next to the fallen tree blocking the pathway. The map showed that he should continue north but he knew if he took a brief detour on the left fork, heading northwest, he would soon come across Kafka's hut. The temptation was too much. Having taken another swig of water, he followed the path that he knew would end at the hut.

It was a steep descent. The sudden appearance of a magpie made him jump. Looking ahead, he saw a dark plume of smoke drifting up into the air. This, he thought, was not a good sign. Picking up pace, he strode forward, his chest fizzing with anticipation. Approaching the clearing, he heard voices. German voices. He stopped, wondered whether to continue. The sensible part of his brain told him to walk away, that he would gain nothing by venturing forward. But he did. He crept forward, his eyes and ears fully alert for danger. Creeping closer, he came across a scene of devastation. He saw that Kafka's hut had been set on fire, the wood audibly crackling as the flames did their work. On the patch of ground in front, where Pierre had done his target practice, a number of German soldiers, wielding spades, were digging. Nearby, lay two German corpses plus another. With a jolt, Pierre recognised the corduroy jacket, now heavily stained with dried blood, with its leather collar, the spectacles glinting in the sun – it was Monsieur Dubois, still wearing his blue beret. From their uniforms, it was obvious that the German dead were privates. Pierre looked round, hoping to see the major. But no, the most senior man here was a corporal. The men under his charge were digging graves while he, the corporal, kept an eye on the fire, smoking a cigarette. The diggers, stripped to the waist, did their work in fine spirits, flicking clods of mud at each other. How could they be so light-hearted in such a grim scene? Gravediggers from hell. The corporal flicked his cigarette into the fire and turned, his eyes scanning the woods. Pierre ducked behind a tree. Surely, he was too far away to be seen. Inching his head from behind the trunk, he saw the corporal urging his men to hurry. Pierre had seen enough; it was time to go.

He made it back up the hill, glancing back frequently, making sure he wasn't being followed. He made it to the fork with the fallen tree, his mind whirling as he tried to imagine what had happened there. Did Kafka shoot them all? He had, after all, served in the war as a sniper. But surely, Kafka wouldn't have shot Dubois? And what happened to the major? Had his father been there? A dreadful thought struck him. Once the corporal had reported back to the colonel, then Claire's situation, perilous enough already, would be made worse. He had to find that lake.

He headed north for another twenty minutes, then, following the map, veered east. Tired, his calf muscles aching, he stopped for a rest and ate his cheese. The apple, he decided, would be best kept for later. His water was already half gone. As he swung his bag over his shoulder, he spied a kingfisher swooping low at great speed. He thought of his mother's brooch. With a lurch, he realised that meant only one thing – the lake was nearby. Eagerly, despite the surging apprehension, he pushed on. And yes, the trees thinned out and behind them lay the lake. He halted, allowing his bag to slide off his shoulder. So this was it, the lake. Slowly, he stepped forward, mesmerized, dragging his bag by its strap. He reached a stretch of sand, a small beach. How blue the water; the gentle ripples, the sun reflecting on its surface, the freshness of the air, the utter quiet of it all, a silence broken only by the sounds of the woods – insects humming, birds singing. This was it; this was the lake he remembered; the place that had haunted him through the years. Yet, there was no island. He could see the far side; the lake was not that big. He let go of the strap. But it could not be Kafka's lake. Consulting his map again, there were no other lakes in the vicinity, this was the only one. Unfolding the map, there was another, much bigger lake, much further north; some fifty kilometres or more. No, this had to be it.

He so wished now he'd brought his father's binoculars. He could see them hanging up on the back of the living room door. He wondered whether his mother had seen his note. She'd be beside herself by now. So be it, he thought;

he had a job to do and he wasn't turning back now.

* * *

If Michel and I had hoped to be cheered up by wandering through the woods, we were soon disappointed. Still, we carry on, picking our way along a little zigzag path. At least it's stopped raining now but we still get caught by big raindrops falling off the leaves. *I spy with my little eye something beginning with 't'.*

Tree.

Yes. Well, that's that game done with.

That was too easy.

I know.

He picks up a stick and smacks it against the trunk of a tree, bringing down a little shower of rain. He squeals and throws away his stick. *I wish we were still playing with our kite. We could have it flying by now. Can we try again later?*

Maybe tomorrow, eh? Hopefully it won't be raining. Listen, if tomorrow Papa says "would you boys like to go fishing?", what do we say?

He giggles at my impersonation of Papa's voice. *We say no!*

No! Never again.

We laugh together. *Have you remembered to bring Munchie?*

Yes, he's in my bag. Where's your satchel?

I left it with Papa. Have you got any lunch left?

No, I ate it all.

Yes, so did I. Oh, look, Mickey, another place for fishing. Maybe Papa would have better luck here. It's almost the same – a stone wall, more like a platform really. This one's smaller, lots of puddles on it. To one side, hanging from a branch just beyond the platform, I see something red. *Look, Michel, what's that?*

We run over. It's a scarf; a child's scarf, all wet.

What's it doing here?

I don't know. Maybe some kid dropped it. Someone's tied it round the branch in case they ever come back, I guess.

We leave it where it is and return to the wall. Creeping up to the edge, I look to the right to see if I can see Papa. I can. I wave but he doesn't see me.

Who are you waving at?

Look, it's Papa.

Considering we'd only left him four or five minutes ago, Michel is excited to see him from here. He calls out but Papa doesn't hear.

He's probably singing to himself, I say.

I wish we could catch a fish for him.

I laugh. *Yes, that would surprise him. I don't know whether they swim up so close to the wall. Step back, Michel.* I yank him back, perhaps a little too hard because he looks shocked, upset even. *Sorry, Mickey, but you had me worried there. Not so close, OK? You could slip.*

I won't slip.

Still. Don't go so near.

A thought occurs to me. *Stay here a minute,* I tell him. If it's a kid's scarf, it might have a nametape stitched into it. I wander over to have a look. And that's what I'm doing when my life changes forever – twisting a wet scarf round in my hands, looking for a nametape.

There was no sound from him. Just a mighty

splash. I know at once, I can feel it as if someone's punched me in the stomach. I run across faster than I've ever run before. I can hear him screaming my name. I stop at the edge and see him in the lake; his arms thumping the water, making huge waves, his satchel round his neck. *Mickey, no.* Quickly, I lie on my front and reach my arm out, stretching out my fingers. It's too far, just too far. He's fighting the water, choking. The water – it's like a beast, an evil thing and I'm frightened of it.

On my feet again, I look round, desperate to find something to throw to him. There is nothing, nothing at all. My satchel? No, I haven't got it. I think about running back into the woods to find a long stick but that'll take too long. I know he can't swim but then – neither can I. He screams my name, screams help again and again. I feel sick. *Hold on, Mickey, hold on,* I shout. I scream for Papa louder than I've ever shouted before, jumping up and down, waving both my arms. This time he hears. We waves at me, grinning, holding up a fish he's caught. But then he realises something's wrong. He stands up slowly, looking over at me. He looks worried. Then, suddenly, he throws down the fish and his fishing rod and runs into the woods. *Michel, Michel, Papa's coming. Try to swim, try to...* But there's no answer; why doesn't he answer me? His arms are still flapping, his body bobbing up and down; he's gagging. Why did he have to wear those heavy shoes?

The scarf; I remember the scarf. I run over to the branch and untie it.

Mickey, take this, I scream. But I can't see him any more. Still, I throw the scarf into the water. It flops just a metre or so out; it's useless.

Michel, just swim, can't you? I'm crying; I don't know what to do. Oh, God, please help me.

I pull off my coat, struggling to get my arms out, and then my shoes, yanking them off. Michel's head comes out again; he tries to scream but there's too much water spewing from his mouth. I have to do this, I have to try and save him; even if it means I drown, I have to do this.

I stand on the precipice of the wall, willing myself to jump. Michel is gurgling, choking. He disappears again, the water claiming him. I can't do it; I'm too frightened. The nausea rises up my throat. He's drowning, I know this for sure; my brother is drowning, and there's nothing I can do. I don't know what that noise is. I look for Papa. Where is he? Please let him come. That noise – it's me; I'm crying; no, more than that; I'm wailing.

Michel, screams Papa, breathlessly arriving next to me, terror written all over his face.

He's there, I yell, pointing vaguely to where I last saw Michel just a few moments before.

He looks at me a second, shooting me a look I don't understand, throws off his coat, before jumping into the water with a huge splash. He swims out, his arms thrashing through that water, but I know it's already too late. Papa swims round frantically in circles. *I can't see him, I can't see him,* I hear him shout.

I can't stand up any more; I feel faint. *Find him, Papa; please find him.*

He does! He's got him. He's pulling him back. One arm round Michel's neck; the other splashing through the water. I pace up and down the wall, crying, begging God to let him be alive.

Help me, Pierre, Papa shouts up at me as he approaches the wall. I lean down but I don't know what he wants me to do. Papa pushes Michel up. I grab him from under the armpits but I can't move him; he's too heavy for me. Papa climbs out of the water, then, pushing me off, pulls Michel up. He lays him on his back. Michel looks like a ghost, his face horribly white, his lips blue. Papa pinches open his mouth and breathes into him. He thumps him on his chest. He repeats it over and over again.

I don't know what do with myself. I grab fistfuls of my hair. And still Papa carries on, sobbing, getting more frantic. Michel doesn't move. I will his chest to go up and down but nothing moves.

Michel, Michel, screams Papa so loud I think the forest will fall round our ears. *Michel, my son, my son...*

He staggers to his feet, his knees bent like an old man in a nursery rhyme. Next to him, like a rag doll, Michel lies still, utterly, utterly still.

Why didn't you save him? Papa cries. *Why couldn't you have...* His words trail off into great, giant sobs.

I tried, I weep. But Papa, collapsed next to Mickey, doesn't hear me. *I tried.*

I see something yellow and green nearby. It's Munchie. I pick him up and hug him as tightly as I can while, all around me, darkness descends.

Chapter 22

'I'm sorry, Michel; I'm sorry.' Retrieving his bag, now covered in dry dust, Pierre walked along the sand. It soon came to an end, and he was faced with a bank teaming with vegetation. Pulling himself up by a root, he realised what a task laid ahead of him. Each step now involved concentration, pushing back bushes, stepping over roots, ducking under low-lying branches. The sound of the lapping water, to his left, never far away, made him more anxious by the minute. He thought back to the stories he read as a child, of famous French explorers battling through the unknown jungles of the Dark Continent. He tried to remember them, tried to keep his mind busy.

He slipped. Trying to retain his balance on the wet bank, he only slewed further. Skidding down the bank, he grabbed clusters of grass and managed to stop himself slipping into the lake. Regaining his balance he stood and eyed the water lapping at his feet.

They buried him three days later – on the southern side of the church. Father de Beaufort had led the service.

Pierre had never seen a coffin before but he was surprised by how small it was. He tried not to think of his brother within. Pierre had only a vague memory of the day; his mother convulsed in sobs, his father speechless with grief. People shook their hands, offered their condolences, but not to him, not to Pierre. No one spoke to him; no one looked at him. It was as if he wasn't there. His father blamed him; he never said it again, he didn't have to, once was enough – *Why didn't you save him?* Pierre knew that how ever long he lived, he'd never be able to erase those words from his memory. It took weeks before Lucienne stopped laying a place for Michel at the kitchen table. She would sit for hours at a time in Michel's bedroom, burying her face into his clothes, breathing in his aroma. Each day she'd go to church but she never came back any happier. Pierre had given her Munchie. She washed it under the tap, then, to remove the dirt from her fingers, she washed her hands – again and again. And ever since, she'd been obsessed about washing her hands, and whenever she felt under strain, it was to the sink she'd go. His father spent his time in the yard building a second shed though they had no need for another. Pierre went to school everyday and returned in the afternoons with no recollection of anything the teachers had said. They never upbraided him for failing to do his homework, for failing to listen. His friends avoided him, not wanting to be contaminated by his grief. His parents never asked him how he was, how his day had been. They lived in silence, unable to speak to one another. All the time, he longed for his mother to hug him, to reassure him that everything was OK. But, more than anything, he longed for his father to say that it wasn't his fault. He never did.

Once he heard children playing outside the house. His heart caved in, thinking for a moment he'd heard Michel's shrill voice.

Weeks later, they erected a little cross at Michel's grave with his name. Pierre and his father never visited it except once a year, the anniversary of his death, when Lucienne took Georges and Pierre there to stand and remember. Lucienne still went almost every day.

He gazed across the water. How calm it looked now. He wondered whether Michel's spirit was still out there. Could he have done more; could he have saved him? He felt lightheaded, dizzy almost. He placed one foot into the water, then the other, the water seeping through his shoes. He never did learn to swim. He'd swim now though; he'd find Michel. Removing his jacket, he threw it behind him onto the bank. The icy shards of water bit into his ankles, into his calves, but still he placed one foot in front of the other. He had to save him; he couldn't fail him a second time; not this time. He realised he was crying, his tears clouding his vision. 'Michel?' he screamed. 'Michel, where are you?' The water now reached the belt of his trousers, lapping around him. His hands skimmed the surface, causing ripples. Wiping away the tears, he scanned the lake, looking for movement. 'Mickey,' he yelled. 'I'm sorry.'

A voice, faraway, it seemed, echoed his screams. 'Michel, Michel, is that you?'

Someone was behind him, splashing. Turning, he saw his father wading through the water. He stopped. 'Oh my dear Lord, I thought...' Throwing his head back, his eyes clenched shut, his mouth opened but there was no sound.

'It wasn't my fault, Papa; I didn't mean to…'

Another voice filtered through. 'Georges, no. Who is

Michel?' That voice – it was the major, Major H. 'It's Pierre,' said the voice, the major. 'Your son, Pierre, not Michel.'

What was that sound, that clawing, frightening sound? He wished it would stop; that screaming; he didn't like it. 'Nooo, no, it's Michel; it's my son; the Lord has delivered him back. My son…'

*

Pierre opened his eyes. He found himself inside a shack of some sort, walls made up of wooden planks. To his right, lying on the wooden floor, the major, soaked through, shivering. On his left, hunched up on a child's wooden chair, also wet, his father. Opposite, perched up on a stool with a rifle on his lap was Kafka.

'He's awake,' he heard Kafka say.

'Pierre, are you OK, son? How are you feeling?'

Someone, presumably his father, had covered him with a blanket. 'Fine, I guess.'

'Here, Foucault, give him some water,' said the major.

'*Monsieur* Foucault to you,' said Kafka. 'Georges, give him that bottle.'

Pierre took the water while taking in his surroundings. Against one wall was a stove with its black flue rising half way up the wall, a bucket of coal beside it; in the corner a bed, next to it, an upturned crate for a bedside table, a paraffin lamp on top. A simple table showed remnants of a meal, metal plates piled on top of each other, a couple of tin mugs, an empty beer bottle. Next to the table, a couple of sturdy-looking chairs. A coil of rope, along with a number of coats and jackets, hung from a large brass hook on the back of the door. On the wall, above a low-lying sink, a portrait of Joan of Arc and a calendar displaying the month of April 1939. Next to them, a crucifix. Somehow, Pierre knew it was the one Kafka had taken from the dead German on New Year's Day in 1918. He looked round for his bag but it was nowhere to be seen.

'What happened?' asked Pierre.

'You fainted in the water,' said Georges, his voice distant. 'We'd heard your screams from here, calling out his name. I'm sorry if...'

'It's OK,' he said, knowing it was far from OK. 'I don't understand, what are you all doing here?'

'Ask him,' said the major.

'And I will tell you,' said Kafka. 'It's simple – your father and I have taken your major as hostage.'

'I'm not part of this,' said Georges.

Kafka laughed again. 'Think the Krauts will believe that? Come on, Georges. All for one, one for all.'

'Trust me with the gun then.'

'Yeah, like I did in 1918. I think not. The Krauts sent your major and a couple of lackeys to find me. That traitor, Dubois, was their guide. I shot the bloody lot of them.'

'As well as the soldier in the square,' added the major. 'You'll never get away with this.'

'Shut up. Your, not totally unexpected, appearance is fortuitous, boy.'

'How did you get away from the town hall?'

'They killed Bouchette; shot him in the back, the murderers. I got away thanks to that truck getting in the way, and got to my *getaway car*.' He said the words in an ironic tone. 'OK, it was the slowest thing on Earth but it brought me enough distance.'

'Hector and Albert's truck.'

'I was going to send your father, but it'd be better if you act as our messenger.' He spoke quickly. 'Go to Colonel Eisler and tell him – release the prisoners from his jail and he can have his major back.'

Kafka's words and the hopelessness of his situation galvanised Pierre. Throwing off the blanket, he leapt to his feet.

'But that's just stupid – as soon as you hand the major back, he'll re-arrest them and have them shot.'

'He does that and your friend here will be a dead man, you mark my words, there'd be no hiding. They won't want to lose a major – far too senior. A private, yes, they're two a penny, but a major with all those years of training and experience, no.'

'The Germans, they killed Monsieur Clément – in the square, in front of everyone.'

'Monsieur Clément? No,' said Georges.

'It was horrible. And they've taken hostages.'

'What?'

'Six hostages, including Claire.' The mention of Claire brought both the major and Georges to their feet. 'If you don't return the major by midday tomorrow, they'll be shot also.'

'You must give yourself up,' shouted the major.

Kafka slid off his stool, gripping his rifle, his face screwed with hatred. 'All the more reason for the boy to get back there and tell them our terms.'

'How do you know I won't just lead them back here?'

The gunshot took them all by surprise. Instinctively, they ducked. A black hole smouldered in the wooden wall just above Georges's head. 'You try it, and it won't just be the major with a hole in his head. You understand? OK, so a few people get shot. Such is war. They'll die in the name of sacrifice.'

'Steady, Kafka,' said Georges. 'The boy said they had Claire.'

'Good, she deserves to be shot, the slut. It was she who denounced us, told the Germans our plans.'

'No,' said Pierre. 'It wasn't Claire; it was never Claire.'

'What? What are you saying?'

'Was it you, Pierre?' asked his father. 'Did you tell the Germans?'

Kafka shook his head in disbelief. 'You're weak. Sucking up to the Krauts. Like father, like son.'

Georges stepped forward. 'I've had twenty-two years of this. Murder is murder, you pig. The rules of war—'

'The rules of war! There are no rules in war. Get back, all of you, get back.' The veins throbbed in his neck, his bestial eyes glared.

But Georges didn't step back, inching towards Kafka, his eyes red with pain. 'You killed that boy in cold blood. I've lived with his memory all these years.'

'Proves my point – you're weak, sentimental. Get back or I'll shoot you now.'

'Papa, get back, please,' screamed Pierre.

Kafka, so concentrated on Georges, didn't see it coming. In a flash, the major was on him, seizing him by the waist. The two men fell but Kafka, holding onto his rifle, was too fast for the German, pushing the major down. He punched him in the chest. Nimbly, rising to his feet, he lifted his rifle and smashed it into the major's face. The major fell onto his back, blood streaming from his cheek. Kafka spun his rifle round, taking aim at him. The major covered his face.

'No,' cried Pierre, leaping onto the major, trying to smother him.

'Pierre, stop,' screamed Georges.

Kafka, with the rifle ready to shoot, shouted at Pierre, 'Stand aside, boy, now.'

'Get off me, Pierre,' groaned the major. 'Don't do it. Just get off.'

'You harm my son...' Kafka turned to face Georges, just as Georges's fist caught him on the chin; just at the moment the gun went off. This time, Kafka fell back. Georges leapt on him before Kafka had chance to right himself. Both men fought for the rifle, grunting, trading ineffectual blows. Pierre stood up, wanting to help but, with a jolt, realised he was afraid. He looked to the major for support. The German staggered to his feet only to fall again, his eyes glazing over, blood pouring from his shoulder. The stray bullet had caught him. Pierre looked round, searching for something, anything, to help. The chair. Get the chair. Georges and Kafka screamed at each other, the rifle spinning loose, sliding across the floor. Both men leapt for it, each preventing the other from reaching it. Calmly now, Pierre picked it up, nestled the butt against his shoulder and pointed it at Kafka.

'OK, OK,' said Kafka, extricating himself from Georges. Puffing his cheeks, he rose to his feet, raising his hands. 'What now, eh?' He stood, hands in the air, his chest heaving. 'Durand and son; turncoats, each as useless as the other.'

Georges, too, got up, dabbing the blood from his lips, stepping to one side.

'Shut up, Kafka.'

Kafka laughed. 'So, are you going to do the Germans'

work for them again and shoot me then, Pierre, like I taught you? Remember?'

'No, I'll do it; nothing I wouldn't like better.' It was the major, panting, leaning against the chair, his face white, accentuated by the deep red hole in his left shoulder.

'Let the boy, do it,' said Kafka, slowly putting his arms down. 'Let's see if he's man enough.'

'Put your hands back up,' ordered Georges. 'Pierre, give me the gun.'

'Man enough? People always want me to be a man.' He was speaking in a whisper, to himself. '*Pierre, you're just a boy. We need men, not children. Come back when you've become a man. He's only a kid.* If this is being a man, I'd rather stay a child.' He tried to focus but realised his tears were obscuring his vision.

'Here, Major, tie him up.' Georges threw the German the coil of rope.

Distracted momentarily by the rope, they didn't see Kafka's hand as it went to his back pocket. Backing against the wall, he pointed his revolver at Pierre, clicking off its safety catch. The two of them faced each other, their guns trained on the other, Georges and the major either side, the German holding the rope. Transfixed by the black hole of the revolver's barrel, Pierre's vision blurred. He knew he could never pull the trigger, even to save his life; the rifle was as useless in his hands as a stick. 'Don't do it,' said the major. 'Like you say, he's still only a boy.'

Kafka's eyes darted from one to the other, his revolver still trained on Pierre, snorting like a bull.

'Please, Kafka, I beg you. I've lost one son, don't take the other.'

It took but a second. The barrel in his mouth, the shot;

Kafka on the wooden floor, the splatter of blood and brain on the wall behind him.

The three of them stood in silence, gaping at the fallen figure, the revolver still in his hand.

'Pierre? Pierre, you can put the gun down now.'

But Pierre didn't hear his father. Images flashed through his mind – Claire's ashen face as she was led away, Tintin at the moment he knew death was about to come, Monsieur Roché with his skull caved in, the exhausted Algerian killed like a dog. *Vive la Framce*. Michel. Poor Michel, at the bottom of the lake, dead at six. The rifle felt heavy now, his arms weak. Gently, a pair of hands circled round the barrel, taking its weight. He saw the glint of the signet ring.

'It's OK, Pierre,' came the reassuring German accent. 'It's over now. It's over.'

Chapter 23

There were perhaps two dozen or more of them, crammed into the waiting area at Gestapo headquarters in Saint-Romain. Parents, spouses, children, siblings. A soldier stood guard at the door kept open on a latch. The atmosphere inside, although tense and full of anticipation, was jovial. They had all believed they would never see their loved ones again yet, here they were, within minutes of being reunited. Everyone seemed to have dressed up for the occasion, the men in suits and ties, the women in their best frocks. Pierre too had worn his father's smart jacket with a blue-collared shirt and matching tie; his mother having helped tie it while he tried to flap her hands away. At least he had managed to persuade her that he didn't need her to accompany him to Saint-Romain. They had gathered earlier in the town square to catch the bus. They greeted each other with hugs and tears. People slapped Pierre's back and shook his hand; the women kissed him – congratulating him on having such a brave father. Pierre, like many of the others, bore a bunch of flowers, wild flowers plucked from the village hedgerows. The mayor would have disapproved – having issued a ban on such activities. But nothing mattered – their loved ones had been spared the bullet, the sun was shining and the world seemed a better place. Major Hurtzberger, Georges and Pierre had left Kafka's body in his lakeside shack. Later in the day, four privates were sent to retrieve it. What happened to it after that, no one knew and no one cared. On receiving back his major, Colonel Eisler called off the town gathering and declared that the six hostages would be released from Saint-Romain at midday.

There had been similar outpouring of emotion when Georges, Pierre and the major returned home. On seeing them, Lucienne cried. And then carried on crying for hours, thanking God, unable to speak coherently, hugging all three of them in turn. It was, she said between sobs, the happiest day of her life. A bottle of red wine was opened, toasts made. Retiring to her bedroom, Lucienne returned a couple minutes later, in her yellow dress, having stuffed, she said, the black dress to the back of the wardrobe. 'I hope not to see that hideous garment again until the day I have to bury Georges.'

'Lovely,' said Georges.

'And let's hope,' said the major, lifting his glass, 'that's not for many, many years to come.'

'Absolutely,' she purred, planting a kiss on her husband's cheek.

Pierre smiled at the memory. The mood in the waiting room became almost hysterical with good cheer. The men swapped jokes, the mothers reminisced about their children growing up, husbands recounted their first dates, wives their wedding days. Even the guard was unable to keep a straight face. Pierre had no history with Claire, and providing an account of boyhood lust and a solitary kiss didn't seem appropriate somehow. A sudden hush descended over the room at the sight of the receptionist, Mademoiselle Dauphin, with her tight skirt, pink nails and bright red lipstick, approaching them. 'Monsieurs, mesdames,' she said, enjoying the moment. 'If you would care to follow me.'

After numerous rounds of 'after you'; 'no please, after *you*', the gathering tumbled past the grinning guard and followed Mademoiselle Dauphin into the courtyard. Despite the jovial mood, a chill ran through Pierre, remembering all too well the last time he'd seen this place with its red brick flooring, its laurel hedge. Along the far wall of creeping ivy, standing to attention under the shade, eight German soldiers, with their rifles against their shoulders. He felt weak all of a sudden, dizzy almost.

'You all right, Pierre?' said Madame Bonnet.

'Something's wrong,' he muttered.

'Wrong? What on earth could go wrong now?'

An arrow of terror struck Pierre's being – this was their shooting range; it was a trick; they were going to shoot the hostages after all. They weren't here to welcome back their loved ones, but as witnesses to their deaths.

'Oh, Lord, no.'

Madame Bonnet had already disappeared, her arms round a friend, giggling with excitement. There was nothing he could do; no way out; they were trapped. With every sense on full alert, he heard the click of the door latch open. They all turned to see the hostages file out, under German escort, one after the other. Screams of delight ensued as they were engulfed by their loved ones.

Claire was last to appear, in her polka dot red dress, now crumpled, her face pale. She waved on seeing Pierre, an embarrassed little gesture, and came towards him, almost stumbling. Pierre pushed his flowers at her but couldn't bear to look at her; too fearful of the soldiers against the wall, distracted by their hateful expressions.

'I can't take these,' she said handing them back to him. 'Everyone despises me. I killed Clément.'

'You had no choice.'

'No, but… Pierre, are you OK?'

He looked up to the balcony, to where he had been, to see if he could spot Colonel Eisler looking down on proceedings. He dropped the flowers.

'What's the matter?' she asked, her expression streaked with concern.

Around him, people embraced, laughing, crying with such gaiety, such joy.

'Claire…' He didn't know what to say. Taking her hand, he pulled her to one side, yet knowing that these four walls offered no escape.

'Pierre, you're worrying me now.'

'When I say get down, lie down and I'll lie on top of you. I'm sorry; it's all I can do. I'm so sorry.'

'For what, Pierre? Tell me, for what?'

'Attention!' The word rang out across the yard, bringing with it immediate silence. It was Colonel Eisler. Pierre's hand tightened on Claire's. 'It's lovely to see such celebrations, but we have work to do, and no doubt you'll be wanting to get home. So I ask you kindly to make your way out now please. Mademoiselle Dauphin will escort you. Good day.'

With a wave and a kindly smile, Mademoiselle Dauphin

beckoned everyone to follow her. The soldiers next to the wall remained static, their expressions unchanged. Still laughing, the gathered trotted back inside, and along the ground floor corridor. Last in line were Claire and Pierre, Pierre continually glancing behind, his stomach hollowed with dread.

He wandered slowly down the corridor, falling behind the others, Claire looking at him with a puzzled expression.

Half way down the corridor, he stopped. His hand on his chest, hardly able to breathe, he said, 'I think we're OK now.'

'I don't understand. Did you... did you think they were...?'

He nodded.

'You said you would have lain on top of me. You...' Pierre felt Claire's hand. 'Come on, let's get out of here.'

The others had disappeared.

'Pierre, I have to leave.'

'Leave what?'

'This town. I'll go back to Paris.'

'Oh, there you are.' It was Mademoiselle Dauphin, holding a clipboard to her chest. 'I thought I'd lost you for a moment. Unless you particularly want to extend your stay, Mademoiselle Bouchez, I'd recommend you and your friend follow me.'

'With pleasure,' said Pierre.

They stood outside, alone, exposed to a shower. Pierre looked back at the grey, foreboding building, a guard standing at the door, oblivious to the rain. He hoped never to see the place, or Colonel Eisler, again.

'Do you have to leave?' he asked.

'Oh, Pierre, you should have heard them in there. The names they called me.' She shook her head. 'I can't stay. They'll never forgive me for what I did; they'll never forget.'

'Take me with you.'

Chapter 24

Perched high above them on a branch, a pigeon cooed. Madame Picard passed by, walking her little terrier, stopping to allow the dog to sniff. She waved on seeing Pierre and Xavier resting against the tree across the green, opposite the library. They waved back.

'How long now?' asked Xavier.

'About five minutes, I think.'

'She must love her work to want to go back straightaway.'

'She's not going back. She just wanted to collect her things.'

'Must have been difficult, thinking, you know, this could be my last night on earth.'

'Yeah.'

'But you, eh? You got the girl in the end?'

Pierre tried to smile. 'I guess.'

'Well, you're one lucky chap, Pierre Durand. Horrible business, though, wasn't it? Everyone was worried about your papa. Has he spoken to you about it?'

'Papa? Speak to me about anything? Hardly.'

'People are saying all sorts of things. How he singlehandedly found Kafka out on that lake, and the wounded major, and killed him. Claire and the others, how do they express their thanks for something like that? I mean, hell, if it wasn't for your papa, they'd be…'

'Yeah, I know.'

'How is he?'

'He's at home at the moment, doing a stone for Monsieur Clément.'

'Oh yeah. Poor old sod.' Xavier pulled up a few blades of grass. 'Fancy a fag?'

'Not really.'

Xavier took a blade of grass and, holding it between the tips of his thumbs, blew on it, producing a high-pitched whistle sound. 'How's that thing of yours?' he asked between whistles. 'What do you call it? The Black Maria thing?'

'Oh that. I don't know if I can be bothered with it any more.'

'You should. It's good.'

'I'm not sure. I think I should have started on something… I don't know.'

'A little bit less ambitious?'

'Yes, that's it. Something a little bit less ambitious.'

'Come on, she should be coming out now.'

'Hopefully.'

They got to their feet and stretched.

'I know,' said Xavier, 'let's have a race. To the library wall and back. Oh no, I'm sorry, I forgot, it's too childish for you now.'

'No, it's not that.'

'What is it then?'

'I wouldn't want to embarrass you. I'd beat you too easily.'

'You… What? Right, that's it.'

'Get ready then. On your marks, get set… go!'

'Hey, I wasn't ready. That's unfair!'

Thus, almost tripping over with laughter, the two boys sprinted across the soft grass of the green, with the wind in their hair, the sun on their backs. Claire appeared, her yellow dress flapping slightly. She stood with her back to the library wall and watched, smiling, as the two boys sprinted towards her. She squealed as Pierre, on seeing her, ran straight at her. Slamming his hands against the wall either side of her, he leant forward, planted a kiss on her lips, before racing back to the tree. And there, bending over, catching their breaths, hands on each other's shoulders, Pierre and Xavier laughed, at nothing really, just the pure delight of being there, of being young and alive.

*

Major Hurtzberger stood in the centre of the living room in full uniform, his suitcase and a shoulder bag at his feet, scanning the room, knowing he would probably never see it again. Georges, Lucienne and Pierre were with him, also on their feet, making the room seem rather small. 'Well, this is it,' he said, with a sigh.

'We shall miss you,' said Lucienne, her hands clasped as if in prayer.

'Yes, well. I shall miss you too.' He cleared his throat. 'I know it hasn't always been easy; I am your enemy, after all. My presence here could not be under more unfavourable conditions. Yet… yet, I could never have asked for kinder, more generous hosts. And for that, I thank you all.'

'You've done a lot for us, though, Major,' said Georges. He had changed into his corduroy jacket and canvas trousers, as if to mark the occasion.

'Perhaps.'

'You will come to visit us, won't you, Major? I mean, after all this is over.'

'Oh, Lucienne, there would be nothing on earth that I would like better.'

Pierre frowned, trying to work out whether that was, essentially, a 'yes'.

'Oh, would you mind?' The major rummaged in his bag. 'I've been given this,' he said, holding up a camera. 'A gift from the men, a going away present. Could I...'

'Yes, by all means,' said Lucienne. 'Where would you like us to stand?'

'Just here, next to the fireplace. Now, which button is it? Ah, here we are.'

The three of them hunched together in front of the fireplace, Pierre in the middle, his father's hand resting awkwardly on his shoulder. 'I haven't had my photograph taken in years,' he muttered. Lucienne fluffed up her hair and grimaced in her attempt to smile.

'Ready?'

'*Ready.*'

Click.

'Perhaps one more – just in case. Keep still...' Click. 'Lovely.'

'Thank you, Thomas.'

'And now, I ought to go.'

'You sure you don't want us to come with you?'

'It's very kind of you, Georges, but no, I think best not.

It wouldn't do to be seen waving off the enemy, would it?'

'No, I guess not.'

The major patted his pockets. 'Oh, before I go, I wonder if I could have a final look at your White Venus, Pierre?'

'Really? OK.'

'White Venus?' said Georges. 'Is that what you call that thing out there?'

'Leave him be, Georges. If it amuses him…'

'Come,' said the major. 'Come with me, Pierre.'

Late afternoon, and the yard was half in the shade, the chickens sticking to the cooler side. The major inspected the sculpture as if seeing it for the first time, circling it, considering it. 'Very good,' he said, rubbing his chin. 'May I take a picture of it?'

Pierre shuffled on his feet. 'If you want. I don't…'

'Yes?'

'I don't really like it any more. It's nothing like the painting.'

'Rubbish, it's an excellent piece of work; you should be proud. Do you think Botticelli managed it in one go?' He took his photograph. 'No, he probably worked on it for months, years even. I'm sorry the town hall said no. I think it would have graced the reception area very nicely. Here, let me take another with you next to it. Go on; don't be shy. That's it. Smile, Pierre, give us a smile. That's it. Good lad.' He turned the camera round in his hands. 'Am I meant to switch this thing off, I wonder? You know, Kafka has been buried.'

'No.'

'This morning. In an unmarked grave'

'Oh.' Bouchette, Dubois and Kafka – all dead.

323

'Why are all your tools here?'

Pierre hadn't noticed but the various shovels, brooms, sledgehammer and hoe were all lined up neatly against the shed wall. 'Perhaps Papa's having a sort out now that's he's started working again.'

'I see that you've become close to Claire.'

Pierre nodded, not sure how to respond.

'That's good. I'm sorry that I…'

'It's… it's fine.'

'You know, don't you? It wasn't her fault. I knew she was under orders and I took advantage of that. If I'd know you were…'

'It's fine,' he repeated.

The major covered his embarrassment with a smile. 'She's a charming girl. You'll make a lovely couple. I'll be expecting an invite now.'

'Sorry?'

'To the wedding.'

Pierre laughed politely, hoping the conversation would end.

'Pierre, listen. I want to give you something.' Placing the camera on the rocking chair, he slid his ring off his finger and held it out in his palm.

'Me? You want me to…?'

'It would have been for Joachim, as you know, but…'

'I… I'm not sure.'

'Please, it would be an honour. You are very much alike my Joachim; you remind me of him in so many ways, I'm sure I've told you. It would make me happy to know you wore his ring.'

Pierre took it.

'Try it on.'

'It fits. Different finger to yours but it fits.'

'Perfect.'

'I'll… Thank you. I shall wear it always.'

The major glanced up at the sky. 'And now, I really ought to be going.'

*

The major had gone, handshakes all round, an embrace and a peck on the cheek with Lucienne, closing the door gently behind him. Georges, Lucienne and Pierre sat in the living room, an air of gloom hanging over them, unable to find anything to say. Pierre had slid the ring off and secreted it in his pocket. He couldn't face telling them why he had it. Not yet.

Eventually, Georges broke the silence. 'I wonder whether they'll send us another guest.'

'I hope not,' said Lucienne. 'Despite the extra food, it's somebody else's turn. I want Michel to have his room back to himself now.'

'Hmm.' He patted his knees. 'Well, this is no good. Did you say you were going out shopping?' Lucienne nodded. 'I think I'll come with you. It'll give me something to do. Did he take his camera?'

Immediately, Pierre could see it in his mind's eye. 'Oh no,' he yelped, springing to his feet. Dashing out in the yard, he saw it where the major had left it, on the rocking chair.

Georges had followed him out. 'Is it there?'

'Yes. What do we do?'

'Well, run after him, of course. He wouldn't have got far with that suitcase. Hurry up, then!'

Pierre rushed out the house, slipping the ring back on.

The major had said a car was taking him from the town hall to the train station at Saint-Romain. He ran up the hill, round the bend and towards the town square. As he approached the square, he could see the car with its swastika pennant, a private, doubling up as a chauffeur, lifting the major's suitcase into the boot. The major, next to the car, was shaking hands with another officer. The two men parted with a Hitler salute. Pierre waved. The major hadn't seen him. The major strode stepped away from the car, as if preparing himself for the journey ahead, pulling the creases out of his tunic.

'Major! Major Hurtzberger.'

This time, the major saw him. Walking quickly towards him, he shouted, 'Pierre, is everything OK? What's wrong?'

Pierre caught him up, slightly abashed to be so out of breath. 'Your camera. You forgot your camera.'

'Oh, thank you!' He took it. 'Silly me. Thank you so much.' The two of them stood facing each other, not sure what to say. 'That's my car.'

'Yes. Your driver's waving at you.'

The major glanced back, acknowledging the summons. 'Yes, I'd better go.'

'Yes.'

'This is it then, Pierre. I hope, one day… You're a good boy.'

'Goodbye, Major H.'

'Major H, yes.'

Pierre offered his hand, another handshake. The major ignored it and, stepping closer, flung his arms round him. Pierre, unable to reciprocate, stood with his arms hanging at his side. The major smelt clean – aftershave and soap.

326

'Goodbye, my boy. I shall miss you.'

Pierre watched him as he marched quickly back to the car, clutching his camera. The driver, waiting at the wheel, started the engine. The major got into the back, closed the door behind him, and wound down the window, looking straight ahead. The driver eased the car off, round the green, round where once had stood the statue of Soldier Mike, and onto the road to Saint-Romain, its pennant flapping gently in the breeze. With his breaths coming in short gasps, Pierre watched the car disappear into the heat rays of the late afternoon. The major didn't look back.

*

Pierre returned home almost in a daze, feeling like a drunk man. Images, uninvited, sprung into his consciousness, of playing with Michel in the fields behind the house, flying a kite, of his father pulling his brother out of the lake, his fist beating Michel's chest, giving him the kiss of life – *Why didn't you save him?* The words, the accusation, had always haunted him. *Why didn't you save him?* He thought of Joachim, killed at nineteen; of the major's last words, calling him 'my boy'.

He stopped, his head pounding. Someone passed by, a woman with a walking stick, a breezy greeting. He wiped his forehead with the back of his hand, felt the unfamiliar gold of the ring scrape his brow. *Generations of my family were cavalrymen.*

He staggered home. The sculpture. He'd only done it for his father, a means by which to finally supplant Michel from the forefront of his affections. It hadn't worked; nothing would work. He knew that now. The major would never see it again, would never see the final work. His mother had never shown any interest, and his father... he was more interested in the chickens. It was Michel he was saving from the water yesterday; Michel, not he, not Pierre. The wrong son. A memory – that of Georges playing with Michel, running round the house, playing hide and seek, Michel almost falling over with such laughter. His brain was full of such memories – Georges and Michel. Michel and Georges. But never him. Not a single one. He kissed the ring.

He burst into the house and found it empty. They'd gone shopping. He raged from room to room, pent up energy threatening to overcome him. He wanted to hurt him, to hurt his father. He gripped his hair, told himself to calm down. Yes, Michel had been the favourite but only by the virtue of his death. It was natural. But why then, this pain, this stabbing of his heart?

He went through the kitchen and out into the yard. The chickens fled upon his arrival. There she stood, the White Venus, her face still without features, mere hollows where her eyes should be. The White Venus – *is that what you call that thing out there?* She was still anonymous, still just a block of sandstone. And how he hated her. She'd known all along that it had been a pointless exercise. *I am not a work of art*, she seemed to be saying, jibing him. *I am a work of desperation. You can't manipulate me, just as you can't manipulate your father. You're weak. Like father and son. Weak.*

'Yes, I am weak,' he said through clenched jaws. 'I let him drown, and no one's listened to me since.' With rapid movements, he scooped up the sledgehammer, taking its weight and bracing himself. With a mighty sideways swing, he smashed it against her head. A cloud of splinters burst; a crack appeared, running from her ear to her throat. A second blow, the head flew off, crashing against the yard wall with a satisfying thud. The chickens squawked. 'I am not weak,' he screamed as he delivered a third blow, a fourth, a fifth. His chest heaving, his hands dry with dust, he carried on and on until like a snowman melted to its core, only a stump of the White Venus remained. Finally, panting, unable to see with dust and sweat in his eyes, he dropped the sledgehammer. He felt sick; he felt evil; he felt triumphant. Wiping away the sweat, he viewed the chaos he'd created, white dust everywhere, the fragments, the shards and bits of sandstone, scattered across the ground. Tears came to his eyes. The White Venus was no more; he'd killed her, and much more besides. He had no need for her any more; he had Claire, his very own White Venus.

He heard the front door open. His parents were home.

THE END

Novels by R.P.G. Colley:

The Love and War Series
The Lost Daughter
The White Venus
Song of Sorrow
The Woman on the Train
The Black Maria
My Brother the Enemy
Anastasia

The Searight Saga
This Time Tomorrow
The Unforgiving Sea
The Red Oak

The Tales of Little Leaf
Eleven Days in June
Winter in July
Departure in September

https://rupertcolley.com

Made in the USA
Monee, IL
27 October 2021